THE DUCHESS EFFECT

Also by Tracey Livesay

AMERICAN ROYALTY SERIES

American Royalty

GIRLS TRIP SERIES

Sweet Talkin' Lover

Like Lovers Do

SHADES OF LOVE SERIES

Love on My Mind

Along Came Love

Love Will Always Remember

IN LOVE WITH A TYCOON SERIES

The Tycoon's Socialite Bride

Pretending with the Playboy

THE DUCHESS EFFECT

A Novel

TRACEY LIVESAY

AVON
An Imprint of HarperCollins*Publishers*

FIRST EDITION

Library of Congress Cataloging-in-Publication Data has been applied for.

ISBN 978-0-06-308456-8

23 24 25 CPI 10 9 8 7 6 5 4 3 2

Printed and bound by CPI Group (UK) Ltd, Croydon, CR0 4YY

To all the couples who found love in a world that made it difficult

Chapter One

WE HOPE TO SPY WITH OUR CUT CREASE EYE . . . WILL DUCHESS DRIVE BY HER BESTIE'S FEATURE FILM BASH?

Bossip

I thought we'd agreed that was *my* job."

Danielle "Duchess" Nelson turned from gazing out the car window to stare at the gorgeous man sitting next to her. "What?"

His Royal Highness Prince Jameson Alastair Richard Lloyd, the Duke of Wessex, flicked his bright cornflower blue gaze to her mouth and with a start, Dani realized she'd been nibbling on her lip.

He narrowed his eyes. "Are you nervous?"

"Why would you think I'm nervous?"

Her personal assistant, Tasha, who'd been sitting in the front seat, all but obscured save the tips of her bantu knots, said over her shoulder, "Is she biting her bottom lip? She tends to do that when she's nervous."

"I'm *not* nervous."

She had no reason to be nervous.

But she probably should fix her mouth. The last thing her makeup artist had said to her, while applying the glossy, shimmering lipstick, had been, "Don't put these lips on anybody or anything until after pictures are taken."

Dani popped open her clutch and pulled out the wand before taking the compact Tasha held out to her. "Rhonda would be so pissed."

Jameson leaned in. "I'm not worried about Rhonda. I'm worried about the fact that watching you do that for the past minute is going to make it difficult to hide the effect you have on me when I stand up."

She shivered, need curling leisurely and thick in her midsection. *God, this man.* And his words.

Not the time, Dani.

"I don't care what *this* is doing," she said, gesturing to her face. "I'm good."

"I can, indeed, vouch for that," Jameson said. His lashes lowered. "Have I told you today how much I love you?"

Her newly glossed lips curved. "Yes, you have."

"Have I told you how beautiful you look?"

She huffed out a laugh and, with her free hand, adjusted the micro-beaded material of the long skirt of her burgundy dress. "How would you know? Until a moment ago, when you were ogling my mouth, you hadn't taken your eyes off my cleavage."

His shrug held all the nonchalance of a man secure in his opinion and views of the world. "Can you blame me?"

She couldn't because it was the reaction she and her stylist had wanted. The strapless gown seemed to defy gravity, making it impossible to discern how the fabric that barely covered her breasts stayed up. "You might have told me. But I don't mind you repeating it again."

"My pleasure. You, my darling Duchess, look stunning."

Despite Rhonda's admonishment and her own rush to rectify

her earlier mistake, Dani leaned over and gingerly pressed her lips to his. "I love you, Jay."

She was lucky that only a little shine transferred from her lips to his. She wiped it with a tissue.

Jameson's stare blazed as he reached for her hand and kissed it. "I love you, too."

Dani was still gooped by how much her life had changed in the past few months. She'd gone from the verge of failure, having all her carefully made career plans disintegrating before her eyes, to being invited to perform at a tribute for the British royal family and meeting Jay. Their romance had been swift, intense, and not without its issues. They didn't have all the answers for how they would merge their two very different lifestyles; they just knew they loved each other enough to try and make it work.

Tasha turned to face them, adjusting the frames of her stylish black glasses. "Vicky says we're the last car in the queue. There are two more ahead of us. The security team wanted me to remind you that when it's our turn, stay in the car until one of them opens your door. Both of you."

Something else Dani was adjusting to.

It's not like she hadn't dealt with her share of bodyguards. She was a celebrity in America. But the more famous she became, the less she could depend on the disguises she'd used when she wanted to go out and enjoy her own company. She'd needed some sort of protection. It's the reason she kept Antoine, her personal security, on her payroll.

But safeguarding a royal was on another level.

Jay's personal security had traveled to the States with him, as members of the royal family were never without protection. The mantra "from cradle to grave" had been mentioned on more than one occasion. As an explanation.

And a warning?

"We're next," Tasha said.

From the corner of her eye, Dani noted Jay's right knee bouncing and, just like that, her own anxiety vanished. In the three weeks Jameson had been in the States with her, they'd kept a pretty low profile, holing up in a spectacular oceanfront home in Carmel, about five hours north of L.A. The days seemed to pass in a hazy orgasmic glow filled with great food, even better sex, and hours spent talking, listening to music, and watching tv and movies. Basically, getting to know each other. It had been Primrose Park, the U.S. edition.

But this was their first public outing since Jameson had defied the queen and declared to the world their love for each other, and Dani, despite protesting way too much, had been nervous. But while her anxiety was new, Jameson had been dealing with his own issues for decades. To say he had a contentious relationship with the press was like saying Beyonce had only been slightly irked by Becky. His father, Prince Richard, had spent a lot of time living his life in a way that the press had found . . . intriguing . . . and they loved hassling his family. When his father had been killed with his mistress in a helicopter crash, the press coverage had been constant and harassing. Jameson had never forgiven them for the way they'd treated him and his mother, and as a result, he'd sworn off his royal duties and retreated further into his world of books. It wasn't until earlier this year, when the queen made him the face of the Royal Tribute in Honor of Prince John, that he'd stepped back—albeit reluctantly—into the spotlight.

Between the two of them, he should've been the one to claim nervousness, not her.

She placed a hand on his thigh and felt the steely muscle flex against her palm. "Thank you for doing this."

His anxious movement stilled. "Of course."

"I know you hate it."

"But it's important to you," he said, not denying her assertion. "And if it's important to you, it's important to me."

The car eased to a stop.

"Let's do this!" Tasha said, already exiting the vehicle.

"Just remember, you don't have to answer any questions. You don't even have to be in the pictures if you don't want to. Tasha can take you a back way and we can meet in the—"

"Dani." His calm voice cut through the angst she was rebuilding. "I'm here for you and with you. However you want me."

"Thank you," she said, yielding to the need to kiss him, but remembering and stopping at the last minute.

Your lipstick.

His door opened and the cheers, yelling, honking of horns, and discordant sounds of traffic invaded their peaceful cocoon. Jay's royal protection officer, Roy, was there, his head on a swivel, searching out any possible dangers with Terminator-like efficiency.

Jameson squeezed her hand. "I'll see you in five seconds."

And then it was quiet again. She took the moment to compose herself.

You did it. They tried to come for you, and they missed. You're on the verge of getting everything you've worked for.

Despite the odds and naysayers, Dani had created Mela-Skin, her own skin-care line geared specifically toward women of color. It had been an immediate success and she'd been close to signing a contract with Genesis, one of the world's largest cosmetics and personal-care companies, when a fraudulent post from Samantha Banks, a fame-seeking pop star, had placed Dani in a negative light and that deal in jeopardy. But Dani hadn't given up. She'd reclaimed her name and found the love of her life.

She looked up, meeting the eye of the driver in his rearview mirror. He smiled and nodded.

You got this, sis.

The unspoken but recognizable affirmation bolstered her and, responding in kind, she straightened. She knew who she was and what it had taken to get here. And she wouldn't let anything, or anyone, stand in her way.

Her door opened and she briefly saw a tall man in a dark gray suit and light blue tie who held his hand out to indicate she wait. And then, true to his word, Jay was there, elegant in a classic black tuxedo. Although Dani loved everything about Jameson, she couldn't deny that in the beginning, it'd been lust at first sight. Six three with dark wavy hair, blue eyes, a straight nose, chiseled jaw, and firm kissable lips, he looked every inch the Prince Charming he actually was.

If Prince Charming were also a university professor.

If all professors looked like him, she would've been willing to get not only her bachelor's degree, but also her associate, master's, a doctorate, her teaching certification, a heating and cooling certificate, and whatever else was available.

The roar when she stepped out of the full-size black SUV was deafening. A large number of people occupied risers that had been erected around the theater. More stood behind the barriers that ran along the length of the red carpet.

What the hell?

A crowd of this size would be expected if this were the premiere of the next Marvel movie, but not for a mid-budget romantic comedy.

No offense to Nyla.

Dani struggled to keep the shock from showing on her face,

knowing that at least one camera was probably trained on the arrivals.

"I thought we'd kept our attendance on the DL?" she muttered to the tall woman who'd materialized at her side.

Dani had wanted to make an appearance at the premiere of her best friend Nyla Patterson's movie, *Boy, Bye!*, but Dani hadn't wanted to do anything to steal her thunder. She knew showing up with Jameson would cause a stir—she and Jameson, individually, together, and the hashtag #RoyalSwirlLove had been trending on Twitter, both Stateside and in the U.K., for the past few weeks—so she'd planned for this, keeping the press in the dark about their presence and arriving at the tail end of the red carpet.

It seemed all their planning had been for shit.

"You know how that goes," Vicky said, professional and blend-in-able in a tailored black suit, her relaxed hair cut into a sharp bob that brushed her jawline. "Nobody could keep a secret *before* the two of you became the most famous couple in the world."

The need for good press was what had sent Dani to the U.K. and it was how she'd met Jameson. Dani's agent had hired the in-demand publicist to deal with what they thought would be the negative fallout of the world finding out about their relationship. But if the feedback she and her agent had received from the executives at Genesis was any indication, her European adventure had worked. What no one had anticipated was that the news of her relationship with Prince Jameson, seventh in line to the throne, would capture the world's attention and increase her goodwill and notoriety a hundredfold. She knew it was a thing people in her business did—use relationships, real or not, for publicity. But not her. She wanted to get ahead on her own merits, based on the work she'd done.

Not who she was screwing.

Of course, once the contract was signed on the dotted line, none of that would matter. She could focus on her life and her business, calling her own shots the way she'd worked so hard to do.

"Don't worry. Whatever happens, Nyla knows you didn't do this on purpose. And any extra attention you bring will only help her and the movie," Vicky said.

"It'll be fine," Jay said, squeezing her hand.

She stared up at her British boo and smiled. Of course it would be.

As they stepped onto the red carpet, Jameson shifted their positions until he was the one nearer the throng of press. Irritation threatened to bubble to the surface but Dani quashed it with a quickness. If any of her other boyfriends had pulled that shit, she'd have called it out for the attention grab it was. Not Jameson. His instinctive protectiveness toward her would take getting used to.

"Duchess! Prince Jameson!"

"Look right here, Duchess!"

"Who are you wearing?"

The flashes and clicks were blinding and loud but she and Jameson ran the media gauntlet. The atmosphere was frenetic, the noise deafening and disorienting. There was no safe place for her gaze to land, nowhere to hide from the relentless scrutiny. Everywhere she looked there were screaming fans holding up cellphones or signs, arms outstretched as if to reach for them or hand them something. Bright lights muddled her vision. And questions. So many questions, shouted and pelted at them in a never-ending torrent.

"How did you snag yourself a prince?"

"Over your shoulder! Are you two going to get married?"

"To your left, Duchess. All the way to your left!"

"Kiss her again, Your Majesty!"

They'd paused at the step-and-repeat to take pictures, when

Dani felt the muscles in Jameson's arm tense where it rested around her waist. She couldn't tell if it was due to the stress of being before the press or because they'd mistakenly addressed him as Your Majesty, something that never would've happened back in the U.K.

They continued moving and while the sensation of being overwhelmed never left Dani, at least one thing was made clear: the negative coverage from Samantha Banks attempting to grab her coattails and run her into the ground had finally been left in the past.

Which meant a contract with Genesis, who was willing to bring Mela-Skin into the fold and make Dani one of the richest women in hip-hop, was in her future.

So, two things were clear.

Those beliefs buoyed her, turning the fake-as-fuck smile on her face real and making it easier to wave to the fans and blow them kisses. "I love you! Thank you!"

Finally, Vicky stopped at the news outlet where they'd agreed to grant a brief interview. The host, Sandra Carlton, was wrapped in a shimmery coral dress, her honey blond hair styled in carefully tousled waves.

"Duchess and Prince Jameson! Welcome!" Sandra projected her voice to be heard. "Our viewers will be thrilled to hear from you."

"Thank you, Sandra. We're happy to be here," Dani said, actually meaning it.

People watching the show's feed would just see Sandra, Dani, and Jameson. They'd hear the background noise and get a sense of the commotion surrounding the event, but they'd never see the teams of assistants, bodyguards, crew, cameramen, and even the guests who didn't make for exciting television but were essential to the running of events like these. It was an entire production.

Sandra's toothy grin rivaled the brilliance of Times Square on New Year's Eve. "You look stunning. Who are you wearing?"

Dani shook her head, letting her bone-straight, waist-length hair cascade over one shoulder. She slid a hand to her hip and thrust a bare leg through the slit in the skirt, shifting into the killer pose she'd practiced for this precise moment. The clicks and flashes rewarded her effort. "Aurora Kerby."

"That's who designed the gown you wore to the tribute ball, right? The one the entire world saw when you and the prince announced your relationship?"

Dani arched a look up at Jay and winked. "That's right."

The host turned to Jameson and Dani watched the transformation from entertainment reporter to royal fawner. "Prince Jameson, how are you enjoying your stay in America?"

"I enjoy being anywhere Duchess is," Jameson said in his deep, cultured voice.

Dani had found his British accent potent when they'd first met, but here in America, where no one in the vicinity sounded like him?

It was lethal. A panty soaking, pussy clenching instrument of devastation.

He would never be called outgoing, but he had a charm and charisma that could put most people under his spell, when he chose to use it. As he was doing now.

And Sandra was falling hard.

Damn, girl. Don't hit your head.

"You two have made headlines around the world and people are obsessed with your love story," Sandra gushed. "Does that include your grandmother, the queen?"

Jameson's grip tightened on Dani, but he continued smiling, speaking calmly and clearly into the microphone the host was holding in his direction. "The queen knows how much Duchess means to me. How important she is in my life."

Truer words.

Especially since being here with Dani went against the queen's wishes. But no one outside of the family and a few members of the royal staff knew that.

"A prince and he's romantic, too?" Sandra's tongue darted out to touch her lip and she drew her fingers through her hair. "He's a catch. You better hold on to him."

Dani met the woman's eye. "I plan to."

"Yes, well . . ." Sandra cleared her throat. "I guess there's no surprise why you're here today."

Assured that her message had been delivered, Dani let loose a lighthearted laugh. "None at all. Nyla Patterson is a great friend of mine. I'm so excited for her. And for all of you," she said, playing to the crowd. "You'll get the chance to see how extremely talented she is."

Someone screamed, "We love you, Duchess!"

Dani smiled and waved in the general direction of the proclamation. Then she nodded to Vicky, who gave the signal to wrap everything up.

Sandra's expression tightened but she carried on. "I'm sure she appreciates you being here. It was a pleasure talking to the two of you. Enjoy the movie."

"Thank you."

They walked the last few yards, but when they failed to stop and talk to anyone else, the questions grew more outrageous.

"Prince Jameson! Prince! Have you dated a Black woman before?"

"Does your mother like Duchess?"

"Did you teach the queen how to twerk?"

"Duchess! They're getting ready to announce the presenters for the 2023 Hip-Hop Awards. Any response to the rumor that you're being disinvited?"

Dani didn't break her stride, knowing the pap was simply looking to provoke a reaction. After the tribute, her team had been approached about having her perform and present Artist of the Year, the top award of the night.

A piercing shriek permeated the din. Two young women broke through the barricade and rushed through the crowd, one carrying a sign and the other holding up a phone. "Duchess! Prince Jameson! We love you! Duchess!"

Dani's heart leaped into her throat and she couldn't look away as fear rooted her to the spot. She wanted to move and had always assumed in this type of situation flight would be her automatic go-to, but her limbs refused to listen.

After what felt like minutes, but was probably seconds, Roy appeared out of nowhere, neatly diverting then ushering the fans over to the security guards hired for the event. Jameson grabbed Dani and pulled her close while the other protection officer and Antoine scanned the crowd.

"Holy shit!" Dani exclaimed, pressing a hand to her chest.

"Are you okay?" Jameson asked, his voice frantic.

She needed a second to catch her breath.

"Dani?"

"I'm fine." Rationally, she knew she hadn't been in danger, but the sudden scream had short-circuited her brain.

"Are you sure?" His fingers dug into her arms.

"Jay—"

But he wasn't looking at her. His gaze seemed to check the area around them, searching . . .

"Jay." She cupped his cheek and forced his eyes to hers. "I'm fine. Just some overzealous fans."

He didn't unwind immediately, but after a few moments, the rigid tension in his jaw relaxed and he pressed his face into her palm. Her heart ached for him and the trauma and pain he'd experienced that still seemed to affect him.

"I wasn't in the U.K. long enough to experience what you did growing up, but it's not like that here. The public attention is a pain in the ass and things like this might occur, but it doesn't get out of control. See? Nothing happened. And there's something else that you didn't have there."

His gaze bore into hers. "What?"

"Me, Jay. You've got me. And I got you."

One corner of his mouth quirked up and his eyes softened the way they did when he was fully focused on her. He pressed his lips to hers and—poof!—like magic, everything disappeared except the feel of him strong and solid. She swept her tongue across the seam of his lips, seeking entr—

Ah hell . . . her lipstick!

They were going to have to figure out something for events they had to do together. The no-lips-touching ban couldn't be allowed to stand!

"I just want you to be okay," she said when they drew apart.

Vicky handed her a tissue and Dani gently wiped away the transfer of color.

His long fingers gripped her wrist, halting her actions. "I *am* okay. I'm with you. There's no place I'd rather be."

"Really?"

He whispered in her ear, "Well, the part about being with you is true. But I'd rather be back at the house sliding into your wet, tight pussy."

Said pussy clenched. Damn, when he said things like that . . .

"Repurposing one of my Nana's favorite sayings—"

"Your Nana had a saying about everything."

"Repurposing!"

"I'm all ears."

She shot him a look from beneath thick, sweeping false lashes. "Don't let your mouth write checks your dick can't cash."

Chapter Two

PRINCE JAMESON & DUCHESS ENJOY A NIGHT OUT IN L.A.

Prince Jameson and his new love, rap artist and entrepreneur Duchess, had a special night out attending the premiere of the romantic comedy *Boy, Bye!*, starring Duchess's BFF, Nyla Patterson.

Leona McLaren
E! Online

It took serious restraint to hold back a bark of laughter at his confused expression. She'd explain that one later, in private, when she could tell . . . and show. Dani waved one last time to the crowd as Vicky escorted them inside the theater.

Done with the spectacle that was the red carpet, Dani was ready to loosen up. But if outside had been the main course, in here was the after dinner digestif. Their arrival to the event had sent attendees into a shouting frenzy. The celebrities in the building were taking the opposite approach. The incessant buzz of conversation ceased almost immediately. But the end result was the same.

They were still the undivided focus of everyone around them.

"Now *this* feels familiar," Jameson said, pressing a kiss to the top of her head.

Dani scoped the pointed looks and attempts to get her attention from some pretty famous faces. An actress smiled brightly when she caught Dani's eye and a player from her ex-boyfriend's basketball team waved. She returned their greetings but didn't invite anyone over.

It had already been difficult socializing in the entertainment business; trying to discern who wanted to be your friend because of who you were versus what you could do for them. Since Jameson's speech, she had found that doubly true. Her DMs had exploded. In and of itself, nothing new; folks were always reaching out to her. But now she was hearing from people who'd once thought her distasteful as a rapper but now felt the royal shine made her acceptable.

Fuck that.

And fuck them.

Dani shook off those thoughts. "That's what I was hoping. We spent so much time by ourselves that I thought you needed a refresher on life back in the spotlight."

"Not necessary. Once uni starts, my time in the spotlight will be greatly reduced."

The fall semester at the University of Birmingham began in early September and, although that was several weeks away, as a professor of philosophy, Jameson had said he'd need to get back to prepare.

They hadn't talked about how they were going to handle the months apart until they could be together again, but they needed to. Dani had been so wrapped up in having him with her that she hadn't wanted to allow the cold reality of their situation to seep in. Back in the U.K. it had seemed so simple. They were both privileged, wealthy individuals who were desperately in love. They could find a way to make it work.

The time was coming when they would have to put that thought to the test.

"Have you heard from the palace?" she asked, adjusting the lapel on his jacket. Not that it was needed. It was perfect, as usual. She just liked touching him. "Do you know if they have any events planned for you? You've been off the radar for a bit. I imagine the queen would love to show you off."

"You make me sound like a fucking show pony," he growled.

"I do think of you as my own personal royal stud."

The heat in his gaze could singe her dress off. "Then feel free to ride me whenever the need arises."

Her lips twitched. "So that's a no?"

He sighed. "I haven't heard from her and neither has my staff."

Dani couldn't imagine why his grandmother hadn't reached out to him, but she hoped he was ready for the very real possibility that the queen still considered him a senior member of the family and a working royal. There was no way she was going to let him take his high approval rating and retreat back into his ivory tower when the events from the tribute and their love story had made him the most popular royal since Prince John.

He slid his hand to her waist. "We'll have to schedule FaceTime calls . . ."

Her heart stalled, then thudded in her chest. "Anything in particular you want to discuss, Your Royal Highness?"

His glittery gaze skimmed her body, leaving ripples of sensation in their wake. "How well you take directions."

Her breasts swelled against her bodice. "It depends on who's giving the directions and what they're asking me to do."

"What if it's me and I'm asking you to spread those thick thighs and show me that pretty pussy?"

Moisture flooded her core and she gasped. Although a telling flush dotted his cheeks as he stared down at her, no one would be able to tell that the proper royal had such a wicked mouth that said such wicked things. That he saved that part of himself for her gave her a thrill like none other.

She looked around. "Do you suppose there's a room we can use real quick?"

She was joking.

Partially.

"There's nothing quick about what I want to do to you," he said.

Good Lord!

"There you are!" Nyla exclaimed, hurrying toward them, stunning in a silver LaQuan Smith gown. "I've been waiting for you!"

"Congratulations on the movie," Dani said, pulling her into a hug.

"Thank you." Nyla's hazel eyes glittered with excitement. When she turned to Jay, she winked before dipping into a curtsy and raising her voice. "Your Royal Highness."

Jameson leaned forward to kiss her cheek. "I told you to call me Jameson."

"I know," Nyla said, "but do you see the jealousy they can't hide because they're not over here with us?"

"Why wouldn't they be jealous? We're hanging out with the star of the mo—"

Nyla waved away the flattery. "Don't even! Look, this is a small rom-com that's projected to do well, in terms of making its budget back, but you guys showing up will turn this into the event of the summer! Talk about a serious case of FOMO! Pics and videos will be posted on Instagram and TikTok, if they aren't already, and when everyone talks about you, they'll mention the title of the movie! It's a win-win, trust."

That's why she loved Nyla and valued her and their friendship. She was a real one.

Dani rubbed Nyla's arm where it was bared by the dramatic cutout sleeve. "Are you excited?"

"Oh yeah. This is insane," Nyla said, gesturing around them at the posters that featured her beautiful face in various expressions and the huge ten-foot display of her with the different leading men from the movie. "How many premieres have I gone to, either as a guest or where my role was so small people barely knew I was in the movie? Now it's my turn."

"It's about time."

"I know that's right. They're saying I'm a 'luminous new face to watch.'" Nyla's nails sparkled as she made air quotes with her fingers.

Dani rolled her eyes. "The entertainment business is always late. Claiming someone is a new star or just discovered when they've been working for ten years."

"And they say we're on CP time!" Nyla laughed.

Jameson's brows met over his regal nose. "CP time?"

Which only made them laugh harder.

"We have to stop," Dani wheezed, touching a pinkie to the corner of her eye, in an attempt to stem a tear from rolling down her cheeks. "You know how Rhonda is about my makeup. She's probably watching this on someone's IG Live and calling me out my name."

Vicky appeared next to them. "Prince Jameson, someone named Oscar Michaels wants to speak with you for a moment."

"We met a few years ago at the queen's birthday celebration," Jay explained, his expression brightening. He placed a hand on the small of Dani's back. "Would you excuse me for a moment?"

His question wasn't a statement dressed up in the requirements of etiquette. He actually waited for her to answer. She loved that about him.

"Go do you, boo."

He gave her the look he reserved for when she was being extra. "I won't be long, love."

He followed her publicist, the ever-present Roy trailing behind.

Dani watched him leave. His tuxedo was cut to perfection, fitting his tall frame as if it was made for him.

Which it probably was.

Her lips parted on an exhale as she remembered that broad-shouldered, lean-hipped form skillfully moving between her thighs last night, wringing one last orgasm from her sensitively spent body.

When she finally dragged her attention back to Nyla, she found her friend also studying him.

Dani widened her eyes. "Ma'am!"

Nyla grinned and shrugged as if to say *sorry not sorry*. "Do you ever get tired of that . . . accent?"

"Not so far."

"Fair." But the humor slowly melted from Nyla's expression.

Dani frowned. "What's wrong?"

"Did you listen to *The Brunch Bunch* this morning?"

The Brunch Bunch was a syndicated morning show and an institution in the hip-hop world. Most artists knew they'd officially arrived when they were asked to "take a seat" at the famous roundtable made up of some of the most influential DJs and music industry personalities in the game.

"No, I missed it. I was going to catch up during my training session on Friday."

Staying in great shape wasn't just about vanity, although she did have to fit into her barely there stage outfits. But as a rapper and performer it was a professional necessity. She worked out with a trainer at least four days a week to maintain her endurance and breath stamina, which allowed her to perform at top intensity. The month she'd been in England, she'd been lax, although rehearsals for the concert had helped.

Wait, why would Nyla ask if she'd caught it this morn—

"Don't tell me . . . they had Samantha Banks on?"

"Oh God, no!" Nyla wrinkled her nose. "But do you know she tried to crash the premiere?"

"This one?"

"Yup. Once I knew you and Jameson were definitely going to attend, something told me to make sure they put her on the 'no admit' list."

"Does she have any shame? You know what, I don't even care. I refuse to give that girl any more of my time and consideration. She is done."

Nyla winced. "I don't know. It's been so bad *I* even started feeling sorry for her."

"Nuh-uh! Nyla—"

"I don't want to. But she is getting dragged up and down the threads on social media."

"It's her own fault. There are consequences to actions. I'm not saying it's right for people to be calling her out her name, but she had nothing to say when it was happening to me." Dani pursed her lips and ignored the pang of sympathy that shifted in her chest. "But you said it wasn't her? What happened on *The Brunch Bunch*?"

Nyla sighed. "They had Cash on."

Cash Hammad was a prominent manager in hip-hop who, up until a month ago, had been *her* manager. When she'd found out he'd rejected the offer for her to perform at the royal concert, without first informing her of the proposition, she'd had to let him go. Dani had fought hard to be in charge of her own life and make her own decisions. She refused to give that up to anyone, even the man who'd given her a start in the business.

"Was he talking about Dirty Junkie's upcoming tour?"

Cash also managed the popular rap group. Dani had recorded a couple of features on their last album, and she knew Cash had wanted them to collab on a joint tour next year. Something she hadn't wanted to commit to because she'd hoped to be putting her focus solely on her own venture between Mela-Skin and Genesis.

"In the beginning," Nyla hedged. "But then they asked about you, and he . . . well, he acted like a dick."

"Why is my name even in his mouth? What did he say?"

Nyla moved closer and pulled her phone out of her Saint Laurent clutch. Tapping the screen, she opened YouTube.

It was the classic *Brunch Bunch* scene, the three hosts sitting around a large oval table in a glass-enclosed room, posters bearing their likeness and the show's logos adorning the walls.

"I love me some Duchess," Kiara, the lone female host said, huge headphones nestled in her natural hair.

Troy, a radio host from back in the day, rubbed his hands together and licked his lips. "And I'd like to love *up* on some Duchess!"

"Shut up!" Kiara said, laughing. "But seriously, I'm happy to see her getting the props she deserves. Not to mention that fine-ass prince."

"Yeah, your girl is everywhere," DJ Len said into the large microphone in front of his face, his long locs twisted into a knot on top of his head and covered in knitted fabric.

"She not my girl," Cash said, slouching back in his chair, a scowl slashing across his face. His cap was pulled low on his forehead and his diamond necklace popped against the plain black T-shirt he wore that looked like Hanes but Dani knew probably cost five hundred dollars.

"What?" Troy rolled back from the table, his arms raised in the air. "You not managing her no more?"

Cash sucked his teeth. "Nah, bruh. I had to let her go."

"That's bullshit and he knows it!" Dani raged, tapping the screen, which paused the video.

Several people glanced in their direction.

She lowered her voice. "That's how he wants to get back at me? Go around telling everyone that he's the one who ended our arrangement? What are we, in high school?"

"That's not the part I'm talking about," Nyla said, pressing play.

There was more?

"I don't know if that's a smart move," DJ Len said. "She's more popular now than she's ever been."

"Yeah, but I don't want that kind of popular," Cash said.

"Why? What's up?" DJ Len asked.

"Look at her. She used to be on the cover of *Hype* and *XXL* magazines and on shows that represent the culture, like yours. Now she's doing royal concerts and hanging out with the queen. I heard next she's going to be on MSNBC." Cash pounded a meaty fist on the table. "What the fuck she know about politics?"

Nyla spoke over more arguing on the video. "Is that true? You going on Joy Reid?"

"No," Dani said, her indignation leveling up, "but I could. I have thoughts about the state of the world. And who is Cash to say what my experiences should be?"

On the video, Troy mugged comically. "Are you saying she's using him or selling out?"

"I didn't say shit. You did." Cash smiled like the cat who ate the damn canary since his attack landed.

She hoped it gave him metaphorical heartburn.

"Yeah, it's like she's forgotten where she's from, getting together with that colonizer!" Troy said.

Kiara rolled her eyes. "Y'all just hate it when Black women out here showing they got options. Nobody says nothing when some rando rap star smashes several white women or an athlete dates some ethnically ambiguous Instagram model. But when Duchess, who has done nothing but represent and prove she's down for us, falls for a prince, suddenly y'all motherfuckers got something to say!"

"That's different," Troy said.

"Why?" Kiara clapped back.

"Cuz it is!"

"Yo, I don't know about all of that," DJ Len said, "but I used some of that body butter on my elbows and that ish is the truth!"

Kiara scooted closer to her mic. "Oh, you gotta try the moisturizing bath bombs—"

Nyla stopped the video. "That's pretty much it. Thankfully Kiara had your back. And Len . . . kinda."

It had been unpleasant, but it could've been worse.

"I need to have Tasha send them a basket with some products. But none for Troy." That fucker. Dani lifted a hand to massage her forehead before remembering and letting it fall to her side. "I can't believe Cash has the nerve to call me a sellout?"

Dani looked at herself in the mirror every day. She was keenly aware that she was a Black woman, with all the beauty and baggage that entailed. In fact, she'd had an idea for a new marketing campaign based on staying true to oneself.

But as she'd learned with the Banks situation, there were always people out there willing to believe bad shit about her. How many people had heard what Cash said and believed it? All because of who she chose to love.

"Are you worried this will affect the Genesis deal?" Nyla asked.

"No! And that's the last we're going to speak on it. This is *your* night and I'm so proud of you. Your first starring role in a major studio film!"

"Now they can add me to the list of Black actresses they call for all the roles. I can look forward to seeing Zendaya, Zazie Beetz, and Zoë Kravitz at all the auditions. I heard they have a group chat." Nyla grinned ruefully. "If I change my name to Zora, do you think they'll let me in?"

Dani laughed. "You are too much."

"Nope. That's what I say about you."

A woman wearing a simple black sheath and a headset mic came up to Nyla. "They're ready for you, Ms. Patterson."

Nyla pouted her lips and shrugged her shoulder. "I'm so very important. I must go do very important things. Seriously, thank you and Jameson for coming. And let's plan something soon. I miss you."

When Dani was in California, she and Nyla usually spent a lot more time together. But it had been difficult with Nyla getting ready for her premiere and starting back on her TV show and Dani hibernating with Jameson. Understanding their desire to avoid publicity, Nyla had flown up to have dinner with them a couple of times, but it wasn't the same. Dani had never been one of those women who dropped her friends when there was a new man in her life.

"I miss you, too. Dinner, just you and me. A girls' night."

"I'd like that. I need to talk about Rhys."

"Oh really?" Rhys Barnes was another *fwine* British professor—you'd think they grew them on trees!—and one of Jameson's best friends. Dani'd had a front-row seat to the fireworks that had sparked to life when the two had met at the tribute ball back in June. "Is something going on?"

"Later. We need wine, Chinese food, and a sinfully gooey dessert."

"Can't wait. Good luck," Dani called after her.

Dani's optimism left when Nyla did. Tapping the toe of her stiletto heel, she turned away from the still-curious gazes and pondered what she'd seen on the phone. Did Nyla have a point? Would Cash's new narrative affect her Genesis deal?

It shouldn't. Everyone could tell he was just jealous, right? After years of telling her that becoming and remaining successful in the game could only happen if she stayed with him, he was seeing her take off to heights he'd never imagined.

On her own.

She bet that was eating his ass up.

And, unlike the Banks situation, her profile and approval rating were, excuse the pun, sky high. The surge her brand was getting from her relationship with Jameson, whether she sought it out or not, was way more than any little waves caused by Cash and his comments.

Are you sure? What if what that guy had yelled out on the red carpet was true? What if you have been disinvited from presenting at the Hip-Hop Awards?

"My apologies. I didn't intend on being away so long," Jameson said. He glanced around. "Where's Nyla?"

"She had to go. I think the movie will be starting soon."

"Noted. But before we go in, I wanted to introduce you to someone. Have you met Oscar Michaels?"

"No, I don't believe so," she said, shaking the hand of the man standing next to Jameson. About half a foot shorter than Jay, he had a presence that made him seem taller.

"A pleasure," Oscar said, his brown eyes sharp and focused.

"Prince Jameson told me about your company. I can't believe I hadn't already heard of it, but I think there's a natural synchronicity between our two businesses."

"What do you do?"

He handed her his business card. *Celebrity Gift Suites, Inc. Oscar Michaels, CEO.*

Excitement zinged through her. CGS was one of the largest marketing hospitality companies in the world. They'd taken the idea of the gift suite, where celebrities were given hundreds of thousands of dollars of free merchandise in exchange for taking photos of the items and posting about them, and brought it to an international audience. The chance to partner with CGS and supply them with Mela-Skin for international events was remarkable. She hadn't imagined she'd have access to opportunities like these until she'd partnered with a giant like Genesis.

"That would be wonderful. I'll make sure to pass your information on to my CEO."

"Looking forward to it. Your Royal Highness," Oscar said, smiling and bowing slightly before striding away.

Dani peered at Jameson. "Why do I think I have you to thank for what just happened?"

Jameson held his hands up, palms out. "There's nothing to thank. He asked me about you, and I couldn't stop talking about my gorgeous girlfriend's accomplishments."

Cash's lies and insinuation that she was using Jameson rushed to the fore and poisoned the triumphant moment. The lobby of a well-attended movie premiere wasn't the best place for this conversation, but now that it was out there, she couldn't go another second when the possibility existed that Jameson would ever believe she cared more about his title than his heart.

"Jay, it's important to me that you know I'm in this because of who you are, not what you can do for me."

He frowned. "Of course. That's never been a question."

"For you. But it may be for others. And I don't want that shit to come between us."

"Why would it?"

"Because the longer we're together and the more things happen, like you talking to Oscar Michaels about my business—"

His expression tightened. "I didn't know that would be a problem."

This wasn't coming out the way she wanted. She tried again.

"I love you. More than I ever thought possible."

"Good. I feel the same."

"I can't imagine not wanting to be with you forever, but in reality, we've only known each other a couple of months, while I've been working on music, Mela-Skin, and growing my business for *years*. We don't know what the future holds. I think it would be best, for the time being, that we focus on nurturing our relationship."

Confusion furrowed his brow. "What does that mean?"

"That we be in love, spend time together, go on dates, travel. Everything a regular couple does. But when it comes to business, we keep that separate. No more red carpets, even for friends. No joint interviews and no god-awful *People* magazine cover shoots announcing *Duchess and Jameson: Risking it all for Royal Love!*"

His laughter gave her permission to release the breath she'd been holding.

"No having a say in Mela-Skin. Or throwing business our way," she finished softly.

"Is that it?" he murmured.

"For now. I reserve the right to make amendments."

A smile teased his lips. "And was that hard to get out?"

She exhaled a laugh. "Oh yeah."

"It didn't need to be, love, because I understand. I don't want you anywhere near the Company."

Jameson had once told her the "Company" was the term the royal family used to describe the business of being the monarchy. It wasn't the "Firm," as a joke by Princess Bettina, the queen's youngest and bitchiest daughter, seemed to suggest.

"And not because I'm ashamed of you or us," he rushed to add when she'd parted her lips to speak, shooting her a look that said she should know better than to even suggest it, "but because it's not the fairy tale it appears to be. People and relationships will always come second to the institution and because of that, they won't think twice about sacrificing your dreams, your goals, your privacy, and your life in service to the monarchy. I witnessed it with my mother, and I'll be damned if I let it happen to you."

She shivered at the grim determination in his tone. "I hear you. So, what are *your* terms?"

"The main one would be no official royal events, although I don't plan on attending many once I'm back at uni. No premieres, or charity galas." He winced. "No formal family gatherings, but I don't usually go to those, either."

"Then this should be easy. Oh wait, does that mean no guest lecturing any of your classes?"

"According to the terms of this agreement, no. Why? Is that something you'd wanted to do?"

"Hell no. I just thought I'd drop by and see if that cute tour guide was still hanging out at the Guild," she teased.

He hauled her close. "You're going to pay for that later."

"I sure hope so." She poked the tip of her tongue between her teeth.

"It's unorthodox, but it might work." He kissed the tip of her nose. "I'm rather looking forward to dating like regular people."

Happiness fluttered throughout her body and Dani didn't attempt to suppress her silly grin.

Fuck Cash and his bitter words.

She was so close to achieving her goals and now that she'd found true love with Jay, life was nearly perfect.

Chapter Three

PRINCE JAMESON TO SPEAK TO SOCIETY OF ENVIRONMENTAL ENGINEERS IN SMALL GATHERING OF SUMMER TERM STUDENTS

"We're extremely excited. It's very rare for Prince Jameson to make appearances, let alone at a university in the States. We understand what a privilege this is . . ."

***The Daily Californian*, Berkeley's News**

It's important to consider the impact of your work. Ask questions *before* you build, mine, or drill. How will you deal with the inevitable byproduct in a way that won't be harmful to the environment?"

Jameson took a sip of water from the glass that had been placed on the table beside him and stared out at the sea of faces in the auditorium. All seats were occupied, and people were standing in the aisles, against the walls, and several rows deep in the back.

Quite the crowd, considering it was summer term.

Two days ago, he'd been nervous facing the press at Nyla's movie premiere, but here, onstage talking to students at the University of California, Berkeley, he felt at home. Comfortable. In charge. After all, it was essentially a large lecture and he'd worked hard to excel at those.

When he'd told Rhys he was going to be in California, his mate had mentioned a former student who was currently teaching at a university there. Rhys had put the two in touch and they'd had an interesting conversation that had led to an invite to the campus to speak to a small gathering of students. Jameson also thought it would be an excellent opportunity to spread awareness in the U.S. about the John Foster Lloyd Prize for Environmentalism, the prestigious prize he'd created in honor of his grandfather that would be awarded annually to individuals or organizations for their work in the field of environmental studies.

"Remember, there are sustainable paths forward," he continued. "Prevention may take more time on the front end, but it's cheaper in the long run. We must continue to prioritize this thinking so we can work towards saving this planet we all call home. I want to thank Professor Graham and the Student Society of Environmental Engineers for having me here today. And you all, for having a listen."

The applause was deafening. Exhaling in relief, Jameson sat back and rested his ankle on the opposite knee.

"Thank you, Prince Jameson," Graham said from the neighboring club chair, his British accent instigating a brief moment of homesickness. "His Royal Highness has been gracious enough to grant us time for a few questions."

Dozens of hands shot in the air. Graham gestured to a student sitting in the second row, who hurried over to the microphone stand in the center aisle.

"Hi, Prince Jameson, and welcome to Berkeley. Thank you for taking the time to speak to us. I know this is a rather broad question, but what would you say to the person who wanted to know just one thing they could do to help?"

"What's your name?" Jameson asked.

"Me?" The student's eyes widened. "Uh, Rodney."

"Nice to meet you, Rodney, and thank you for your warm welcome. To answer your question: you're doing it. This is a massive problem and not one that can be solved with a single law or initiative. It'll require a change in thinking. So those of you"—he shifted his gaze to encompass the entire room—"who recognize this is an issue, and are willing to devote your career to it . . . *you* are the change we need."

"Next." Graham pointed to someone sitting in the back.

"I'm Bailey," said a female student dressed in a Berkeley jumper and shorts. "You've said this is a huge concern. Do you think it's dire now? That we're too late to effect any real change?"

He'd anticipated this question. It was the one most people asked when they learned, and actually believed, the data on environmental impact. The trick to answering was to be truthful but encouraging.

Jameson shifted forward in his chair. "Maybe. But the work I've done setting up the JFL Prize has really opened my eyes to the fascinating ways the younger generation is thinking about this issue. And, of course, coming here, meeting with students like you, Bailey, and listening to you, I'm full of optimism for the first time in a long while. However, it's critical we take action now, to prevent even more harm from occurring."

"Cool." Bailey smiled. "And thank you for giving us more information about the prize. It sounds exciting."

"My pleasure."

Bailey beamed, pressing her palms to her cheeks. She turned to walk away, bumped into the person standing behind her, looked around as if hoping no one was watching her, and hurried back to her seat.

Graham shot him a knowing look before announcing, "We have time for one last question. Make it a good one."

"Hi, Prince Jameson. My name is Samreen." The young woman wearing a blue hijab bit her lip and grabbed the microphone. "Are you and Duchess getting married?"

Whistles and catcalls filled the auditorium.

Heat singed the tips of Jameson's ears and the back of his neck. He should probably get used to that question being thrown at him. The public was still fascinated with them as a couple and it's not as if marrying Dani wasn't something he'd already been considering. Though their time together had been brief, Jameson knew he wanted to spend the rest of his life with her.

And therein lay the problem. What would his life entail?

If he were just a professor at uni, it would be easy. But he was a member of the British royal family. And a lot came with marrying into the Company. Since the last time he'd spoken to the queen he'd disobeyed a direct order from her, he wasn't even sure what his own position in the family was. He was aware Dani thought him naive for thinking he could go back to lecturing, but he had to believe that was a possibility. He'd meant what he'd told her at the premiere. If he was destined to live his life as a working royal, he couldn't commit to a future with Dani until he'd worked out how to keep her safe. His mother had been born into the British aristocracy. She'd grown up seeing and understanding the cost. And in the end, it hadn't been enough to protect her.

Graham narrowed his eyes. "That's not what I meant."

At least he had guidance on how to handle these questions going forward, thanks to his discussion with Dani. He could feel the subtle anticipation in the room, as if everyone were holding their breath waiting for an answer.

One, he knew, that wouldn't satisfy them.

But he couldn't let the event end on a negative note.

"Why?" he asked, curving his lips in the smile that had unwittingly caused the tabloids to resuscitate his father's unwelcome moniker, Sexy Wexy, a reference to his title as the Duke of Wessex. "I assume it's not because you're making me a better offer?"

Samreen gasped, and her hands flew to cover her mouth. Her cheekbones rounded and flushed becomingly as the room erupted in applause and laughter.

The perfect time to make your escape.

A chorus of yeses pelted the stage. Jameson stood and gestured for Graham, who seemed confused as to how things had gotten so out of his control, to join him.

Welcome to my life.

"Thanks again for having me," he said, as they strode off the stage.

"That was wonderful, Your Royal Highness."

"Jameson. Please," he said.

"Oh no. I may have been over here for close to five years but I'm still a proud Brit with tea flowing through my veins."

"Understood," Jameson said, shaking the other man's hand.

"Tell Rhys the next pint is on me when I see him, yeah?"

Jameson smiled. "Will do."

"Sir?" Graham hesitated before continuing. "I'm not a big gossip hound but in light of your presence here and your current situation, should you find yourself wanting employment in the States, there's a position here for you. My dean made me promise to mention it, although I told him it wasn't necessary . . ."

Jameson nodded then strolled toward his protection detail waiting just out of sight.

Lecturing here, at Berkeley? He already had a job, but would he be willing to uproot his entire life and relocate to be with Dani? Was that even a viable possibility?

"We're going out the back, but there's still press," Roy informed him.

Exiting the building, he ignored the roar of clicks and the calls of "Prince Jameson!" "Jameson!" "Over here, Prince Jameson!" and practically dove into the waiting large black SUV. Only as they were making their way off campus did his breathing return to normal.

Despite the planning and logistics involved in making this speaking engagement happen, he was happy he'd done it. In many ways the university reminded him of Birmingham and the visit reinforced that while earlier in his career, he might have sought out the ivory tower to get as far away from royal life as he could, it now was a place he genuinely loved. Where he thrived. Where he felt he made a difference.

It also got him in the right frame of mind for going home at the end of the week.

So while the feeling of leaving Dani in a few days would be akin to his chest being ripped open, the thought of Birmingham helped ease the ache. There was a possibility the school would need to put protocols in place for his return, with the fervor surrounding his increased profile. It was unfortunate, especially after all he'd done during the initial hiring process to convince the dean that he wouldn't be a distraction. He was amenable to reducing his schedule or just lecturing upper-level courses until it all died down. Whatever they required, he would do if it meant getting back to work.

THE DRIVE BACK to the house had taken a little more than two hours and it was only in the last twenty minutes or so that the echo of the flashing lights had disappeared from behind his eyelids, the click of the shutters and the yelling from the photographers receded from his ears. Would he ever get used to that experience, one it seemed he was destined never to escape? He'd spent so many years avoiding that situation, swearing he'd never live in the hot glare of the spotlight, and yet in the past few months he'd been burned by the almost constant exposure.

Jameson nodded to his PPO, then entered the large house that he and Dani had been occupying for the past few weeks. He'd initially thought she owned it, but she'd corrected his assumption.

"I do well, but not *this* well," she'd said, laughing. "Bennie thought it might be better for us to rent something versus risking the chance that one of my neighbors would sell us out to the tabloids."

Placing his phone on the circular glass table in the middle of the foyer, his gaze strayed to the floor-to-ceiling windows and the magnificent ocean beyond. He found it remarkable that one could live and have access to this type of view, white puffy clouds dotting an endless blue sky that seemed to meet azure blue waves somewhere in the distance. During his time here he'd gotten used to spending his evenings on the stone patio off the main bedroom, watching the glorious sunset produce trails of orange and purple on the water's surface.

He needed certainty and routine, craving the sense of calm and organization it brought him. But loving Dani was akin to setting a bull loose in the china shop of his life. Sure, he could try to stop it, but it would be useless. Instead, he gave in to it, his anxiety soothed and repaired by the consistency of her affection. No matter the craziness they would have to deal with—and given the nature of their lives there would be a lot—he knew they'd get through it together. Because she'd earned his trust.

Such a sentiment would've been unfathomable not too long ago. But Dani had changed that for him.

She'd changed everything.

"It's about time! Where have you been?"

Speaking of magnificent views . . .

Dani stood in the doorway, lovely in a purple cropped T-shirt and ripped jeans, her hair in big puffy curls.

She took his breath away.

Every.

Single.

Time.

He crossed the distance between them in three strides, pulling her into him and fusing his mouth to hers, his eyes closing as shards of pleasure splintered throughout his body. Kissing her was more than lips touching and tongues tangling. He breathed her in, allowing her essence to seep into his bones, reminding him that with her, he'd found his forever.

He broke the kiss and pressed his forehead to hers. "I had the speaking engagement at Berkeley. I told you about it."

"I know." She shuddered. "But that was over hours ago and I've been texting you!"

"You have?" He turned to look accusatorially at his phone.

Right. He'd switched it to airplane mode before the presentation to make sure it didn't go off during the event. And on the drive back to the house, he'd been so lost in thought he'd forgotten to turn it back on.

Her hands gripped his waist. "When was the last time you talked to your family?"

"I spoke to my mother yesterday." Other than her and Rhys, he had no reason to talk to anyone else. "Why?"

"I need to tell you something."

Fear skittered down his spine. "Is something wrong? Is it my mother?"

She cupped his cheek. "Calanthe is fine. But something has happened."

"What? Love, don't keep me in suspense."

She pulled him into the spacious, wide-open living room and over to the enormous sofa they'd spent many an afternoon lounging on.

Moisture fled his mouth, but he kept trying to swallow, wondering what she had to tell him.

He'd lost his job at the university, and he had to be a working royal permanently.

There had been a freak accident that had taken out everyone ahead of him in the line of succession and he was the next king of the United Kingdom and the Commonwealth realms.

She'd been in a fugue state for the past three weeks, but now that she'd had a moment to think clearly, she'd decided she didn't love him enough to deal with his family.

"Have you seen this?" She handed him her phone.

It was a text from Louisa Collins, who'd once been the senior events coordinator for the royal family during the tribute, but who now worked for Dani as a royal family liaison.

Who else had a girlfriend who needed an intermediary to their family?

He read the message. Julian's wife, Fiona, was pregnant.

The arm holding the phone dropped to his lap and he sagged back into the plush cushions, a shaky laugh all he could manage.

"Can you believe it?" Dani asked.

Julian was his uncle, the Prince of Wales and the next in line to the throne. After his marriage to Fiona sixteen years ago, it had taken some time, but they had done their duty and produced an heir. The little girl was ten years old and took after Julian in looks, but her mother in temperament. Thankfully. So, this would be the couple's second child.

"It isn't an issue of belief. More like surprise. And relief."

Her brown eyes searched his. "Is some small part of you disappointed?"

The chances of Jameson ascending to the throne were already slim and with every child born to Julian and his aunts, he slipped further back in the line of succession.

He pulled Dani onto his lap and nuzzled her neck. She smelled *goood.* One of Mela-Skin's tropical-scented body butters. "Not in the slightest."

Dani kissed his cheek. "You're a good man, Jameson Alastair Richard Lloyd. That's the very reason you *should* be king. They don't deserve you."

"But you do?"

She snuggled close. "Absolutely."

His time in the States had been filled with moments like these. Periods of contentment and peace he never thought he'd get the chance to experience. And now that he had, he didn't want to lose it.

"This is good news for them, right?"

He sighed. "Nothing like a royal baby to garner positive press."

She looked up at him. "You sound just like the queen."

Because he knew the articles that would come out when the palace made this announcement. His uncle would be forgiven and granted grace and latitude because royal baby fever would send a blissfully happy country on a spending spree for royal baby-themed paraphernalia.

"I wonder how much she has to do with this?"

Dani shifted to face him. "What would she have to do with it? Does she actually have to be there to put Julian's dick in—"

"I meant," he interrupted, giving her a pointed look, "Julian's extracurricular activities are well-known. He didn't have a lot of time for Fi and Isabella, leaving them on his country estate while he lived in London. They probably would've been happy to keep it that way, except for the scandal surrounding Samantha Banks—"

Dani nodded. "And the queen making them come back to pose pretty for the cameras."

"You know what? It doesn't matter. If this is what Fi wants, then I'm happy for her. I'm certain the palace is thrilled. They love the idea of the Princess of Wales being pregnant. And it bears repeating, the positive press will be beneficial to Julian."

"But not so much for Fiona."

"Why do you say that?"

"Because you're thinking about this like a man. The media will talk in glowing terms about Julian becoming a dad again, but Fiona will be on constant bump watch. If it's anything like it is here, they'll take pictures of her, with a focus on her midsection, which is something no woman wants, even if she's pregnant. They'll discuss her weight gain and swollen ankles. They'll critique her choice of maternity clothes. Can't be too matronly or too sexy. They'll judge whether she touches her belly too much or not enough.

"Then, a day after she gives birth, she'll be trotted out to do that god-awful stand on the steps of the hospital, looking like someone who just pushed something the size of a watermelon out of something the size of a stretchy turtleneck, while he stands there slim, rested, and fashionably put together. Those pictures will be transmitted around the world and referenced for the rest of her life. And then, just when that indignity isn't enough, they'll start harping on when she's going to lose the baby weight!"

He stared at her, wide-eyed. "Had some feelings about that, didn't you?"

Her brows lifted and she nodded. "I didn't realize how much, but yeah. It's hella unfair."

"Well, when you're pregnant, you're going to be gorgeous," he said, pressing a kiss to her curls.

She stiffened, then said, "Funny you should mention that . . ."

His breath caught in his throat. Was she saying what he *thought* she was saying?

"Is there something you want to tell me?"

She picked at the button on his shirt, denying him eye contact.

Were they ready for this when their situation wasn't settled? The media interest in their lives was already at an astronomical level. Add in a pregnancy and a baby? His chest tightened. How would he protect them?

"Dani, are *you* pregnant?"

She finally met his gaze, and her eyes searched his for . . . something.

He waited, tense.

"No."

He exhaled and closed his eyes. Relief?

Almost certainly.

But what was that other feeling?

Was it disappointment?

"But for a second, I thought I might be. I was trying to think back to when it could've happened. We've been very careful."

They had been. He'd stopped that night he'd come home to Primrose Park and found her watching *Four Weddings and a Funeral,* because he hadn't had a condom. And since then, they'd made sure to always have one. Except . . .

"It was that time during the opening reception," she concluded. "When I'd left to go to the bathroom."

And he'd gone after her. They'd been pushed outside the bubble they'd created for themselves at Primrose Park, and he hadn't liked it. He'd needed to be close to her, to remind them both of what they'd been feeling, and he hadn't considered the consequences of surrendering to his impulses.

Neither had she.

They could've been facing a big-ass consequence now.

"I still can't believe we got carried away like that."

"Did you take a pregnancy test?"

"I did. Do you want to see it?"

"That's not necessary. But it was negative?"

She nodded.

"Did you throw it away?"

She pushed away from him. "Are you crazy? I can't throw it away!"

He frowned. "You're going to keep it?"

"No! I was going to have Tasha take it to the city dump. Although . . . I wonder if they burn?"

"Don't you think that's a little extreme?"

"After what you just said about the press and Julian and Fiona, I can't believe you're not offering to light the match! I'm not being paranoid. People *have* gone through my trash. Can you imagine the headlines if this got out? I didn't even purchase the test. Bennie keeps a stash, and she had an assistant drive it up to me."

He hadn't considered that. A headline touting their pregnancy scare made his skin crawl. And if the palace had seen it without him giving them a heads-up . . .

He wrapped his arms around her. He hated that she'd done it alone, without him.

And he needed to know.

"Are you happy about the outcome?"

"Are you?" she asked, a slight tremble in her voice.

He took her hands. "I would love to have children with you . . . someday. We're not ready. For all the reasons behind our agreement times a million. You're getting ready to start your new partnership with Genesis—"

"And you have to figure out your situation with your family."

"My family. Can you imagine? Are you ready for what would happen if you were actually carrying a potential heir to the throne? At the same time as Fiona?"

"I guess we got lucky."

He wasn't buying her airy tone. They *were* fortunate. But in all the discussions they'd had, they'd never discussed the prospect of children.

"Do you even want kids?"

She moved off his lap. "I don't know. I never thought about it."

"Never?" he pressed.

"I mean, I've thought about it enough to make sure it didn't happen. But nothing beyond that. Do you?"

"Yes."

He knew that with a certainty. He'd always accepted it as something that would happen, but he'd assumed he'd raise them on the margins of the royal stage. It had never occurred to him that he wouldn't have children. Or that he and his partner might be raising them in front of the entire world.

"My parents weren't ready to have me," she said, "and I don't want to repeat that same mistake. I have goals to achieve. Goals that won't be helped by having a child right now."

He understood and agreed.

Then why are you bothered because she didn't unequivocally state she wanted to have children with you?

But she wasn't finished.

"What I do know is that when we start a family, it won't be some publicity stunt to detract from bad press. It'll be because we're ready and want to bring our beautiful babies into this world."

He loved her so much. "And you won't be alone. I'll be there every step of the way. I'll even make sure I'm not—how did you put it?—'fashionably put together' when it's our turn on the hospital steps."

She wrapped her arms around his neck. "We're gonna have to talk about them steps."

However he felt about his uncle, Fi's pregnancy was good news for everyone, including Jameson. The fanfare from another royal baby was news the queen could capitalize on for a long time.

Meaning, she wouldn't need him.

One thought formed just before Dani reclined flat on the couch and he prepared to lose himself in her:

He just might get back to his ivory tower after all.

Chapter Four

IS PRINCE JAMESON GOING INTERNATIONAL?
How the Duke of Wessex Charmed the Students at One Prestigious American University
Daily Mail

So, do *you* like wearing this in public?" Dani asked, her tone playful.

Jameson instinctively touched the front of his blindfold and regretted the action when he stumbled. Dani's grip around his waist tightened and he kept one hand slightly in front of him, focusing on not falling and hoping he didn't look as ridiculous as he felt.

"No. And I'm sorry I didn't fully comprehend how much I was asking you to trust me when I did this to you."

"Thanks, baby. But it's okay. Even then, I knew I was in good hands."

Hip-hop music played, and the bass seemed to vibrate the molecules in the air around him and change the rhythm of his heartbeat until they were both synced, but its muted volume suggested the sound originated elsewhere, like on the other side of a wall.

Finally, she squeezed his arm and they stopped.

"You can take this off now. We're not quite there yet, but there's steps."

He removed the satin mask and winced at the brightness that immediately assaulted his eyes. He blinked several times until his vision returned to normal.

"Where are we?"

"One of my favorite places in L.A."

"We're in a building, so I can rule out the Hollywood Walk of Fame, the Santa Monica Pier, and Disneyland."

"I'm not a fucking tourist, Jay," she said, rolling her eyes.

He glanced around at the bare walls, steel steps, and concrete floors. "I'm not gleaning any clues from the environment. Can you give me a hint?"

"Because I'm generous like that, I'll give you three." She started up the stairs and he followed. "Outside. Double Feature. 'Big Mistake. Big. Huge!'"

Hmmm . . . She had to be referencing the time he'd taken her to Open Air Cinema at Baslingfield Court to watch *Pretty Woman* and *Notting Hill*. And one of those movies took place in Los Angeles—

"Are we going on a tour of the *Pretty Woman* locations?" he asked once they'd reached the landing.

She laughed. "Well, you got the movie right."

He'd take the win. He was shocked his brain retained its ability to function considering his eyes hadn't strayed from the tempting sway of her hips in light blue jean shorts that cupped her ass, with frayed hems that barely reached her upper thighs.

"But no," she continued. "We're going to do a little shopping."

"For you?"

"Nope. For you."

His head jerked back. "Me? I don't need any clothes."

"No one who shops here *needs* clothes. Just humor me."

He looked down at his blue quarter zip polo and khakis. "You don't like the way I look?"

"I love the way you look. I love *you*. But you toggle between two styles: professorial or royal."

"Because that's what I am!"

"But there are so many spaces in the spectrum where you could experiment. You're always so classically composed. Let's dirty you up a bit. Do something a little more"—she moved her shoulders and hips—"swaggy."

What did she bloody mean by that? *Swaggy?* Like a rapper?

He clenched his jaw. "I'm pretty certain swaggy isn't my style."

Dani sighed. "Jay, I'm not trying to change you. I know exactly who you are. I wanted to play a little dress-up; have some fun. You know how loving me is diversifying your life? I thought we could diversify your wardrobe. And you could experience a little bit of my culture and take that back home with you. But if you're not into it . . ."

Her lashes fluttered and she shrugged her shoulders.

Fuck! When she put it that way . . .

He'd let his own insecurities surrounding who he was almost prevent him from enjoying an adventure she'd planned for them. One that would allow him to learn more about her and what she liked. And discerning her preferences had easily become one of his primary goals in life. So, if that meant getting swaggy, well . . . he'd do it with the best of them.

He cupped her cheek. "I'm yours to command."

She pressed her hands to his chest and gazed up at him, her expression softening. "I'm going to remind you of that later."

"I hope so."

Smiling, Dani pushed a button next to a slatted steel door. "On the first floor is Backtrack, an iconic upcycled streetwear store here in L.A. The owner has his offices and personal design studio up here."

There was a loud *click* and the door rolled up bit by bit to unveil a well-lit, sleekly designed space. Black piping ran the length of all four walls showcasing clothes hung on thin black hangers and organized by color. Glass display cases featuring hats, trainers, and accessories dotted the open space.

"Yo, Duchess. My girl! What's poppin'?"

A Black man of average height with light skin, a bald head, and a thick beard strode over to meet them.

"C-Swizzle! Long time no see!"

The two embraced and when they parted, he grabbed her hands and held her arms out. "Look at you! I recognize that cropped bomber jacket."

Dani put a hand on her hip and struck a pose. "You know I had to represent! But seriously, thank you for taking time out of your schedule to accommodate us."

"Anytime, Duchess. We Gucci, you know that."

"I do." Dani reached back and grabbed Jameson's hand. "C, this is His Royal Highness, Prince Jameson Alastair Richard Lloyd, the Duke of Wessex. And my boo. Did I get it all?"

Jameson winked at her and nodded.

"Whew!" She laughed. "Jay, this is Corey Solomon."

"Nice to meet you," Corey said. "Uh, do I bow or—"

"No, please don't." Jameson held out his hand and they shook. "And it's a pleasure meeting any friend of Duchess's. She spoke highly of you and your work."

"The respect is mutual. No doubt. She's a beast. So, I pulled some pieces like you asked," Corey told Dani, shoving his hands into the pockets of his extremely oversized khaki overalls. "Some from the floor of Backtrack and a few from my newest collection. My assistant has everything on racks in the first dressing suite. Imma head back to my office, but if you need anything, holler."

"I appreciate you, Corey," she said, kissing him on the cheek.

"No worries. Good meeting you, Prince Jameson."

"It's Jameson. And thank you."

Corey nodded and disappeared through an arched doorway.

Jameson glanced around, struck by the strangeness of their situation. They'd barely ventured out in the three weeks that he'd lived here. Why was it suddenly safe to be in a building during the day in the middle of central Los Angeles without worrying about photographers or regular people with their phones out, cameras recording?

"Is this okay? Can we trust him?"

"Do you know how many celebrities shop here? Corey would lose that clientele if he was selling everyone out. Besides, he prides himself on restricting the spectacle to Backtrack."

With a start, Jameson realized he could no longer hear the music that had been so audible when they'd been outside.

"Only a select few are provided access to *this* experience," Dani continued. "And we go way back. Now, stop stalling. Time to shop. Do you trust me?"

His response was instantaneous. "With all that I am."

"Right answer, Your Royal Highness."

Corey's assistant led them through white barn doors into a large room that continued the urban sophisticated decor from the previous one. Industrial styled track and pendant lighting illuminated the space that featured white throw rugs, metal accent tables, and a dark grey low profile sofa situated across from black drapes opened to reveal several racks of clothes.

Dani headed for the garments and began flipping through them.

"Nice. Nice. I like that," she muttered to herself.

In addition to the clothes, the space included a small half moon–shaped platform, surrounded by mirrors on three sides, and a rust-colored chair with matching ottoman.

"Come here. Okay, these are all different. Just as there are infinite numbers of BBC TV channels—"

"Hey!"

She grinned cheekily. "—there are many different styles of streetwear, from skatewear to Hypebeasts. You can't be inauthentic, though. It'll look the best when you feel it. That's why we're trying out lots of styles. To see which one rocks best with you. Each outfit is already grouped together, so you should put them on that way."

"Yes ma'am," he said.

She stuck her tongue out and retreated, sinking down on the sofa in the main seating area. When he started to draw the curtains closed, she complained, "What are you doing? It's not like I haven't seen it all before?"

"Consider it part of the experience," he said, shutting the drapes on her astonished expression.

The first outfit was a pair of blue jeans—Good God, were both knees torn open? How impractical!—and a voluminous red jumper with blue flames drawn along the hem and sleeve. She wanted him to wear this? He checked the tag on the jeans.

"How did you get my size?" he called to Dani.

"Margery."

Of course.

He needed to have a discussion with his chief housekeeper. Remind her who she actually worked for.

Quickly donning the clothes, he stared at his reflection in the mirror.

Would you step one foot out of your house dressed like this?

Absolutely not. He didn't want to leave the privacy of *this* room. But he promised Dani an "experience," and he truly loved making her happy.

Taking a deep breath, he pushed the curtain aside.

"Wow!" Dani leaned back on the sofa and studied him. "You look different."

"Not like a prince or professor?"

"Oh no," she said, with a laugh.

He turned away. "So, I look as ridiculous as I thought."

"No, no!" She rose, her palms facing outward. "You could never look bad. But this style may not be for you."

"Glad we're on the same page."

Her response to the second outfit—olive-colored cargo trousers with loads of pockets and zippers, a fitted, white, tissue-thin T-shirt, and a khaki-colored anorak—was warmer. "I like it but it's giving me Buckingham Palace 2074!"

He agreed. It wouldn't go into his regular rotation, but he could see wearing it to the right event.

"I'd wear my trainers with these?"

"I'm pretty sure none of your shoes would go with this. But never fear." She pointed to a tall, rolling shoe rack that hadn't been there before. "I had Corey's assistant pull some kicks for you. The white-on-white Air Force 1s would work with this outfit and the shoe is so ideal it doesn't hurt to have several other color combos. The classic black-and-white Adidas Superstars go with everything, and no collection is considered complete without the Air Jordan 1s."

She might as well have been talking in a language he didn't understand, but he nodded as if he did.

"She also brought some light refreshments, to keep up your energy," Dani said, helping herself to a glass of champagne and a strawberry from the fruit-laden tray on the table.

"Maybe later," he said, remembering the number of garments he had yet to try on.

The next two outfits had hits and misses, but he liked the green bomber jacket with the black collar from one of the ensembles and the black-and-white joggers from the other.

As he changed into the next outfit hanging on the rack, he thought about calling it a day. Is this what all shopping excursions involved? It really was much simpler to have his valet purchase clothes he could try on at his leisure.

When he finished, he turned to look in the mirror and—

Bloody hell.

He looked good. He'd thought the black jeans a little snug, but he had to admit the proportions worked on his body. The black hooded tee was soft to the touch and not at all bulky beneath the buttery black leather jacket. Now, this was something he could get used to. He shoved his hands in the pockets and tilted his head back, staring at his reflection.

Was this what Dani meant by feeling it? Was this *swaggy*?

He left the room, holding his arms out to the side and spinning slowly. "You like?"

Dani glanced up from her phone and froze. Her eyes swept him from head to toe and her lips parted. Pleasure at her obvious approval warmed his chest.

She nodded, setting the device down on the cushion next to her before standing. "Most definitely."

She glided over, her shoulders back and hips swaying in a silent rhythm that drew him into her spell. When she reached him, she took his mouth in long, slow drugging kisses that plundered his soul.

"You're so fucking hot," she murmured against his lips, sliding her hand beneath the lapels of his coat and pushing the item off his shoulders.

"And you're exquisite." He cupped her cheek.

She trailed her fingers over his chest and down his stomach, leaving goosebumps in their wake. She grasped his buckle and dropped to her knees on the plush carpet.

He quickly glanced around and whispered, "What are you doing?"

"This isn't our first time," she said, intent on her task.

"You want to do it here?"

"Why not? We won't be disturbed. And why are you whispering?"

"Are you sure?"

Her task completed, she tugged the pants over his hips and down his legs. "Uh-huh."

He would've asked more questions but when she dragged her tongue along his cotton-covered cock, his brain went fuzzy.

"Beautiful," she said, pulling it out of his boxer briefs and stroking him with long, slow pulls.

His lashes fluttered and his head fell back. Of their own accord, his hips began to move, thrusting into her hold. He hissed in pleasure and covered her hands with his, pressing her grip tighter around him as he rubbed in and out of her palm.

So. Damn. Good.

But his head snapped forward at the feel of her tongue brushing against his thick crown. He looked down in time to see her sweep a bead of pre-cum from the tip.

Bloody hell.

"Hmmm. . . ." She licked her lips and looked up at him from beneath long lashes.

This woman would be the death of him.

And then she took him fully into her mouth.

Desire seized hold and he bucked, struggling to hang on to control. Her hands squeezed the base of his cock and her tongue caressed its underside, the combination driving him wild. It went beyond what she was doing; it was where they were, the carnality of being in a public location adding to his fervor exponentially.

He staggered back several steps, pulling out of her mouth. "That's enough. I don't want to come in your mouth."

"Next time," she promised.

He hauled her to her feet and reclaimed her lips, his tongue dueling with hers in a battle they would both win. He savored their mingled taste, more potent than the best wines in his cellar at home, and shivered, the need to be inside her more pressing than his body's demand for air.

"My pocket," he said, gesturing to the chair where he'd neatly folded the pants he'd initially been wearing.

He used her brief absence to rid himself of his pants and undies and when she was back, the condom nestled between two of her fingers, he took it, tearing it open and quickly sheathing himself.

In for a penny, in for a pound . . .

He led her over to the platform facing the mirrors in the middle of the dressing area.

"Turn around."

Her smile became positively wicked. She faced the mirror, and he met her gaze in its reflection.

"Take those off."

She lifted a brow, but acquiesced, slipping out of her shorts and knicks.

Fuck!

He clasped the base of his cock and it pulsed in his hand. *That ass!* "Bend over."

The tip of her tongue appeared and moistened her upper lip as she leaned forward and braced her hand on the dais. She spread her legs and glanced at him over her shoulder.

"It's all yours, big boy."

"You're damn right," he said, surging into her.

Their joining ripped the air from his lungs. The action propelled her forward on the balls of her feet and she gasped.

He stayed in her snug warmth for several long moments before he slowly withdrew until the head emerged, glistening, from her cleft. He gripped it again, dragging his cock head through her folds, teasing her clit, using the evidence of her desire to coat himself. She moaned loudly and the sound arrowed straight to his erection.

Looking in the mirror, he met her gaze and reseated himself, inch by torturous inch. Her lashes fluttered and she arched her back, lifting her hips higher. He took the hint, gripping them tightly and starting to move. There was too much to take in and he alternated between staring at the ecstasy on her face and watching his cock slide in and out of her pussy. Her curvy ass bounced as she pushed back against him and he smacked the pillowy globes, turned on by the stinging of his palm.

"Fuck, yeah," she cried.

He varied his strokes: shallow and fast, deep and slow, and her soft, panting *yeah*s and *do it*s drove him out of his mind. He curled forward to press his chest against her back and wrap an arm around her midsection, his hips pistoning his cock inside her yielding flesh. The musky scent of sex mixed with her perfume and filled the space, making him dizzy with desire.

When he licked the space between her neck and shoulder, she clenched around him.

"Jay, baby, I'm coming!"

Her torso trembled and shivers racked her body. He took her chin and covered her mouth with his as she came, her inner walls pulsating the length of his cock.

That did it! He was going to explode!

And then he did, his own powerful orgasm tearing through him.

Good God!

His chest rose and fell with the labored efforts of his breathing as sanity and awareness returned.

"I hope you like those clothes," Dani said, relaxing against him, her laughter wrapping itself around his heart, "because I think they're ours now."

Chapter Five

THE SPARE! QUEEN THRILLED NOW THAT FIONA'S PREGNANT WITH BABY NO. 2!
The Morning Star

You were an asset to the faculty. We wish things were different . . ."

"This is an institution of higher learning, not some posh social club!"

"Parents entrust their children to us for their education and safety. To see them on the front page of some tabloid is unacceptable."

"We really do hate to do this, but we've decided not to ask you back this semester."

"That's fucked, mate. I'm sorry," Rhys said, leaning forward and bracing his elbows on his knees.

Jameson nodded and took a sip of his whisky. The fact that they were having this conversation here in his home office at Primrose Park, instead of at the Bell and the Crown, the pub near the uni, only caused the fire in his gut to burn hotter. He had no reason to ever visit the pub again.

He'd lost his job at Birmingham.

So much for the pregnancy announcement getting him back in his ivory tower.

Jameson shook his head. "I've worked there for more than a decade, and they made me a permanent lecturer a year ago. It's not as if my being a member of the royal family is a new condition. They knew that when they hired me."

Rhys slouched back and reached for his own drink. "But you have to admit things are different now."

"They are?"

"A year ago, you were a reluctant royal. You didn't want anything to do with your family and you made it very clear that you pictured a life in academia for yourself."

"I still do!"

"But look at it from their point of view," Rhys persisted. "Despite your protestations, you became the face of the royal tribute honoring your grandfather. An event that made you the most popular member of the most famous family in the world."

Jameson tensed. Was Rhys taking *their* side?

"You know why I did that! The queen forced my hand!"

"I *knew*," Rhys emphasized, "they didn't."

Jameson leaned back in his chair and stared at the ceiling, the ornate scrollwork and medallions in the plaster as familiar to him as a child's favorite book. He'd known from the moment the queen had drafted him into service that his life would change.

He hadn't foreseen the good—Dani.

Or anticipated the bad—losing his job.

"There was the press coverage before the event and then we couldn't escape your mug the entire week of the festivities. Not to mention—"

"But you will anyway," Jameson muttered.

"—the incident where the press breached the campus."

Jameson's hand clenched into a fist, thinking back to the moment when he'd accidentally bumped into a student crossing the quad only to discover it was a paparazzo, looking for a comment about Jameson's newly increased royal responsibilities . . . and the scandal surrounding his father's death.

When he'd initially been hired, the press had practically salivated at the thought of a young royal teaching at uni. How would all those young, impressionable female students deal with having Sexy Wexy in their midst? But when no titillating tidbits managed to escape, they gave up. And thus, a tentative unspoken agreement formed: as long as he stayed out of the spotlight, save only his attendance at the required family events, they'd leave him alone. But as Rhys had helpfully pointed out, when Jameson had "agreed" to be the face of the royal tribute, the press had taken that as a signal that the tentative truce was broken.

No one had been brazen enough to breach the campus before, but once word got out that it had been achieved, more were sure to follow.

Jameson sighed. "That's essentially what the committee said."

"You could fight it."

As a permanent lecturer, Jameson could only lose his post due to an unwillingness to perform his duties, gross misconduct, or redundancy. And though he knew he could argue his innocence on all counts—

"No, I can't."

"You couldn't," Rhys agreed. "Especially if you want to reduce your media footprint."

The headlines generated by his filing a lawsuit would make him look like a spoiled prince in the best scenarios and like an entitled prick in the worst. Based on that alone, even if he wanted to challenge the dismissal, the queen wouldn't allow it.

The university knew it, too.

"Did they mention Dani?" Rhys asked.

Then there had been *that* little nugget . . .

"Your involvement with this vulgar American rapper . . . What are we supposed to say to the parents who call and inquire about the appropriateness of the lecturers on staff?"

A red mist of rage had clouded his vision. How dare they judge Dani without knowing her?

"Her performances are what she does for a living, not who she is. But of course, that was beyond their comprehension. They've spent their entire lives in academia. They are what they do."

Rhys pointed at him. "You know this is really jokes coming from you."

"Oh, sod off." Jameson exhaled and sat up, bracing his elbows on his desk.

"What are you going to do now?"

Jameson fiddled with a pen. "Find another lecture position."

"Where exactly? The higher-ups may have been right prats about it, but their concerns are valid."

"Not for long. With the royal tribute over and the palace's announcement about Fiona's pregnancy receiving front-page treatment, I have no need to be the family's representative again."

"But you're still with Dani."

Forever, his brain and heart emphatically stated.

"So?"

"She's one of the hottest celebrities on the planet right now, thanks in part to your relationship. If you're going to be together, you have to expect the press attention will be intense. Everywhere. Do you see another university wanting to put up with that?"

"It'll only be intense if Dani and I feed into it. We've already decided to keep our relationship separate from our work lives. If we're not showing up at celebrity events or royal functions, the interest will diminish."

Rhys shook his head. "That won't make the problem go away. There are many reasons why the two of you will always be news."

"I know. Me being royalty, her being a rapper. Me being British, her being American. Me being white, her being Black. Believe me, I get it." He raked his fingers through his hair. "If I fail to find a position here, I guess it's time."

"For what?"

Jameson drummed his fingers against his tumbler of whisky. He'd relayed Professor Graham's wishes, the reception of which pleased Rhys. But he hadn't mentioned Graham's job offer. Or that Jameson was now considering it.

"To relocate. Graham offered me a position at Berkeley."

His statement erased the perpetually disinterested look from Rhys's face. "Are you serious?"

Jameson nodded. "I am."

"Can you do that?"

"I don't know yet. Up until a few hours ago, I was still employed. But I'll find out."

"That's major. And you're willing to make that transition for someone you've only known a couple of months?"

He'd asked himself that very question, so he wasn't angry at Rhys for challenging him. From the outside, it would seem fast. But he and Dani had weathered a lot in their brief time together. He believed she was the one for him, even if they hadn't figured out how it would all work.

And speaking of making it work—

"If things progress with you and Nyla, would you make the move?"

"Fuck, mate, I don't know. We're nowhere near that yet."

"Well, where are you and how's it going? I was surprised you didn't make it to the premiere."

"I know." Rhys dropped his chin to his chest. "I wanted to be there."

"Then why weren't you?"

"Because attending her movie premiere on another fucking continent seemed a bit serious. You know I love an adventure and Nyla and I had some fun, but neither of us are ready for what me showing up as her date would mean."

Jameson's cellphone buzzed with a text from Edgar, the queen's private secretary:

"The queen requests your presence at Buckingham Palace, tomorrow morning at eleven A.M."

Time to pay for the way he'd handled things back in June.

He shoved his phone across the desk and was on his feet refilling his drink before the device stopped spinning, perilously close to the edge.

Rhys arched a blond brow. "You may want to be done with the royal family, but it appears the royal family isn't done with you."

THE MORE THINGS change, the more they stay the same.

He hadn't been ushered into the Den of Despondency, the bright yellow sitting room where he'd always received unwanted news that changed his life.

But the queen was still late.

Jameson shifted in his chair, attempting to protect his eyes from the rays of sun that managed to break through London's perpetual cloud cover. Thankfully he'd made the right choice last night, putting the bottle of Glenmorangie away when he'd wanted nothing more than to drown his sorrows and ruminate on everything he'd recently lost: his privacy, his sanity, his career.

But you gained Dani.

And that was worth everything.

He knew that.

He meant it.

It should've made the misfortune easier.

It didn't.

He wished he'd had the chance to talk to her this morning. Hearing her voice helped ground him, reminded him of life beyond the Buckingham Palace gates. But she'd told him she was going to be out of touch for a couple of days. She'd text him but there was nothing like hearing her voice.

Except seeing her face.

Or having her with him.

Another glance at the closed door and he reached into his inner blazer pocket and pulled out his phone. He was ridiculous, reduced to checking her Instagram feed like some lovestruck fan.

The most recent post showed her in the cabin of a private plane, one foot—clad in black high heels, with straps that wound up and around her calf—perched on the cream-colored leather seat, a black romper molded enticingly to her curves.

His body stirred. *Beautiful. And all mine.*

But she was projecting Duchess instead of Dani.

She'd been hired to perform for a private birthday party in Dubai. He'd been amazed that she'd even consider traveling halfway across the world to do a few songs for a handful of people, but she'd tilted her head and said, "They're paying me a grip! For *three* songs. You don't turn down that type of money . . . unless you're a member of the royal family."

When she'd told him how much an oil tycoon was willing to pay her to give a mini concert for his wife, a huge Duchess fan, he'd blinked, then promptly disagreed with her.

"Members of my family would certainly fly around the entire world for that amount of money."

And probably had.

After the performance, she was heading back to New York for her meeting with Genesis. Between the travel, her work, the time difference, and preparation, he didn't expect to talk to her for a few days.

He didn't know how he'd bear it.

"Her Majesty the Queen."

Jameson hadn't seen his grandmother since he'd walked away from her at the tribute ball a month ago. He'd expected her to look the same as she had then. As she always did.

Imperious. Regal. No-nonsense.

Queen Marina II was still regal. She'd been the ruling monarch for more than three decades; one didn't just lose that presence, even in the face of other emotions. She was only of average height, but with her trim figure impeccably styled and her cloud of silver hair, she always seemed taller. But she looked weary, as if she carried the weight of the entire Commonwealth on her shoulders.

The palace had recently announced the impending birth of the third in the line of succession to the British throne. What could she possibly be worried about?

He stood, as he always did when meeting with his grandmother, but instead of sitting down, she walked over and gazed up at him. Emotions darted across her features, too quick for him to discern, before she masked them. Nodding once, she ended her scrutiny.

What was that about?

He waited until she'd perched on the edge of her chair, before retaking his own seat.

"Welcome home." Her voice was cool and measured, as if he'd imagined the moments before.

"Thank you, Your Majesty. I wish it would've been under better circumstances."

"Yes, I heard, and I'm sorry."

He didn't respond but she must've read the skepticism in his narrowed eyes and pursed lips.

"I am," she insisted. "I may not have understood your need to renounce your duties and immerse yourself in the scholarly world, but I know how much you loved it."

He swallowed past the sudden lump in his throat. "I did."

"It's for the best, really. Now you can continue on as one of my Counsellors of State," she said with finality.

Counsellors of State were senior members of the royal family who could carry out official duties on the queen's behalf. Once an appointment was made, one was unable to refuse acceptance. The queen had appointed Jameson back in March.

He frowned. "I thought you'd had me removed?"

"Why? You're a valuable asset to this family."

"That was our deal. In exchange for acting as the face of the family for Grandfather's tribute, you'd appoint me as the patron of his charitable trust and I could go back to lecturing at Birmingham."

"I did turn over John's charitable trust to you. Edgar said the paperwork had been sent to your household. And since Birmingham is no longer an option, there's nothing preventing you from being incorporated full-time into the Company's schedule."

Jameson pinched the bridge of his nose. What was that quote from *The Godfather*? *Just when I thought I was out . . .*

"What happened with Birmingham was unfortunate, but I still intend to teach at the collegiate level. I'll find another position."

"How?" Divots appeared between the queen's white brows. "You're a disturbance. You come with a lot of baggage and a new high-profile romance. There isn't a prestigious university in the country that will invite that bedlam onto their campus."

That sounded suspiciously similar to his department chair's sentiment. Had Birmingham consulted with his grandmother? Or worse, had *she* intervened?

He straightened, annoyed by the attempts to steer his life. "That's only a problem if I stay in this country."

Now *she* was the one scrutinizing *him* through narrowed eyes. Conversations with his grandmother weren't just an exchange of information and ideas. They could mutate into verbal chess matches, battles of wit from start to finish.

"So, your speaking engagement at the university in California? It went well?"

A bold opening gambit, letting him know she was aware of his movements. Did his grandmother have people spying on him?

It wouldn't be the first time.

"It did."

"And you'd do that? Turn your back on your lineage? Your family and your responsibilities? For her?"

He would, but this wasn't about Dani. It was about how he wanted to live.

"I would've been perfectly happy going back to life before the tribute."

"Sometimes I rue the day I ever came up with that damned idea," Marina muttered, looking away.

"Stunned" wasn't a strong enough word to describe Jameson's reaction to what the queen had just shared. The tribute had been essential to distract from calls for the abolishment of the monarchy. She'd pinned everything on its successful occurrence. He'd never thought he'd hear she may now be regretting it.

Before he could come up with a proper response, Marina patched up the crack in her armor. "We are where we are. This family needs you, Jameson, and you will do your duty."

"I have. I did what you asked me to do and now I'm done."

The air thickened in the face of her incredulity. Jameson held her stare, making it clear he meant what he'd said.

Check.

Marina dropped her gaze first, smoothing out the already immaculate fabric of her navy skirt. "And will this new life in America include your mother?"

The hairs at the nape of his neck stood at attention. "What does my mother have to do with this?"

"She is the mother of a royal child, but she married into the family. She's not a Lloyd by blood. She was allowed to live at Primrose Park and Kensington Palace and enjoy our privileges and protections while she raised you, but now that you're 'done,' why should the taxpayers continue subsidizing her lifestyle?"

Her threat rang in his ears and a heaviness settled on his chest. "She hasn't done anything to warrant what you're suggesting. She's given her *life* to this family. Your son got her pregnant at seventeen, and to save his reputation—and yours!—she was forced into a loveless marriage. She endured his affairs and scandals with dignity while being constantly harassed by the media. She's kept the family's counsel when she could've profited from it. She's been nothing but loyal. Yet you'd kick her out of her home and deny her protection just to force my hand?"

The queen merely stared at him.

Son of a bitch!

He exhaled a shaky breath through his nostrils as rage—hot, thick, and destructive—flowed through his body. He wanted to leap from his chair and roar, turn over a table, kick something. Anything. Starting with that large French porcelain vase in the corner. But he didn't. He couldn't. Some formalities were too well-ingrained to toss off like an unnecessary jacket. He settled for flexing his hands on the arms of his chair and breathing deeply in an effort to calm down.

No wonder this family was in its current predicament. The only way they could relate to one another was through blackmail and a series of power grabs. Would it ever end? Or would he always be a puppet on a string, subject to his grandmother's whims? What would she do, who would she use the next time he refused to do her bidding?

Dani?

Fuck no. This was the last time he'd allow himself to be in this position. He had research to conduct, plans to make. In the meantime, he couldn't let his mother lose the lifestyle she'd earned and the protections she deserved. Jameson's increased profile meant his father's scandals were back in the press and his mother was in their crosshairs. It had been terrifying for her the first time around. He'd do whatever it took to protect her.

A fact the queen knew and had been counting on.

Checkmate.

"What do you want me to do?" he pushed out through a jaw clenched so tight he was surprised he hadn't cracked a molar.

"I . . ."

Again Jameson thought he detected a . . . softening?

But she shook her head and lifted her chin. "You will take over the events on Julian's calendar. Catherine will take his official meetings."

As the Prince of Wales and heir apparent to the sovereign, Julian was charged with helping Marina in the performance of her duties.

Jameson frowned. Was everything okay with Fiona or were

there complications with the pregnancy? Could Julian actually be taking time off to be with her and Isabella?

"We need to provide a united front," the queen was saying.

"Is there something going on other than Fi's pregnancy?"

"Fiona's fine, but we have the St. Lucia state visit coming up next month and it's important that everyone acknowledges we're still a strong ruling family."

"That's never been a problem before."

Her hands fidgeted in her lap. "They haven't discussed declaring their independence before."

Oh. "The Commonwealth has had realms declare their independence but remain members."

The Commonwealth of Nations was a voluntary association of fifty-six countries, once British colonies, that the queen had sought to uphold throughout her reign. Many of them still recognized Marina as their head of state. Including St. Lucia.

"It's not the same. Independence means they no longer trust my leadership. And the more it happens, the more our people begin to question our usefulness!"

It explained his grandmother's actions. All around her, the thing she loved the most, the monarchy, was ripping apart at its seams.

Jameson sighed. "Fine. But I'll attend these events alone. I don't want Dani involved."

Per their agreement. Which was looking more prescient as time passed.

"Believe me, I have no intention of involving that woman. This is a family matter, and she isn't family."

"Not yet."

The queen stiffened. "Haven't you skipped a step? You're still close enough in the line of succession that you need my formal consent to get married."

"If that's your way of asking if I've proposed to Dani, the answer is no."

She released a huge breath. "That would be absurd. You've only known each other for two months!"

He narrowed his eyes. "But it's only an issue of timing, not confusion. Because it will happen. And I won't require anything from you when the time comes."

"You will if you expect her to be a part of this family."

"Do you think that matters when a majority of the time *I* don't want to be a part of this family?" Frustration tightened into a knot in his chest.

"But you are. And we need you. You were quite effective during the celebrations. Everyone remarked upon it. You reminded me a lot of your father."

He inhaled sharply. "I don't want to talk about my father. But I do want to know why you need me to do this. Julian, with a pregnant Fiona by his side, would project a healthy and secure future for the monarchy—the exact image you're trying to put forward. Why aren't you using them?"

Lines of tension bracketed her mouth. "I take it you haven't talked to your girlfriend today?"

"No." He scowled at another reminder that it would be days before he'd have the pleasure.

But what did this have to do with Dani?

"Apparently, Fiona isn't the only one expecting. That girl Duchess was involved with, Samantha Banks? She's also claiming to be pregnant. By Julian."

Chapter Six

FROM LONDON TO DUBAI: DUCHESS TAKES THE WORLD BY STORM

People

"Here." Tasha waited until Dani had stepped out of the massive black SUV before handing her the large iced vanilla coffee.

Dani accepted the drink from her assistant with a tired smile. "Thanks."

She'd flown almost sixteen hours through eleven different time zones, performed her ass off—as usual—and flew another fourteen and a half hours to New York, all in the span of four days. Sure, she did it with first-class accommodations, and she was grateful, but—

A bitch was tired.

And she missed her man.

She didn't have time for a layover in London though she'd seriously considered it. With exhaustion coming for her, all she'd wanted was to snuggle up against Jameson's tall, solid frame, close her eyes, and forget about the outside world.

As soon as that thought entered her mind, she'd immediately sent it packing. She loved Jameson, but nothing could get in the way of this deal. She'd put in the years of hard work—always hustling and on the grind—and had kept going in the face of overwhelming doubt and skepticism.

Now Dani was about to reap the rewards. This was the meeting where Mela-Skin would ascend to the next level, finally granting her the control over her life that she'd always craved. So while a bitch was tired, and longing for her man, no one outside of her inner circle would ever know it. Certainly not by looking at her.

She was the epitome of business . . . Duchess style.

The bright pink corseted jumpsuit with matching heels popped against her dark skin. Her face was beat to perfection and her hair was slicked back into a low tight ponytail that fell to her waist. With a gray plaid print blazer draped over her bare shoulders, she hoped she projected the image of the rapper turned mogul she aspired to be. All her dreams were about to come true. She knew how to show up and show out.

Dani and Tasha glided through rotating glass doors and into the large steel and glass skyscraper that housed Genesis's U.S. headquarters. The foyer was enormous, and echoes of heels and voices bounced off the marble floors. On the walls, large gold letters spelled out the luxury brand-name tenants, whose headquarters and retail spaces could be found within.

A tall Black woman wearing a classic navy suit with gold-tipped dreds brushing her shoulders waved from her position at the base of the massive three-story staircase.

"You look incredible," Mela-Skin's CEO Andrea Thompson said when she reached them.

"I hope so. I wanted to project the right image." Dani shook her head. "I can't believe it's finally happening."

"I knew it would. I never doubted you."

"I appreciate that. I had the vision, but it was your business savvy and management that got us here. So, thank you."

Andrea clasped Dani's hand and squeezed. Dani tossed a smile to Tasha and then the three of them crossed the lobby like members of the Dora Milaje, ready to kick ass and take names.

And Dani didn't plan on writing anything down, not with these two-inch stiletto nails!

The last time she'd been in this elevator she'd been extremely nervous. And while her stomach was still in knots, it wasn't due to anxiety over their reaction to the Samantha Banks ordeal.

This time it was excitement.

Dani had completed the charge Genesis had given her. Get amazing press to counteract the Banks scandal and get people on her side again. Her time in London had been a success, her coverage had been stellar, and the press she'd received after she and Jameson had gone public with their relationship had only added to her positive image.

What a difference a couple of months made.

The doors slid open and they stepped into a bright, sleek, welcoming area. The receptionist, who wasn't the fan from last time, greeted them.

"Welcome to Genesis, Duchess," she said, tucking a lock of blond hair behind her ear. "Can I get you anything? Water? Coffee?"

Dani lifted her cup. "Already taken care of."

She took one last fortifying pull before reluctantly handing the drink over to Tasha.

"I'll be here when you're done," her assistant said, taking a seat on one of the bright orange lounge chairs.

"They're ready for you in Garamond A. If you'll follow me . . ." The receptionist gestured for them to precede her down the hallway that led to the same conference room they'd met in for their previous meeting.

"I'll take it from here." Dani was stunned to see Barbara, a Genesis executive, hurrying over.

"Certainly, Ms. Moore." The receptionist retreated to her desk.

"Duchess, Andrea! It's great to see you." Barbara, every inch the business professional in a black sheath dress and pearls, was smiling, but there was a jerkiness to her movements and her eyes darted around them.

"This *is* a surprise! Am I getting the VIP treatment?" Dani asked, shaking Barbara's outstretched hand.

"Always. We're so excited to have you," Barbara said, her voice unusually loud and chipper as they passed several people who openly stared at them.

Dani shot a look over her shoulder at Andrea, who frowned and adjusted her horn-rimmed glasses. Something was wrong. Dani didn't know the other woman well, but she'd gotten a feel for her at the first Genesis meeting, since she'd been the only Black woman on their team. The behavior Barbara was exhibiting today didn't jive with her prior impression.

"Is everything okay?"

Barbara slowed her steps. "I was hoping to intercept you downstairs, but I had a phone call that went long."

Intercept them? What were they, spies?

"What's going on?" Andrea asked, as they finally reached the conference room door.

Barbara sighed. "There's been some changes. Just know that I tried to talk them out of it, but—"

The door swung open, and a tall man stood there, his face beaming. "Duchess! I've been looking forward to this day for weeks. It's a pleasure to finally meet you."

Dani's brows rose. *Who was this dude?*

"Where's Henry?"

Henry Owens was Genesis's point person and the man Dani *had* been dealing with.

"Henry has the day off. I'll be leading today's meeting."

"And you are?"

"Greg Martin. I'm sure you have many more questions. Come on in and I'll do my best to answer them."

Dani shot Barbara a look as they walked into the room and saw many of the same faces she was used to seeing at these gatherings.

"It's like a family reunion," Dani said, spreading her arms wide, excitement beginning to take hold, despite her current confusion.

"I hope so. Because we consider you and Mela-Skin a part of the Genesis family," Greg said, his hand on the small of her back, leading her to a chair at the front of the room, where large floor-to-ceiling windows offered a magnificent view of downtown Manhattan and One World Trade Center.

So, the deal was still on?

Dani managed to sink into her seat at the rectangular-shaped wooden table before relief swiped her knees. She didn't know why Barbara was worried or what she'd wanted to tell her and Andrea, but as long as they were still on track, Dani could roll with anything else.

"And at family reunions," Greg was saying, "sometimes you meet long-lost relatives, right?"

A smattering of laughter circled the room.

Oh, snap! He was good. As someone who spent years engaging in rap battles, she appreciated someone who was quick on his feet.

"But enough with the metaphors," Greg said. "Let's get to business. How does it feel to be the woman of the hour?"

"Oh, you underestimate me, Greg." She shrugged the blazer off her shoulders and sat back, crossing her legs. "I'm planning to stretch this out way longer than that!"

Greg's smile was playful. "I've been doing my research and I've learned it would be a mistake to underestimate you. Case in point, your trip to London. I have to say, you've definitely exceeded our expectations. The coverage has been phenomenal. Focus groups are overwhelmingly positive and all anyone can talk about is your real-life fairy-tale romance with Prince Jameson."

Her stomach fluttered at the mention of Jameson. "Going to London changed my life. I guess I have you guys to thank for that."

More laughter from around the table but when Dani's gaze landed on Barbara, the executive's mouth was pinched, like she'd tasted something sour.

What the fuck was going on?

"Duchess? Please—" Greg directed her attention to the large digital screen built into the wall behind her.

It came to life and Dani gasped, thrilled to see enlarged versions of the Mela-Skin and Genesis logos. There was also a third logo she'd seen before but couldn't place; however, her elation at her dreams finally coming true dulled the sharp edge of her normally suspicious nature.

"We're excited about Mela-Skin and the place it can occupy in our portfolio."

"You won't regret your investment," Andrea said. "We have some fantastic ideas for the company moving forward and Duchess has come up with a new campaign we think will kill. Be Your Own BAY."

Greg frowned and glanced at Barbara. "I don't get it."

Of course. Dani clarified. "Bae. B-A-E. It's slang for a person's significant other. But our bae will be spelled B-A-Y and it'll stand for Be Authentically You. We're encouraging women to love themselves."

The wattage of Greg's smile dimmed slightly. "Uh, okay. We can definitely . . . consider that, but I think we're getting a little ahead of ourselves."

"What do you mean?"

Greg cleared his throat. "Duchess, everyone in this room is privy to information that you and Ms. Thompson do not have."

"Really?" Andrea pushed her shoulders back and set her jaw. "Because my job is to ensure that rarely happens."

That's right. Get him, Andrea!

"You couldn't have had this information. If you did, someone would be getting fired." This time he was the only one who laughed. "So let me let you both in on the secret. I'm the VP of Mergers and Acquisitions for Parcellum and our company recently acquired Genesis."

Parcellum?

"The real estate company?" Andrea asked.

"Yes. I should've been clearer in the beginning but it isn't every day I get to chat with a rap icon."

The muscles in Dani's cheeks eased as her smile faded away. She didn't bother peering over at Barbara. *This* was why the other woman had tried to warn her.

"I don't understand. I thought Genesis was investing in MelaSkin."

"It is. It's just that *we* acquired Genesis. And this deal—"

Dani couldn't decipher another word Greg said. He might as well have been Charlie Brown's teacher.

Wah-whoa-wah, woah-wah-wah.

Another company had purchased Genesis? When had that happened?

Andrea had the same question.

"The acquisition has been in the works for more than six months," Greg said.

So when they'd been here four months ago, Genesis had already been dealing with Parcellum, and Henry and his team had known about it? Shouldn't they have disclosed that information to her? Didn't she have the right to know who she was in business with?

"We have some amazing ideas about what you can do—"

Dani held up a hand. "You have ideas?"

She'd just learned these people would be a party to any deal she made with Genesis and now the fucker wanted to share *his* ideas?

"Just a few things. Marketing pushes and ad campaigns. Strategies you can use to take your brand further. Packaging, commercials, that sort of thing."

A few things? That was a hell of a lot!

Andrea pursed her lips. "Our partnership with Genesis was only going to involve increased manufacturing and distribution, expanded research and development capabilitics, and the ability to expand into more retail doors and bigger markets. We would maintain control of day-to-day operations and they would certainly have nothing to do with product marketing."

"That's correct," Greg said. "Mela-Skin is your company. How you want to run it, the direction you want to take it, the products you want to bring to market, that's all up to you. And let me be clear, your contract would still be with Genesis. But Genesis is now a Parcellum holding. We're investing a considerable amount of money. We expect to have *some* say."

Dani blew out a breath and laid her palms flat on the table. "It's a lot to take in. Mela-Skin has been my baby for a long time. I'm not interested in making a deal where anyone else's input is more important than mine."

"We understand. This isn't our first time at the rodeo. We've dealt with other business owners who've felt similarly, but in the end, we always manage to come to an understanding. We all want what's best for your company. Our focus is on giving Mela-Skin an optimal chance to grab its space in the marketplace."

Dani pressed a hand to her chest. "That's what I want, too."

"Good." Greg clapped his hands together. "Now that's out of the way, are you interested in seeing what we've set up for Mela-Skin once you sign the contracts?"

"Of course," Dani said, her posture thawing as they inched closer to finalizing the deal.

"This part I'll turn over to Barbara."

Barbara shook her head, as if she couldn't believe he'd asked her, but she was nothing if not a professional. She stood and reached for the remote that controlled the screen.

"Thank you, Greg. Duchess, we'll start with a press release announcing that we're bringing Mela-Skin under the Genesis umbrella with all our other top-tier luxury brands. We'll discuss the potential we see and how we plan to help you increase the scope of your customer base, as well as educate and enrich ours."

Andrea nodded. "We like the sound of that."

"We'll follow that up with an in-person launch party that we'll also live stream. We'll invite beauty industry insiders and influencers and make it glamorous, sexy, and unforgettable, like you."

Barbara was smiling but it wasn't genuine, and Dani couldn't shake the feeling that the woman was bracing herself.

For what?

"I love a party," Dani said, trying to reclaim her earlier enthusiasm.

"And this will be a great one, with you and Prince Jameson as the guests of honor."

Bloop, there it was.

"You and Prince Jameson as the guests of honor."

Dani frowned. The agreement she and Jameson made aside, why would Parcellum invite Jameson as a guest of honor? The company, the products, the launch—they were all hers. *She* should be the guest of honor, not him.

Slow your roll, Dani. Maybe it's the royalty thing. You've seen people and the press in America lose their minds over that angle of the story.

"We'll also produce tutorials showing the major beauty influencers using your products. We think several of you talking about your favorites will do well online." Barbara paused a beat before continuing. "Prince Jameson could give his insights, as well."

What insights? Jameson was a white British aristocrat. What would he know about beauty products created for women of color?

Dani interjected. "While Prince Jameson has been very supportive, we lead separate lives. I don't show up to his classes or any of his royal events and he's not featuring on my songs or getting involved in Mela-Skin."

She was proud of the way she'd handled that. Cool, calm, professional. No need to get turnt up and cause things to go left. It wasn't Barbara's fault and Dani didn't blame her. Hopefully, they all got the message, and they could move on, Martha, move on.

Barbara gave Greg a look that had "I told you so" written all over it, before she sat down.

Around the room, executives shifted in their chairs or fiddled with the documents and tablets on the table in front of them.

"But he'll be at the launch event with you, right?" Greg persisted. "I'm sure he wouldn't mind a couple of pictures?"

With a sense of dread, Dani sighed. "What do you want?"

"Our focus groups showed that while you are very popular, linking you with the prince sent your approval ratings through the roof. Not just with young people but in all demographics. Consumers are going bonkers over the fairy tale and they're willing to pay to be a part of it. So"—Greg firmed his lips—"we're going to need Prince Jameson to be a part of the campaign. In some way."

Did her mouth drop open? It felt like it was open. Dani was so shook she wasn't sure she was in control of her body.

This was outrageous! For fuck's sake, they'd only been dating a little over a month. What made them think Jameson should have *anything* to do with a business she'd built on her own before she'd even known he existed?

"No! Mela-Skin is my company. It has nothing to do with him."

"But there's more interest in your brand with him attached."

"There was tremendous interest in Duchess's brand before him," Andrea pointed out. "Not only interest, but actual sales. Our products are bestsellers, profits rise steadily year after year, and we have a great social media presence with a loyal and consistent customer base. That's why we were here originally, correct?"

Greg shrugged. "True. But things have changed. We can't unknow this information. It would be a breach of our fiduciary duty to the company."

"Not to my company. Please, unknow away!"

"The eyes of the world are on you now, which translates to your products. That's prime international exposure we won't have to pay for."

Dani uncrossed her legs, letting her heel hit the floor with a hard, satisfying thud. "First, you—or rather Henry—call me in here and tell me that because of some made-up controversy with Samantha Banks, I need to rehab my image before you'll invest in my company. Then I do what you ask and you tell me it's not good enough, that my boyfriend has to be involved!"

Barbara was watching her, compassion and understanding etched on her striking features.

Dani sought to breathe in the cool air of reason. Why was her company, the one she'd started by herself when no one else believed in its potential, suddenly besieged with white people making crucial decisions about its identity, when they had nothing to do with the product? She couldn't even imagine a scenario where the owner of a urinal company was brought into a meeting with mostly women and told he needed to incorporate their input into his marketing!

"I thought this was about *my* image. *My* brand. You said the eyes of the world are on *me* now."

"It is and they are," Greg said. "But the prince is a part of that. And Parcellum, via Genesis, plans to take advantage of that association. We're prepared to invest a considerable amount in you and Mela-Skin, even more than before. We're going to make your company a household name by this time next year. But only if Prince Jameson is involved."

She shook her head. "For what I hope will be the last time I need to say this: Jameson is not involved in Mela-Skin."

Greg's amiable demeanor receded, and she saw the ruthless businessman beneath.

"Maybe I should be having this conversation with your CEO. I was led to believe that despite being a rapper, you were more than a figurehead for Mela-Skin. That you understood the business."

The condescension practically rolled off him.

Dani curled her lip. "I do."

"Then for what I hope will be the last time *I* need to say *this*: you need to find a way to get Prince Jameson involved or the deal is off."

The emotional trinity of resentment, fear, and anger burned like acid reflux in her chest. She'd pushed through the lack of thoughtfulness, excitement, and enthusiasm because people didn't understand the purpose of what she was proposing. She'd dealt with the racism and misogyny of men not taking her seriously because she didn't look like their idea of a businessperson. She'd burned the candle at both ends—and sometimes on the sides!—to work on the business without compromising any of her music endeavors. And she'd invested her own money to develop and implement this idea she knew had merit.

All to get here. To sit at this table and sign a contract that would give her the control and freedom she'd been craving since Nana died when she was fourteen. When people she barely knew began deciding where she would live, what she would wear, and how she would act.

Ironically enough, Dani had learned that becoming a famous rapper hadn't shielded her from being "handled." She was still told where to live, what to wear, and how to act—only now the economic benefit of controlling her involved way more than monthly assistance checks from the government.

In Mela-Skin, Dani had finally found a way to seize authority over her life. She'd started and nurtured it the way she'd wanted to. She'd brought on staff and an executive team who understood and carried out *her* vision. And early on in all her negotiations, Dani had been clear that she was looking for a partner who would respect Mela-Skin's products, customers, and branding.

She thought she'd found it in Genesis. But they wanted her to jump through so many damn hoops she felt like a fucking circus poodle.

It was time for her to go. She needed to get the fuck out of Dodge before she said or did something that could permanently harm Mela-Skin. Thankfully, she trusted Andrea to manage the rest of the meeting on the company's behalf.

"If you'll excuse me . . ."

She didn't wait for their response. Ignoring Greg's cold stare and the shocked faces around the table, Dani stood, draped her blazer over her arm, and strode from the room, head held high.

What were you just saying about things not going left?

Chapter Seven

> Me: Coming out of Tory Burch @HudsonYards, happy & minding my business after purchasing my monogram ladybug sneakers
> Life: Duchess getting on the elevator
> #fyp #lifemade #bowdown #skyhigh #duchess
> ***@camdampsey, TikTok***

On the rooftop terrace of the hotel's penthouse suite with the black-and-white-striped umbrella providing maximum shade from the midsummer sun, Dani popped the last piece of crust in her mouth and reached for the glass of water on the table in front of her. She took a long sip, leaned back in the chair, and said, "What the fuck are we going to do?"

Tasha looked up from scrolling on her phone. "She speaks! I was wondering if you were ever going to talk."

Two hours had passed since Dani had stormed out of the meeting at Genesis, directed her driver to take her to the nearest place where she could get good NY-style pizza, and headed back to her hotel.

"It was a lot! Trust me, I needed some time and space. And food! I wanted to make sure I was doing the right thing and not feeling some type of way because I was hangry."

"It definitely wasn't what we expected," Andrea added from the seat across from her, tapping her nails on the table's glass top. She'd gotten back to the hotel half an hour before.

"How did you leave things?" Dani asked.

"I told them we were disappointed that they chose to spring this on us at the meeting instead of giving us a heads-up and that since they'd done so, we'd need some time to consider this new requirement."

Dani was still outraged at their treatment. That man had sat there with a straight face and said that Jay should be included in the marketing for Mela-Skin.

The caucasity of it all!

"I did everything they asked of me," Dani said. "The press I generated knocked the scandal with Banks off the front pages."

"Can they do that?" Tasha asked. "Just change the contract?"

"There is no contract," Andrea said. "We hadn't gotten that far. The stipulation regarding Dani's reputation was a precondition before we even got to the contract."

"Which I fulfilled," Dani reiterated, to make sure the universe heard and understood.

"You did," Andrea agreed.

Thank you, universe.

"It's also why they weren't obligated to disclose their own deal with Parcellum."

Tasha frowned. "Isn't Parcellum a residential real estate company? I've seen their 'For Sale' signs on lawns."

Andrea smiled slightly. "Parcellum is a multinational conglomerate based here in the U.S. They have their fingers in everything including energy, manufacturing, media, retail, and real estate."

"I have a finger for them," Dani muttered, pulling a pepperoni from a slice in the box.

"Think of Parcellum as a holding company. They don't manufacture or sell anything or conduct any other business. They exist solely to hold controlling stock in other companies. All their subsidiaries operate independently and Parcellum has no input or oversight into their day-to-day operations. So, there was no reason for them to get involved in Genesis's deal with Mela-Skin. But as we've said again and again, your relationship with Jameson has raised your profile to another level. One that even an organization like Parcellum can't ignore. They want in on it."

"Fuck that! I'm so done with them! And clearly, it's not being hangry. It's how I feel."

"I understand. But while they were busy being greedy, they failed to recognize things have changed," Andrea said.

"What do you mean?" Dani asked.

"Before the tribute, Genesis was in the position of power. They were able to call the shots because they were the only company willing to come to the table after the scandal broke." Andrea held up her phone. "Since the tribute, we've been contacted by all the companies who initially bowed out plus several others. The field is once again wide open."

What was that lighthearted feeling bubbling in her chest? Was it hope?

Dani slammed her palm on the table. "Let's tell Genesis and Parcellum to fuck off and then commence negotiations with the other companies. But not the ones that canceled on me. They can fuck right off, too!"

Tasha shook her head. "You hold a grudge like it's your religion."

"Petty-ologists of the world, unite!"

"I wish it were that simple," Andrea said, through their laughter. "We may not have a contract with Genesis, but there's a letter of intent to contend with—one that's been signed by both parties."

Dani leaned forward. “But letters of intent are not a contract. You said it was just a record of the understanding between us and Genesis. What their company intended to do in acquiring Mela-Skin.”

“It is. But there are parts that can be binding. We’ll need the lawyers to look at it closely and advise us on how we should proceed.”

“Then let’s do that.”

“We will. And we should tread carefully until we know for sure. You are one of the most popular women in the world and one half of the most exciting couples to come around in a long time. Parcellum isn’t going to allow Genesis to let you go now. They could take us to court, claim we didn’t negotiate in good faith. If we get involved in a long drawn-out legal battle, Mela-Skin can be tied up for years. So, we probably shouldn’t tell them to fuck off. At least not yet.”

“You’re joking?”

“I’m afraid not. Any asshole can file a lawsuit, whether the case has merit or not. Parcellum has money to spend and time on their hands. If they sue, no other company would want to come near us until everything was resolved.”

Goddammit!

Dani wanted to pull out her hair. She was just a woman, with a company, seeking control over her life and choices.

Why did it feel like it was getting more and more difficult to manage?

“With that said, they don’t want to sue you. They want to be in business with you. Because of your increased public persona and interest from the other companies, we do have leverage. The trick will be in determining how to use it to our advantage.”

Tasha placed a large iPad in the center of the table. “Bennie texted to see how the meeting went and I told her what happened. She wants to chat."

Dani nodded and leaned back in her seat as a small breeze flowed across her heated skin, rare for the usually humid summer weather. Tasha tapped the screen several times and Dani's agent appeared, her strawberry blonde hair falling sleekly around her face.

"Are you okay?" Jane "Bennie" Benedict asked, stylish rimless reading glasses perched on her nose.

"Not really. I thought we'd finally be done but things now feel further away than ever."

Bennie nodded. "I get that. But they still want to go through with the deal, right?"

"If Jameson is involved!"

"It makes no sense and yet I see why they want it. The two of you generate a lot of media attention, and in an environment where advertising and related marketing costs are escalating, organic reach and engagement for any brand is of great value."

"I can't do it, Bennie. And you know why."

One, she and Jameson had made a pact to keep their personal relationship separate from their other obligations. Hell, it had been her idea! What would it say to him if she suddenly changed her mind because it benefited her? He'd think she was using him just like others had in the past.

Two—and most importantly—it was *her* company. She felt like that kept getting lost in the discussion.

Why should her business be tied to who she was dating?

Were people asking Tim Cook, Elon Musk, or Mark Zuckerberg to market their companies by playing up their relationships with their significant others? Were the deals Jay-Z, Dr. Dre, and 50 Cent signed contingent on the contributions of their wives or girlfriends?

As much as Dani loved Jameson, things were still new for them and she didn't know what the future held. What if she changed her mind? Or he changed his? What if he decided he couldn't be with someone as high profile as she was? If people felt positively about Mela-Skin and purchased the products because they bought into the fairy tale, who would they blame if the fantasy ended? Would her company bear the brunt of that disappointment? How would that affect its value? Her brand? Would she lose everything she'd worked so hard to build? Because of a failed relationship?

It was unfair to ask that of her.

But if she didn't find a way to involve Jameson in the marketing, Genesis could keep Mela-Skin hindered by legal proceedings for the foreseeable future.

What should she do?

"We're going to have the attorneys look at everything, Bennie," Andrea said.

"Good. And if you could loop me in on those discussions, I'd appreciate it. Now, I'm not trying to get involved in your business," Bennie said, "but it occurs to me that neither side benefits from drawing this out, right?"

"That's true," Andrea said, her tone cautious. She met Dani's gaze across the table and raised her brows.

"And it's the publicity Parcellum wants to capitalize on?" Bennie asked.

"Yes."

Bennie shifted her blue-eyed laser-focused gaze to Dani.

"Then let's give it to them."

Say what now?

During the past several months, Bennie had worked hard at earning Dani's trust. In fact, the only reason Dani even found out about her invitation to perform at the royal tribute concert was because Bennie had brought it to her attention after Cash had declined on her behalf.

Without her consent.

Still, what part of the previous five minutes had her agent missed?

"Dani?" Bennie called her name as if it weren't the first time she'd tried to get her attention. "When are you heading back to London?"

"Next week."

"And how long are you staying?"

"About a week. I wish it was longer, but I thought I'd have my hands full with Mela-Skin and Genesis business."

"Well, now you don't, so you should extend your visit. I can work with Tasha to shift your schedule around because—"

"Wait a minute!" Dani pushed forward in her chair. "How does staying in the U.K. longer solve this problem with Genesis and Jay? He won't want to do it and I can't ask him. I shouldn't have to."

"The two of you just being together will generate publicity."

"But—"

"Look, I agree with you that formally involving Prince Jameson in the marketing for Mela-Skin is ludicrous. But Parcellum wants to capitalize on your increased exposure. We know that you are your brand. So, let's focus on *you*. The more you and Jameson are photographed together, the more it feeds into the fairy tale narrative. People will buy Mela-Skin to support *you*, to be like *you*, to believe they can get their own prince—as crazy as that sounds. It all benefits *you*, which benefits the brand and gives Parcellum the organic reach they want."

Andrea nodded slightly, a grin curving her full lips. "That's not bad. And you wouldn't have to ask Jameson to do anything he wouldn't already be doing. He has to attend events. You would go with him."

Bennie dusted her hands together. "Pictures will be taken, you both stay popular and relevant. Problem solved."

Wow. It was no wonder Bennie was one of the most sought-after agents in the game. To come up with that shit, on the fly . . .

"Jay has only been in the spotlight so much because of the tribute," Dani said. "He fully expects to go back to lecturing full-time once the semester starts."

"Is he going to stay home the rest of the time? Tell him you want to go out to eat or have him take you sightseeing. You can figure something out."

Bennie's suggestions left a bitter taste in her mouth. Dani appreciated that the other woman had her best interests in mind, and sure, it seemed like a simple ask. Except it wasn't. Not for Jameson.

"Would Parcellum accept that? Because they were clear that they wanted Jay to be a part of the actual campaign."

Bennie shrugged. "They say you know it's a good compromise when both sides are equally dissatisfied."

"Mela-Skin goes where you lead, Dani," Andrea said, "so this is what I need to know: Do you still want this deal?"

Dani exhaled and fell back in her chair, lifting her gaze skyward.

How was that even a question?

A nine-figure investment that would take her company to the next level and afford her more freedom than she'd ever known? *That's* the deal she wanted, the one she'd been ready to sign today before they'd added that dumb-ass Jameson stipulation.

But now?

If she had to, she could let this deal go and start the process all over again with another company, but with the time and effort they'd already spent on Genesis, Dani would prefer to avoid it if necessary.

"I want the deal with the terms we initially agreed upon."

"Then you have three choices. You can agree to Jameson being part of the marketing for Mela-Skin. You can tell Parcellum to fuck off and hope they walk away. Or we can approach them with this compromise and see if they bite."

"It's worth a shot," Tasha said. "If you have concerns about Prince Jameson, talk to him. See what he thinks. He may be willing to endure a little uneasiness if it gets you closer to your dream."

Why was she even considering this?

Why not just walk away?

Because she was soooo close to living on her own terms.

Because after a childhood of being passed from family member to family member, Dani needed to be in control of her life.

Because she couldn't leave the fate of her business in the hands of other people.

Having Jameson in the official marketing for Mela-Skin was absurd and she refused to entertain it.

Walk away from the deal while knowing Parcellum could still make a move? They'd continue exercising control over her actions. She'd be loath to approach another company for fear that Parcellum would institute a lawsuit just to fuck with her.

But the compromise . . . She'd be grabbing her destiny by the balls; acting instead of reacting, something she'd had to do her entire life.

Jameson believed he wouldn't be called on to attend many royal affairs because he'd go back to being a full-time lecturer. If that was true, would he mind if she accompanied him to the few he'd be invited to? Was Tasha right? Should she talk to him? If she explained the situation and stressed her intention to inconvenience him as little as possible, would he play ball?

What if he didn't? What if he reiterated his desire to not be in the spotlight? What if he referred to the promise they'd made to each other, just a week ago? Was she willing to put a monumental decision that affected her life solely in his hands? Trust that he would put her childhood trauma ahead of his own?

Could she bet Mela-Skin's future on it?

Fuck if she didn't want to. But she couldn't. History and experience had branded an unforgettable lesson on her memory: when your ass is on the line, you have to depend on yourself. Jameson loved her, but it was too much to ask too soon.

She knew what she had to do.

Dani pursed her lips. "Let's do it, Andrea. Call them with the compromise."

"You made the right decision. Keep me in the loop," Bennie called out from the tablet before ending the call.

"I'm on it," Andrea said, pushing back from the table and rising to her feet. She excused herself and headed back into the penthouse, phone in hand.

Despite the warm afternoon, Dani suddenly shivered as a chill wrapped itself around her bones and set up camp. The whiplash of emotions in the span of a few hours and her Jules Verne–level jet lag were conspiring against her. It was time to go inside, curl up on the couch under a blanket, and watch a good movie.

Hell, who was she kidding? It'd be lights out before the opening credits finished crossing the screen.

But she could feel Tasha staring at her. "What?"

Tasha's brows rose to meet her sideswept bangs. "Considering your mood, I'm not sure if I should show you this, but . . . I think you'd want to know about it."

Dani had heard there was a time before social media. She'd give anything to experience the world back then. When every minute wasn't a potentially life-changing land mine, ready to blow.

"What now?"

Tasha grimaced. "It's Samantha Banks."

Dani threw up her hands. "Don't even joke about that."

Since the eruption of the scandal involving Banks and Prince Julian, the palace had been working overtime to prevent discussion of it from gaining traction. Anytime the hashtag #PrinceJulianSparkleAffair was trending on social media, it would suddenly disappear and be replaced by something far more positive about the royal family.

#RoyalFamilyRules #JuliananndFiona #BabyWales

Social media worked hard. Queen Marina and her staff worked harder.

Other than learning that Banks had tried to sneak into Nyla's movie premiere, Dani hadn't heard a peep from her or her Sparkle Sammies. And, at least in the media, Dani had been vindicated. Someone had come forward with the unedited video, proving what Dani had said all along and causing calls for Banks to be canceled on multiple platforms.

Dani hoped the young woman had learned her lesson.

"Is Samantha talking about me?" she asked.

"No," Tasha said, her tone slightly bemused.

Thank God.

"Then I don't care."

"Are you sure? Because this is ju-say," Tasha said, drawing the word out into two sassy syllables.

"Oh, what the hell." Dani took the phone.

She almost choked when she saw the headline: *Royally Knocked Up?*

The article linked to a TikTok of Samantha Banks walking into a high-end baby boutique. As Britney Spears sang her iconic intro, "Oh baby, baby," on a loop in the background, the video cut from a profile image of Banks thumbing through tiny clothes on a rack to looking at baby toys to staring longingly down into an empty crib.

It ended on a torso shot of her—in a Union-Jack T-shirt!—cradling her still flat stomach and looking beatifically into the camera.

Dani shot widened eyes at Tasha. "No!"

Tasha shrugged. "She never explicitly says, but if you look at the comments, when people asked, she replied with these cryptic responses like, 'Spring is a time of rebirth,' and 'Guess we'll see in March,' with a baby emoji . . . and a crown!"

Dani bracketed her head with her hands, attempting to process this new information.

Samantha Banks was trying to claim she was pregnant with Julian the Prince of Wales's baby?

Holy shit!

Chapter Eight

"There's an uproar over the news that Prince Julian may be expecting more than one spare to the throne. Speculation is growing that American singer Samantha Banks has named HRH as the father of her unborn baby. A scandal of this magnitude will be hard for the royal family to overcome. Many are doubting whether the Prince of Wales can ever be king. Just another in a long line of scandals making headlines and further damaging a monarchy in crisis. Abigail Tindyre, BBC News."

The queen has to be shitting bricks right now," Dani said, the twinkle in her brown eyes clear through the screen of his phone.

Jameson laughed. "I wouldn't know. We're not that close."

Her responding chuckle caressed his heart. "Good point. And to think . . . she'd been worried about me!"

"Clearly a lapse in her judgement."

Among others.

"You look beautiful, love."

Dani's shoulders were covered in a bright pink fabric that did marvelous things for her glorious skin. Her hair was pulled back from her face, the style emphasizing her high, sharp cheekbones and full, kissable lips.

"Thank you." Her expression softened. "I miss you."

"I miss you, too. I didn't expect to talk to you today. I thought it'd be a few more days, at least."

"I know, but when Tasha told me about Banks, I had to call and check on you. See if you'd heard."

"I'd heard." He shoveled a hand through his hair. "Is it gaining traction over there?"

"Like a car with no brakes going down a very steep hill."

Fuck. He shifted on the large window seat, the floor-length curtains brushing his arm. "What are people saying?"

She tilted her head to the side and a large diamond stud caught the New York afternoon sunlight. "You care?"

"I have to care, whether I want to or not."

"What does that mean?"

His gaze strayed out the window and the purplish hue of the dusky London sky caught his attention. His apartment at Kensington Palace boasted one of the more pastoral views, as it was bordered by a small garden, but it didn't give him the same peace and serenity he felt looking over his land at Primrose Park.

But heading out to his estate hadn't been an option. After his meeting with the queen, he'd contacted his household's private secretary, who was charged with providing administrative support for his new duties, including organizing his diary of events and arranging the logistics of his travel, security, and meals. Essentially, each part of his life would now be accounted for and coordinated with the other working members of the royal family. It was just as stifling as he'd always imagined.

"I lost my job."

"What?" Dani's hand flew up to cover her mouth then moved to press against her chest. "At the university?"

He nodded.

"Wait, do you mean the queen pressured you to leave or—"

"No. They fired me. They said my presence, quote, impaired their ability to provide a safe and distraction-free place to educate young minds, end quote."

"Those fuckers!"

Despite the sting he still felt over this dismissal, the corner of his mouth tilted upward. He was a lucky bastard to count himself as one of the few recipients of her fierce loyalty.

"That's not all . . ."

She shook her head and muttered, "Damn. When it rains, it fucking monsoons."

"Pardon?"

"Just something my Nana used to say."

"Did your Nana have a saying for *every* occasion?"

"Pretty much. Go ahead, lay it on me. What else?"

He exhaled. "The queen is drafting me into service. Again."

"Oh no! Baby . . ."

The compassion on her face nearly broke him. He wanted her here. Being with her would make everything better.

"Since you're no longer lecturing, she's probably thinking this is your job now. I know it doesn't help, but you understand why she did it, right? She needs to go into damage control mode."

"I'm aware. It doesn't mean I have to like it."

He'd taken for granted the leniency he'd been offered when he was younger. After his father's death, his mother had intervened with the queen on Jameson's behalf, requesting that he be allowed to hold off on his royal duties and pursue his studies. The queen had allowed it but now his royal promissory note had come due.

As a Counsellor of State and a senior working royal, his life was considered a tool to help carry out the queen's duties. Some members of his family soothed the bite of royal servitude by indulging in the lifestyle and riches the monarch provided. For Jameson, it would never be enough.

"You're a shining star in that family and the queen knows it. They all know it. You might shy away from it, but people want to be around you. They're drawn to you."

Had he gotten so good at pretending that even Dani had been fooled? The only reason he'd been proficient at presenting a charming persona during the tribute was because he'd known there was an end in sight. Could he still call on that persona if he'd be doing the same thing for the foreseeable future?

He'd do it for now. The threat to his mother's way of life ensured that. But he'd also begin planning for the future. He wouldn't subject himself to the queen's whims any longer than necessary. Once he had a viable exit strategy in place, he'd share it all with Dani.

"So, love, what's the take on this pregnancy scandal on your end?"

Her mouth parted and he could tell she wanted to say more, but she followed his cue. "Tasha gave me the lowdown. Her fans, the same ones who came after me, I might add, are excited by the fact that she could be pregnant with a little prince or princess. And that's where Banks is keeping *her* focus on social media. But the gossip sites and magazines are focusing on the scandal part of it. Although very few of them are talking about Julian's role in this. Sure, Banks isn't an angel and I wouldn't cut her any breaks, but Julian is the one married with a child and another on the way. He's the one who's the next in line to the throne. He definitely should've known better."

His uncle had rejected the notion of "should've known better" ages ago.

"This can't be the first time this was an issue, right?" Dani continued. "Julian didn't wake up and suddenly find Samantha Banks so irresistible she was worth risking everything for. I mean, I can tell that by how he treated me and the things he said."

"Bloody hell, I thought her videos were sexy. She looks fucking unbelievable in person."

"You look like a delicious chocolate treat wrapped in gold. Do I get the chance to unwrap you and see if you taste just as sweet?"

"You see how she moves? Can you imagine all of that riding your cock?"

Jameson flexed his hand, the memory of his uncle's vulgar statements bringing forth a phantom pain from when he'd punched Julian in the nose. It had actually felt good, considering all the things the other man had said about Dani from the moment he'd found out she'd be performing at the tribute concert.

"It's not the first time, but it's usually handled with a bit more discretion. Samantha Banks isn't the typical woman he deals with. She's playing by a different set of rules."

"Ain't that the truth!"

"The queen only found out a couple of hours before the news broke. Samantha told Julian about the pregnancy, but she promised not to go public. I guess her word is worth as much as his."

"She's unpredictable. I'm sorry Julian got involved with her, not because of how it's affecting him, but because you're bearing the brunt of the fallout."

"I'll be fine. And I'm not going to waste the pleasure of this unexpected time with you talking about my uncle and Samantha Banks. Tell me how your meeting went with Genesis."

He was so proud of Dani. When he thought back to his reaction upon learning who she was, he was ashamed of the assumptions he'd made about her character and personality. She'd disproved all his preconceived notions.

"Well . . ." Her gaze flicked sideways, and her tongue darted out to wet her bottom lip. "It was obvious the trip to London was a success . . ."

He arched a brow, waiting.

She swallowed. "They were really excited to see me and they have lots of thoughts about announcing their investment . . . and the marketing . . ."

Why wasn't she more excited? Unless, it didn't go well?

"Did you sign the contract?"

"Not yet. There are a few more sticking points we have to iron out."

He frowned, wondering at the reluctance that was palpable even through the screen.

"That's good." He guessed.

"It is. I mean there's more, but . . . I'm exhausted. You know, the jet lag is catching up with me. Yesterday I was in the Middle East. At least I think it was yesterday . . ."

"Of course." He felt like a right prick, grilling her when she was certainly ready to crash. "I understand. Get some rest. I'll check on you soon."

"Yeah," she said, biting her bottom lip.

He groaned. "Stop that. We agreed that was my job from now on."

There was that smile he loved. The tightness in his chest eased. He rose from the window seat and rounded the small writing table that served as his desk when he was here.

"Hey, Jay? There's something else."

"Do tell."

"Remember how I said I'd be able to visit you at the end of next week?"

Remember? The fact was tattooed on his brain. He'd had three weeks of waking up with her in his arms or curled against him like an appendage he'd grown overnight. Of not being denied the privilege of giving her pleasure whenever the mood struck either of them. These five days apart had seemed endless. Knowing he'd see her soon was what had been getting him through it.

That vise in his chest constricted. "Have you changed your mind?"

"Sort of. What if I could shorten that time frame?"

Excitement overtook him and it was all he could do not to throw his fists in the air in triumph, as if he'd scored the winning goal in the final match of the Queen's Cup polo tournament.

"By how much?"

"I can be there in a few days."

His heart beat maniacally against the protection of his rib cage, as if it sensed her impending presence and wanted to be physically closer to her.

Get in line, mate.

"Love, you've just made my day."

Her eyes flashed and her lashes lowered. "I can't wait to see you. I've been thinking about you so much. More specifically, what I want to *do* to you."

The temperature in the room rose ten degrees. His cock throbbed. "You always have my attention. Now even more so."

What this woman did to him!

He settled back, getting comfortable. This wouldn't even be the first time that thoughts of her caused him to stroke himself to completion in one of his home offices.

"Are you home, baby?" she asked, her mind appearing to run along the same lines as his.

"I'm in my apartment at Kensington Palace."

She moaned and the guttural sound of pleasure roused all his nerve endings. "We never did spend any time there together. Would you like to pre-christen it with a little solo play?"

Fuck yeah.

He slid his hand down along the imprint of the bulge in his—

A knock at the door ripped through his growing sexual haze.

Bloody hell.

"Jay?" A long, polished nail rested against Dani's glossy red lips. Blood shot straight to his dick, making rational thought impossible.

The knock came again. "Sir? You have a visitor."

A visitor? He shook his head, trying to clear the fog. Who in the fuck would be visiting him here at this time of night? Not Rhys. Could it be his mother? Possibly, but she wouldn't be announced, she'd just stroll in.

Which was why it was probably best that he not jerk off in the drawing room.

"I have to go, love."

"Awwww . . . I guess we'll have to wait then. Give my best to Calanthe and I'll see you soon. I love you."

She blew him a kiss and ended the call.

He exhaled, tossed his phone down on the desk, then called out, "Come in."

His butler, Townsend, entered. "Her Royal Highness, the Princess Royal."

Jameson's head jerked back. His aunt was here? What would warrant visits with both his aunt and the queen in the same day? There might be something to Dani's grandmother's saying about rains and monsoons.

Doing his best to surreptitiously adjust himself, he stood as Catherine appeared, serenely majestic in a violet blue dress and matching cardigan, her hair loosely pulled back from her face.

He executed a crisp bow. "Catherine."

"That isn't necessary," she said.

"Try telling your mother that. Or mine."

"Fair point. Do you fancy a chat?"

"Of course."

He gestured, then followed her over to the rarely used seating area. The room was lavishly decorated in tones of green, gold, and cream. Gilt-framed mirrors and oil paintings graced the light-colored walls and thick carpet muffled their steps. Jameson couldn't take credit for the decor. His mother had spearheaded the renovations of the apartment that had once belonged to his father.

He waited until Catherine was settled on the forest green sofa before he sat on the matching green and gold armchair across from her.

She placed her purse on the wooden antique table between them. "How is Duchess?"

Shocked, he raised a brow.

"What's that look?"

"Just surprised that you asked," he said.

"Of course, I was stunned when you invited her to perform," Catherine began, "and I'll admit, because I judged her, I wasn't keen on spending any time getting to know her. But I admired how she stood up for herself in some very intimidating company. And you love her so she must be special."

"She is. And she's doing well."

Catherine nodded. "What you did was really brave. I've never seen anyone stand up to the queen in quite that manner."

"What about Julian? He rarely does what she wants."

Catherine's gaze flicked upward. "He's like a naughty toddler, misbehaving behind our mother's back. But you declared your intention to her and followed through. It was . . . impressive."

He smiled but eyed her steadily. Catherine had inherited her mother's steely resolve, her father's compassion, and both parents' intelligence. Had she been born first, she would've made a fantastic queen.

Those same traits also made underestimating her extremely dangerous. This visit and her complimentary words weren't as unstudied as she'd wanted them to appear.

"I'm going to be blunt—"

When had she been anything but?

"—We're in a bind here and we need you. Full-time."

Not more about his duty to the Company and his family! Did these people think about anything else?

He'd been so naive. He'd created this situation the moment he'd agreed to be the family representative for the royal tribute. He'd foolishly thought he'd be able to slip back into his life from before. Even after his mother and Dani had warned him, he'd deluded himself into believing he could achieve what no one else had been able to, outside of dying: escape his obligations as a member of the royal family.

He sighed. "The queen already talked to me."

"I know. Just as I'm aware of the reprehensible way she gained your cooperation. I'm truly sorry she did that, but I hope you recognize just how desperate she is to have taken that action."

"The reason *why* doesn't change *what* she did. In the end, she got what she wanted."

"But we require more than your begrudging participation. You showed your potential during my father's tribute. We're going to need that and more during the coming months."

Months?

"Where's Julian? Have you talked to him? He made this mess. Shouldn't he be involved in fixing it?"

Brackets formed around her mouth. "Julian has his hands full.

Between Fi and this girl from America . . . Honestly, the less he's seen, by the public and the press, the better for all of us."

Jameson didn't see how him attending the opening of a new hospital or meeting with tyre factory employees and their families would blind anyone to the spectacle of the heir apparent possibly impregnating two women.

"Don't you get tired of cleaning up his messes and of pretending that you shouldn't be the one who takes the throne after the queen? At least you're actually prepared for the job!"

His grandfather often said that being the sovereign required duty before self, an understanding his aunt had also inherited from her mother.

Catherine's expression didn't alter in the face of his comment. She crossed her ankles and shifted in the chair. "I didn't have the luxury of pretending I wasn't royal while I was growing up. From my earliest memory, I was taught that being a member of this family meant responsibility and sacrifice."

Ouch. A velvet-covered whip still delivered a sting.

"As Prince of Wales, Julian is given a lot of latitude. That won't be the case when he ascends to the throne, no matter what he believes. The monarchy will make sure of that."

"You speak of it as if it were a person."

"Not a person, but it's kind of like a sentient being. Julian will learn, as my mother did and her father before her, that the people in these buildings are loyal to the institution, not the individual."

Even though the institution could demoralize the individual.

"And so, I must sacrifice and do my duty?"

"Yes," she said, as if it were the most reasonable response in the world.

He pushed to his feet and strode over to the fireplace, bracing his hands on the sleek stone mantel.

"Jameson?"

"I hear you. And it's not my intention to be difficult. I know what I have to do. But if you expect me to pretend that I'm happy to do this, then you're expecting too much. For God's sake, the queen has essentially blackmailed me. Twice!"

"I understand chafing under the restrictions of the Crown. For all the reasons you so astutely and, I hope, confidentially, stated. But none of us chose this life. It chose us and we must act within its restraints."

"And so by virtue of my birth, every choice in my life is to be taken from me?"

"Stop acting as if this is a hardship. You've benefited from it. I'm not saying you haven't worked hard. But you've had the softest of cushions known as the royal family behind you, ready to catch you if you fell. Or rather, to guarantee you never did. Who you are has made what you've achieved easier." She took a deep breath. "You've made your feelings clear about being a working member of this family. If you seek to venture beyond its protections, can I assume you have a plan in place?"

"I'll be working on it."

She nodded. "Then while we still have you, I'm asking for your help. We have our own strategy in place. First, there's the St. Lucia state visit in a month. Mother is worried about the family's influence with the Commonwealth of Nations. Then there's the matter of the third in the line of succession. When Fi gives birth in six months, despite everything going on, it will bring goodwill to this family. It always does. In the meantime, we're working on making this Samantha Banks situation go away."

"Good luck with that."

He knew how much she'd affected Dani and why. Now that she

may have her hooks in the royal family, there was no way she'd willingly let go.

Which meant he'd be caught up in this charade for the foreseeable future.

"If you help us, not begrudgingly, but as if you valued the institution and what it means, showing all the charm and charisma you displayed during the tribute, then you have my word your mother will be fine."

He narrowed his eyes. "Meaning?"

"My mother doesn't like when people oppose her will. You've done it twice already, by failing to take over your father's duties when he died and by choosing Dani when she expressly forbid it."

"The queen already promised to let my mother be if I did what she asked."

"She made that same promise to you before the tribute; said you'd be able to go back to lecturing at uni. Yet here you are, doing exactly what she wants you to do."

He curled his hand into a fist, realizing Catherine was right. What could he do? In the end, all he had was the queen's word that she'd hold up her end of their bargain.

"And if you're coming up with some sort of plan to leave the family, she'll see it as an attack on her legacy and she'll do whatever she can to try to stop you. But I can guarantee she won't use your mother again as a bargaining chip. As long as we're here, Calanthe can stay where she is and have all the protections she needs."

"You can do that?"

Catherine stared back at him, her confidence evident in her steady eye contact. "It's what my brother would've wanted."

He nodded, trusting what he saw in her principled gaze. "Okay."

"Thank you, Jameson. Can I give you a piece of advice?" She

didn't wait for his response. "You are the Duke of Wessex. You need to stop fighting it and accept it. We can never escape being a member of this family, no matter how much we may want to. But you don't have to occupy the title the way your father did. You can make it fit who *you* are."

The way Catherine had done as the spare.

She stood and reached for her purse. "The queen's private secretary will contact yours and set him up with the information from the others."

He clenched his jaw but nodded.

"You may not like everything we do in service to the monarchy, or even understand it. That's because your focus is on what will make you happy today, tomorrow, or next week. But we have to look far ahead, and I don't mean next year but the next fifty or one hundred years." She pressed her hands together, her blue eyes steady and resolute. "Julian will do what he's told. And he will be king. That's his role to fulfill. Ours is to ensure there's a throne for him to ascend to."

Chapter Nine

> Remember when y'all were on here calling out Duchess & siding with Sa-messy Banks? I do, screenshots don't lie! Banks still desperate to be a Duchess even if she has to pop out a baby. 🙄 #Isaidwhatisaid #julianmybabydaddy #justiceforduchess
>
> ***@InDuchessIStan, Twitter***

"Welcome back to Primrose Park, Ms. Nelson."

Past the guarded, gated entrance, beyond the tall trees that lined the long private road—Amos timed his words perfectly, and when the view opened up, Dani pressed a hand to her chest as emotions overwhelmed her. Not because of the house, although the large three-story gray stone building, bordered by a lake, was absolutely stunning. But because this is where she and Jameson had fallen in love.

"When I was told the prince had invited me, you definitely weren't what I had in mind."

"Did you just throw your sponge at me?"

"What are we going to do . . . about this . . . thing between us? Aren't you tired of fighting it?"

"Jay, I like you."

"I like you, too, Dani. A lot."

This house had been the cocoon that had protected them and allowed their feelings to grow.

Where they'd been just Dani and Jay.

Before the world knew about Duchess and Prince Jameson and believed their opinions on the couple's relationship should be heard and validated.

Amos pulled the car into the circular drive and Jameson stood waiting, the wind tousling his dark hair. Dani gave thanks to the guards who must've called down to the house and let them know she was coming. Now she wouldn't have to search eleven thousand square feet to find him.

Although she would've.

Dani barely allowed Amos time to put the car in park before she'd thrown open the door and hurtled herself into Jameson's arms.

"He—"

His lips crushed hers and she gave herself up to the kiss, meeting his tongue as it swept inside and tangled with hers.

Heat suffused her body, hardening her nipples and creating a delicious sensation as they pressed against his chest. Her hands gripped his broad shoulders and trailed down his back, the muscles beneath his skin reacting to her touch.

She shivered. He was so big. So masculine.

When she reached his firm ass, she clenched her fingers into the denim-clad flesh and ground into the hardness waiting for her. He moaned and hauled her closer and she thrilled in the barely leashed passion.

Always so controlled, her Jameson. But not with her. He tasted her, drank from her, as if every kiss before her was an unsatisfying experience and only she could ease the ache within. This is what she needed. What she'd craved. It had been nine days since their last kiss.

Entirely too long.

How was it possible that several months before she hadn't even known this man existed, and now she couldn't imagine living her life without him?

Seconds . . . minutes later, when they finally broke apart, he stared down at her. A flush tinged his cheekbones and his blue eyes blazed. "I missed you."

Her heart swelled and she palmed his cheek. "I gathered as much. Unless you treat all your guests to such a welcoming greeting."

He laughed and she hung on tight, closing her eyes and staying in what had easily become her favorite place. Where she felt safe and cherished.

"Come on, let's go inside."

She slid an arm around his waist, he draped his along her shoulders and they traveled together up the stone steps as if neither wanted the other to be too far away. They passed through the stately double-door entrance, which was flanked by four pillars. Margery and the entire staff stood waiting in the large foyer.

"Margery," Dani said, going forward and enveloping the older woman in a hug.

Jay's chief housekeeper made a sound of surprise before lifting her arms and returning Dani's embrace.

"Good to see you, ma'am," Margery said.

"Would you see to it that Dani's things are brought into the house and settled?" A tiny smile played upon Jay's lips.

"Yes sir."

"Where did you put me this time?" Dani asked, as Jay hurried her in the direction of his office. "Back to my tower in the east wing?"

"You have a suite near mine in the west wing. But don't plan on sleeping there. I wanted you to be comfortable, so it's your own space to design however you like. But at night, this ass will be within caressing distance at all times," he said, grabbing the aforementioned part and squeezing.

She stopped and stared at him. Had she heard him correctly? "You're giving me my own space? To do with what I want?"

A frown marred his brow. "Yes. As long as this is my home, I want you to consider it yours, too."

This man. So loving and generous. How did she get so lucky?

She kissed him again, chastely this time, before snuggling close and pressing her nose against his neck, inhaling his essence.

"Mmmm . . . my strategy to get you here more often and keep you longer appears to be working," he boasted.

When they reached his intended destination, he closed the door and pulled her down next to him on the couch.

"Now, where were we," he murmured, as he slid the light pink cashmere wrap off her shoulders and buried his face in her cleavage, bared by the white scoop-necked halter top.

Goosebumps erupted all over her body. She clutched his head to her chest, the crisp strands of his hair yielding to her pressure.

"When we parted after the tribute," he said, nuzzling her neck, "I thought I'd lose my mind if I didn't see you soon. But after our time together in California, I assumed I had a handle on it. How is it possible that I missed you more this time around? Being without you is going to be torture."

She moaned, throwing her head back, allowing him easy access to . . . whatever he wanted. "Good thing we don't have to worry about that for a while."

He paused and looked up at her, confusion breaking through the inferno blazing in his blue gaze. "We don't?"

"Uh-uh," she said, wrapping her arms more firmly around him. "I'm going to be here for a while."

"Define 'a while'?"

"A month. Maybe more."

He frowned and straightened, dislodging her hold. Cool air intruded where there had once been heat. That wasn't the reaction she'd been expecting to her news.

She tilted her head. "What happened to losing your mind, sweet torture and all that?"

"I'm not complaining; I *do* want you here as long as possible. But when we talked about your visit, you said you'd only be able to manage a week. Two, if you turned off your phone and locked it in my wine cellar."

It was her turn to pull away. She scrambled off his lap, going over to rest her hip against his desk.

She bit her lip. "Things have changed."

He moved to the edge of the sofa and braced his elbows on his knees, staring up at her. "Does this have anything to do with your meeting with Genesis? You sounded strange when we talked but I ascribed that to jet lag. Was there something more? Something you're not telling me?"

How could she tell him? What would she say?

"Jay, I know you hate the spotlight, but can you please suck that shit up and help me get this contract? They want you to be a part of my official marketing campaign, which is ridiculous, since you don't use the products and they're not targeted to you and before this summer you'd never heard of me or Mela-Skin. But that doesn't matter because you're hella famous and Genesis's new parent company wants to use you.

"I said no but I agreed that we would go out and take lots of pictures together and stay relevant and trending and even though

neither of us are happy with this arrangement, Bennie said that meant it was a good compromise. No pressure, it's just that if you don't agree, it could affect everything I've worked for. Also, once you do this we can't break up. Ever. Because it'll affect my brand. Which you're now a part of. So . . . what do you say?"

Mental Dani was panting by the time she was done.

Nope, that wasn't happening.

Dani trusted Jameson. And yet . . . no matter how much people *said* they wanted to help you, in the end, all you could count on was yourself. People might not mean to let you down and the disappointment wasn't always intentional—she knew Nana didn't die on purpose!—but the result, Dani having to take care of herself, was still the same.

Her team had approached Genesis with their compromise and after some back-and-forth, the beauty company had agreed it could work. But no one was signing the contract.

Not yet.

Apparently Greg Martin, the VP of Mergers and Acquisitions for Parcellum, had concerns about whether she and Jameson would honor their end of the deal. Jameson wasn't a party to their contract; legally, he couldn't be forced to act. So Martin had required a one-month trial period to ensure Dani followed through and to evaluate the proposal in action. If their joint public appearances continued to increase Dani's brand awareness and sales, Parcellum would allow the investment by Genesis to go through.

She wouldn't have to ask Jameson for help.

And he wouldn't say no.

Or leave her because she wasn't worth the hassle.

She cleared her throat. "They were extremely excited by the coverage I got from the royal tribute."

"That's wonderful," he said, smiling. "You were worried whether the announcement of our relationship would derail all the work you did that week. So, it didn't?"

"No. Actually our relationship has raised my profile."

"The deal is going through? You got what you wanted?"

"Almost." She was really skirting the line here. "We need to figure out one mo—"

She broke off when the phone on his desk rang. He closed his eyes. "Damn."

"Is everything okay?"

"Years ago, I asked Margery to remove that phone and she informed me all royal residences were required to have a working landline. In more than a decade, that phone has rung twice. This past week? Several times daily." He exhaled and stood. "Let me take care of this and we'll get back to our conversation."

He kissed her forehead and reached around her to pick up the black receiver.

"Yes?" His tone was clipped, and tension seemed to stiffen his shoulders with every second that passed.

His expression hardened and, that quickly, he morphed from Jay to Prince Jameson. This was the man she'd first met when she'd arrived back in June. The one who'd been arrogant, judgmental, and dismissive.

And yet, even in that persona, she'd still found him sexy as fuck.

"What's wrong?" she asked, when he'd hung up the phone.

He stared into the distance, his hands perched low on his hips.

"This Julian and Samantha Banks scandal is affecting everything."

"I'll bet. The next in line to the throne impregnated a woman other than his wife. Who was half his age! There must be protocol for something like this?"

"There is." He shook his head. "But Samantha Banks defies protocol. Apparently, she goes on social media every day with a new post!"

It was true. Samantha had hit the motherlode with this one. Her feud with Duchess had helped her to stay relevant and get more followers. But her affair with the prince and possible pregnancy would help her make history. Her followers increased with each post. And she'd started doing daily IG stories where she'd update everyone with how she was feeling. #RoyalSparkleBabyBumpWatch.

In a way, Banks was still biting off of Dani, trying to copy her life. Dani had found her prince. Samantha was determined to do the same.

Dani would actually feel sorry for Julian if he hadn't brought it all on himself. He'd welcomed Samantha Banks into his life as a way to hurt both Jameson and Dani. Now he was reaping what he'd sown.

"What is the palace doing about it?"

"Besides removing Julian from his scheduled events and trotting me out in his stead?"

"You can't solve the problem single-handedly!"

"I've told them that. Repeatedly. Friday, I was in Blackpool. Between briefings on the town's challenges, investments, and regeneration efforts and tours of the community gardens and parks, I was constantly asked about the scandal and the truth of the rumors. And about you and our relationship."

"Poor baby," she said, rubbing his back.

He must've hated doing that. Unless he was lecturing or giving a speech on the issues he was passionate about, he didn't like being the center of attention, even as he'd charmed everyone he'd met while they'd been in the U.S.

Which is why you know he's not going to like doing what Genesis has suggested.

"I was so close to saying, Sod it! To telling the queen I refused to get involved."

Dani gasped. "You can do that? I thought you had no choice once she appointed you a Counsellor of State?"

"That only matters if I remained a senior working member of the royal family. I could've said no."

This was all news to her. "What would've happened?"

"Most of it comes down to money. I could've lost financial backing, my home, my titles. It all belongs to the monarchy. But my father and grandfather left me money and I've never had to touch the income I've earned as a lecturer. Let's just say I won't starve. Outside of money, the queen could've stripped me of my titles. Again, not a hardship. And it would hurt my mother more than me."

"Then why didn't you say no the last time?"

He shoved a hand through his hair. "Because she played on my grief and love for my grandfather while assuring me it would only be temporary. And since my dealings with the queen had been quite limited before, I believed her. Once I knew better, she turned to blackmail using someone I loved."

"Like when she threatened to turn over pictures of us kissing to the press and saying I was trying to trap you."

Which would've all but guaranteed Dani lost her deal with Genesis.

"Right."

"So why are you doing this now?" The words had barely left her lips before comprehension dawned. "Who has she threatened this time?"

"My mother," he said, his fingers clenching into tight fists at his sides.

"Calanthe?" she asked, stunned.

Jameson quickly outlined the current state of affairs.

"My mother is financially secure, but she's been a part of this family since she was seventeen. She's never known any other life. Can she survive outside of the royal family? Of course. Should she have to out of spite? No."

"And you trust the queen to keep her word?"

"Not really. But I trust Catherine. And she's promised me that my mother will be fine." He squeezed his eyes shut and pinched the bridge of his nose. "I'm sorry. I didn't want to spring all of this on you on your first day here."

"No, it's okay. Really. I understand."

"With my increased duties I may not be able to spend as much time together as I wanted."

His situation *had* changed. Now that he was taking over Julian's duties, there would be more opportunities for those appearances and photos she needed.

This fairy tale *will* be televised.

Her stomach twisted into knots. "Don't worry. We'll figure it out."

He brushed a lock of hair off her forehead. "Enough of that intrusion. Let's finish our conversation. What were you going to tell me about needing something for the deal to go through?"

Tell him! He might help you!

"It can wait," she said. "Just know that everything will turn out just as we anticipated."

"I have no doubt," he said, walking over to his door and locking it. "Anything else we need to discuss that requires my full attention."

"No."

"Good," he said. He moved quickly and scooped her up into his arms. "Because I can't wait another moment until I'm reacquainted with the feel of your body and the taste of your sweetness on my tongue."

The couch's supple leather was cool against her back. Above her, Jameson's features were taut, a hint of a blush staining his cheekbones, and she was awestruck by the sharp line of his stubbled jaw and the inferno sparking in his eyes. The man had been overly blessed. It wasn't enough to possess drop-dead gorgeous looks. He had to have intelligence and humor, too.

Their lips met and she gave herself to it, dazed by the hungry possessiveness of the contact. He seared a blazing trail of kisses from her ear, along her cheek, and down her neck, causing her to moan, her heart thudding in her chest, her breath coming quickly. Exquisite sensations rippled through her and her nipples beaded and abraded deliciously against the fabric of her bra.

Everything about him called to her and she wanted to be closer to him than what was humanly possible.

Do you?

She tried to block out the inner critic that wondered if she should be doing this. Was it right to enjoy all this satisfaction if she wasn't being honest with him?

But when he gripped the edge of her shirt, the back of his hand scorched her lower belly, and she could give a shit about anything else.

He kissed every plane of skin revealed, his tongue dipping into her navel and curving the sensitive underside of her breasts. He palmed the lobes, squeezing them, and flicking the hardened nubs in a way that had her thrashing, the sensations so overwhelming.

He licked the valley.

"Next time I'm going to place my cock here," he said, patting her sternum, "and watch it slide in between your tits."

The mouth on this man! No matter how he was using it, he was a skilled master.

"Will you hold them together for me?" he asked gruffly. "Tight like this?"

He demonstrated, pressing them close until he'd created a snug channel and the phantom ache of her body missing what he'd promised, shot straight to her core.

"Yes," she panted.

She thought she would come out of her body as desire pooled thick between her thighs. His chest rose and fell with effort, as if he'd just run a marathon and the hard ridge of his cock pressed against her leg. He ground it against her, and she hummed low in her throat.

That's how much he wanted her. And recognizing the extent of that need turned her on even more.

She loved being intimate with him. He never thought about his own pleasure until hers had been achieved. Often multiple times. And because he took such good care of her heart, she felt comfortable doing things with him, to him, that she hadn't done with anyone else before. He made her feel safe in her vulnerability.

With your body, you mean.

Enough!

She shoved all thought away and dove back into passion, something she could handle.

He kneaded her pussy through the fabric of her pants and the action sent a rush of moisture to meet his palm, as if he'd called it forth. He pressed hard and she met him, grind for grind, the sweet agony compelling her to arch off the couch, bound only by the weight of his body.

He slipped his fingers in the waistband of her pants and yanked them down, freeing one leg and settling it along his left hip. When he released her other leg, he kissed its ankle and she fucking melted. Like a dropped ice cream cone on a summer sidewalk. Tenderly, she reached out and combed her fingers through his hair. He kissed her inner forearm before turning his attention to the scrap of red material covering her.

He toyed with the lacy band on her hip. "Is this what I think it is?"

She peered at him from beneath half-lowered lids. "It is if you think it's a thong."

"You're killing me, love. I have to see."

He flipped her over and slid his hands into the grooves of her hips, lifting them until they were high in the air and her face was pressed against the sofa.

He groaned deep in his throat. "Your ass is perfect."

He stroked it, his touch gentle but firm. Her lashes fluttered and she hissed as he pressed wet kisses along each curvy cheek, nipping then soothing the sting with the pad of his tongue.

He pushed aside the strap of material nestled in her ass. The cool air teased her hot, swollen flesh and then his mouth was there and she screamed, grabbing a throw pillow to catch the sound before it was audible. His tongue worked her snatch with an expertise that would've made it difficult for her to remain on her knees if it weren't for the steel band of his arm against her lower back.

A finger feathered between her creases and then two long digits slid inside and she bucked.

"Your pretty pussy is so greedy. I wish you could see how much it wants my finger."

His breath titillated her folds, his words teased her mind. His fingers thrust in and out of her drenched channel, and, unable to remain still, she fucked them, wanting everything he could give her and more.

Like his mouth.

"So sweet," he murmured. "Do you know how much I missed you? Missed this? I need it like the air I breathe and the food I eat. It's essential to my survival. I can't live without you, I merely exist."

He sped up, the velocity of his words matching his motions.

"You know I'm only getting started, yeah? I'm going to make you come at least two more times before I fuck you. Before I claim what's mine."

The pads of his finger scraped her G spot, his tongue sucked her clit, and the tingling started low in her belly before spreading up and out. She raced to meet it, tightening her pelvic muscles, drawing it forth—

She screamed into the pillow, as bliss totally consumed her, the rapture on the right side of unbearable. She collapsed on the sofa, breathing hard, as another involuntary shiver racked her body. He fell on top of her, his clothes scraping her sensitized skin, his cock pressed hard against her ass.

"Watching you come is the most beautiful thing I've ever seen. I'll never tire of it," he said softly, kissing the curve of her shoulder.

In the aftermath of her orgasm, his tenderness was almost her undoing. She closed her eyes.

Easier to share your heart and your body than your soul.

Oh, shut the fuck up!

Chapter Ten

MAKING HIS GRAN PROUD! PRINCE JAMESON STEPS IN AS JULIAN'S SEX SCANDAL SURGES

The Times

Two glorious days.

Two glorious days holed up at Primrose Park with Dani.

Two glorious days holed up at Primrose Park with Dani where they never left their suite of rooms.

Where the only time he'd taken a break from indulging his overwhelming need for her had been when he couldn't deny the sustenance his body needed to survive.

Once that had been tended to, he resumed tending to her. Kissing her lips, caressing her skin, sinking into her tight, hot body until time had no meaning, and the world, outside of the two of them, ceased to exist.

But no matter how much he wished otherwise, they couldn't hide away forever. That's what they'd done initially, and they'd underestimated the shock of stepping back into the real world together. Jameson didn't intend to make that mistake again.

When he'd been in California, Dani had shared the private parts of her life with him. He'd wanted to return the favor by officially welcoming her into *his* life, not the royal one.

Hence, the small, informal affair with some of his closest friends, now taking place in his sitting room. He'd invited Rhys and two of their poker buddies, Lord Jasper Strathmore, the Viscount Hastings, along with his wife, Lady Harriet, and Oliver Camden and his long-time girlfriend, Mary Baldwin. Months ago, the notion of hosting a social gathering in his house would've been an anathema. But he was enjoying tonight's festivities. Maybe because it involved people he actually liked instead of the usual peerage crowd he'd had to endure.

"It was all over social media that you performed at a private birthday party in Dubai. How exciting! Do you do that sort of thing often?" Mary asked.

"I've done it a couple of times," Dani said, from where she sat on the arm of Jameson's chair, her fingers absently combing through his hair, "but that was the first time I'd traveled so far! And lots of celebrities do it, not just singers. More than you'd think."

"We live a pretty good life," Harriet said, "but I have to admit your IG feed leaves me a little envious."

Jameson had first met Jasper at uni before reconnecting with him and Harriet about seven years ago. While Jasper and Harriet were titled, they were unpretentious about it in a manner that was rare to find.

"Sure," Dani said, incredulity evident on her expressive face.

"It does! All the parties, fancy clothes, and meeting celebrities."

"You're a viscountess! I thought parties, fancy clothes, and famous people were just a regular Tuesday for you?"

"She wishes," Oliver smirked.

"No one's talking to you, Ollie," Mary said.

"He should be used to that," Rhys said. "Just like secondary school, right, mate?"

"I hope not," Oliver said. "It was absolute torture. Hormones surging through my body. A stiff wind could give me a woody. And in this weather, that meant I was constantly hard. I was jerking off so often, I developed carpal tunnel."

"How is any of that different now?" Mary asked.

"That's my girl!" Oliver said, leaning over and giving Mary a loud kiss.

"But seriously," Harriet said above the laughter, "*I'd* trade places with you."

"Really?" Jameson said, raising a brow and trying to suppress a smile.

"Hey!" Jasper cried at the same time.

Harriet dropped her blushing face into her hands. "I'm making a right mess of this, aren't I?"

"I'd say so," Oliver smirked.

Dani pressed her palms to her face. "Stop it! I'm laughing so hard my cheeks hurt!"

"Let me start over," Harriet said. "I adored Jas from the moment I met him. How could I not? Smart, handsome, and from a good family."

"I was attracted to her top-notch tits," Jasper said, helping himself to another hors d'oeuvre from the tray Margery had brought in earlier.

"You ass!" Harriet rolled her eyes at him but continued. "I certainly didn't marry him for his title, but I can't deny that a part of me thought being Viscountess Hastings would be a bit more . . . magical."

"Like a fairy tale," Mary added.

"Exactly."

Dani reared back. "And you're saying it's not?"

"Not even close. These days it's rather naff."

She studied them all for a second before shaking her head. "Sorry, I don't know what that means but I'm not buying it. If you ask any two ordinary people if they'd rather be a rapper or royalty—"

"Rapper, no question. Look at how Jameson is dressed," Rhys announced, pointing to the black-and-white joggers and white trainers Jameson had gotten during his shopping spree with Dani.

Jameson dusted a hand down the front of his basic black T-shirt. "I know it's difficult for you, Rhys, but you're permitted to try new things."

"I think he looks great," Dani said, bending down to give him a quick kiss.

A kiss he would've deepened if they'd been alone.

Harriet nodded. "I agree."

"Oh, we know how you feel," Jasper said.

Jameson shook his head. "Come now, mates. There's no need for jealousy."

"Jealous? Because you fancy yourself to be the new David Beckham?" Oliver asked, giving rise to another round of laughter.

A relaxing evening full of fun and laughter, spending time with good friends and the woman he loved? This is what he'd been missing; what he'd always wanted. Even though he hadn't known it.

"We haven't gone over this yet," Jameson said, sliding his hand along Dani's thigh and squeezing, "but Jasper and Harriet aren't royalty."

Dani pursed her lips. "But he's a viscount."

"Yes, but there's a difference between royalty and nobility. Royalty only includes the immediate family of the ruling monarch. Nobility is much broader; it involves class and hereditary titles."

"I guess I still have a lot to learn. Do you guys get hounded by the press the way Jay's family does?"

"No one is stalked by the rags more than the royal family. Jas and I will get our picture taken if we attend a notable event, but we're too boring to sell papers."

"The papers can be merciless," Oliver said.

"Just ask Julian," Mary said, still managing to smirk while taking a sip of her wine.

Silence blanketed the room and glances bounced around, landing on Jameson before quickly flitting away.

"And on that note . . ." Rhys rattled the ice in his empty tumbler and pushed to his feet.

"Oh, come on! We've said much worse," Mary said, crossing her arms and sinking back into the settee.

"Only after Jameson starts," Oliver said.

Jameson shrugged a shoulder. "Feel free to dispense with that formality."

"In that case," Harriet said. "Jameson, you must be concerned. At the Children's Village reception that Jas and I attended two weeks ago, Julian strolled in as if nothing had occurred. The poor bastard seemed stricken when he realized he wasn't getting his usual welcome."

That was part of the problem. Julian was rarely denied what he wanted. That's how he'd ended up in this position. And despite what Catherine seemed to think, Jameson didn't believe his uncle would pivot and be the monarch the country needed when it was his time to ascend to the throne.

"Don't feel sorry for him. He made his own bed." Realizing what he'd said, Jameson winced and closed his eyes while his friends laughed.

"The one I feel sorry for is Fiona. Everyone knows she's wanted to have another baby for a while now. It's her duty as the Princess of Wales. The whole heir and a spare. She finally gets pregnant and she can't even enjoy it because of that pop star."

Dani shook her head. "It may make me a bitch to say it, but I'm just glad that pop star's attention is focused on someone else. It was exhausting. So, I personally want to thank Julian! If he hadn't gotten involved by trying to trip up Jay, he wouldn't have brought her here."

"He's been a sleaze since he was in knee pants," Harriet scoffed. "That's why it took so long to marry him off. The queen probably threatened to disown him . . . or to live forever."

Dani laughed and snapped her fingers. "You are one shady bitch, Harriet."

Harriet tilted her head and pressed a hand to her chest. "Call me Hetty and awww . . . Thank you!"

Nothing they were saying was news to Jameson, yet it was a telling indication that his family was no longer held in the same high regard as they had been in the past.

Give his grandmother credit for seeing the precarious situation the monarchy was in and trying something—anything—to right the sinking ship.

He wished the something she tried didn't have to include him.

"I saw the pictures. Fiona's barely showing, but the dress she wore emphasized her tiny bump perfectly," Mary said.

"She looked gorgeous." Harriet sighed. "I'd hoped seeing her in person and pregnant meant everyone would behave."

"You mean you'd hoped the queen had found a way to muzzle the press for just one event," Jasper said.

Harriet nodded.

Jameson curled his lip. Ah, the naivety.

"There will always be one who figures the short-term gain of getting the scoop is worth whatever punishment the palace metes out," he said.

"And when the *Daily Standard* asked if Fiona was going to have a joint baby shower with Banks . . ." Jasper's grimace was absurdly comical.

"That actually happened? At a royal event?" Dani asked, eyes wide.

"It was brutal watching the clips on Twitter. I can't even imagine seeing it in person," Mary said.

"She rushed off and left Julian standing there. He seemed to forget all of his press training and proceeded to go on a tirade about the media's lack of deference and how things were going to change when *he* ascended to the throne."

"It was not a good look," Harriet summarized.

"That part wasn't on Twitter," Mary said, her voice rising in shock.

"Security escorted the reporter off the premises after his question to Fiona," Jasper continued. "I guess the other invited outlets didn't want to risk the palace's wrath. And the rest of us in attendance, well . . . we know better than to say anything publicly."

Jameson knew that well. Other than Dani, everyone in this group had been put through loyalty tests to ensure they were interested in his friendship and not his ties to the royal family. Everything from telling Rhys the toes on Jameson's left foot were webbed to see if he'd leak that "fun fact" to the media to "confiding" in Ollie the James Bond–like machinations Jameson and his cousins plotted to get into the hottest bars in London, including the use of the code name Buttocks Whimplesnatch, and waiting for the hordes of their Eton mates to attempt the scheme.

However, as he sat there, basking in the laughter and camaraderie, he realized while they'd earned his friendship, he'd never truly let them in. He'd seen them socially, but they hadn't enjoyed many evenings like this one. In his efforts to protect himself from the limelight, he'd withdrawn into the darkness.

How lonely he'd been.

"Damn!" Dani brought a closed fist to her mouth. "It's like a real-life soap opera! I wish Nyla was here. She's always saying she needs to write her own stuff to get good material to play. This would be perfect."

"You aren't the only one wishing she were here," Rhys muttered into the depths of his glass.

"Are you missing her?" Dani asked in a singsong voice. "Do you want to see her?"

"Yes!" A chorus of agreements from Jameson and their four friends.

"Don't make me sound like a sodden wanker!" Rhys scowled.

Dani frowned. "Jay said you didn't come to her premiere because you wanted to take things slow."

"That was a month ago. Now he's bingeing that drama she's on." Mary turned to Rhys. "Since when are you interested in fashion?"

"It's a great show. In the cutthroat world of fashion, it takes determination, cunning, and just a little bit of luck to rise to the top!"

Everyone glanced around at one another for a second.

"Isn't that the tagline of the show?" Mary whispered.

"Aren't you seeing each other in two weeks?" Dani asked, her lips twitching.

Rhys sighed and shoveled a hand through his blond hair. "We both had to cancel. The uni has scheduled a weekend retreat for senior lecturers and professors to answer questions about the change in personnel and on dealing with the press—"

"Sorry, mate," Jameson said.

"—and her new movie is doing so well, they're adding more promotional appearances to her schedule. It seems inconceivable that in this modern age, two people who want to see each other can't.

But the timing hasn't worked out. She started shooting the new season of her show in July and now I'm preparing for the semester."

"Do you think it's a sign from the universe?" Oliver asked.

"Ollie!" Mary hit his arm.

"What? I'm just asking. I mean, should relationships be that hard?"

"Sometimes I ask myself that very question. Like now," Mary muttered. She tapped Dani on the knee. "Can I ask you something?"

"Go for it."

"Da Real's annual Pajama Jammie Jam. What's it like?"

Dani cackled. "You know about that?"

Ollie raised his hand. "I don't."

"It's an over-the-top party thrown by this rapper, Da Real. He does it every summer at his house in Beverly Hills. You have to wear pajamas to get in, but not the comfy kind. Women show up in Louboutins and La Perla. Dudes'll be blinged out while wearing Versace boxer briefs. And the Veuve Clicquot and tequila be flowing. Think Diddy's White Party but sexier and more exclusive."

Jameson's mind conjured up an image of Dani in four-inch stiletto heels and barely there lingerie. He'd need to plan their own private version of this party; he didn't intend to share that vision with anyone else.

"That sounds like my kind of party," Rhys said. "How do I get an invitation?"

Dani winced. "*You* don't."

Mary laughed. "I have a friend who worked for Stella McCartney and she got to go a few years ago. She said the guest list was iconic: athletes, musicians, actors, models—"

"It can get crazy, but it's a lot of fun."

"Why did you decide not to go this year?"

The smile slowly dissipated from Dani's face. "This year?"

"It was a few weeks ago. And I didn't see anything on your IG."

Dani blinked rapidly several times and turned her head away from Mary, dipping her chin to her chest. It looked as if she'd recalled something disturbing.

Jameson broke the awkward silence. "I was visiting her during that time, and I don't think us attending a pajama jam is the best way to keep a low profile."

"I hate to break it to you, mate," Oliver said, "but you don't seem like the Pajama Jammie Jam type."

"I must've forgotten about it. I've had a lot on my plate lately. Don't tell anyone, but I've started this new relationship," Dani said with a laugh—that didn't sound genuine to Jameson's ears—and a look of gratitude in his direction.

What was that about?

Jasper tapped Jameson on his shoulder. "A little birdie told me *you're* taking on more royal duties."

Jameson tensed but then shrugged it off. Only Catherine, Dani, and Rhys knew the full extent of his arrangement with the queen. Still, he shouldn't be shocked that his friends would wonder at the unlikely development. "Just a few events."

"But you hate them!" Jasper frowned. "Is it because of what happened with Birmingham?"

"Partly. And with everything going on with Julian, the queen asked for my help."

"It's more dire than we thought if they're drafting you into service," Oliver said.

Dani laughed and stroked his thigh. "He was wonderful during the tribute. I have no doubt he'll be great!"

He snaked a hand around her waist and pulled her down onto his lap. She shrieked and he laughed, nuzzling her neck, his heart full of love for her and fortifying his belief that he was doing the right thing to get them out of this life.

"What do you have coming up?" Harriet asked. "Visiting a children's hospital? Meeting with a foreign dignitary?"

"The new royal exhibit at the National Portrait Gallery on Thursday," he said, sure his voice conveyed the correct level of his enthusiasm.

Which was pretty low.

"Are you going?" Dani asked.

Harriet shook her head. "Oh no! We didn't get an invite to this one. Only those in the innermost circle will be there. You'll enjoy it."

"Dani isn't going." At the various surprised and concerned expressions he explained, "We have an arrangement. In exchange for my promise not to damage her coolness with my bungling presence, I'm shielding her from having to attend these dreadful functions."

He glanced at Dani, hoping that their shared smiles would ease the anxiety some were still emoting, but she averted her gaze and rose from his lap.

"I don't know, Jay. It sounds like fun."

That was unexpected.

He narrowed his eyes and shifted in his seat, trying to decipher his feeling that something was . . . off. "I wouldn't call it *fun*, but it's a beautiful museum and it houses an extensive collection of portraits of the most important and famous British people in history. If you're truly interested, I'll arrange to take you at some point."

"How about Thursday?"

"Thursday?" He stiffened. "You want to come to the opening of the exhibit? With me?"

She bit her lip before releasing it and lifting her chin. "Yes."

He pushed to his feet, ignoring the room's sudden deviation in atmosphere and the other occupants watching them as if they were witnessing the finals at Wimbledon.

"But we agreed that we would keep our relationship separate from our 'jobs.' That it would be the only way to protect it."

The last thing he wanted to do was expose Dani to the press here. And not just the press. There was an entire strata of people who lived for the vicious gossip that occurred at these events. Hadn't they just spent ten minutes talking about Julian and Fiona? Jameson never wanted to subject her to that.

"That was before, when I thought I'd be busy with Mela-Skin and you believed you'd still be lecturing. Now you'll be doing something for the Crown almost every day while I have all this time on my hands. Unless"—she jammed her hands on her hips—"you expected me to stay at home all day, waiting for you to return?"

"Oh shit," Oliver coughed into his fist.

Jameson didn't know what he'd thought about how they'd spend their time while she was visiting. In truth, he hadn't done much *thinking* since she'd gotten here; he'd been busy ensuring they both were too busy . . . *feeling*. Eventually they would've discussed it, preferably without an audience.

But what he did know was—

"That's the furthest thing from the truth."

Mary winced and raised her hand slightly. "Sorry, but you guys have been together for several days and this is the first time it's come up?"

"They're two months into a new relationship," Oliver said, his eyes wide. "If you think they would reunite and spend their time alone together discussing his royal schedule, then we're just as old and settled as Jas and Hetty!"

"You should be so lucky," Jasper said.

"We're not a secret," Dani continued, as if his friends' community theatre interlude hadn't occurred. "Everyone knows we're dating. And I'm in the country. Why wouldn't you take your girlfriend on a date?"

"'Girlfriend on a date'? Wait. Dani, I'm sorry. I thought you understood." Harriet set her glass down. "You're out, cleverly done, by the way, and you're right, everyone knows you're dating. But you've spent the past month in the States where the press fawned over the both of you. This will be your first time together in public in the U.K. since the royal tribute. The press, and the country, will have feelings about that."

Mary leaned forward. "Hetty is right. Jameson is our prince, and the people here feel entitled to his life and the lives of his entire family."

"This is not the two of you appearing at an event in Hollywood," Harriet said, "or captured holding hands here in London. You're going with Jameson to a royal event where he's attending as the family's representative. You need to tread carefully. You can't be so cavalier about this."

Resentment burned in his gut. He loved Dani. Having her with him would make all the times he had to put himself out there bearable. But he'd never be a normal man, taking his woman out on a date. He was a member of the royal family. And any outing involving them would turn into a state event that required a briefing.

Jameson took Dani's hand. "You've managed an impressive amount of time in the public eye in the States, so some of the nuances may seem silly to you. But when people find out you're there with me, it's going to turn into a circus. The press is going to be there in full force. It can be ruthless."

"Stop talking to me as if I'm a child. I know what I'm asking. If your answer is no, just say so."

He sighed deeply and shook his head. "I can't say no to you."

Her chin quivered and her lovely eyes softened behind a sheen of moisture.

His chest constricted and he palmed her cheek, ready to catch any falling tears. "Don't cry, love. Please. It's not worth it. Of course you can come with me."

"No, it's . . . I'm not—" Her hand covered his and she kissed him, her lips briefly clinging to his before she pulled away. "We knew it wasn't going to be easy. I'll be fine. And I'm prepared. That's why I hired Louisa as my royalty whisperer."

Harriet nodded. "Then you'd better call her now. She'll appreciate the heads-up."

"See"—Dani smiled, though it was strained—"nothing to worry about."

Famous last words, Jameson thought, unease prickling the base of his neck at the thought of Dani being presented to the wolves. He was supposed to protect her. Instead, he was walking her down the red carpet and straight into their den.

Chapter Eleven

Female 1: Speaking of exciting news, I just have to talk about it. Duchess is here. In the U.K.

Male 1: We have a lot of those here. I don't see how that's news.

Female 1: Cheeky. You know I meant American rap star Duchess. Prince Jameson's newest girlfriend.

Female 2: Still so romantic, the declaration he made about her on the plane. I believe it has over 10 million views on YouTube.

Male 1: Did she just get here? I haven't seen her.

Female 1: That's the point. No one has seen her. Is the palace hiding her?

Female 2: Maybe they're not as supportive as they said in their statement.

Good Morning, London

Blinding lights from camera flashes?

Check.

The deafening chaos of hundreds of people behind security barricades?

Check.

Paparazzi shouting her name?

Check.

It was all familiar to Dani, even if the location was not.

The walk from their vehicle to the National Portrait Gallery took less than thirty seconds, yet Jameson's grip on her hand telegraphed his unease and discomfort with the situation.

Dani was conflicted about her own feelings, and guilt burned like acid in the back of her throat. Jameson had been right; they'd agreed to keep their professional lives separate. And for her to go back on their understanding without telling him why *and* in front of his friends . . .

"I can't say no to you . . . Don't cry, love. Please. It's not worth it. Of course you can come with me."

Her heart hurt at the knowledge that he'd been agitated thinking he'd upset her when it was actually her own shame that had brought tears to her eyes.

But what choice did she have?

You could tell him about Parcellum and ask for his help.

But what if he said no?

Everything was still so new and so good. She could see breaking up because they had different goals and values, or one of them was an asshole, or—God forbid—one of them cheated. But to risk it over something when there was another way? It made about as much sense as having Jameson be the face of Mela-Skin.

He glanced down at her, signs of stress and strain all over that gorgeous face. He was so worried about her, he couldn't focus on what he needed to do. She hadn't lost sight of the fact that the only reason he was here was to save his mother. Dani wouldn't let him mess this up because of her. Releasing his hand, she reached up and smoothed her thumb over his brow, appreciating when the rigid muscles thawed beneath her touch.

"It's going to be okay. Remember, you've got me. And I got you," she said, recalling her earlier words to him on the movie premiere red carpet.

"I love you," he murmured.

"I love you, too."

The cameras clicked, catching the moment.

She smiled, elated that when they entered the building, his clasp had gentled and his smile was more natural.

She also knew that picture would end up all over the news and social media.

She was going to hell.

Inside, they stopped at the base of the staircase to chat with the brunette who'd introduced herself as Gillian Wickstead, the museum's director.

"Your Royal Highness, Duchess. Thank you for being here," she said. "We're really excited about this exhibit. We've been working on it for three years."

Curators had searched the globe and pulled together a top-notch collection celebrating the royal family for the opening of the House of Lloyd exhibit at the museum. Dani didn't claim to be an art lover, but she knew what she liked and she appreciated pretty things. She was looking forward to seeing the pieces.

And it could've been worse. At least it wasn't a hospital.

She hated hospitals!

"We've gathered oil paintings, photographs, and prints. The history of your family is spectacular. We learned so much. The queen had a private audience several days ago and she was shocked at some of the things we managed to unearth."

Gillian gestured for them to precede her, and they did, ascending the stairs . . . to the waiting throng of more photographers. Dani made the mistake of looking up and catching a face full of flashes that blinded her for several seconds. She briefly lost her balance.

"Are you okay?" Jameson asked, his hold tight on her arm.

"I'm fine. Looked into the flash. Rookie error."

"Bloody photographers," he cursed, his expression becoming unyielding once again.

At the top of the steps, Gillian introduced them to the curator of the exhibit and several other museum employees and they all chatted briefly. With the angle of his body and his purposeful gaze, Jameson did his best to ignore the cameras. Dani placed her hand on his lower back, feeling the rigid muscles beneath the exquisitely tailored suit. Did attending these affairs always cause this level of agitation? Or was her presence making it worse?

Gillian escorted them down a long hallway where statues and busts punctuated every several feet.

"We were able to borrow a handful of pieces of sculpture from the Royal Collection. We thought they would be a wonderful prelude into the exhibit itself."

They walked through an arched doorway and into a room adorned with art. It was such a feast for the eyes that Dani didn't know where to look first. The sounds of a live string quartet and the murmur of voices filled the room. Jameson had been told that the guests would be top tier level patrons of the museum, members of the aristocracy, and distinguished guests. Dani recognized several actors and actresses who'd been granted the title of Sir or Dame, as well as some faces from the tribute ball, although she'd never recall any of their names.

"Your Royal Highness," an older woman in a beige tea-length dress said, dropping a brief curtsy to Jameson.

"It's wonderful to see you, Ellie," he said, shaking her hand when she straightened. "Have you met Duchess?"

Ellie arched a thin black brow. "No. I haven't had the pleasure."

"Duchess, this is the Countess of Salsbury, Eleanor Cameron, an old friend of the royal family. Ellie, this is Duchess."

"Oh, I know who you are," Ellie said, the cut of her black bob sharp against her pale cheek. "You've caused quite the stir in these circles."

"That wasn't my intention."

"I'm sure," she said, a little snidely. She refocused on Jameson. "I couldn't believe it when I heard you were replacing Julian. But I'm glad you did. What was he thinking?"

"Only he knows," Jameson said, diplomatically. "Have you had the opportunity to view the exhibit?"

Ellie waved her hand dismissively. "No one's here for the art! We've seen it all before. The only thing anyone in this room is interested in is the fallout from the various scandals."

Dani could see the realization dawning on Jameson, the look of dread coloring his eyes.

Ellie grabbed his arm. "Oh no, my boy, don't you dare turn into a nervous wreck on me. You're here representing not only the queen, but all of us. If the monarchy goes down, it'll take the aristocracy with it. So, buck up."

Dani didn't like the tone the woman used to speak to Jameson, but she couldn't deny the advice was good. He couldn't fall apart, not with his mother's future on the line. She tried to think of a way to snap him out of his feelings.

"Jay, have you told the countess about the JFL environmental prize you announced?"

"I haven't." Jameson smiled, a genuine one that brightened his eyes. "We're finalizing the funding and I've been struck and moved by the response we've received. We've exceeded our initial projections."

"That's very interesting," Ellie said, as she narrowed her eyes at Dani.

Dani stared back. The countess had wanted him to buck up.

Consider him bucked.

"Grandfather would've approved of—"

From experience, Dani knew Jameson would be occupied for a while. She squeezed his arm and went to take in the exhibit. While the hands she left him in weren't friendly to her, they *would* make sure he was taken care of.

She grabbed a flute from a circulating waiter and regarded the room. The walls were painted an olive green and the color complemented the golden frames, from ornate to minimalist, that seemed to recede into the wall and make the painting, photograph, or print pop.

Stares scalded her skin—made possible by the slate blue strapless gown that molded to her breasts and hips, snatched her waist, and flowed out in a skirt with structured waves that showed off quite a bit of leg. She ignored the looks, however, her interest solely on the artwork. She wanted to see more of Jameson's family and understand the legacy that was so important to the queen that she was willing to do anything, sacrifice anyone, to protect it.

It might be a concept Dani could never comprehend. Other than Nana, she didn't know or wasn't close to her family, so she didn't place her faith in the concept or hold it in high regard. Other than Nana, family had done nothing but let her down.

As conversation buzzed around her, Dani studied the display. The presentation began with paintings of his ancestors, featuring bright colors and stoic people. As time progressed, she began to recognize the subjects. There was an oil on canvas of a younger Marina standing with a man Dani knew was Prince John. Marina still had the same presence, but there was a glow about her, a happiness in her eyes as her husband gazed down at her with obvious tenderness. It was clear to see why the committee had chosen this picture.

There was a painting of Julian when he was named the Prince of Wales—the title placard called it the "Investiture of the Prince of Wales"—and while there was no denying he was a handsome man, his character was evident in the smirk he didn't hide and the soft rounded curve of his jawline. What her Nana would call a weak chin. It was so apparent, Dani wondered how the artist got away with it. Any layperson looking at the portrait could see they hadn't thought much of the subject.

And someone had chosen it for the exhibit.

"I'm not a fan of my uncle's," Jameson said, coming up next to her and sliding an arm around her waist, "but choosing this picture didn't do him any favors."

"Have you seen any of these portraits before?"

"Most of them. Some were hung in Buckingham Palace when I was growing up."

An oil portrait of the queen and Julian—her sitting on a red velvet chair, wearing an elaborate crown, while he stood slightly behind her in full royal regalia—held a solo spot on a prominent wall.

"In case you were still confused about who's next in line," Dani whispered.

They strolled along arm in arm, looking at the other offerings. There was a photograph of Princess Catherine in her early twenties, at what looked like an official event.

"That's a beautiful picture," Dani said.

Catherine was listening to someone, and people were gazing at her, their admiration and respect clear and freely offered.

There weren't any candid shots of Princess Bettina. Most of her solo portraits were official ones where she was posed, her expression serious, but bored.

Dani stopped to examine several black-and-white photos of the entire family from decades past, including one where the queen was sitting on a settee surrounded by her entire family. It stood out because it was oddly casual and came close to giving off a "Royals! They're just like us!" vibe.

From the corner of her eye, Dani caught sight of a face that was startlingly familiar, and she moved toward it, drawn. Jameson tensed, but he didn't stop her.

And then there it was, an extremely large portrait of a breathtakingly handsome man. Golden blond hair that curled ever so perfectly over his brow. Bright blue eyes, ringed with lines, that proved he smiled often. A clean-shaven square jaw softened in amusement. The subject was glancing away from the viewer and had been caught mid-laughter. It was as if Jameson had donned a wig . . . and an air of cavalierness.

"Is that—?"

"Prince Richard John Alastair Lloyd. My father."

"Wow."

"He did tend to have that effect on women."

"How can you blame them? Look at him."

"I have," he said.

"You look a lot like him."

"So they say."

The bitterness in his voice finally penetrated.

Oh.

It wasn't Prince Richard that she was enamored of. It was the parts of Jameson she saw in hi—

The flicker of a flash bounced off the portrait.

Dani glanced around. They were the center of attention. And at that moment, hundreds of pictures were being taken of the two of them. Of Jameson staring up at his father with the bitterest of expressions on his face.

Jay would hate the idea of the media, once again, witnessing then feeding off his pain and vulnerability.

"Tell me something you loved about your father."

His head jerked back. "Excuse me?"

"You've always focused on the bad things he did. But he was your father. There must've been some good things about him."

He pinched his lips together and glared up at the painting.

"Many people found him funny and charming. Particularly women."

Well shit, that didn't help. If anything, the scowl made him look downright hostile.

"Do you have any positive memories of him? Of any time the two of you may have spent together?"

A muscle ticked in his jaw and several moments passed where Dani wondered if she'd made a mistake by wading into familial waters with no clue of their depths.

But then he said, "My father was athletic and participated in many sporting events, and he'd collected numerous trophies. There was this one polo trophy that I'd always liked and when he wasn't home, I would sneak into his office, where I wasn't allowed, and pretend it was mine. One day, I was playing around, imagining I'd beat out Adolfo Cambiaso, when he caught me. I was so startled that it slipped from my grasp and crashed on the floor. The topper broke off. I knew he was going to be angry."

Dani marveled at this tiny glimpse into Jay's childhood. "And was he?"

"No. He said, 'You can get your own. I'll show you how.'"

A slight smile curved his lips and this time, his tall frame was relaxed when he glanced at his father on canvas.

"He was home for a month, and we spent every afternoon together. He taught me how to play the game and to love it as much as he did."

She moved closer and stroked his arm. "And did you win your own trophy?"

"The following season I won the junior club championship."

"Do you still play polo?"

There was a twinkle in his eyes. "Occasionally."

Her breath quickened. "I want you to know I find that incredibly sexy. Those tight shirts and britches." She smoothed a hand along her sleek hairdo and peered up at him from beneath her lashes. "You'll have to wear your uniform for me sometime."

"I will, if you promise you'll ride me like I'm your personal stallion," he murmured in her ear, his voice, scent, and nearness causing her nipples to bead against the bodice of her dress.

But when he straightened, he looked stricken.

"What's wrong?"

"I've spent years suppressing those memories, as if remembering the good times betrayed my mother."

Dani could definitely co-sign having conflicting feelings about one's family. "Nana used to say very few people are all good or all bad."

"Do the Nana sayings ever end?" he murmured, his tone scornful.

Dani raised her brows. "I get that seeing this portrait and talking about your father may have you feeling some kind of way, but don't take that out on me. And don't fucking insult my Nana."

If he wanted to be in a mood, she'd let him.

Alone.

She walked away but he grabbed her hand, halting her. "Dani. Love. I'm sorry."

She instantly forgave him, smoothing the frown from his face. "I know how you feel about him and how much hurt he caused you and Calanthe. But you're not your father. Thanks to your mother and your grandfather, you turned out different. Your father is still a part of you but you can take the positives from him and let his negatives guide you to make better choices."

His gaze heated her blood. "I don't know what I would do if I didn't have you in my life."

Leaning into him, she pressed her lips to his, offering all the adoration, affection, and comfort she had to give. She loved this man. Loved his vulnerability and the way he didn't play games or hold back how much he loved *her.* He gathered her close, accepting the care.

When they broke apart she realized the room had gone quiet. She peeked around his large frame to find all eyes on them.

Dani's first concern was Jameson, but she had a job to do. She didn't know how often she'd be able to convince Jameson to let her accompany him, so she needed to make each event count. She needed to give the media what they wanted, so she could get what she rightfully deserved. And if that meant smizing and booty tooching her way through this exhibit, to get the photos that sold the fairy tale, then that's what she was going to do.

And she couldn't shake the feeling that securing this contract might be more important than she'd initially anticipated. She hadn't made a decision one way or the other as to her music career, and she liked having the option available. But Cash appeared to be going out of his way to poison that well for her. First, he trash-talked her during his *Brunch Bunch* interview, and then she'd missed Da Real's party. She'd played it off, saying she'd forgotten about it and that was true. Only because she hadn't received an invitation. If she had she would've remembered. She'd even checked with Tasha. She'd been invited every year for the past five years. Why not this one?

"I need a moment," he said, for her ears only.

"Of course." She darted a look to her right, confirmed the media and photographers were still watching, and patted his chest, right over his heart.

Flash! Flash! Flash!

A warm sympathetic hum whispered across the room.

He closed his eyes, and she watched him wrestle with his emotions. She took one of his hands in both of hers then reached up and cupped his jaw, a silent one-woman show.

Flash! Flash! Flash!

Her stomach churned and she dropped her arm. *There! That should do it.*

His lashes lifted and his blue eyes were bright with gratitude as he brought their clasped hands to his lips.

Flash! Flash! Flash!

You are one dirty bitch! Hope it was worth it.

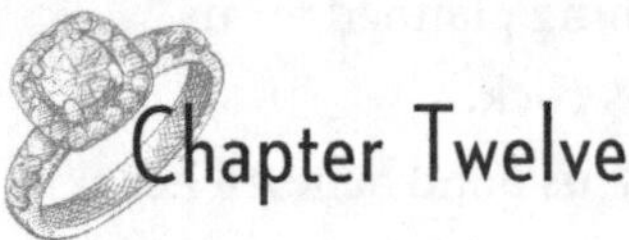

Chapter Twelve

A ROYAL FIRST: PRINCE JAMESON AND DUCHESS ATTEND HOUSE OF LLOYD EXHIBIT AT THE NATIONAL PORTRAIT GALLERY

CHELSEA GIBSON, NEWS CORRESPONDENT, *DAILY MIRROR*

While royal watchers have been waiting to catch a glimpse of Prince Jameson and his lady love, the venue where they made their official debut was unexpected and, according to some, a tad inappropriate.

It's unusual for a royal couple not yet affianced to attend a monarch-sponsored event. But then, everything about this couple has been unconventional. Which may be just what the royal family needs. Prince Jameson and Duchess's love and respect for one another was obvious to everyone in attendance. It's nice to see at least one royal couple that seems to be on the right track.

Duchess sparkled in a . . .

I promise the next time we're in the back of a car, it will be in the fun way," Dani said.

Jameson glanced at the empty front seat before peeking out the window and into the night. He didn't recognize where they were, but even if he did, he wouldn't have the best view. All he could see was the black-suited back of one of his protection officers.

"Why wait?" he asked. "I'm game if you are."

She flattened a hand on the seat between them and leaned close until her lips were barely an inch from his. "I'll take you up on that another time, but tonight, I have something planned for us."

Anticipation sent blood surging to his cock.

"Something better than this?" He slid his hand beneath her skirt and up her bare thigh, watching her lips form an O.

"You can be so naughty," she moaned, her lashes fluttering as her head fell back on the headrest and her deep burgundy curls splayed against the black leather.

He nudged aside the delicate fabric of her panties and ran his middle finger along the seam of her folds. He whispered, "Only with you, love."

"No, no, no," she said, laughingly pushing on his shoulders. "I won't be distracted."

"Pity," he said, removing his finger.

Never releasing her gaze, he stuck the digit in his mouth and tasted the evidence of her arousal.

So sweet.

Her nostrils flared and he smiled now that both of them were balanced on the edge of need. He pulled away and readjusted himself, so his hardness wasn't so evident when he stood.

The car door opened behind Jameson and Roy said, "All clear. If you'll follow me . . ."

He didn't want to. He wanted to close and lock the door and explore backseat car sex with Dani. But she'd planned this evening and he hated disappointing her. But he *would* hold her to her promise.

When he reached Dani's side of the car, he held out a hand to help her up and his breath caught in his throat. How did he get so fortunate?

Thick white strips of fabric crisscrossed her bust line and ended in a black skirt cut just above her knee. The design was simple, yet shockingly sexy, as it bared her upper chest and emphasized peeks of dark skin along the sides of her torso and belly. Red strappy heels completed the ensemble.

"You're gorgeous."

"Thank you, baby," she said, her expression soft. She lifted her arms as if to say *ta da*! "This is it."

Jameson looked around them. Now that he was out of the car and had a better view of their surroundings, he recognized that they were on a side street in the historic center of London next to a tall building with a wooden, stone, and metallic facade.

As if by magic, a nondescript door materialized, held open by a woman clad in black.

"What is this?" he asked.

"It's a surprise," Dani said, giggling with childlike excitement. She shared a look with the young woman before seizing his hand. "Come on."

They slipped inside and walked down a dark hallway that led through another door and to a majestic flight of stairs that seemed to be carved out of a giant tree. Peering up, the large skylight let in the night, lending everything a surreal note.

Where had she brought him?

He followed Dani down the winding white oak staircase, into a room with amber lighting, dark wood, and an ambience that seduced all his senses. He felt as if they had been transported to a lush, sophisticated enchanted forest.

"Welcome, Your Royal Highness and Duchess." A server dressed similarly to their guide gestured toward the sole tablescape in the room. "If you please . . ."

The horseshoe-shaped booth was large enough to seat a big party but was intimately set for two. Dani sat on the leather banquette and slid along until she faced out of the booth. Jameson undid the button of his suit jacket and moved to sit next to her.

"I can say with certainty that no one has ever gone through this much trouble just to take me out to dinner," he said.

Her wide, dark brown eyes shone. "I wanted to enjoy a night out with you, and I figured it would be a bad idea to make reservations at some trendy place in Shoreditch."

"You can make a lot of things happen, but you won't convince me you called up this morning and made a reservation for tonight."

"Not quite. I've been planning this for about a week and a half with Tasha's help."

"She deserves a raise."

"Already done."

"Right." He laughed. "Is there a menu?"

"Yes, but you don't need it. I have curated our dinner for this evening."

"Oh, have you?" He pinched his chin between his thumb and forefinger. "You think you know what I like?"

Her lined glossed lips curved upward. "I feel like I have an idea."

He took her hand and placed it over the thickening bulge in his pants. "I feel like you might be right."

Dani squeezed his cock then nodded across the room. Two servers emerged from a kitchen cleverly hidden behind the staircase and came over to the table.

"For your first course, we have a crusty baguette, topped with an avocado Parmesan mash, poached egg, and a white balsamic vinegar glaze. To drink, we have a racy and vibrant New Zealand Sauvignon Blanc."

"Thank you," Dani said, as their plates were placed in front of them.

"Avocado toast?" Jameson recalled bemoaning the idea that his new houseguest would eat the millennial, Californian clichéd dish when she'd first arrived at his estate, before he'd gotten to know her. When he'd visited her, he couldn't escape the fare and every restaurant's interpretation of it.

She smiled. "It took two weeks before you would even try it, but, admit it—you like it."

He couldn't give her the satisfaction. He shrugged. "It was acceptable."

"'Acceptable'? That's why you ate it every morning the last week of your trip?"

"That was for you. I didn't want you to go through all the trouble of making two separate dishes."

"Stop it!" she said, laughing.

He took a bite, and though the dish was more elevated than what they'd eaten, the taste invoked the memory of brunch in California, together on the patio overlooking the ocean. He could almost feel the breeze and smell the salt-tinged air. His blood simmered as he remembered what happened when she'd climbed onto his lap afterward.

"That was fantastic," he said, putting down his utensils and taking a sip of the wine.

"I'm glad you enjoyed it." She covered his hand where it sat on the table. "I know you're nervous about how your life has shifted in the past couple of weeks. It's not what you saw for yourself. But, like avocado toast, you might be surprised by what happens. And no matter the outcome, I'm going to be here with you every step of the way."

Appreciation expanded his chest until it felt close to bursting open. He didn't know it was possible to love someone as much as he loved her.

"Do you remember this?" Dani asked, leaning back as the server slid two covered plates in front of them.

When the cloche was removed, he rubbed his hands together. "I never imagined something this gross-looking could be so delicious."

Dani sucked her teeth. "Says a British person. Have you seen *your* food?"

The server's mouth quirked but she didn't react to either of their statements. "The chef has prepared a buttermilk drop biscuit with a white wine and sausage gravy infusion. And he's paired it with a Blood Orange Bourbon Sour. Enjoy."

It smelled delicious but the small fluffy discs and creamy smear—

"This doesn't look quite like what we had."

"This is the fancy version with petite portion sizes. A plate piled with a mound of biscuits and topped with a vat of sausage gravy like we'd get at home? I wouldn't do that to you. Or to me. I'm trying to look cute for you tonight and there's nothing sexy about bloating and gas."

He'd trust her judgment as to the portion size, but he disagreed with her conclusion. She'd introduced the southern cuisine to him so he would always find the dish sexy. Because when he ate it, he would think of her.

"What if I get a craving when you're not here? I can't call up and order biscuits and gravy. I'd get cookies and meat stew."

"I'll make sure to give my Nana's recipe to Margery."

"Good idea."

"Of course it is," she preened. "That's why you keep me around. My job is to alleviate your stress."

"Which you do, every time I see your beautiful face."

"You are too sweet."

Dani broke the silence that had descended as they savored the fare. “I had a good time at the exhibit the other night.”

“Surprisingly, so did I.”

Her expression brightened. “That’s great. I thought you would.”

“It doesn’t mean I wasn’t blindsided by the suggestion and your desire to attend. Especially after our agreement.”

“I know.” She pushed a bite of biscuit around on her plate. “It wasn’t fair of me to do it that way. And I’m sorry.”

“My life is different from what it was when we had that discussion—”

“Same,” she muttered.

“—and I’ve made a choice to take on more duties. But how I feel about it hasn’t changed. I want it to have as little impact on our life as possible.”

“I understand. I just . . . I want to spend time with you. It may not be appropriate for everything on your schedule, but for the events where it is, I’d like to go with you.”

He realized that her happiness had become more important to him than his own.

How had that happened? When had that happened?

They’d been under a microscope at the exhibit but things had gone well. Even with the media present, no one had gotten out of line. And he couldn’t deny he’d enjoyed it more because she’d attended with him.

But he also refused to stand by and watch the media destroy her the way it did so many others in its ravenous glare.

There had to be a middle ground.

“How about I look at my upcoming schedule and select a few functions?”

“I’d love that. Thank you.” She bit her lip. “You know I love you, right?”

"If you love me, why are you trying to put me out of business?" He nodded at her mouth. "My job, remember?"

"And I do love your work." She grinned into their kiss.

When he caught the scent of the next course, moisture flooded his mouth. "This one . . ."

"We'd just driven past a Taco Bell—"

"And I'd asked you what that was—"

"I flipped out! Who hasn't heard of Taco Bell?" Dani shrieked. "You wanted to stop in and I put my foot down. No offense to the Bell, but I didn't want that to be your first real taco. So, I called Tasha and sent her to my favorite taco food truck—"

"If you'd told me in advance that you were turning down a restaurant for food from a vehicle—"

"But when you tried it, you had to admit it was the bomb, right?"

He knew what this one meant. "Yes, it was delicious."

Dani spread her hands. "And so . . ."

The server took over. "The chef has prepared sweet and spicy carnitas tacos topped with pickled cabbage, pineapple mango salsa, and jalapeño avocado crema. On the side, a shot of premium tequila."

"You want to get me hammered?" he asked.

"Of course not. That's just a nice bonus." She winked and lifted her shot glass. "One drink is good. Two at the most. Three, I'm under the table. Four, you're under the host!"

The liquid burned going down but settled warm in his belly. He picked up his first taco and took a bite.

Life couldn't get any better.

"Ready for dessert?" Dani asked a little while later, after the dishes from their third course had been cleared.

"Let me guess: Apple pie? Peach cobbler? Cheesecake?"

If it followed the theme of the rest of the dishes, it would definitely be American.

She winked.

"And for our final course . . ."

The server removed the silver lid and Jameson stared at the dome of steamed pudding sprinkled with dried currants and a serving dish of rich, creamy vanilla custard.

"Spotted dick," he said, emotion clogging his throat at the sight of his favorite dessert. "How did you know?"

"I asked your mother. Although let me tell you, it took me a good five minutes to stop cackling when she mentioned it. I thought she was fucking with me."

He was surprised she'd consulted with his mother although he shouldn't have been. His mom adored Dani and the feeling was mutual. They hadn't had a chance to visit since Dani had arrived, but he knew they'd had several FaceTime chats.

Being with Dani was intoxicating. He looked forward to even the most mundane things when he knew he'd be with her. He'd never thought he'd find someone who stimulated him mentally and physically, and who, more importantly, was as unimpressed with his royal status as he was.

The server plated two slices with accompanying sauce.

Dani inhaled a huge breath. "I'm not eager to put my mouth on any dick that's spotted, but if you love it, I'm willing to give it a try."

She dipped her spoon into the wedge of pudding drizzled with sauce, then took a tentative bite. She perked up immediately.

"This is good! It's not what I was expecting. At all. It reminds me of bread pudding."

Tingles of happiness lightened his limbs. He didn't question the pleasure he derived from her enjoying something that had been a part of his life since he was a kid. He just dug into his own serving and reveled in the air of quiet contentment as they enjoyed the delicious dessert.

When he'd taken his last bite, he put his spoon down and sighed. "I can't express enough how much I've enjoyed this. A night out in London with you and we weren't mobbed by press? Thank you." He lifted her hand and brushed his lips against her skin.

"You're welcome. And while I totally did this for you, I also had an ulterior motive. I wanted to see if we could get away with it and figure out how much our life would be impacted by the press. And I'm happy to report we *can* do it. It just takes a little planning and trustworthy people."

She was fearless. She really believed she could control everything in her orbit. He found her confidence incredibly attractive.

And her certainty made him want to believe she was right. That maybe he was overreacting to something that could be managed. Especially with Dani by his side.

He wiped his mouth with his napkin. "Are you ready to go?"

"We're not done."

She gestured and a server came over with another covered dish.

"Love, I'm stuffed. I don't think I could eat—"

Dani lifted the cloche and he stared at the package wrapped in white tissue paper. He picked it up and looked at her inquisitively.

She rolled her eyes. "I wouldn't have taken the time to wrap the gift if I was just going to tell you what it is."

"This is a first edition of Aristotle's Discourses of Government!" Wonder softened his tone as he held the leather-bound folio in his hands.

"I know."

"It's considered the world's most important and influential political text derived from philosophical truths."

"That's what they told me when I bought it."

"But how? First editions are exceptionally rare. I've never been able to find one."

"Can I tell you a secret?"

"Always," he said, although he didn't take his attention from the book.

"You and I are a pretty famous couple, and people tend to want to help us. I put some feelers out and here we are."

Here we are . . .

She watched him, her expression unsure. "Do you like it? I checked and you don't already own it."

Without answering he carefully put it down and claimed her mouth in a kiss that he relished more than anything they'd sampled that evening.

"I love you."

Her eyes were dark liquid pools. "I love you, too."

"The fact that you did all of this for me means everything."

"How about we head home, and you can show me how much."

Home.

Thanking their servers and the chef, they headed up the stairs. Jameson felt a little wistful leaving their enchanted forest and returning to the real world. Roy held the door open for them and they exited the building, holding hands.

"I don't know if I can wait until—"

"Welcome back, Duchess. Have you seen the queen?"

"Prince Jameson! Duchess! Are you getting married?"

"Duchess, did you introduce Samantha Banks to the prince?"

The throng wasn't only surprising, it was large. The click of cameras seemed loud after the intimate calm of the restaurant. The lights were blinding.

"What the fuck?" Jameson growled.

"Come here often, Duchess?" a photographer asked, getting too close to Dani.

Jameson saw red. "Back off!"

The photographer continued taking pictures of Jameson.

"Does that make you angry, Prince Jameson?" He moved closer to Dani. "What are you going to do about it?"

Rage erupted and Jameson started for the man, when he felt a steel grip on his forearm.

"Let's go," Roy said, and hurried him toward the car.

He dug in his heels. "Not me! Get Dani!"

"Sir, you're my responsibility. Nicolas has got Ms. Nelson."

Jameson turned his head and saw the other man sheltering Dani from the press as they hurried to the car.

Dammit, he should be the one doing that!

He felt powerless and knew he wouldn't be settled until they were safe. He picked up his pace and stopped fighting Roy, something the officer probably appreciated, but Jameson had only done it to accelerate them getting out of the situation.

He climbed in the car and the moment after he was seated, Dani was next to him, waving to the press.

"Thanks, guys," she said.

"Were you waving at them?" he asked incredulously.

"Yes. If you give them a little bit, they tend to let you be faster. It's only when you give them attitude that they get crazed and act like jackoffs!"

"Dani! How many times do I have to tell you they're not like the press in the States and you can't treat them that way?"

Jameson pulled her into his arms and inhaled her scent, using it to assure himself that she was unharmed.

The drive back to Kensington Palace took twenty minutes.

When the Land Rover drew up in front of his apartment, Jameson ordered, "Leave us."

He would apologize for his rudeness later. But his grip on his composure was slipping and he needed to be alone with Dani.

Now.

He didn't fully understand where this frenzied imperative of keeping her safe came from, but he gave in to it, his being not allowing him to do anything else.

"Are you all right?" he asked, after everyone else had exited the vehicle.

"I'm fine! You're the one still shak—"

He pulled her onto his lap, so that she straddled him, and crushed his lips on hers, his tongue immediately sweeping inside to tangle, nibble, and taste. And still it wasn't enough to soothe or convince him that she had emerged unscathed. His heart was beating so loud it drowned out any other sounds.

And reason.

"I need you," he panted, attempting to drag breath into his tight chest.

"You can have me," she responded and his spirit soared.

Their hands fumbled over each other, undoing his belt, trouser button, and zipper.

"Condom?" she rasped.

"Yes." He'd started keeping one on him at all times, having learned the hard way he couldn't always anticipate when the mood struck.

Dani leaned forward and her breasts pressed against his chest.

The pleasure that soared through him was staggering. She wiggled her hips, raising the tight skirt until it was bunched around her waist.

"Lean back. Let me see it."

With one arm draped around the headrest of the driver's side front seat, she used the other to spread the lips of her pussy, revealing it for his heated possessive stare. The beautiful contrast of the pretty pink against the dark satin of her skin made his cock swell and bob against her thigh.

He slipped his thumb into his mouth, getting it nice and wet before transferring the moisture to her clit and gently rubbing the tender button.

"I love this pussy so much."

She moaned, her head falling loosely, her lips parted in a silent *oh.* He reached up and wrapped the long strands of her hair around his fist before pulling her to him and pressing hard, firm lips to hers.

"Is it mine?"

She nodded.

He gripped her hips and lowered her down as he pushed up, his aching cock nestling in her slick, tight heat. The muscles in his ass worked overtime, allowing his hips to drive upward, increasing the friction between the outer rim of her entrance and his corded length.

It was fast, hot, and carnal.

"Feels so fucking good," she said, the words staccato as his strokes kept up a feverish pace.

"I'll never get enough of this," he pushed out through clenched teeth. "Will always want more."

He shoved aside the thick strap of material crisscrossing her bodice and latched on to her nipple.

"Fuck me, baby. Fuck me," she screamed.

He did, the sounds of her arousal and the writhing of her body soliciting his release. But he willed it back, wanting her to come first.

It wasn't long before her pussy clenched his cock and her orgasm ripped through her. Three more hard strokes and he followed, pleasure tingling at the base of his spine as his balls contracted and a surge of paralyzing energy curled his toes and exploded from his body.

Their combined exertions caused the windows to fog. Anyone watching from the outside would have had a pretty good idea what had just happened, not needing Dani's lazily drawn *Jay & Dani, 2-gether, 4-ever* finger writing across the glass.

He exhaled shakily as his heartbeat slowed and his breathing returned to normal. Pressing a kiss to her damp forehead, his mind clicked back on.

"We must ascertain how they found us. Was it someone at the restaurant?" he asked.

Dani stretched and softly kissed him. "Try not to worry about it. They didn't ruin our night."

"But if there's a leak, I need to plug it. We didn't attend a gala or take a stroll down the Mall in front of the palace. You tried to keep this moment for us only to have someone sell out our privacy."

Dani's chin dipped down and she averted her gaze.

He hated that they'd sullied her surprise for him, but the experience only strengthened his resolve to seek a life away from his family. Was it a crime to want to enjoy a simple meal out with the woman he loved without it turning into a fucking circus?

Chapter Thirteen

PRINCE JAMESON AND DUCHESS ARE #ROYALCOUPLEGOALS!
Get Details of Duchess's Date-Night Look!
POPSUGAR

Dani crossed her legs, barely noticing her left foot, clad in nude Rebecca Allen heels, bouncing.

Wait, that's not how they did it.

She shifted, bringing her foot down and pressing her knees together, sliding her legs to the side and then crossing her ankles.

Yes, that's right.

Only—

Who could sit like this for any length of time? It was hella uncomfortable.

She bit her lip.

"Don't be nervous," Jameson said, stroking her thigh. The warmth of his touch singed her skin through the fabric of her yellow skirt.

"What? Nervous? Who? Me? No," she said, waving off his statement.

The few times she'd visited Buckingham Palace previously had been for large, ceremonial events. And the last time she was here, she'd experienced one of the worst moments of her life. What was she in for this time?

She glanced around the drawing room, decorated in shades of blue. Jameson assured her this was a private family room, but it didn't look like any family room she'd ever been in.

"You said she could be calling us in because of what happened with the photographers outside the restaurant last night."

"It's possible."

"Then how can you be so calm? What if she's angry and she takes it out on your mother? And it's all my fault because being there was on me?"

"It'll be fine," he said, his hand rubbing comforting circles on her back.

She leaned into his touch, unable to resist. "Says you. The last time I saw the queen, she wasn't exactly warm."

Warm? Really? You should've just called it out: she was a real bitch!

"I'm not saying she's going to be warm *this* time," he said. "But she did request your presence."

Dani narrowed her eyes at him. "I was here by her invitation last time."

"I promise, if she starts insulting you, we'll leave."

He would. Of that Dani had no doubt.

"You can have your choice of anyone or anything in the world . . . But not Jameson. Not this family. I won't allow it."

The queen's words to Dani at the tribute ball still stung. And as much as she'd like to tell the older woman, "Yes, Jameson. All up in his family's house. And I could give two shits about what you will and won't allow," she wouldn't.

Dani was petty but she wasn't stupid.

She and the queen didn't need to be biffles, but it would help if they were cordial.

For Jameson's sake.

And yours.

"I do have experience in rushing off dramatically," she said, able to semi-joke about it since things had worked out in her favor.

"And I have experience in getting you off dramatically," he said.

Sir!

Her pulse quickened and moisture pooled at her core. Their eyes met and in his she could see all the things he'd done—and still wanted to do—to her, but she did what was best for both of them and looked away. If she did what she *wanted* to, they'd scandalize the queen.

Dani cleared her throat. "So I remember some of the protocols from the crash course we were given for the tribute festivities, but this is less formal and not public. Do the same rules apply?"

"In a manner of speaking, yes. You still need to curtsy and let her lead the conversation."

Dani fought down her contrariness that practically screamed, *Curtsy to her? Bitches supposed to bow down to me!* "And what do I call her?"

"Your Majesty," he said, his furrowed brow indicating his confusion that she thought there would be any other option.

"You mean all those times when she called you here and it was just the two of you, you called her Your Majesty?"

"Well, 'ma'am' after the initial address." He shrugged. "I told you we don't have the closest of relationships."

"I know, but—"

The woman was his grandmother. Dani had grown up around a lot of relatives she didn't consider close, but she'd still called them by their designation: Aunt, Uncle, or Cousin. Sure, there were roles to play in public and rules to be followed. But in private, the queen really required her grandson to refer to her the way everyone else did?

Jameson looked at his watch and frowned. "Why am I always the one on time when I have to travel the longest to get here? She lives in the building."

At his words the door opened, and a footman announced, "Her Majesty the Queen."

Dani's belly roiled. In the immortal words of Slick Rick, *Here we go.*

Jameson shot to his feet and Dani followed suit. The queen strode in, her bearing as regal as ever, even though she was dressed less formally in a startling bright white blouse and lilac skirt that fell to mid-calf.

"Jameson, thank you for coming."

He bowed. "Of course, Your Majesty."

Her blue eyes, the same color as Jay's but devoid of his warmth, swung to Dani. "Duchess."

One word, and all the feelings this woman invoked in Dani at their last meeting came flying back.

"Not Jameson. Not this family. I won't allow it."

Prickles of embarrassment, shame, and anger tingled across her skin and warred inside her, forming a boulder that hardened in her stomach. She fought not to give in to it. Not to blame herself, make herself smaller, or, heaven forbid, run away. Despite everything the queen had threatened, Jameson had chosen Dani.

Choke on it, she wanted to fling at the other woman.

But such impetuousness would also be a mistake. This was more than being face-to-face with the sovereign of a nation who had no power over her. She was meeting the family of the man she loved.

And that, plus the image of Nana pinching her arm for showing her ass, made Dani swallow back her words.

Dani curtsied. "Your Majesty."

Marina's eyes flickered with an emotion Dani couldn't identify before it was concealed. "Thank you for coming. I know it couldn't have been easy given our last interaction."

Though her tone was brisk, the words were more considerate than Dani had expected.

"It wasn't," she conceded. "But Jameson said you wanted to see us both."

"I do," Marina said, settling on a blue tufted club chair with rolled arms and a gold frame.

Jameson clasped Dani's hand and they sat on the love seat they'd occupied before the queen's arrival.

United.

Dani appreciated the gesture.

"I understand the two of you have been getting out some during this visit," the queen said, her hands folded in her lap.

Dani glanced at Jameson, noted the tick in his jaw and decided to take this one.

"In the past, my visits to London have been for work only, so I've never had the opportunity to just enjoy the city. I'm looking forward to doing more."

"Doing more? Hmmmm." She angled her head and nodded. "The press seems to have taken an interest in your activities."

"As you are aware, ma'am, controlling the media can be difficult," Jameson said, his gaze steady. "We did our best to keep our plans secret, but they found out."

Guilt bloomed in Dani's cheeks. He'd worded it to suggest *he* had planned their restaurant outing and that the paparazzi being there had been a miscalculation. But Dani knew exactly who was at fault for the photographer's presence. She hadn't seen the harm in them getting a few pictures *after* dinner. She certainly hadn't anticipated Jameson's response!

Crap! This was too much. She didn't want him to lie to his grandmother.

"I marvel at how they managed to discover your whereabouts," Marina said, sarcasm coating her words. "Especially when the two of you showed up to a royal-sponsored event."

They'd gotten it wrong? This *wasn't* about the incident last night?

Jameson shared a look with Dani before responding. "Dani attended the exhibit opening as my date."

"I gathered as much." Marina sniffed. "Although I recall a conversation where you insisted on attending these functions alone."

Because he'd wanted to protect her. Dani placed a hand on his thigh and squeezed. "Don't blame Jameson. I was the one who insisted on going with him."

Marina's gaze followed Dani's action and it took many long moments before she responded. "It appears you're being rewarded for your boldness. The coverage has been glowing."

She pressed a button and a second later, a footman entered carrying a stack of print newspapers on a silver tray. He sat the platter on the side table and left as quickly as he'd arrived.

Dani was used to having people work for her, handling the tasks she could no longer do because of her schedule and her notoriety, but that kind of service was unreal. She had one of the best and most loyal teams around and yet she couldn't imagine them jumping to attention without a look of acknowledgment or words of appreciation.

The queen pulled the first one off the stack and read the headline. "*Has the prince found his Duchess Charming? Taming of the Wessex*," she read. Marina shook her head. "They always think they're being clever. Ahhh, and this one: *Can this couple save the monarchy?*" She spun the paper and Dani saw a picture of her and Jameson at the museum's opening: Dani looking up at the large painting of Prince Richard while Jameson stares at her, his affection visible on his face.

It appeared the queen planned to put on a show. If Dani had known, she would've brought popcorn.

She was starting to see what Jameson had meant about his relationship with his grandmother. It didn't feel like a family visit. They truly had been summoned by *The Queen* with all the pomp and circumstance it entailed.

"But they're better than these," Marina continued, brandishing more papers like they were case-cracking courtroom exhibits. "'Julian caught cheating with American popstar!' Then there's 'It's over: Wales a' Wailing as Fiona walks out on Julian!' And 'Can the love child heir take the throne?'"

Dani dipped her chin, willing her lips to remain neutral.

Wales a' Wailing. Good one.

The queen, however, wasn't in the mood to appreciate the clever alliteration.

"Centuries of service and our family has been reduced to descriptions of lurid novels!" She tossed the periodicals back on the tray. "This thing with the American pop star is unseemly. She refuses to go away."

"Don't I know it," Dani said, before she could stop herself.

The queen looked at her sharply. "This is all because of you. You brought her here."

"Don't put that on Dani," Jameson said.

Damn straight.

"Samantha Banks is a lot of things, but your son is the one who sought her out, slept with her, and possibly got her pregnant. None of that. Had anything to do. With me." Dani spoke clearly and concisely to make sure she was heard and understood.

The muscle in Marina's jaw ticked for several seconds before she exhaled. "You're right. My apologies. This entire ordeal has me stressed."

In that moment, she looked more like an old woman and less like a monarch and the transformation softened Dani. She knew what it was like to have tons of people depend on her and look up to her. To know that every decision she made would affect the livelihood of so many. It was her responsibility, but it was also a burden. And it was the reason Dani found it difficult to handle things when her life was negatively influenced by the selfish actions of others.

The queen had to feel that tenfold.

"What I'm about to tell you is information that would never be given to anyone outside of this family. But Jameson has made it clear how important you are to him, and I'm sure he's shared much of this with you already, so he's left me no other choice." Her gaze hardened. "I expect it to remain between the three of us. And Catherine."

Dani nodded, recognizing the seriousness of the queen's tone and understanding the significance of the disclosure.

"John's tribute had the desired effect. People remembered the good of the monarchy, remembered we are the visible embodiment of the British nation. All was going according to plan. We thought the announcement of Fiona's pregnancy would be the start of another round of good press. But Julian ruined it. I guess it was too much to ask for him to be faithful to his wife!"

"When will this family learn that forcing people to marry never ends well?" Jameson asked.

"When will *the men* of this family learn that duty supersedes all?" Marina shot back. "If you want the privileges and benefits that come with being a royal, you have to accept the responsibilities and disadvantages."

"Oh, I have," Jameson murmured.

"Have you? Is Catherine the only one who comprehends how tenuous our current position is? It's bad enough that here at home we're faced with a younger generation that questions our very relevance, but abroad, a number of the Commonwealth nations have begun questioning the necessity of my leadership. They want to leave the organization and lead themselves. And this new scandal, featuring the heir to the throne, isn't helping on either front.

"But my plan was working. The nostalgia of John's tribute made us beloved again. And the public, especially young people, took a specific liking to your coupling. When Fiona told us she was pregnant"—she closed her eyes, sighed, then continued—"I thought we'd be able to ride that sentimental wave for at least two years, through the pregnancy and up until the baby turned one. Past that point, they're only charming in pictures. Toddlers refuse to follow protocol and it's hard to control them in public."

Wow! Come on through, cynicism.

"Julian's affair with this American singer and the possibility of her being pregnant has undone everything. People are questioning Julian's leadership and the very notion of the line of succession. It's been quite a distraction. That's why I thought having Jameson take over some of Julian's duties would help. And it has." The queen narrowed her eyes in Jameson's direction. "The press coverage of the both of you is the one thing that's been consistently positive. Even the incident outside the restaurant was spun as a romantic act of protection."

So she *had* heard about that.

"Despite my earlier misgivings, your relationship is like a breath of fresh air to the public. It gives everyone something more positive to focus on."

It wasn't a ringing endorsement, but . . . "That's good . . . I guess."

"It is. Which is why—"

Next to Dani, Jameson stilled.

"—I hope you would consider doing more."

Jameson stood. "Absolutely not!"

"Don't forget yourself, Jameson," the queen said firmly, but quietly.

There was subtextual shit going on here. Dani swallowed hard. "I don't understand. What are you asking?"

"Something unprecedented," Marina conceded, never taking her eyes off Jameson. "But desperate times call for desperate measures."

Jameson circled the love seat and braced his hands on its frame. "No. Don't bring her into this."

Instinctively, Dani bristled at Jameson making a decision for her.

"I didn't want to," Marina said. "But you did."

The tension between Jameson and his grandmother was palpable as they engaged in a death stare showdown. It was feeling eerily similar to the last conversation Dani had with the queen, when everyone in the room had known what was going on except Dani. And she didn't like it.

Not one damn bit.

"Someone better tell me what's going on right now, or I swear—"

"She wants us to officially do events for the palace!" Jameson raged. "Together, as a couple!"

Cue the confused little blond girl gif!

Dani didn't know what she'd expected, but that had been downright anticlimactic.

"What's so wrong with that?"

Unbidden, her problem with Genesis and Parcellum came to mind. This played right into the compromise Dani's team was proposing. Doing these events with Jameson would be an official acknowledgment of their relationship by the palace. That could only elevate her status, which would increase her brand awareness, which is all Parcellum really cared about.

And she wouldn't have to mention any of it to Jay.

The relief she felt was almost orgasmic.

She wouldn't have to keep coming up with reasons to go to places where they would be photographed, and, most importantly, she would never have to divulge her reasons for going against their pact to not get involved in each other's business. Because by agreeing to participate in what the queen was asking, Dani would be helping Jameson, too.

They could both get what they wanted. A win-win situation all around.

"Maybe it won't be that bad," she told him.

He stared at her, his gaze imploring her to listen. "You don't understand. If we do this, we're inviting everyone into our relationship. The palace, the media, the world. Right now, we still have a modicum of privacy. Even with Nyla's red carpet, and the restaurant, and the exhibit . . . all of that was on our terms. But once we let them in, once they realize you're not a charming American outsider but an actual cog in the royal wheel—" He shook his head. "No. I can't let you do this."

Marina's expression hardened and Dani knew it would be a mistake to ever underestimate the queen.

"I'll allow you to step away from royal life. For good."

"What?" they asked, simultaneously.

"Jameson, you're a member of this family and that will never change. But this is important, and I will do whatever it takes to save the Company. I know being more involved these past few months has not made you happy. So, if you and Duchess agree to this, I promise you'll never have to work as a senior royal ever again. I'll permanently remove you as a Counsellor of State and you can recede back into the shadows, if you so choose."

Dani shifted to look at Jameson. "This is what you've wanted, Jay. More than anything."

"I know." He appeared as dazed as he sounded. "But not more than anything. I can't ask you to do this, love."

"You're not. She is." Dani directed her next question to the queen. "And you'll keep your promise and allow Calanthe to retain her position in the royal family?"

The queen's snow-white brows lifted. "You know about that?"

"As you said, Jay tells me everything."

"I will. And to be clear," Marina said to Jameson, "removing you as a Counsellor of State is only about official duties. I'll still expect to see you at family functions."

Uncertainty hung tightly on Jameson's features. "I knew what I was doing when I agreed to this, Dani. I know what I'm getting myself into. You don't. Trust me, love, this isn't a good idea."

Was he right? Jameson was more familiar with this world than she was. Shouldn't she trust that he might have a better understanding of how agreeing to this could impact their relationship?

But it wasn't just their relationship. It was about Mela-Skin and the opportunity to finally be in control of her life. And in the end, it would benefit them both. Dani couldn't let anything stop her from doing what was necessary to ensure this deal went through.

Not even Jameson.

"This doesn't need to turn into a melodrama. Are you in?" Marina asked. "Do we have a deal?"

Jameson stared at Dani and whatever he saw on her face caused him to dip his head and shake it slowly. Glancing up, he pursed his lips and nodded.

Dani faced the queen. "We have a deal."

Chapter Fourteen

THE PRINCE AND THE POP TART
• A brewing crisis as Julian is pulled from his royal duties
• Questions about the future line of succession
DAILY MAIL

Dani drifted into their suite and sat on the edge of the bed. "They're fast."

In the adjoining dressing room, Jameson approved the clothing choices his valet recommended and nodded his thanks. He went to join her. "Who?"

"The queen's staff." She wrinkled her nose. "Or is it her household? I remember Margery explaining that to me last time. That households don't refer to the house where you live but the staff that assist you in your public duties."

"Right."

"Thankfully, I have Louisa as my one-woman household. She's got my schedule and it appears our first event is a reception at Buckingham Palace honoring the winners of an essay contest." She grinned. "That seems right up your alley."

It was. He always enjoyed meeting with students or attending events that touched upon education. They had been some of his grandfather's favorites, too.

He'd be prepared, as he always was. But Dani mentioning their first joint event was the in he needed to discuss an issue that continued to plague him.

"I want to talk about our meeting with the queen yesterday," he said, sitting in the leather accent chair that faced the bed next to the fireplace.

She tucked her legs beneath her. "What about it?"

Was she serious?

"We agreed to keep our individual responsibilities separate from our relationship because we didn't want it affected by outside forces. You brought it up first. But then you caved and agreed to her request. You heard everything I said and disregarded it, like it didn't matter."

The sting of the slight still bothered him.

"That's not what I was doing. You heard her. If we do this, you won't have to be a working royal anymore. You can go back to teaching. Not at Birmingham, but somewhere else. And your mom's place in the family will be safe. How could I not agree?"

"Because it's not worth the risk to our relationship."

"Our relationship is fine."

"It is *now*. But what happens when people begin commenting on how we perform at an event, criticizing you and praising me or vice versa? When they start questioning why you're being treated in an unprecedented manner? When some 'enterprising' journalist decides to tie you to Samantha Banks again and questions your role in the Company's latest scandal?"

It was clear she hadn't considered that. She averted her gaze and dropped her hands to her lap, absentmindedly tangling her fingers.

Good.

She needed to consider what he was saying. This wasn't a sound idea.

"What about Mela-Skin? Can you be gone from the company for so long? Just as you're about to sign the contract with Genesis?"

She looked up and he was surprised to see the determination in her gaze. She scrambled off the bed.

"This is too important, Jay. Mela-Skin is in good hands. And if anything urgent comes up, I'm a video conference call away," she countered. "As for our relationship, I love you and I want to be with you. As long as we keep that in mind and put our relationship first, we can spend the next few months helping your family. Especially because we'll get what we want out of it. And then we'll have the rest of our lives together."

She smiled beatifically and fluttered her lashes.

Damn. He'd thought mentioning her company would be the pièce de résistance of his argument. Instead, it seemed to have had the opposite effect.

"I hope we don't regret this," he said, surrendering.

"We won't," she insisted, leaning down for a kiss.

He palmed the nape of her neck and captured her lips, deepening the embrace as if doing so could wrap them in a spell of protection against incoming royal mischief.

He wanted what she said to be true.

He was terrified it wouldn't be.

"IF YOU'LL PLEASE wait here, I'll check that they're ready," the palace aide said, ushering them into a small ante room.

Jameson immediately began to pace, unable to remain still. There were a million things he'd rather be doing than waiting at Buckingham Palace for their first official joint Company event to begin. What he had yet to figure out was how they'd ended up in this situation. Especially when he'd never intended for Dani to be involved with his family, let alone participate in royal engagements.

Dani thought they could handle it. Jameson wasn't as sure.

"So we're meeting a group of high school students today?" Dani asked, her eyes sparkling.

Clearly she was excited. But then, she had no idea what she was getting herself into.

"Secondary school, mainly students finishing Key Stage four."

Dani stared at him. "I know you're speaking English because I understand the words coming out of your mouth, but I have no clue what any of that meant. Are we meeting middle school or high school students?"

He laughed. "In the U.K., education is broken down into parts and stages. The secondary stage equates to what you call middle and high school, and stage four are the upper levels. You did read the dossier?"

"Yes, but they obviously thought I knew the systems were so different. I'll mention it to Louisa for the next one."

She walked over to check her reflection in the large gilt-framed mirror that hung on the gray tapestry-covered wall, but she needn't have worried. Black wide-legged, high-waisted slacks hugged her curves and the sheer white gold-edged ruffle blouse tucked into them emphasized her waist. Her hair was pulled into a ponytail, the long ends braided and wrapped into a high knot. Diamond and gold hoop earrings completed the look. She was ravishing, sexy, and polished. He knew she put a lot of thought into her outfit, wanting to be respectful, but still quintessentially Duchess.

Mission accomplished.

However, as excited as she was, he could sense an anxious energy reverberating between them. "Are you nervous?"

"Why would I be nervous?" She winked. "This is what I do."

Good point. Was *he* the source of this jitteriness?

"Hey," Dani said gently, her brows drawn together. "How are *you* feeling?"

He adjusted his jacket. "I thought I was fine. But it's possible I'm more bothered than I thought."

"You were the face of the family during the tribute, and you've done several of these engagements since you've been back. Are they dredging up any memories?"

He considered her question, then nodded. "My parents used to do these. I rarely participated, but I'd be here in the palace, reading in one of the private drawing rooms. It was never fun. There was so much tension. Even as a child I could tell they didn't want to be there or with each other."

"Well, that's *not* our situation, okay? I'm happy to be here with you."

Warmth filled his chest, and he leaned his forehead against hers in a moment of gratitude and affection before kissing her cheek.

Suddenly, she clutched his arm. "We should come up with a distress signal!"

"What's that?"

"A word or action that'll let the other person know you're in trouble and need to be rescued. Sort of like our own personal bat signal."

"Did you know that during the tribute's opening reception, even as I hated being there, I remember looking at you and thinking I could handle these events if you were by my side."

Her expression softened. "You did?"

"Yes. And after this suggestion, I know I was right." He took both of her hands in his. "What should we use? And should we each have different signals?"

"That might be too much to remember. If we have the same one, we should be fine. But instead of a word, what if we come up with a gesture? Finding a safe word you can drop naturally into a conversation but that's odd enough to be noticed is difficult. And what if I'm across the room and I can't hear you?"

"A safe word?" He arched a brow. "For a reception or a secret BDSM room?"

One corner of her mouth curved upward. "We could be talking both. You never know."

He hauled her closer and lowered his voice. "I know you're lucky we're here right now, or there are some things I could do to you where a safe word might come in handy."

"Then I'm not sure I'd call myself 'lucky.'"

She stared up at him, her pupils dilated, her lips parting slightly. Moisture flooded his mouth and his pulse pounded in his ears. In that moment he ached to pull her into his arms and kiss her until she was out of breath and begging to be fucked.

And then he'd happily oblige her.

Someone cleared their throat. Without moving apart, they turned in unison to see the aide standing at the door, a leather-bound folio clutched to her chest.

"They're ready for you," she said, a blush staining her cheeks and her neck.

Dani squeezed his hand. "You'll be great."

"Are you sure you want to say a few words?"

Under normal circumstances it would be seen as highly inappropriate, and Jameson wouldn't have offered because he would prefer to lessen her time in the spotlight. But it had been "suggested" that she prepare brief remarks.

"Are you kidding? They'll be sorry you ever gave me the microphone."

"Said none of your fans, ever."

"And pull on your earlobe," she whispered as they left the room.

"Pardon?"

"Our signal," she shared conspiratorially, like they were two spies. "We'll pull on our earlobe. It's an innocuous enough gesture and we can do it several times if the other person doesn't notice, without it looking suspicious."

"You're a beautiful genius."

"And don't you ever forget it."

Together, they followed the aide down the hall. Footmen opened the doors and they were shown into one of the many rooms used to host receptions for the public. It was beautifully appointed in tones of cream and gold, with the chairs covered in teal silk and paintings and sculptures placed strategically around the space.

A group of students, teachers, and parents waited for them, turning when Jameson and Dani entered. Their faces brightened in varying levels of excitement, enchantment, and awe. The sudden sound of cameras clicking and the accompanying flashes captured the moment for posterity.

And publicity.

There were a few who appeared unsettled, biting their nails or fidgeting with their clothes. The irony didn't escape Jameson, and they'd probably be shocked to discover he'd been acting similarly just a few moments ago. He squeezed Dani's hand then walked to the lectern placed in the corner of the room.

"On behalf of my grandmother, Her Majesty the Queen, and the rest of the royal family, I want to welcome you all to Buckingham Palace. It is a very special pleasure to be here with you this afternoon, and I'm rather flattered to find you agree since none of you ran from the building immediately upon learning that I would be your new host."

The children cackled and the adults laughed, though there were some nods and a few knowing glances from those aware that Julian had been scheduled to be present.

He continued. "I don't take your generosity lightly. And because I wanted to reciprocate, I invited an actual celebrity to join us."

He smiled at Dani and the attention, en masse, swung her way. She smiled and waved, dipping her head at the smattering of applause.

"But the main reason I was asked to step in and represent Her Majesty today is because my fondness for education is well known. I prefer to think of myself as a scholar. Others have called me a nerd."

More laughter. That was a good sign. His shoulders lowered and he relaxed a bit more.

"Whichever term is used, I embrace it because I believe in the written word. So do you. It's why you're here. You were chosen for this honor, based on your excellent essays honoring the role of women in society. And if you are an example of our future generation of scholars, then I posit we're in very good hands indeed. Duchess, would you like to say a few words?"

He understood the sounds of surprise and distress that greeted his invitation. Dates had been invited to events, and it wasn't unusual to see a significant other watching from the sidelines, but to have a person who wasn't a member of the royal family be asked to say a few words on behalf of the queen?

Outrageous.

He knew the comments, segments, think pieces, and social media posts that would result from this gesture, and he planned to prepare her for it, but he was also very proud of her. Of the way she carried herself as she made her way to stand at the lectern.

As if she owned the building.

But for good measure, he skimmed those assembled with a quelling glance.

"Thank you, Prince Jameson. And thank you to the royal family for allowing me to be here today. When I learned about the event, and who was being honored and why, I begged Prince Jameson to let me attend. Not because I was a good student; I was not. But because I know a little something about honoring kick-ass women." Dani gasped and swung to face him. "Can I say kick-ass?"

He widened his eyes. "You just did. Twice."

The audience chuckled and her expression was so adorably dismayed it was all he could do not to kiss her. Handholding had been pushing it; the palace would go apoplectic if they actually embraced during the festivities.

"Strong women," she amended, laughing. "I wouldn't be here without the strong women in my life. And on that note, I'm going to stop while I'm slightly ahead. Congratulations to the essayists and to the parents and teachers of these creative students! I look forward to meeting you all."

She pressed her hands together and nodded at the applause.

"Now, if you'll please," another palace aide said, as others assembled the guests into a line.

Jameson briefly touched the small of Dani's back when she rejoined him. "You were wonderful."

"That bit works every time."

He frowned. The part when she'd "accidentally" cursed in her enthusiasm and had been charmingly remorseful? That hadn't been genuine?

The aide gestured to him and Dani. "Your Royal Highness. Duchess."

They moved along the procession, greeting the students and their families. He shook hands and spoke to everyone, asking their parents questions and chatting with the students about their studies.

But he couldn't help being entranced by Dani to his left. He received his usual smiles and respectful regard, but Dani was greeted with such warmth and appreciation, especially by the students. They were drawn to her, like a beloved family member. It was startling to bear witness to it, as he hadn't seen anything like it . . . ever.

Did the power lie in her not being a member of the royal family or was it a quality innate in her?

And was that a part of the show, too?

Jameson exhaled a silent sigh of relief when he reached the last student. "Hello, Candice. Congratulations."

Candice took his hand and dropped into a shaky curtsy. "Your Royal Highness."

The guests had been told that bowing or curtsying wasn't required, nevertheless, most of them made an attempt.

He mentally flipped through all the essays he had read and linked up Candice's name with the corresponding paper. *Oh!* "I really enjoyed your perspective on the imperative of prioritizing the education of women globally. The Brigham Young quote you used was particularly effective: You educate a man, you educate a man. You educate a woman, you educate a generation."

Candice had been the only student to approach the essay with an eye toward racial and class disparities.

"Thank you so much, sir," she said and beamed, pride straightening her posture. Her gaze flicked to Dani and her mouth dropped open. "Oh my God!"

"How you doing?" Dani asked, flashing the teen a brilliant smile.

Candice bounced from foot to foot, flapping her hands. "It's actually you."

Dani laughed. "Last time I checked."

Candice raised her hand to cover her mouth and began to sob.

"Oh no. Candice, are you okay?" Dani asked, with a look of concern. "Where are your parents? Do you need a br—"

"No, no." Candice dashed the tears from her eyes and took a deep breath. "I'm sorry. I don't know why I'm crying."

"Give me one sec." Dani hurried over and whispered in an aide's ear.

The aide looked startled, but she reached into her bag and handed something to Dani, who patted her arm and hurried back. She gave Candice a tissue. "Here you go. It's okay. You can't always help your emotions. I totally understand. This is all a bit overwhelming."

"It's not this," Candice said, dabbing her eyes. "This is amazing and it's wonderful to be recognized for your work. No, it's you."

"Me?" Dani pressed a hand to her chest.

"You can't imagine what it feels like to be here and see someone who looks like you. Someone who looks like me. Here. Not just staff, but, essentially, as a member of the royal family. It's major."

"I can imagine. Not in this setting. I mean, I barely understand being here myself. But I do know how it feels to see women of color, especially Black women, in certain places and positions. Even more so when we've never seen them there before." Dani held out her arms. "May I?"

Candice nodded and Dani gave the girl a hug. They must've been the center of attention because the room got quiet, save the incessant clicking of the cameras. But Jameson stayed focused on the interaction between Dani and the teen.

"I'm sorry it's taken so long for this to happen, but if my being here helps you dream bigger and set your goals higher, then I'm proud to have been a factor in that."

When they parted, they shared a smile and Jameson's heart shifted in his chest. He felt silly remembering how hard he'd protested involving Dani in the business of the Company. If he'd gotten his way, this incident wouldn't have happened, and he could see that meeting Dani would have a positive impact on this girl's life.

Did he need to protect Dani or was he being overprotective? Dani had the ability to be an asset not only to him but to the Company. Maybe he was wrong in his assumptions about how Dani would be treated. Maybe things were changing. And the rules might be different for her. She was already famous, with her own fan base. The British tabloid media might think twice about trying the usual schtick with her.

Was it possible this could all work out?

Chapter Fifteen

DUCHESS SHARES SWEET MOMENT WITH STUDENT ESSAY WINNER DURING RECEPTION AT THE PALACE

EVENING STANDARD

Jameson leaned an elbow on the round rustic mahogany table and propped his chin on his fist. "Are we going to play anytime soon?"

"What's the rush? You got someplace to be?" Rhys asked.

Not someplace to be, but someone to be with. When he'd originally been roped into hosting poker night, he'd thought Dani would've come and gone by now. He enjoyed his friends, but he hadn't put a dent in making up for how much he'd missed Dani when they'd been apart.

However, Dani wouldn't hear of him canceling his plans. "Go. Hang out with your boys. I'll be here when you're done."

"That would be really rude, considering you invited us here," Oliver was saying.

"And how long has it been since he's done a proper poker night?" Jasper asked.

"All right, all right. I get it." He leaned back and picked up his tumbler of whisky. "Who needs to actually *play* poker on poker night?"

Oliver took a homemade sausage roll from the tray of highly curated snacks and popped it in his mouth. "Margery prepares the best spreads."

"That she does," Jasper said, picking up and studying a bacon-wrapped date. "Hetty told me I couldn't come home unless I found out where Margery got those marvelous tea cakes she served when we were here for Dani's party."

"Is this *The Great U.K. Baking Championship* or bloody poker?" Rhys drank from his whisky.

Oliver's brow rose. "You either need to hit the gym or get laid."

"Please," Jameson urged. "You've been far too grumpy for far too long."

"Do you act this way with your students?" Jasper asked. "The school would probably pay you to go to Los Angeles if it meant you'd come back in a better mood."

Rhys gave him the middle finger. "Want to play poker? Here you go."

He threw more chips onto the pot.

"Son of a bitch. That was Jameson who complained, not me," Oliver said, before tossing his cards towards Jasper. "I fold."

"Well, well, well," Dani said, propping her hip against the doorway, lovely in one of her cozy matching lounge sets, this one a mint green. "I thought you said it was poker night? This looks like a scene straight out of that James Bond movie."

His smile was automatic, as were the particles of joy that radiated through him. He loved having her here. Her presence did more to liven up this old building than anything since his mother's time. Dani was also having the same effect on his life. Yesterday's event had been tolerable—enjoyable, even—because he was able to share it with her.

A thought that had kept him up all night. It shouldn't be this easy. The good press. The queen's welcome. The promise to let him leave royal life behind. It all seemed too good to be true. He never would've imagined the queen allowing someone's girlfriend, not to mention said girlfriend being an American rapper, to participate in royal events on behalf of the monarchy!

Was he missing something? Was there a move his grandmother had available that he couldn't see? Or was he looking for trouble where there was none?

"Why, thank you," Jasper said, looking up from his hand to doff an imaginary hat to her.

She laughed and moved around the table to stand next to Jameson. "Do you always wear tuxedos to play poker?"

"It's a stupid rule Oliver came up with," Jameson said, resting his hand on the small of her back.

"There's four of us," Oliver said, spreading his arms wide, his black and diamond encrusted cuff links catching the light. "I wasn't outvoted."

"Because it doesn't matter what I wear," Rhys said. "I'll still take your money."

"Ooh, shit talking! I love to hear it!" Dani said. "And you look good doing it! There's something about a handsome man in black tie."

"Hey!"

"No worries, Jay," she said, sitting on his lap and giving him a kiss. "You're the handsomest of them all."

"That's more like it," he said, placing his cards facedown and giving her a squeeze.

Jasper revealed the turn.

Jameson should've been deciding how he wanted to play his hand, but it was unreasonable to expect him to concentrate when he had Dani's soft warm body on his lap. He nuzzled her neck, seeking the source of her scent that was spicy, full-bodied, and would always remind him of her.

"Jay!" she said, simultaneously giggling and pushing against his shoulders. "Pay attention!"

"I thought that's what I was doing."

"For fuck's sake," Rhys growled. "As I recall, there are five hundred rooms in this place. You two are free to pick any one except this one. In this one, we're playing cards!"

"I would like to refer you to Ollie's earlier comment about hitting the gym or hitting the sheets," Jasper said.

"Or I could hit you," Rhys deadpanned.

Jameson ignored the fraternal back-and-forth, inhaling and then gently pulling Dani's smooth skin between his teeth, tugging, as if he could draw her essence in.

"You're wicked," she moaned. "Down, boy. I'm going to go and let you all get back to it. No need to rub Rhys's nose in it. Plus, I'm really underdressed."

"No. Stay. We're almost done," Jasper said, revealing the final card.

Jameson picked up his hand and grimaced. "Yeah, Rhys is getting ready to clean me out."

"You're not good at this, are you?" she asked.

"Cards aren't where my talent lies."

Dani pursed her lips. "But you play poker regularly?"

"And Mary and Hetty are part of a monthly book club where cases of wine are consumed but nary a spine has been cracked," Oliver said. "And your point is?"

"That it's a shame four grown men aren't cool with saying they want to hang out together, so instead they come up with a fancy pretext." She fluttered her lashes.

"Bloody hell, woman! What did I ever do to you?" Oliver asked, leaning back in his chair, his hand over his heart, as if wounded.

Dani blew him a kiss.

"You're not supercompetitive are you, Dani?" Rhys smirked.

"Have you met me?" She laughed. "But seriously, where I was raised, cards were a big deal. We played a lot. And either you have juju or you don't."

"If you do, just take a course of antibiotics and it'll clear that right up. Ask Jasper, he knows," Oliver said with a wink.

"Fuck you," Jasper said.

"Isn't indiscriminate fucking what caused you to get the juju in the first place?"

"Oh my God," Dani said, laughing. "You guys are too much!"

"That's one way to put it," Jameson muttered. "Ignore them. What's juju?"

She tilted her head, her brow furrowed. "Do you really believe cards are all about skill?"

"Of course."

"Oh, my naive, privileged sexy prince." She smacked a kiss on his lips. "Skill is a part of it, but there's a lot of luck and what we call juju. It's like the cards having an affinity for someone."

"And I suppose you have it?"

"Of course I have it. There would be games where the cards I needed would show up at the perfect time. That had nothing to do with skill. That was juju."

"Well, that settles it," Oliver said. "Rhys definitely has juju."

"You can borrow my antibiotics," Jasper said dryly.

Rhys nodded towards the table. "You want us to deal you in?"

"I appreciate that," Dani said, sliding off Jameson's lap. He felt her absence keenly. "But poker isn't my jam."

He loved her little sayings and looked forward to the years it would take to learn them all.

"What *is* your jam?" he asked, curious.

"Spades."

He met his friends' confused gazes and shrugged. He was just as clueless as they were. "What's spades?"

Her eyes widened. "So, it's white people everywhere, not just the ones in America? You've never heard of spades?"

Everyone shook their head.

"Now, *that's* a card game. The next time you guys get together to kiki"—she grinned—"I'll have to school you."

Oliver hit the table with the palm of his hand. "No time like the present."

"Aren't y'all in the middle of a game?"

"Not really," Rhys said, displaying his cards.

Everyone groaned and Jameson and Jasper threw their hands in.

Oliver gaped at the ace and six of hearts Rhys had revealed that joined the three, seven, and queen of hearts on the table. "A fucking flush?"

Dani clapped. "Juju."

Rhys laughed and pulled the pot to his side of the table. "Now, tell us about spades."

She looked around the table. "Y'all sure?"

"Here, let me get you a chair," Jameson said, snagging an extra one from the corner of the room. "Would you like a drink?"

"A glass of champagne, babe, if you don't mind."

Her favorite. "Does anyone need a refill?"

All hands shot up.

He dropped a kiss on Dani's lips and strolled over to the bar cart.

"Spades," Dani began, a smile in her voice. She shuffled the deck. "When I was growing up, there wasn't a get-together, picnic, or barbecue that didn't somehow end up with grown folks around a table playing cards. Even as kids we played, but we stuck to war, gin rummy, and crazy eights."

"Look at that fancy shuffling. Jameson, you brought in a ringer."

She smiled slyly. "The sound of cards being shuffled always signifies a good time to me. I'd watch them playing and I'd want to be like them so bad. I remember the first time one of my cousins decided to teach me how to play. It was like I was being let into this secret world."

He could imagine a young Dani, being so excited to learn a card game.

Adorable.

"I also remember the first time I was brave enough to call 'next' on a game. I promptly got my feelings hurt."

"What do you mean?" he asked, immediately protective.

"You gotta have a thick skin. When you sit down to a spades table, age or relationships don't matter. It took years to get to the point where I could play without shedding tears."

"That sounds hard-core," Oliver said.

"It is. You gotta come correct or don't come at all. I've seen husbands and wives run the table during a spades tournament. But if they end up on separate teams, I've seen that same wife call her husband out his name. People in my family still talk about the time Cousin Edward and his wife ran a boston on Uncle Sammy and Aunt Myra . . . in 2008."

"Run the table?"

"What's run a boston?"

His friends were all staring at her in rapt attention. It appeared he wasn't the only British gentleman susceptible to her charm.

"Let's start with the basics. The object of the game is to win the number of books you bid before a hand starts. You can play solo or in teams, but if you have four players, you typically play in teams."

"What's a book?"

Jameson opened his mouth to quip and Oliver shook his head. "Not you."

"Books are the cards of any play. Now, the person who goes first leads with a card. Whatever suit that card is—heart, club, et cetera—is the suit everyone has to play. If you have it in your hand, you have to play it. Highest card wins the book."

As Dani further explained the rules of the game, including cutting, reneging, and bidding, Jameson marveled at the turn his life had taken. And there were more changes to come. A time when he could do the work he wanted and live his life outside of the royal spotlight, with the woman he loved, was in his future.

"—The more you play, the more you'll get into the strategy of bidding. But we don't have to worry about that right now," Dani concluded.

There was a long pause.

"That doesn't seem too hard," Oliver quipped from his spot away from the table, the charcuterie board in his hand. "Not at all."

They all laughed.

"Is this for real? It sounds like you need several advanced degrees just to take part!"

"It'll make sense as we play. I can stop and explain some of the minutiae, like the method behind cutting, playing with a kitty, taking blinds, sandbagging—"

"Sandbagging? That sounds naughty," Oliver said.

"That's teabagging, you git." Jasper looked over at Dani and winced. "My apologies."

"Trust me. It's not the first time I've heard that word." She looked at Jameson and winked.

“Are you blushing?” Rhys asked.

Jameson could feel the heat on his cheeks and the tips of his ears. Bloody hell!

“Okay, okay, enough talk,” Jameson said. “Let’s get on with it.”

“Usually, the score is to five hundred, but let’s start out at a cap of three fifty. Just so everyone gets a taste for it. Jay, you want to play with me?”

“Always, love,” he said, standing to round the table and sit across from her.

“Uh-uh. She’s played this game her entire life.” Rhys pointed at Jameson. “And he’s bloody brilliant. Plus, who know what signals they’ve worked out. Jameson, you play with me.”

Dani shrugged and continued shuffling. “Whatever. I’ll take Jasper.”

“Funny. That’s how Hetty accepted my marriage proposal.”

They switched chairs until they were each paired up with the correct partner.

Jameson turned to Dani, who was seated on his left. “Are you going to go easy on me?”

Her expression hardened briefly before she arched a brow and smiled. “No.”

They began the game and as Dani predicted, it only took a few hands before they got the gist of it. In the beginning, when someone would make a mistake—like when Jameson played a spade to win a book even though he had the correct suit in his hand—Dani would go back and explain his error, without penalizing them for it.

Once, when Jasper laid down a card that won a book, Dani picked it up and slapped it down again with a flick of her wrist.

“For those special occasions when you want to emphasize an ass whooping. We say, ‘Put some English on it!’ ”

Jameson intended to.

Observing her took him back to the feeling he had watching her perform. Of his pulse thumping in his throat and his breath fleeing his body as he was dazzled, mesmerized, and fucking awed by the woman before him.

But at a certain point she declared they were "taking the training wheels off" and she . . . changed.

When he cut a book she'd been about to win, she eyed him so fiercely he couldn't believe those beautiful eyes had ever looked at him with love. Her string of curses when Jasper took a book with a king that she'd already won with a jack had Rhys's eyes widening. Over the course of the game jackets were discarded, bow ties undone, and sleeves rolled up. She made daring moves, consistently taking risks that shocked him.

When he commented on her assertive style she said, "You play to win the game."

On the last hand, she played with a single-minded focus he remembered from her tribute concert rehearsals. With mastery and precision, she won the final five books of the game, slamming each card down in the center of the table with a flourish that bordered on ruthlessness.

"That's it! We won!" Jasper whooped and rushed around the table to sweep Dani into a hug.

Jameson sagged back in his chair and looked over to see Rhys looking as dazed as he felt. As if they'd been through a battle . . . and lost.

"I've never seen anything like that. Especially the ending. It was . . . wow. If that's juju, I'll take it over pure skill any day." Oliver cleared his throat. "Dani, do you think you can teach Mary to play spades?"

Dani laughed. "Of course. I forgot to mention that side effect. Spades can be sexy as hell."

"Hetty will be joining those lessons, if you don't mind."

Dani patted Rhys's arm. "Don't worry. Nyla knows how to play. We've hosted a couple of Black Hollywood tournaments over the years."

Dani and Nyla playing spades? The drinks, the trash talking, the intensity?

Jameson refused to let himself travel down that mental road and he glared at Rhys when it looked like the other man was going to forge ahead, ignoring the caution signs.

Jasper stood. "And with that, I'm going to shoot off."

"Hold on," Dani said. "Margery mentioned having some snacks for you to take back to Hetty."

"Excellent," he said, rubbing his hands together.

"You can call and have someone bring that for you," Jameson said.

Her nostrils flared. "I'm perfectly capable of walking to the kitchen, Jay."

It wasn't the first time she'd expressed her annoyance when he'd suggested she delegate certain tasks to the house staff. He knew she was independent, and he loved that about her. But some of the housemaids believed she didn't trust them to do their jobs.

After she'd left the room, Jasper said, "You're one lucky bastard. She's bloody cool."

"Mary really liked her. After the party last week, she couldn't stop talking about how down-to-earth Dani was," Oliver added.

"And it's nice to see you happy. She's good for you."

It meant a lot to him that these men, whom he held in high esteem, appeared to support his feelings for Dani and their relationship. Not that he sought their approval or would be swayed by their withholding of it. But he was pleased, knowing they endorsed his choice.

"Thank you." He pushed from the table. "Come on. I'll walk you out."

Dani met them in the foyer and handed Jasper a parcel. "Margery said you can freeze any extras for up to three months."

"I doubt that'll happen but I'm much obliged." He kissed her cheek and saluted Jameson. "See you in a bit."

Oliver and Rhys followed, hugging Dani and shaking Jameson's hand, their "Cheers" and "Later" almost lost as his butler closed the great door behind them.

"Thank you, Ellis."

"Of course, sir." Ellis bobbed his head and headed to the back of the house.

Jameson was suddenly struck by the simple domesticity of the evening's ending. The two of them seeing their guests to the door, as if they'd hosted an event together. Would that be in their future? Would Primrose Park come alive again the way it had, for a brief period, when he'd been younger?

He could see it. If he could only dislodge the splinter of uneasiness lodged in his mind from her demeanor during the game . . .

"I didn't say this last time, but your friends are great. Thanks for letting me crash poker night. I had fun." She frowned. "You okay?"

He blinked. "Yes, of course. Why would you ask?"

"Because you're looking at me as if you don't know me. Tell me, Jay, are you the type of guy who has feelings about losing to a woman?"

She tossed her head, her tone defiant, her countenance harsh. This was the Duchess everyone else saw, the one who had to fight for everything she had.

Jameson didn't care that he'd lost a *card* game. He'd actually found her competitiveness attractive. But there was competitive and there was a need to win. And he'd been privy to that kind of need, had been burned by it in his dealings with the queen, who was willing to do anything and sacrifice anyone to achieve her goals.

There had been a moment when he'd glanced at Dani and he'd recognized that cutthroat look in her eyes. Victory at all cost and damn everything else. Yes, it was only a game, but that's why it had been so jarring, and he couldn't shake the chill that skimmed his spine as he wondered how far she would be willing to go to come out on top.

"I have no problems losing to you, love," he said quietly. Meeting her gaze so she knew it was true. "When you win, we both win. Congratulations."

Her face softened and she was once again his Dani.

"Thanks, baby." She held out her hand. "How about we go upstairs and celebrate *our* win? I'm dying to tell you more about . . . sandbagging."

Chapter Sixteen

"Is an engagement just around the corner? Between recent photos of that hot royal date, the inclusion of Duchess in official events for the queen, and sources who say she's made herself at home in Prince Jameson's eleven-thousand-square-foot country estate, Primrose Park—even hosting parties—all signs point to yes!"

ENTERTAINMENT TONIGHT **WEBSITE, EMBEDDED VIDEO**

How many events had she and Jameson done in the past week? Two? Three? Five?

Together, they'd hosted a palace reception in honor of Caroline Batley and her second-place finish at the U.S. Open. Dani had actually liked the woman, who'd quietly told her it was okay if she'd cheered for Yolanda's win, since Caroline knew Dani and Yolanda were friends.

The following morning, Dani and Jameson had taken a day away to visit a fifth-generation farm and talk with the family about the challenges of modern-day agriculture. Two days later, they'd visited an ambulance station in East London and taken a private meeting with executives from the JFL Trust to get an update on the progress.

So four. Four official engagements in five days.

Before this she hadn't ever given a thought to what royals did all day, but if pressed she probably would've admitted she didn't believe they did much.

She'd have been wrong.

A lot of planning and preparation went into a royal event. Briefings on security and protocol took hours, and on top of that, Dani put additional time into reading the dossiers and researching the issues and the establishments they were visiting, so she understood the purpose behind the meeting and could be a useful part of the conversation.

She knew the engagements were taking their toll on Jameson, but there was no doubt he was great at them. His growing celebrity wasn't born from being slick and glib, but because he was earnest, smart, and captivating. Dani always took a moment to glance around during each occasion and she'd never failed to find everyone under his spell.

Today, he'd had a rare day off and had been summoned by his mother. Dani had received a summons of her own.

"I'm surprised you invited me to this event with you," Dani said, glancing over at the car's other occupant.

"You shouldn't be," Catherine said, lovely and serene in a kelly green dress with a bow and a pleated skirt. "You're very popular."

Dani couldn't tell from her tone whether the Princess Royal felt that was a positive or negative thing.

But it was true. The coverage of Jameson and Dani's new role in the royal family had been overwhelmingly favorable. She'd never been more popular—as determined by the increase of followers across all her social media platforms and the fact that she was trending or mentioned almost daily—and Mela-Skin products were in high demand, practically flying off the shelves or perpetually sold out online.

Their plan was working. During a phone call with Andrea, her company's CEO had informed Dani that Parcellum was thrilled with the developments and they were working to get a meeting on the schedule for both sides to sign the contract.

Dani should've been ecstatic.

But keeping her motivations from Jameson was taking its toll on *her*. And she'd heard from Tasha that the Hip-Hop Awards had announced their presenters and performers and she hadn't been listed. The slight hurt more than she'd anticipated, and she could only link it to Cash continuing to bad-mouth her within the community. It seemed the more prominent she became on the worldwide stage, the more Cash resented her.

"I'd give Bettina a wide berth for a while," Catherine said.

"Why?"

She had a small smile. "She was supposed to do this with me. Not that she'd been excited about doing it. But the idea that I would pick you over her . . ."

Dani shrugged. The other woman hating her wasn't anything new.

Dani felt she had a good feel for the members of Jameson's family. She knew what to expect from them. Julian was a perv. Bettina was a bitch. The queen was the queen.

But Catherine . . .

Dani hadn't forgotten the older woman's manner after she and Jameson had been outed at the tribute ball. Unlike the others who'd been so clear with their disdain, Catherine had been honest and genuine with her concern. But that didn't mean she'd been warm and cuddly, either.

So, when Louisa had told Dani she'd be doing an event with Catherine, she hadn't been sure what to expect.

She still wasn't.

"Did you read the dossier on today's event?"

"No."

Catherine shot her a sharp glance. "Why not?"

"There wasn't enough time. I was only notified a couple of hours before you picked me up. But Louisa said it was essentially a meet n' greet. I do a lot of those."

Catherine pursed her lips. "I really wish you had. This isn't like the other appearances you've done."

Dani sighed. *Well, they were off to a great start!*

She changed the subject. "This is one of your patronages?"

"Yes. One of my favorites. I have a soft spot for this children's hospital. I spent a lot of time in it when I was younger."

There was so much to unpack in that statement.

Catherine had spent a lot of time in hospitals when she was little? Had she been sick?

But, more importantly, they were going to a children's hospital? *Fuck.*

Dani shivered. She wasn't a big fan of hospitals. Her only meaningful interaction with them had led to the biggest change in her life, Nana's death. During her career, Dani had done her best to avoid functions that took place in medical centers, although she tried to make up for it with donations. She couldn't help it. Hospitals still freaked her out.

But before she could ask more questions, the car stopped and Catherine said, "We're on."

The protection officer opened the door and they both exited the black Range Rover. The press had been corralled into a space behind metal gates, but their flashes were still noticeable.

"Ignore them," Catherine said beneath her breath. "This isn't the time."

Dani bristled. *You have your priorities and I have mine.*

She didn't say anything, but just before she walked into the building, she turned and gave them a full photo op moment, showing off the sleek, knee-length, off-white wrap-front dress that draped beautifully over her body. Diamond and pearl accessories and her favorite Rebecca Allen nude heels completed the demure, for her, look.

The clicks and flashes confirmed that the picture was taken.

"These are the doctors and nurses who've treated her and some of the first responders," the hospital administrator was telling Catherine when Dani joined them.

Men and women of different ages, races, and sizes lined a low-ceilinged hallway, decorated with bright letters and murals. They bowed or curtsied to Catherine, who smiled and shook each person's hand.

"The children are lucky to have you," the Princess Royal told them, and they beamed under her praise.

A reporter and two photographers had been allowed to join their group and cover the event. Louisa had schooled Dani on the pact between the palace and the media. The Company needed publicity for their working lives, the causes they championed, and to allow people to see why they were necessary. In exchange, they endured the media's attention in their private lives.

The antiseptic smell was taking Dani back to memories she'd thought she'd hidden. She nodded, trying her best to keep her composure. The hospital administrator made small talk as they followed her down the hallway, around a corner, and through a set of double doors. Immediately ahead of them, a couple stood outside a hospital room.

"Your Royal Highness," the woman said, her dyed blond hair swinging forward to cover her face as she curtsied. "Thank you so much for coming."

"Ella will love seeing you," said the man, bowing over Catherine's hand. He was wearing a Black Sabbath T-shirt and Dani assumed he was the child's father.

Their gazes flickered to Dani and their eyes widened in surprise. "Wow, you're here, too. This is right posh, innit?" The mother dipped and rose in some sort of half curtsy, half jump of excitement.

Dani forced a smile. "I hope you don't mind me crashing the party?"

"No, we'll budge up. Ella's a proper fan."

"Wonderful." Catherine smiled. "Can we meet her?"

They followed the couple into the room. It was large, meaning it was semi-private and probably had more than one bed in it, but the curtain was drawn so Dani assumed the other bed was empty. And everyone—the medical staff, the media, Catherine—was focused on the little girl in the first bed.

She wore a light blue short-sleeved T-shirt and lay back against the raised head of the hospital bed, her dark blond hair falling in lank strands against her pale face. A nurse checked the machines and froze when they walked in.

"Oh no, no," Catherine said. "Please, don't stand on ceremony. And I know that sounds strange considering the source, but really. Continue what you're doing." She looked at the little girl. "Hi, Ella. Do you mind if I talk to you for a second?"

"No, Your Royal Highness," Ella said, her light-colored eyes wide as they flitted over everyone in the room. She looked as if she couldn't believe who was there.

That makes two of us, Dani thought, the sterile smell and beeping sounds placing her in a mindset she was struggling to escape.

"Thank you. How are you feeling?"

Ella shrugged. "Okay now. I'm still a little scared, though."

"Of course you are. It was all very alarming. I can't even imagine going through what you had to."

Dani refocused on the conversation. Had the little girl been in some sort of car accident? Had the doctor explained but Dani missed it?

"Everyone's been smashing. We're chuffed to bits," the mom said.

"That's wonderful. I know many organizations are really interested in helping everyone affected."

It must've been a really bad accident if people were responding in this manner. Maybe a drunk driver?

Dani didn't want to bring more trauma to the girl, but it was clear she'd missed something. She could ask around the issue, maybe use context clues to figure out what had happened. She moved to stand on the other side of the bed.

"I see your cast," Dani said, pointing to her left arm, wrapped from her wrist to her elbow. "Did it get hurt during your accident?"

Instinctively, the girl lifted it and then grimaced. "It got pinned 'neath the rubble."

The rubble? From a car accident? Dani thought that was possible, but it appeared her context clue sleuthing was failing her at the moment.

"Where do you go to school, Ella?" Catherine asked, smoothly.

Dani clasped her hands in front of her and tried to focus on their conversation when she heard a sound on the other side of the curtain, like someone shifting then trying to stifle a moan. She peeked around the fabric and saw a young Black girl lying in the neighboring hospital bed, her face turned away from Dani. Where Ella's half of the room was brightly lit, this side was dim and shadowy.

The teen moaned again, and the sound pained Dani. She swallowed and moved closer to the bed.

"Would you like me to get a nurse?"

"No," the teen said shortly, her voice raspy.

"Are you sure? There's several dozen over there."

"I said no! Can you crack on?" the girl snapped.

Dani stiffened instinctively. "What's your problem?"

"Are you daft? I'm in hospital. What do you think?"

Dani pursed her lips and squeezed her eyes shut. What the fuck was wrong with her, arguing with an ill young girl?

"My bad. I'm sorry to disturb you."

The girl turned her head. "Duchess?"

Dani couldn't stifle her gasp when she noticed the side of the teen's face and neck scarred with what looked like angry and raw third-degree burns.

"Don't worry," the girl said. "It's not catching."

Compassion caused an ache in her throat. Dani forgot her manners and hurried over to sit in the chair next to the bed. "I know and I'm so sorry. What happened?"

"A bombing. At our after-school center."

"A bombing?" Dani pressed a hand to her midsection, shocked. When had this happened? She didn't read the British papers, outside of noticing the headlines . . . had it been on the news? Had she been so caught up in Jameson that she missed hearing about the bombing of children?

"It got pinned 'neath the rubble."

"And is that what happened to the girl in the other bed?"

She nodded. "Most of us on this floor. Although, it's funny—"

Dani couldn't imagine anything humorous about this situation. "What's funny?"

"She doesn't go to our center. It's mostly migrants. That's why we were targeted. Her family just moved to the neighborhood. It was her third day."

Dani's stomach twisted. "Targeted?"

"People here have lost the plot when it comes to migrants. Think they're nicking their jobs."

The levels of wrongness about the entire situation! Dani opened her mouth, then closed it. What should she do? What *could* she do? A sexy dance followed by a "Duchess is here, Bitches better bow down" call and repeat seemed highly inappropriate and ineffectual given the circumstances.

The side of the girl's face unaffected by trauma tightened. "You're off your trolley. I saw you when you were here for the tribute. You didn't act like this. Is it 'cuz you pity me?"

"Not pity. Sympathy. And great sorrow. Is that not allowed?"

"It is. What happened to us was shitty."

Dani raised her brows. "Wow, I can see why they're not using *you* in the promo materials."

The teen's eyes widened.

Goddammit, Dani!

But the girl laughed out loud only to immediately wince.

Dani half rose from the chair. "Are you okay?"

The girl nodded then asked, "What gave it away? My mouth or my face?"

"I didn't mean it like that."

"It's cool. I flipped my lid and you called me out on it. That's so Duchess."

"I think having an attitude is the least of what you're allowed." Dani frowned. "Me calling you out is okay but not knowing what to say offended you?"

"Yeah, 'cuz calling me out is so Duchess. You're treating me regular. But the other thing is you treating me like charity."

Dani's heart broke. The years seemed to melt away and she was once again that young girl who needed help but hated the side of pity that came with it. She understood not wanting to be seen as a charity case when she'd been fucked by circumstances outside of her control.

"What's your name?"

"Kabira."

"It's a pleasure to meet you, Kabira, although it saddens me it's under these circumstances."

"Thank you. I'm a big fan," Kabira said, her burgeoning smile morphing into a grimace and a moan, her back arching off the bed.

Anger misted her vision. Jaw set, Dani jumped up, marched over to the curtain, and yanked it back.

"Now that we're done with the pretty photo ops, can someone come over here and take care of this patient, please?"

Gasps and various looks of shock and guilt colored the faces of the hospital staff against the sudden backdrop of the clicks and flashes of multiple pictures being taken.

Catherine's jaw went slack for a nanosecond before she reeled it back in. She rose smoothly from her chair, as if all hell hadn't broken loose.

"I'm sure you need to see to your patients, so it's probably time for us to leave. Thank you again for allowing us to visit with you, Ella. Duchess?"

Dani curled her lip. "I'm not going anywhere until someone comes and checks on Kabira."

The administrator's expression tightened but she jerked her head, motioning one of the nurses over. The woman hurried to the machine and pressed a few buttons. Kabira's posture relaxed and it was clear the medicine was kicking in.

Dani returned to Kabira's side, mindful of the pictures being taken, but for once not caring about the contract or her public image.

"Get some rest," she said, working hard to keep the fury off her face as she looked down at the young girl.

"Nice meeting you," Kabira said, her lashes fluttering. "I can't believe I'm finally getting the chance to meet you but it's only 'cuz of what happened. Cosmic joke, really."

That was one way to put it.

"Can I come back to visit?"

"You don't have to," Kabira protested.

"I know. But I want to."

Another half smile. "For sure."

"Then I'll set it up." Dani leaned low and whispered, "And I'll try to sneak something good in for you, okay?"

Kabira nodded and her eyes drifted shut.

It took everything Dani had to contain herself until they were outside the hospital, past the press, and back in the car.

Dani affected her best Whitley Gilbert voice. "Well, that was loads of fun! Thank you ever so much for asking me. I had a fantastic time."

Catherine ignored her.

Then direct it was. "What the fuck was that about?"

Catherine's personal secretary turned to look at Dani. "You forget yourself. You're speaking to Her Royal Highness, the Princess Royal."

Dani shot the man a hostile look. "Trust me. You don't want this smoke."

"It's all right, Antony. Duchess and I can speak frankly with each other." Catherine pressed a button, creating privacy between the front and back seats. She adjusted the material of her skirt over her knees. "That was us visiting some children in the hospital who have gone through something traumatic."

"No, you went to visit *one* child! A child who'd only been at the center a few days when this all happened!"

"Does that mean she's less entitled to my sympathy?"

"Don't do that, Catherine. Those children were hurt because of a hate crime but no one wants to call it that. What are you going to do about it?"

The family was all about events and using the media. Why couldn't they shine some light on what happened and who'd done it? Were they on the trail of the perpetrators?

"It's not our job to do anything."

"Bullshit!"

"Your language!" Catherine exhaled. "Do you use any other words?"

"Forgive me for being outraged. Aren't you?"

"Of course!"

"Then fucking say something about it!"

"I did! That's why you were here!" Catherine asserted, spots of color dotting her pale cheeks.

Dani frowned. "What?"

"We're allowed in because we stay out," Catherine said, as if it were a nursery rhyme or personal mantra.

Dani wasn't in the mood to banter with the fucking Riddler.

"What does that mean?"

"Quite simply, we're allowed to remain a monarch and live the lives we do by keeping our noses and opinions out of politics. It's the only reason we've survived the changes in legislative power. If we start 'speaking out,' the people can decide to get rid of us just like any other bureaucrat."

"That's ridiculous! In fact, it's all a joke. No wonder Jameson wants as little to do with the Company as possible."

Catherine exhaled impatiently. "As you've seen from the official engagements you've done with Jameson, we get a lot of coverage. Depending on the event, that coverage can be local or international. Over in America, would this event have gotten any press?"

The conversational whiplash with this woman!

Dani shook her head. "No, I don't believe we would've broken into a sports event or the latest *Housewives* episode to watch a member of the royal family going to visit people in a hospital."

"That's what I thought. But everything you've done while you've been here? Covered not only in the States but across the world. *That* is why you are important."

It was like Dani was finally being let in on a secret. Her being there meant there would be press attention and the reason the children were in the hospital would get coverage as well. And maybe some pressure would be put on those in power to do the right thing.

Game recognized game.

This woman wasn't to be underestimated.

Dani sat back. "So, you knew the bombing of that after-school center was a hate crime?"

"Of course. The anti-immigrant sentiment has been growing out of control. But if the government and media refuse to label it as a hate crime—"

"You can't call it that," Dani finished for her. And took it a step further. "But I can."

"Exactly."

"But I didn't. I didn't say anything." She reached into her purse for her phone. "But I can fix that."

"No." Catherine put her hand over Dani's screen. "We definitely do not need a social media post."

"Then *what*?" she lashed out, brimming with frustration.

"I wanted your presence. That's it. That would've been enough. Now . . ." Catherine shook her head.

Dani stared at the Princess Royal, the one-eighty shift in her comprehension making her unsteady.

"Did you know Kabira was in the other bed?"

"No."

"Do you care?"

"Yes! That poor girl and her face . . ." Catherine's lips trembled.

"But you chose the more palatable optics of the little white girl with blond hair and her arm in a cast?"

"That's who the *hospital administrator* chose for our visit," Catherine clarified.

Oh.

"You don't have a problem expressing your opinions, do you?" Catherine asked.

"No, I don't."

"I can tell. Even during the ball when you confronted my mother, you spoke your mind. I respect that about you. I have my own opinions, too. But those are private. In public, there's a party line and you're expected to follow it. Especially if you want to remain a working senior royal."

It was like being in a fun-land house of mirrors.

"People looking in from the outside always think they understand our way of life. And they come in believing they can handle it. We aren't insular for any nefarious reasons, but because it's easier to slot in someone who's grown up in, and understands, this world."

Catherine may have a point. Dani had assumed she understood what she was stepping into by agreeing to do these engagements. And she could admit her assumption had been bolstered by her need for the exposure her participation would bring. But Dani didn't have a fucking clue. Those events with Jay had been like dipping her toe in the water. This one with Catherine was akin to being caught in a rip current, pulling her offshore and into water above her head.

"My mother is very aware of this. And yet, she's granted you unprecedented authority and access you haven't earned."

What did that mean? At this point, Dani was tired of asking. And irritated. Why did everything have to be so fucking cryptic with this family?

"Do you remember your last event with Jameson and what you said?"

Dani frowned. "I said a lot of things. You need to be more specific."

"'I'm sorry it's taken so long for this to happen.'" Catherine pulled the quote as if it were sitting on the tip of her tongue, waiting to be called to action.

"Yes. The girl was crying because she'd never seen anyone who looked like her in the family that was supposed to represent her country. And I wanted her to know what that meant to me."

"But it was seen as a criticism of the royal family."

"By who?"

"The palace wanted to pull you from events."

"This came from the queen?"

Catherine shook her head. "The palace!"

"I don't understand what you're trying to tell me!"

"Just . . . be careful. I love my mother and respect her more than anyone I've ever known. It's taken a lot for her to hold this all together. But that doesn't mean she should be trusted. Keep your eyes open."

Catherine turned to gaze out the window, signaling the conversation was over.

"Oh, and Duchess?"

Apparently, Dani was wrong. Catherine had more to say.

"Yes?"

"I'd already spelled most of this out and I hate repeating myself. So, if I ever request you to do another event with me, read the bloody dossier!"

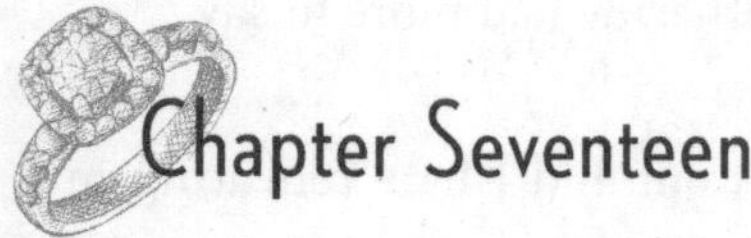

Chapter Seventeen

"Who does she think she is? She's a rapper, and a mediocre one at that. As Prince Jameson's girlfriend, for the time being, she needs to stick to looking pretty and keep her big nose out of our business."

VIVIAN FENDER, *GOOD MORNING, LONDON*

The mostly cloudy sky hid much of the sun but it didn't take away from the loveliness of the Primrose Park scenery. Rolling green hills and manicured lawns caressed the eyes, for as far as one could see.

"This really is beautiful," Dani said, squeezing Jameson's hand as they strolled along an asphalt path on the enormous seven-hundred-acre estate. "You know, Nyla would love this."

"Why?"

Dani pictured her best friend and couldn't help laughing. "She's definitely an outdoor person. All I think about are allergies and bugs but she'll drop everything and hike Runyon Canyon at a moment's notice if the mood strikes."

He stopped midstride. "You have allergies?"

"I took a pill," she said, tugging him forward. "I'm good."

He nodded. "You sound wistful. Do you miss her?"

"I do. I haven't seen her since the premiere. We text but it's not the same. As you well know. But we're both busy. We'll catch up when we can."

"Speaking of catching up, I'm glad you agreed to come on a walk with me. Getting some fresh air can help elevate your mood," he said, a slight smile curving his lips.

"It's working," she conceded, "but I'll admit to much side-eye about the walk part. I was waiting for you to grab your gray cardigan and say it was time for our daily constitutional."

"Pardon? *Where* do you see a cardigan?"

He'd been making an effort to incorporate some of the pieces they'd purchased from Corey into his wardrobe. Today he wore army green cargo pants and a fitted white T-shirt that hugged his broad shoulders and slim torso. Her mouth literally watered.

And he was all hers.

"Okay, sir. What I see is you, feeling yourself," she said, rolling her eyes.

"I know you like when I do that," he said, pulling her close and giving her a brief kiss. "But don't get too excited. I can't guarantee it'll be another thirty years before you see me in a cardigan."

"Thirty years? Now you're getting *ahead* of yourself."

"Am I?" He shrugged. "Maybe. I'm constantly thinking of our future together."

"And what do you see? In our future?"

"I haven't fully worked it out. All I know is whatever it holds, you're in it."

She wanted to believe him, but she had to admit she'd been shaken by yesterday's event at the children's hospital. And the country's reaction to it.

"I love you and I want to be with you, too, but—"

He wrinkled his forehead. "I don't like how that sounds."

"No, no." She waved a hand. "I'm just thinking about what happened with Catherine."

"I wish I'd known she was going to ask you to do that event. Or that you'd told me about it before you agreed," he said, his voice quaking with resentment. "Doing them without me wasn't part of the agreement."

Dani pursed her lips. "I'm a grown woman, Jay. I don't need your input or permission to decide how to spend my time."

"But look what happened! You weren't ready."

Dani bristled. He may have had a point, but she hated knowing he doubted her abilities or thought she needed protection like an outsider or a child.

She dropped his hand.

"And I never said you needed my permission." He recaptured hers, entangling their fingers. "I only meant Catherine wouldn't ask you to attend an event solo without having a reason. An agenda."

"She had one. She knew my presence would bring attention to what happened in a way hers wouldn't."

"Yes, and in the process, put you in the crosshairs of the media, the racist, xenophobic fringe, and the Company."

Is this what she had to look forward to in a future with Jameson? She was happy to participate in these royal engagements because it was vital to her business concerns, but it was more than attending events. There were so many rules and protocols, and no one said what they meant, choosing to talk in riddles and issue cryptic warnings. Dani wasn't in the mood, and she wasn't sure she wanted to deal with this for the rest of her life. She understood intrigue and backstabbing because she worked in entertainment, but she didn't want to spend her days maneuvering accordingly at home!

"It seems this will be something we'll need to figure out, right?

For our future? How much we're going to have to deal with your family?"

"I don't want you to worry. You're my priority. I won't let them hurt you. And as soon as the state visit is done and we've satisfied our part of the deal with the queen, we'll start thinking about our life together."

Dani couldn't wait for that either. Although her reasons were a little different from his.

She turned to walk backward, tapping his chest with her finger. "You'll be unemployed. You're gonna need to find a job because I'm not into being your sugar momma. That's not my kink."

"I'll have you know I'm highly employable."

"What did I say? Feeling yourself!"

"If I'm wrong, we'll still manage. I'm quite well off."

"Really?" As far as boasts about money, it wasn't the most grandiose she'd heard, but for Jameson it was bombastic. She nudged his shoulder with her own. "How much?"

He scoffed. "We don't need to get into the particulars."

"Uh, yeah we do." She rubbed her hands together. "Are we talking Jeff Bezos or Rihanna?"

His quick-witted reply wasn't forthcoming and Dani frowned. She'd hadn't really expected him to tell her how much he was worth—at least not at this moment!—but his discomfort was telling.

After several long, awkward seconds, he jammed his hands into his pockets and cleared his throat. "We would be quite comfortable. For a long time."

Dani clenched her jaw. "I'm not after your money, Jay."

"I never thought you were."

"But if we have a future—"

"If?"

"—we'll have to talk about money and our approaches to it."

He'd be entitled to know about her finances, too, though the thought sank in her belly like a leaded stone. If it were up to her, they would put this conversation off for the distant future. Still, she'd seen so many relationships destroyed behind fights about money. Dani didn't want that issue to come between them, when it didn't have to.

"I don't want you to worry . . ."

God, not *this* again.

"But I do worry. We grew up different."

They came across a grove of trees that sheltered an antique stone bench. Dani dragged him over to it and they sat.

"Have you ever had your utilities turned off? Or come home to find a 'pay or quit' notice on your door?"

"No." He shoveled fingers through his hair. "Fuck, Dani, I'm—"

She held up a hand to forestall his apology. "My grandmother did the best she could, but there were times when her best wasn't enough. We got by but I told myself I'd never be in that position again."

A drop fell on her cheek. She brushed it away.

"And you won't be," he said.

"You're right. But not because of you."

He narrowed his eyes. "Why does any mention of my wanting to take care of you have to turn combative?"

Tension flattened her lips. Combative? Like aggressive? Or angry?

Several more drops fell on her head, and she flicked a look skyward, noticing what little sun there'd been was now gone.

Probably irritated by this conversation, too.

"Because you say it as if you can do it better than me, when I've been doing it on my own for a long time. And very well, I might add!"

He frowned. "Dani—"

The heavens opened and sheets of rain cascaded down, penetrating the thick foliage shielding them.

Dani yelped and hopped up, instinctively raising her arms and using her spread fingers as ineffectual umbrellas. They'd been walking for at least half an hour; they were in the middle of nowhere!

"Come on!" Jameson grabbed her hand and took off running.

Damn, he was fast.

She did her best, grateful she'd decided on sneakers and hadn't tried to be cute with sandals, but she felt as if he were dragging her along. She was drenched and about to give up when she saw the clearing up ahead. It housed a small stone structure that looked remarkably like one of the single-story circular wings that flanked the main part of Primrose Park.

They scurried up the stone steps and Jameson tried the thick wooden door. Initially, it didn't open, but on his third attempt, aided by a little brute force, it yielded. They hurried inside, shutting it behind them.

Jameson shook his head, then pushed his wet strands back. "Welcome to the beauty of an English summer rain shower."

"Reason eighty-two of why I don't do walks," Dani said, wringing out the hem of her silk cashmere blend T-shirt. "At least I threw these braids in this morning. I don't even want to think about what my hair would look like if I hadn't."

"It doesn't matter," he said, looking around them. "You'd still be beautiful."

"Oh, you sweet, delusional man." She laughed. She shifted her focus to their literal port in a storm. "What's this place?"

"It's called a folly. You'll find them on many of the great estates built in the late eighteenth century."

"What do they do?"

"Nothing. They're purely decorative."

"Well, thank God for architectural extravagance."

"I haven't been in here since I was a boy." Jameson crossed the space in several long strides. "Here's a trunk that doesn't look too old. Maybe there's something in it we can use."

While he rummaged through his new discovery, Dani studied their surroundings. Colorful stained-glass windows allowed a small amount of light to filter in from outside, otherwise the space was dark and damp, the stone walls and floors doing little else except keeping the rain out.

She crossed her arms over her chest and ran her hands up and down them to combat her sudden bout of shivering. The temperature had already been on the chilly side; it must've dropped several degrees with the showers.

"I believe it's some sort of rain survival kit. It's stocked with towels, blankets, a battery-powered torch, as well as a couple of macs, wellies, and brollies." At her silence he added, "Raincoats, boots, and umbrellas."

"That's very thoughtful," she said, through chattering teeth.

"You need to get out of those clothes. It's the only way we'll get you warm."

Dani made quick work of the task, toweling off and allowing Jameson to enfold her in one of the blankets. Then he spread out a thick comforter before copying her actions.

"Typically, these storms don't last long," he said, reclining on the homemade pallet. "We can wait it out."

Jameson opened his blanket and when she tossed hers aside and ungracefully sprawled next to him, he pulled her back against his broad chest, spooning her so the heat from his body slowly seeped into hers. He was so hard and strong behind her; she reveled in the contrast. He made her keenly aware of her femininity, the only man who'd ever affected her in this way.

She lay quietly, lulled into sensual relaxation by the sound of the rain hitting the structure and the heated comfort of his arms. His voice, subdued when it came, didn't break the spell.

"I would never suggest you couldn't take care of yourself. I'm frustrated because growing up I learned you cherish and protect the people you love." He hugged her tight and kissed the top of her head. "And I love you. More than I ever thought it was possible to love someone. I'm just trying to show you how much."

Her heart expanded in her chest, and she snuggled closer, marveling at the feel of his skin against her cheek and the exquisite sensation of his muscled, hair-roughened thighs pressed to her bare legs.

She felt him stirring behind her. He nuzzled the curve of her neck and her nerve endings sparked to life. He covered her breasts and she arched into his touch, moaning as he pulled her nipples into hard nubs and swirled his tongue in her ear, causing shivers of a whole different sort.

"One second, love." He reached over her and grabbed his wet pants.

He really did carry condoms with him at all times!

He stroked a hand along her curves and when he reached her thigh, he lifted it and positioned it slightly forward, leaving her pussy exposed.

"Put me in," he said, his breath tickling the hairs at her nape.

Reaching back, she grabbed his covered length and slowly inserted him. Her breath caught in her throat at the slight burn of not being fully ready as she usually was. But she liked the bite as it added to the overall debauchery of the situation.

He groaned and his forehead fell onto her shoulder. "God, I love being inside you."

"You. Me. Same," she panted.

She grasped the hard ridge of his hip and tried to pull him deeper, whimpering as he fucked her with long, slow strokes that drove her out of her mind. He lifted an ass cheek, stretching her open more and when she looked at him, he took her mouth, his tongue staking claim as thoroughly as his dick.

Outside the rain continued to pummel the folly, an accurate soundtrack to what she was feeling. Jameson sped up his strokes and his hands were everywhere, her hip, her belly, her neck, her breast. He grabbed the crook of her knee and lifted her leg, placing it over his thigh, revealing her throbbing core to his caress. While he worked her clit she closed her eyes, wanting to take in every sensation she could.

"Look at me, love."

She did and his gaze seared into hers. Dani was struck by all the emotions on display for her: love, lust, happiness, fear . . . but then her body began to convulse as the tension spiraling in her lower belly broke and waves of immense pleasure started at her core and pulsed outward. She focused on holding his stare so he could see what he did to her and how much she loved him, too.

It also allowed her to see when his orgasm hit. His eyes widened, dropping to her mouth and then back to hers, before he gripped her shoulder and her waist and roared into the resulting silence that hinted the storm outside had passed.

Dani fell back on her extended arm, trying hard to breathe, wishing she could say the same about the turmoil currently circling her life.

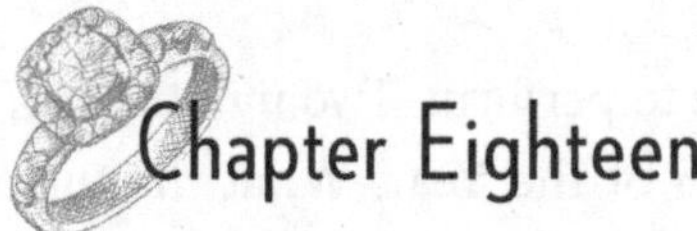

Chapter Eighteen

> I get having Duchess attend events w/Prince Jameson. I mean, that's her bae. But after this hospital thing, anyone else worried our girl being used? 👀
> ***@DuchessLeftAzzCheek, Twitter***

Dani held the phone with one hand and massaged the pounding pulse in her temple with the other. "Were you able to contact anyone?"

On the screen, Bennie's brows had gathered close. "It took some doing, but yes."

"And?"

"It was what we thought. Cash got to this year's producer of the show."

"Fuck!"

Dani let her head fall back on the sofa. Men who got their egos bruised were the worst! She hadn't gone around their industry bad-mouthing *him*. She'd exercised her right as an artist to no longer have him represent her. And the fact that *she*'d made that choice had him so up in his feels that he was willing to mess with her livelihood.

Another reason why she needed the deal with Genesis. Signing the contract would make her financially independent and then *she* could decide when and how she would step away from performing. She'd be damned if she'd leave that up to another person.

Especially Cash!

"Four months ago, they invited me to perform. Two months ago, they asked if I'd also present Album of the Year. What the fuck happened between then and now to make them withdraw their invitation?"

"No one will go on the record, but word is Cash told the producers if you participated in the ceremony, he'd pull his acts. Dirty Junkie is up for Best Video as well as Album and two of his other acts are performing. It was a numbers decision."

The scalding heat of tears burned behind her eyes. Yeah, being excluded from the Hip-Hop Awards hurt, but it was a physical indication of the disconnection she'd been feeling.

Since her arrival she'd had very little interaction with people who looked like her and shared her cultural touchstones. She was certain she could find a version of that community here, but the Company kept everyone so isolated. The only people she consistently saw on a daily basis were Jameson and certain members of the family and the staff, and attempting to venture out on her own involved so much red tape, she'd stopped bothering.

Dani found she not only missed being around her people, she missed the multiculturalism of her world. She missed seeing different skin tones, hearing different voices and accents, learning new fashions and hairstyles. She missed making a reference and knowing *someone* around her would get it. And she missed engaging in hip-hop with others who loved and appreciated it.

The deficiency was affecting her more than she'd ever imagined it would.

But what she wasn't going to do was roll over and let Cash believe he'd gotten the best of her. "Can we change their minds?"

"I'll keep working on it and I'll get back to you. I got a few aces up my sleeve."

"Thanks, Bennie." Once again, Dani was grateful to have the other woman on her team.

"You're welcome. Switching gears, it looks like everything is going well with your main mission."

Despite herself, Dani laughed. "My 'main mission'? What am I, double oh seven?"

"You could be. Just say the word. I know some people at the company that produces the films."

"There are many reasons that's probably a nonstarter, but I think you'd agree I have enough on my plate at the moment."

"Okay. But in my mind there's no limit to what you can do. Remember that. Anyway, Andrea and I talked, and she said Parcellum has been happy with your performance so far."

Dani pursed her lips. That was before last Friday.

As if she'd read Dani's mind, or facial expression, Bennie said, "That was one misstep. At least you brought attention to an attack many in the world hadn't been aware of. I read some schools in the U.S. are setting up fundraisers to send money and supplies to the kids injured in the bombing."

It was true. One of the positives that had come out of the whole debacle.

The doorbell chimed.

"I gotta go. I'll talk to you soon," Dani told her agent as she rose from the couch.

"Yes, you will. You keep your focus on what you need to do over there and I'll deal with Cash and the awards show."

Dani disconnected the call and headed out to answer the door.

The first time she'd attempted such a feat at Jameson's Kensington Palace apartment, she'd thought she'd been locked inside! There was no door handle! She'd spent several minutes looking for one until Jameson had come by, taken pity on her, and explained the high knob on the mounted lock was used to pull the door open. It made zero sense to her, but Brits tended to get touchy when one pointed out those discrepancies, so she'd kept her opinion to herself.

A divot appeared between Louisa's brows. "Why are you answering the door? Where's Townsend?"

Dani stood back and allowed Louisa to enter. "The butler? I don't know but it seemed ridiculous to sit there and wait for him to let you in when I was closer. I'm sure he'll rat me out to Jay anyway. Come on."

She led Louisa from the large elaborately decorated foyer through a curved doorway into the adjacent drawing room. They'd found that when they had back-to-back events, staying at the apartment in London was more convenient and it had the added bonus of being a quick walk to Jameson's mother, who lived one courtyard over.

"Is His Royal Highness here?" Louisa asked, lovely in a sky-blue dress and pearls, her usual composure in place.

"No, he's practicing for the regatta."

Dani hadn't even known what a regatta was before yesterday, but the Royal Regatta was the most famous rowing event in the world. For five days, thousands of spectators came and watched as crews from all over the globe battled it out on the Thames. There were competitions for all ages and experience levels, from school teams to Olympic champions. The highlight of opening day was a race featuring selected rowers and a member of the royal family acting as the umpire. This year, that privilege had been assigned to Julian.

Which meant it would be carried out by Jameson today.

"Good. Even though His Royal Highness is stepping in at the last minute, the regatta is getting the better option. Prince Jameson enjoys rowing. Prince Julian prefers sitting in the royal tent opposite the finish line, drinking and socializing."

Drinking and socializing. The reason his family was currently scrambling to cover up his mistakes.

"Thank you for coming. I really need your advice." Dani gestured for Louisa to sit next to her on the large beige feather-and-down-filled sofa.

"How can I help?" Louisa asked.

"Have you seen the tabloids?"

Louisa nodded. "Hard to miss them."

Dani sighed. The event with Catherine hadn't been far from her thoughts since it'd occurred four days ago. "I can't believe I let that happen."

"One thing I learned working for the Royal Household is they don't spend a great deal of time pondering their errors. They assess and move forward to rectify them. So, how did a simple visit to hospital go wrong?"

"I wasn't on my A game, and I was caught off guard by the location and some news I'd received." She grimaced. "And I didn't read the dossier."

"Dani!" Louisa slapped her own thigh. "What's one of the first things I told you about these official royal engagements?"

She squeezed her eyes shut, not wanting to see Louisa's horrified expression. "To read the dossier, I know. But everything had been going well with the events Jameson and I did together and when this function came through at the last minute I thought, how hard could it be?"

She knew better. She truly did. But—

Louisa bobbed her head. "You assumed it would be easy."

"Yes, okay, I can admit that! And I thought if something tricky came up that I needed to worry about, Jameson would—"

"No," Louisa said, holding up an index finger. "You and Prince Jameson are in two different categories. He loves you and he would never intentionally mislead you, but you can't rely on him for guidance about *your* actions. He's a prince and seventh in line to the throne. *He* will be forgiven almost anything."

Her unspoken message was explicit. That wouldn't be the case for Dani.

The dichotomy in treatment between her and the members of the royal family was already starting to show itself. In one of the major Sunday papers, the story about Julian's affair and the pregnancies had been removed from the front page. In its place, side-by-side photos of Dani, saucy smile firmly affixed, posing outside the hospital versus Dani, an enraged look on her face, yanking open the curtain between the beds. The disturbing—and embarrassing!—collage had run beneath a headline proclaiming:

DUCHESS'S DARK SIDE?

She knew she wasn't the only one who noticed the undertones.

But, as Bennie had alluded to earlier, the U.S. coverage was totally different, focusing on the underlying incident and questioning the way the British government had handled the bombings.

Just as Catherine had intended.

Dani stared out the windows, but she wasn't looking at the beautiful greenery or well-kept lawn. "Nothing's turning out like I planned."

"Can I let you in on a secret?"

Dani shook her head slightly and focused on Louisa. "Okay."

"We've all had that feeling here. When most of us come to work for the royal family, we do so with a bit of the fairy tale in our eyes."

Dani huffed out a bitter laugh. "After my last experience I am well aware there's nothing magical or enchanted about this place."

Except Jameson.

"But you still believed you could handle it?"

"Because I've been handling things since I was fourteen years old! But it's like I'm playing a game where I've been given a set of rules in English, but I still have no idea what they mean. There are so many different agendas. Take Catherine. I thought we were just visiting sick children, only to learn she requested my presence so I would call attention to a political issue because she couldn't do it on her own."

"I'm sure she told you the royal family can't be seen as political."

"Yes. But she used me. And I'm the one who ended up on the front page of the newspapers looking like a raving lunatic."

She was aware that complaining about being used for press coverage was hypocritical, but Dani's actions weren't hurting anyone while this sudden negative attack could harm her brand and decrease the likelihood of signing the contract with Genesis. In spite of that, Dani sensed Catherine could be an ally. Which was crazy considering the position Dani was now in. Maybe she was giving Catherine the benefit of the doubt because she was the only royal, other than Jameson, who appeared to care what had happened to those poor little Black and brown kids.

"Louisa, I know Jameson and I have just started dating but, say we got married . . ." Something fluttered in her stomach and Dani didn't know if it was excitement at the notion of Jameson being her husband or nervousness about Louisa's answer. "Would those rules on speaking out politically apply to me?"

"Yes."

So, if Dani saw something, she couldn't say something?

They really expected the woman who'd found success speaking her mind in lyrical form to remain quiet?

"Louisa, set her up for etiquette and comportment lessons and a meeting with the Press Office. We'll need to begin incorporating her into Jameson's schedule. And we'll need to figure out how to deal with her music and videos. We can't have that sort of image associated with the prince's girlfriend . . . You'll act accordingly until you're no longer needed."

The queen's decree, when she'd thought Dani would play ball, immediately after she and Jameson had been outed as a couple.

"The same protocols that govern the rest of the royal family—how they dress, how they act, what they do—would be expected of me?"

Louisa's face was blank. "Yes."

Dani fell back, stunned. And, simultaneously, annoyed by her disbelief. Had she wrestled control of her life away from Cash only to turn it over to the British royal family? As much as she loved Jameson, was she willing to do that?

"And since you brought up protocols about dress," Louisa said, her features softening, "I got a call from the palace."

Oh, joy.

Louisa cleared her throat. "They want to know what you're going to wear today."

"Not sure." She bristled, doing her best to remember Louisa was only the messenger. "Was there a problem with what I've *been* wearing?"

"Her Majesty has found your attire more celebrity-forward instead of royal."

Dani crossed her arms over her chest. "She told you that?"

"Oh no. I got a call from Edgar, her personal secretary. Since I no longer work for the palace, I don't have the same access I once did."

"To think: taking a job with me is considered a demotion."

"Not to me. Both Bernard and I are much happier now," Louisa said, referring to her husband, who was the stable master at Primrose Park. "But if you ever repeat it outside of this room . . ."

"Don't worry, it'll be our secret." Dani inhaled. "Celebrity-forward, huh? That tracks because I am a celebrity."

"Yes, but they assert you're representing the royal family now and they've requested you wear something more toned down."

Dani clenched her jaw so hard she could've produced a diamond from a lump of coal. "Didn't you, Tasha, and I go over the dress code for women?"

Louisa and Tasha made quite the dynamic duo, with Louisa taking care of things on this side of the pond and Tasha handling things back in America. Louisa had given them both a rundown on the regatta and the clothing requirements. It was a traditional sport, and until a few years ago, women could only wear blazers with dresses that hit just below the knee. While hats weren't a requirement, they were customary.

"We did. And I informed Edgar of that."

"Let me guess. That wasn't enough?"

"No."

Dani pursed her lips. "Just say it."

"According to Edgar . . . even within the guidelines, there's room for . . . poor taste."

Bile rose in the back of Dani's throat, and she tried to ignore the decades-old voice that lingered, questioning whether she was good enough.

"Don't let them rattle you. Remember, you're doing this for Jameson, and he adores you. Trust in that and you will be fine."

Oh God!

Louisa couldn't be more wrong. This wasn't just for Jameson. Dani's company and her financial future were on the line. Parcellum might be willing to overlook one bad turn in the news cycle, but if that narrative gained momentum and continued to grow . . .

Dani needed to nip it in the bud and toe the line so she could turn the press coverage positive again.

She exhaled. "I will take their advice and dress appropriately. Thank you, Louisa. I'm sure that wasn't easy for you."

"You're welcome," Louisa said, looking relieved that the conversation was over. "Please ring me if you need anything else."

After showing Louisa out, Dani went into the adjacent sitting room she'd co-opted as an office and stared at the rack of outfits her stylist had sent her. Her glam squad—Rhonda and one of her alternate hairstylists, because Miss K had to head back home to deal with a sick relative—was due to arrive shortly. Dani wanted to gain inspiration for a look they could use as a jumping-off point.

Apparently, in keeping with the changing times, women were now allowed to wear longer dresses or trousers to the regatta, although the blazer was still a must. However, with everything on the line, Dani would stick with tradition. She'd do it her way, playing around with colors and textures, but she'd keep it conventional.

Willow, one of her favorite stylists, had selected several sheath dresses in bold, vibrant colors with contrasting jackets. She was trying to decide between a tangerine sheath and a cranberry-colored flared dress when the front door's buzzer sounded.

"Add this to the report you give Jay," she yelled out to Townsend.

She'd been expecting her glam squad, so she was surprised when she opened the door to see a white woman, dressed in a plain light blue shirt and tan pants, standing on the threshold.

"Can I help you?"

The woman shifted the large tote bag she was carrying. "The palace sent me to help you get ready."

Damn! They were really keen to micromanage what she wore.

She shook her head and waved her hand dismissively. "I'm sorry they wasted your time but I'm good."

"They thought you could use some help with your . . . hair," the woman said into the space before Dani had fully closed the door.

Dani halted mid-action and her hand flew up to touch the softness of her natural curls and coils. She narrowed her eyes.

What the fuck did she say?

She swung the door wide. The woman had assumed it was an invitation to enter, but when she read the look on Dani's face, she smartly reconsidered that action.

The woman swallowed. "I . . . they told me . . . to . . ."

"I said, I will not require your services," Dani gritted out, sure the baring of her teeth was giving more grimace and less smile but granting herself grace because it was the best she could do under the circumstances, "but feel free to bill them for your time."

She barely refrained from slamming the door.

The nerve! The fucking gall! It was bad enough they wanted input on her clothes and her behavior, but her *hair*?!?!

Dani set her jaw. The palace had a problem with what she'd been wearing before?

They'd seen nothing yet.

THE SCENE AT the Royal Regatta was like something out of a novel about the Roaring Twenties. On both sides of the river, grandstands were erected and arranged for spectators to watch the races. Several enclosures were situated along the bank, including the most prominent one, the Royal Enclosure. Inside, there was riverside seating in the form of teal-colored canvas-backed deck chairs bearing the queen's royal crest, a smaller grandstand, several tented areas for formal dining, a bar, and scattered tables of varying heights for people to visit with one another.

Men walked around dressed in pastel-hued and/or striped blazers with pants and hats that wouldn't look out of place in a barbershop quartet. The women were dressed in colors that spanned the spectrum of the rainbow. Dani was happy to see other women wearing pants, but she could tell from the looks she'd been garnering since she'd arrived that no one managed to look quite like she did.

She was dressed in a blush pink, wide-legged, three-piece pantsuit that was meant to be worn with a shirt underneath. Dani chose to go sans blouse, so the vest covered her breasts but left her chest bone and the valley between said breasts bare.

Or it would've been if she hadn't accessorized with gold hoop earrings and layered gold necklaces that lined her sternum and glistened against her skin. She'd worn her hair natural with added extensions to boost the fullness and highlight her coil pattern. And she'd topped it all off with a coral-colored fascinator that nestled in her curls at a rakish angle over her forehead.

She felt amazing; she knew she looked it.

But traditional Anglo Saxon, she did not.

She'd been at the event for a while and she'd yet to see Jameson. He'd umpired the previous race and had texted her that he'd be along to the Royal Enclosure soon but that had been more than an hour ago. She'd wanted to see him, needed that connection after everything that had happened that morning. But he hadn't been here, and she'd been left essentially on her own, surrounded by people who weren't inclined to include her. She understood Jameson had duties to attend to, but she couldn't help feeling a little abandoned.

A condition with which she was all too familiar.

In the meantime, she watched the races, chatted with the few brave souls who dared to speak to her, and tried not to react to some of the comments she overheard when liquid coverage outweighed decorum.

"This is a phase for him, yeah? He'll get over it," one of the men said as she passed near the bar.

"But until he does, I'm sure he's having a hell of a time! Look at her. I know I would!" Raucous laughter followed that statement.

She tensed but kept moving, over to the four-foot-high fencing that bordered their area. Drinking the delicious champagne she'd been served, she ogled the half-naked rowers walking past with their boats held overhead—have mercy!—and did her best to ignore Bettina and her friends, the only other member of the royal family who'd been scheduled to appear today.

"Why would she wear that color?" Bettina asked, in a tone Dani knew was meant to carry.

"I think she looks spectacular," another voice said.

"Spectacularly out of taste. Did she think she was coming to an Easter egg hunt?"

Dani placed her now empty flute on the flat wide railing cap, determined to give Bettina an answer to her question and tell her where *she* could go, when she heard a peppy, percussive tune. Spinning, she saw a brass band comprised of men dressed in white linen shirts and pants strolling down the grassy area parallel to the Thames and where the VIP tents had been situated.

She'd never been a person who could ignore music and her shoulders were already shimmying, the notes seducing her to leave the Royal Enclosure and head over to meet the troupe.

"What are you doing?" Bettina asked, her tone shrill.

Dani ignored her and grooved in a rhythmic walk, her wedge-heel sandals providing purchase on the grass. When she got closer, they started playing an instrumental version of her song "Sky High"! She was amazed at their talent and how they were able to pivot on a dime. That they obviously knew her music meant a lot to her.

If she did one last tour, she would seriously consider incorporating a section with this type of arrangement.

The music was so vibrant and welcoming, it thrummed her southern roots and took her back home. She could feel the stares, but she didn't care. Everyone and everything else faded away. The expectations, the judgments, Genesis, Parcellum, Cash, the queen, even Jameson. In this moment it was her and the music and she submitted to it, moving her shoulders, shaking her hips, swaying her body in time with the drumbeat.

Remember when life was this simple? When you thought becoming a rapper would solve all your problems?

Instead, it had led her on a journey to ever bigger destinations where none of the pit stops provided the answers she'd originally sought.

The band finished with a flourish, bringing her back to her surroundings . . . and the sound of applause. She opened her eyes and gazed around to see mostly smiles.

And some frowns.

Standing tall, she adjusted her clothes, pulling on the lapels of her vest, dusting off the bottom of her jacket.

"You're a peng ting," the band leader, an older Black man, said.

"Thank you, I think." Tears welled, and though Dani wanted to release them, this wasn't the place. She forced them back and gave a watery smile. "For a minute there, y'all really made me feel at home."

"Then we did our job. Good to see you, ma'am. Cheers!"

He started a new song and moved on, the members of the band following and nodding at her as they passed. She shivered in their wake, almost as if they took the warmth with them.

"I've never been so embarrassed," Bettina hissed, when Dani returned to the enclosure.

"Really? There was the unveiling of your tit pics from the South of France and your brother knocks up a pop star, but it's me and my dancing with an orchestral band that's got your panties all twisted?" Dani rolled her eyes. "Get the fuck out of here with that."

Bettina practically vibrated with her outrage. "You're representing us. Look around. People are staring. You need to act like you're dating a member of the royal family!"

"But what I don't need is advice from you. Jameson and I are fine."

"Really? Then where is he?" she smirked. "The men in this family can do what they want. That's the only reason you're here. But mark my words: eventually, he'll settle down and find a proper wife. They always do."

Not Jameson.

Dani bit her lip.

Their lives were so different and they both would have to make huge compromises. When the novelty wore off, would he still want to? And if he didn't, where would that leave her? If they parted ways, would the royal family retaliate, like Cash? Or go into spin mode like they were doing with Julian? Her heart would be completely broken, but where would that leave her business?

"My apologies, love. I didn't mean for that to take so long. I was practically accosted by Imogen and her family. They're in the enclosure down the bank," Jameson said, sliding an arm around her waist and kissing her cheek. "You look stunning."

Jameson's dark hair was slightly damp and curled back from his forehead, the way it did after he showered. Next to the candy-colored stripes and polka dots favored by many of his contemporaries, Jameson appeared classic and regal in a royal blue blazer over a white dress shirt, golden yellow tie, and beige slacks. A multi-blue-hued pocket square, polished brown leather belt, and shoes completed his impactful ensemble. He was every inch the insider, someone born to this life.

And for once, his presence failed to bring its usual pleasure.

Lady Imogen Harrington? His ex-girlfriend who'd come out of the woodwork during the tribute events vying to be his *next* girlfriend?

"You left me alone here for hours while you had a cozy family reunion with Imogen?"

His head jerked back. "What's wrong?"

"Nothing." She turned away from him, wrapping her arms around herself.

"It's not nothing. You're clearly upset. Dani, what happened?"

"I'm fine," she snapped.

She could feel his confusion and anxiety and wanted to assure him she was all right. But she couldn't. It wasn't true. Too much shit had happened today.

He moved closer. "Let's not do this here."

"Why? Are you afraid I'll make a scene in front of your friends?"

"These people aren't my friends. I don't care about them," he said, his voice low. "They're all watching and the last thing we need is to give them more ammunition to come after us in the press."

Oh. "Like I did at the hospital?"

"Fuck, Dani!" He shoved a hand through his hair, seeming to give himself a mental shake. When he spoke again, he was calmer. "I don't know what's going on and I'm sorry I wasn't here, but whatever it is, you can't let it get to you."

"Easy for you to say, *Prince* Jameson, *Duke* of Wessex. Everything rolls off your back because they have to kiss your ass. They could give a fuck about me." She huffed bitterly. "While wanting to fuck me."

"What the hell?" His heated blue gaze scanned the enclosure. "Who?"

"It doesn't matter."

"Dani—"

"There was the fallout from the hospital visit, I lost an opportunity back home, and your grandmother offended me by insulting my taste and sending someone to do my hair!"

He frowned. "And that's not good? It sounds like she was trying to help."

"Oh my God, Jay! Seriously? One, I don't let randos I don't know do my hair. And b, your grandmother is essentially saying my hair is too wild and she wants to tame it! Do you not remember when we had the Black Hair 101 talk? I told you it's a sensitive issue!"

He rubbed the back of his neck. "You didn't have to be here."

She slowly tilted her head to glare at him. "Excuse me? Where was I supposed to be, Jay?"

"Back home. Not here dealing with all of this."

Back home? As in the apartment at Kensington Palace? Or Primrose Park?

Or the United States?

"I warned you how it would be. The negative coverage, the judgmental stares and gossip, everyone having an opinion about what you do. This is it. This is the job." He sighed and looked at his watch.

"I wanted to stop by and see you for a quick second before I made my final rounds, but now I have to go."

Dani curled her lip. "You would've had more time if you hadn't stopped to shoot the shit with Imogen."

A muscle ticked in his jaw. "I'll be back in thirty minutes and then we can leave."

Fuck waiting here another half an hour!

"Don't bother. I'll see myself home. Have fun. Tell Imogen I said big ups!"

She pivoted on her heel and strode away, feeling his stare sear into her back.

But he didn't follow her.

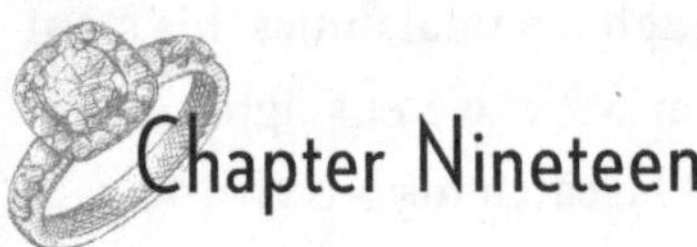

Chapter Nineteen

MEMO TO DUCHESS—
It's the Royal Regatta not a Backyard Cookout!
DAILY STAR

A cookout!

Jameson put his iPad down on his desk as his pulse pounded in his ear. It was happening, just as he'd feared.

The coverage had possessed a similar tenor for the past week, since Dani's event with Catherine, but it had intensified after the regatta. The same British press that had fawned over her now went into phase two of their plan, knowing they could make even more money tearing her down. They only cared about the sales and the clicks, with no regard for the life of the actual person.

Thankfully he and Dani had some time off before his scheduled three-day trip to Northern Ireland. The palace had initially planned for Dani to accompany him, but in light of the recent press trending negative, he'd received word today that he was to travel alone.

He knew Louisa had been informed, but he wasn't aware if Dani knew yet. He hoped she wouldn't be too disappointed, especially when she learned about the surprise he'd orchestrated to take her mind off their current situation. He'd started planning it after the hospital visit, but it appeared to be more timely than he'd thought.

Tension had simmered between them since their argument at the regatta. He'd hated quarreling with her, and the altercation left him tormented as it brought back feelings from their breakup during the tribute ball. He'd rushed through his final duties, his stomach twisted in knots until he'd gotten back to Kensington Palace and found her there. Only then could he catch his breath and calm his racing heart.

She was still upset, but she'd calmed down. She'd asked for some space and since she hadn't left, he assented, grateful that whatever was going on, she wasn't fleeing back to America.

That space had continued as they'd packed up and headed back to Primrose Park, where they'd stay until he left for Northern Ireland.

And she received her surprise.

Speaking of surprises . . .

"Well, this is a disaster," Dani said, flopping down on the sofa in his office.

"I know," he said, bracing his elbow on the arm of his chair and watching her.

She was informally attired in a navy, white, and orange colorblock dress that zipped up the front and lightly skimmed her curves. She'd pulled her hair up into a pouf on her head with two thin braids framing her face.

She was so goddamned pretty he wanted to go over and pull her close. But he didn't dare.

Not yet.

She bit her lip and gazed up at him from beneath lowered lashes. "If you say I told you so, I will kill you. I will literally kill you."

His hand started shaking as relief and gratitude surged through him. He cleared his emotion-blocked throat. "No, you won't."

"No, I won't." She pouted. "But I will scream."

"I'd allow it."

She blew out a huge breath. "It was my fault."

He gave in to his urge, abandoning his desk in favor of the cushion next to her. Cautiously, he slid his arm along the back of the sofa. "Don't blame yourself for what the press says—"

She snuggled close and his soul settled. He'd missed her touch, even the casual instinctual ones.

"Not that," she breathed and . . . was she inhaling his scent? "What they're printing is racist and fucked-up. But I gave them the ammunition."

"That's ridiculous."

He hated that she thought anything she did entitled the media to produce the trash they did. His mother hadn't deserved their attention. Neither had he. All Dani had done was override good common sense and fall in love with him, something he was thankful for every single day.

She stiffened and pulled away from him. "Don't call my feelings ridiculous."

Bloody hell! "I just meant nothing justifies what they're doing."

"True, but I didn't have to act out. I was so furious with your grandmother, your entire family really, except your mom."

He was intimately acquainted with that feeling. "They can be infuriating."

"It's not easy growing up in a society that says anyone who looks like you isn't beautiful or valued. I know I seem confident, but it didn't come naturally. It took a long time to learn to love what I see in the mirror. My hair. My complexion. My lips. So when the queen made those comments and I received them while I was already feeling vulnerable . . . I let them reduce me to that little girl who had been judged and found lacking. And that little girl was a fighter."

His heart ached for her. "Of course you were angry. And hurt.

And you wanted to make a point. That doesn't give the press the right to—"

She inhaled and held up a hand. "Stop."

"What? I'm agreeing with you."

"You don't get it!"

Why the fuck was she yelling at him?

"You're right, I don't. Explain it to me."

She stared at him without blinking. Then she opened her mouth and yelled.

Loudly.

"What was that for?" It took a second. "I didn't say I told you so!"

"I don't need you to fix everything, Jay. Sometimes, I just need you to listen."

"I do listen. And I hear the media is, once again, targeting a woman I love. Do you really expect me to stand by and take no action?"

"Yes! If I ask you to."

"But *why* wouldn't you want my help?"

She pushed to her feet and moved away from him. "Because I've been doing things on my own for a long time now."

He tilted his head. "That's my point. You no longer have to. I'm here."

"And what about when you're not? I can't afford to let myself depend on you and then you're gone!"

Shock and hurt held him momentarily immobile.

He didn't know why she didn't believe him when he said he wasn't going anywhere, but it didn't matter. He would do anything to shield her. He refused to remain on the sidelines and watch the voracious media whet their appetite with her.

Having made a decision, he tossed aside his injured feelings and joined her next to the fireplace.

He slid his arms around her waist. "We don't have to do this anymore."

"Thank you. Let's talk about something else," she said, snuggling into his embrace. "I hate fighting with you."

Having her close always short-circuited his nerve endings. He kissed the top of her head. "I don't mean this discussion. I was referring to these events for the Company. We've done enough. Let's collect our promise and go."

She stiffened. "There you go, trying to fix things!"

He clenched his jaw, annoyed by the ever-shifting surge of emotions. "I will never apologize for wanting to protect you."

"And what about Calanthe? Are you willing to sacrifice her home, her security, and her way of life? All on the altar of my protection?"

"You're being dramatic. I'll talk to Catherine. I'm sure—"

"Jay, you made a promise. And the state visit is next week. We can wait."

Why was she fighting him so hard on this? He still hadn't fully understood why she'd gone back on their agreement to further entwine their lives outside of their relationship, but he'd appreciated that she'd been willing to do so for his mother. But neither he nor his mother wanted her to be harmed for her assistance. Knowing that was happening and how important her good name and brand were to her, why would she stay and allow it?

"What if I don't want to wait?"

She jammed a hand on her hip. "What if I do?"

"But *why*?"

She threw that same hand in the air. "Because we gave the queen our word. And I don't want her or anyone else to think you're backing out because of me. How would that make me look?"

"What does it matter what people you don't like think about you?"

"It matters because I don't have the privilege of it not mattering. If you decide to back out, be clear that it's all on you. Don't pretend you're making that choice for me. I'm telling you right now, I fucked up but I'm willing to stay and see this through. For you. For us."

The air between them was heavy and thick. How had they gotten here? In California they'd only quarreled over what movie to watch, what food to eat, and whether cheerleading was an actual sport.

(She swore it was.)

But here they were. Neither one of them inclined to break the silence.

That would fall to Margery.

"Sir, Mr. Barnes is here."

Fuck. Jameson shoved a hand through his hair. He'd forgotten he'd had plans with Rhys.

"We were supposed to head over to the club and catch a game tonight." But when he'd made those plans, he hadn't thought they'd come on the tail end of two arguments with Dani. He exhaled. "Give me a minute. I'm going to tell him I can't go and then we can finish this—"

"Pardon my interruption, sir, but Mr. Barnes said if you mentioned canceling, I should tell you that you twisted his balls to get him to do this and you bloody well can't back out now." Margery cleared her throat. "His words, sir, not mine."

He couldn't help the tiny smile. "Thank you, Margery."

Dani sighed and spoke for the first time in several minutes. "It's fine. Go."

"You're not fine."

"I'm not. But if things go bad, we'll need our friends. You going is good for us."

"If things go bad . . ."

What the hell did that mean?

He opened his mouth to ask, but one look at her rigid posture and tense expression let him know that line of questioning would only lead to another argument. He reached out and trailed his thumb down her cheek.

"I'll be back."

She didn't respond.

He hauled her close, her gasp of surprise allowing him to sweep his tongue into her mouth and immediately deepen the kiss. He needed to be close to her, craved it more than his next breath. He hated the distance their argument had forged between them and he'd determine how to mend it later. Right now, he knew he couldn't leave until he'd at least physically bridged the looming gap between them.

She moaned and slid her hands up to grip his shoulders, her body softening into his. He shivered at the submission and slanted his head, rasping his tongue against hers, wanting more than this one kiss could give him but knowing now wasn't the time nor the place to claim it.

He ended the embrace and, breathing heavily, leaned his forehead on hers. "I said, I'll be back."

Her hand migrated to his cheek and his heart jolted at the heat simmering in her gaze. "Okay, Terminator."

Much better.

"That's my Dani," he said, brushing one last kiss to those exquisite lips, and leaving, while he still had the strength to go.

***"AND WHAT ABOUT** when you're not? I can't afford to let myself depend on you and then you're gone!"*

The words circled Jameson's mind, like water around a clogged, slowly emptying drain. Where did she think he was going?

Or did he have it wrong?

Had he been preparing for their future while she'd been planning a life without him?

"Have you heard a word I've said?" Rhys asked.

Jameson started then shot a look at his friend. "No."

Through the partially closed door of their sitting room, the din of male voices, clinking glasses, and the clack of billiard balls provided a soothing background noise. By virtue of his father belonging to Vault, the oldest, most exclusive private club in London, Jameson had been entered as a member shortly after his birth. He'd rarely come, not being a fan of the antiquated customs and elitist atmosphere and preferring the pub near uni when he'd needed a drink and to be near people. Since his ouster from Birmingham, he had found the private sitting rooms here to be a refuge when he wanted the spirit of being in public but the peace of being left alone.

"That's something. At least you didn't lie about it," Rhys said, taking a sip of his whisky.

"Why would I?" Jameson leaned back against the supple leather of the chair. "I can admit my mind was elsewhere. Something is going on with Dani."

"I'll say. The media has been bloody relentless. That whole bit about a cookout at the Regatta . . ." Rhys shook his head. "How can you stand it?"

"Me? I wouldn't dare center myself. It's about how Dani's handling it, not me." However . . . "What the fuck is wrong with these people? Grown men and women printing such vile, racist garbage. Do they think it's a game? How do they live with themselves? I wish the fucking lot would sod off."

Rhys's eyes widened. "Such language from a member of the royal family. And I imagine they're so far up their own asses in their perceived importance they no longer question their morality. They're going in because of who you are, what you represent, and their belief she threatens it."

He didn't need Rhys's reminder. The guilt constantly ate at him.

"Of course, but that's not what I was referring to." An unease had grabbed hold of him. One he couldn't shake. "I told her we could leave. That we'd essentially done what the queen had asked. We could get away for a while and let the attention dissipate. She refused."

"So?"

"She's close to signing a very important contract for her business but there's a few matters they've needed to resolve. *That's* where her focus should lie, but she's here because of me and this issue with my family. And for her efforts she's being pilloried by the press!" Saying it aloud fortified his belief in the logic of his reasoning. He continued slowly, almost to himself, "She should be happy to go."

"But she's not?"

"No."

Rhys pursed his lips. "Did you ask her about it?"

"She said my grandmother wouldn't let us out of the deal and Dani didn't want to be blamed if my mother was forced to leave her home and the family."

"She's got a point."

"No, she doesn't. We've spent the past month undertaking numerous official engagements to help generate positive press for the Company. Until recently, I'd say we've more than upheld our part of the bargain. Dani doesn't need to be at the state banquet. And considering the tone of the latest coverage, her absence would probably be a relief. Once that's done, the queen should remove me as a Counsellor of State, this nonsense of ejecting my mother from her position will cease, and the entire ordeal will be behind us."

Rhys's eyes widened and his jaw went slack. "Do you honestly believe that?"

Jameson hoisted a brow. "I don't have to believe it. It'll happen."

"You'll never be free. You'll always be a member of the royal family. And if you plan to be with Dani—"

"—I do—"

"—then she's going to, at the very least, have to interact with them. And she might care how they see her."

"I don't know." Jameson rubbed his chin. "Would that really explain why she's so opposed to leaving?"

Rhys stared into his tumbler as if the answers to the mysteries of the universe could be found at the bottom of his glass. He cleared his throat.

"You know I like Dani and I think she's good for you. But . . . are you sure she's in this for the right reasons?"

Jameson inhaled audibly, as if Rhys had punched him in the stomach. "Why the fuck would you ask me that? Of course I'm sure."

"Mate, you're rich, famous—"

"So is she!"

"You're a prince."

"And she's a famous entertainer who's adored internationally."

"She's used you before."

Jameson frowned. "When?"

"When she first came for the tribute. She needed the good press for her business."

What a complete load of bollocks!

"Being with me almost ruined the deal for her! Have you forgotten what the queen threatened to do?"

"But it fared well for Dani. That's all I'm saying."

Jameson's heart thumped wildly in his chest and the air around him heated. "You're way out of line."

"Maybe." Rhys set his glass down on the marble-topped side table with a thud. "But I'm your best friend. And it's my job to be suspicious and overprotective; to question the things you can't or won't. Out there, in public, I'll always support you, Dani, and your relationship. But in private, when it's just the two of us, I'm urging you to be careful. You're risking a hell of a lot to be with her. Are you sure she's worth it?"

Jameson met and held his friend's gaze. "One hundred percent."

"Then consider it another version of the webbed toes test you pulled on me back at Oxford." Rhys picked up his drink and stood. "A top-tier conversation like that between mates needs a fresh one."

As Rhys left to get them another round, Jameson's bravado slowly ebbed away. He hoped his trust was properly placed. Because if *Rhys* ever had the need to say 'I told you so,' it would be Jameson who would be doing the screaming.

Chapter Twenty

QUEEN RAGES:
WHAT WAS PRINCE JAMESON THINKING?
Duchess Too Different. Not Princess Material.
MAIL ONLINE

Dani pulled her knees to her chest and snuggled beneath the blanket on the settee in the drawing room she'd taken over since she'd arrived. It was one of her favorites, as it had once belonged to Jameson's mother. Dani often felt she could perceive Calanthe's warmth and empathy in the space, two things she desperately needed at the moment.

She laid her cheek on her knees and sighed. Which was worse, the press coverage or her arguments with Jameson?

It should've been the coverage.

But it wasn't.

The critical headlines and articles had been coming in fast and furious. Every British newspaper, news program, blog, and social media account had something to say about her behavior at the hospital and her appearance at the regatta. She'd immediately sought out Jameson, wanting his comfort, but he'd just had to be a man about it, rushing in with his solutions, trying to fix things, when she'd only needed his ear. And his strong arms. And that broad chest.

Can he really fix anything when he doesn't know the full nature of the problem?

Oh, stuff it!

She got his need to defend her. He'd spent years being gutted because he'd been unable to protect his mother from the paparazzi after his father died, in a scandal still felt by the Company. But Dani was a grown woman and had been living for twenty-eight years before she met Jameson.

She could take care of herself.

But her emotions had been too high for them to have a constructive conversation and she'd been grateful when Rhys had shown up and dragged him off. The time apart seemed to help them both put everything in perspective. Sometime during the night, he slid into bed and spooned her, his body hard and hot against hers.

"I missed you," she'd murmured, waking to his kisses on the nape of her neck.

"Then I should go away to the club with Rhys more often?"

"I didn't say all that."

His chuckle was low and delicious in her ear.

"I love you, Dani," he whispered, sliding his hand between her thighs.

She moaned. "I love you, too, Jay. And I'm sorry."

They made love, healing the rift between them. But when she awakened the next morning, he'd already left for his trip.

Despite the pain of their argument, Dani was confident they'd get past it.

The press, on the other hand—

She should've known better. She'd acted like a complete noob.

The press thrived on building people up before tearing them down. To them, it wasn't even an issue of morality. It was business. They made money by hyping a celebrity; giving them pithy memorable nicknames; declaring them the next best thing; raving over their looks, talent, or fashion sense; and swooning over their possible love interest—all to increase magazine sales, click-through rates, and ad revenue.

Once the person was beloved, with stratospheric levels of popularity, the press would begin their campaign to wrench them back down to Earth. Unflattering photos, where concerned sources claimed the culprit was drugs, alcohol, or food; gossip about feuds with people in their industry that turned into declarations of being "difficult" and "not bankable"; and speculative articles about their partner cheating with someone . . . better. Little by little, all drawn out to make the most money possible.

Want to increase profits? Throw in a redemption arc. Two sources of income for the price of one celebrity.

No care about the person's well-being or their mental state.

Or how disruptive that constant attention was to their lives.

"It's supply and demand," she'd heard on more than one occasion. "If there were no appetite for it, we wouldn't do it."

Just the type of bullshit these people spouted to explain their part or assuage their guilt over their role in the process.

She knew this; had seen it play out again and again. She was also aware the British tabloid press was notoriously more aggressive. And yet she'd been so gratified by her reception over here, not to mention stressed by her need to make a great impression, that she'd let her guard down.

Nana was probably looking down on her, angry that she had allowed these people to goad her into showing her ass.

"Ms. Nelson, you have a guest."

Dani shot a look over her shoulder, startled. "Margery? I thought you were heading into town to run errands?"

She'd given up trying to convince Margery to be more informal with her. It had worked when she'd been staying with them as a guest before the tribute, but now that Dani was officially dating Prince Jameson, Margery had reverted to form. Such etiquette ran through her blood. But despite her formality, she'd remained kind and welcoming and Dani had grown to care for her quite a bit.

Margery nodded. "I am. I had a few things to finish up first. I was actually on my way out when Ms. Collins arrived. May I show her in?"

Dani frowned. Louisa was here? Why? They'd talked that morning. What had possessed the other woman to drive all the way out here? Had Dani sounded that bad over the phone?

"Yes, please. Thank you."

"How long is this going to last?" Louisa asked, sweeping into the room with an air of briskness, switching on several table side lamps.

"What? I'm just relaxing. I was watching some stuff on my iPad."

"I see. A saggy posture, downturned mouth, and vacant stare screams relaxation. Especially when there's no tablet in sight," she said scornfully after a moment, her eyes narrowed. "You're not relaxing. You're sulking."

Dammit. "No I'm not."

Louisa slowly shook her head. "I've been working with the royals for a while now. I know sulking when I see it."

"I'm not a royal."

"Royal adjacent."

Ouch. "That's not nice."

"I don't suppose it is. I thought it would give you the oomph you needed. But since it didn't, I'm really worried." Louisa sat on the sofa at Dani's feet. "You're a professional. You know how the game is played and what they're doing."

"Of course I do. But it doesn't help our standing with the queen and it isn't easy to live through. Plus"—Dani picked at a loose fiber on the blanket—"I got into a fight with Jay."

"Don't worry about Her Majesty. We will turn this around before the state visit with St. Lucia next week." Louisa patted Dani's knee. "As for Prince Jameson, it will be okay. I'm aware I keep saying it, but it's true. That man *adores* you."

"The feeling is most definitely mutual. And I know this is silly. I guess I didn't expect it to catch me so off guard."

"You're not alone. Royals who know better have gotten swept up in it."

"Is that why you're here? To tell me pip pip and chin up?" She rolled her eyes. "You could've saved yourself the time and the gas and delivered that speech over the phone."

"No. I was heading out here anyway. I wanted to assure you that we will deal with it, just not tonight." Louisa smiled. "Tonight, you're booked."

"If by 'booked' you mean consuming a bag of potato chips and a pint of Ben and Jerry's chocolate and caramel swirl ice cream all while bingeing the latest season of that show on Netflix where the best friends organize everyone's house to make them look like a rainbow vomited, then you have that right."

"That isn't what I meant. Ladies!" Louisa called out.

Dani dropped her feet on the floor and shifted around to see five similarly dressed women stroll into the room. "What's going on?"

"These are massage therapists and aestheticians from the Bulgari Hotel London. They're here for you."

"I don't understand."

"It's a surprise. From Prince Jameson. As I said, he adores you.

He knew how hard this past week has been for you and he wanted to give you something to help you *truly* relax."

Dani's heart swelled in her chest. That wonderful, wonderful man. He made her feel so special and cherished. Everything *had* to work out. She couldn't lose him.

She wouldn't.

"There's five of them! I know I'm every woman, but not literally. I think one or two would suffice."

"I believe they're for us," a familiar voice said, wryly.

Dani shrieked and jumped off the couch! "Nyla!"

"And me," another voice chimed in.

"Yolanda!"

Dani rushed forward to meet her friends, excitement and happiness combining to make her giddy. She felt suddenly energized, as if her insides were doing the good knees challenge. "What are you doing here?"

Nyla hugged her. "I missed you."

"I missed you more," Dani said. "When we texted earlier you said you were working on a new project."

"I am," Nyla said, her grin wide on her beautiful face. "This."

"And what about you?" Dani asked Yolanda Evans. She'd met the tennis star at the ESPYs several years ago and they'd easily become friends. "Shouldn't you be taking some time off? You just won the U.S. Open."

"I'm planning to," Yolanda said. "I get three weeks in Curaçao. But I could take a couple of days for you. Thank you for the flowers and champagne, by the way. They were beautiful."

"You're welcome. I'm so proud of you." She turned to Louisa. "Jay planned this part, too?"

"He did."

"Then I'll have to thank him when he returns. And thank all of you for being here. I didn't know how much I needed this until I saw your faces."

"Is there room for one more?"

Dani's eyes widened and she sent an incredulous look to her friends, before moving to welcome the older woman who stood confidently just inside the door, beautiful in a cream fit and flare dress with cap sleeves, her dark hair twisted into an elegant bun.

One of these things is not like the others . . .

"Your Royal Highness," Dani said, sliding into a curtsy.

And cursing the fact that she was doing so in cheetah yoga pants, a black off-the-shoulder tunic, and Ugg slippers.

"I told you that isn't necessary," Jameson's mother said, reaching out a halting hand.

If they were alone, Dani would have heeded her wishes, as Jameson's mother insisted on informality each time they visited. But in a room full of people, half of whom were strangers, it didn't seem right not to follow the correct protocol.

She motioned Nyla and Yolanda over, hoping she remembered to do this properly.

"Calanthe, you remember my friend Nyla Patterson from the tribute ball. And this is another of my good friends, Yolanda Evans. Ladies, this is Her Royal Highness Calanthe, Duchess of Wessex."

Louisa gave her a little nod that Dani took as indication she'd gotten the introduction correct.

"A pleasure. You must be really good friends to travel all this way on a mission of mercy." Calanthe shook their hands before they could descend. She directed her attention once again to Dani. "Don't blame Louisa. I forced her to include me."

"That's not true," Louisa said.

Calanthe's blue eyes twinkled. "Jameson told me what he was planning and why. It made me proud to behold my son being a thoughtful partner. I only wanted to stop by for a quick chat. If you don't mind."

"I'd be happy to," Dani said, biting her lip.

With her usual efficiency, Louisa shepherded the group toward the door. "I'll take everyone to the suite of rooms where Nyla and Yolanda can change, and the spa technicians can set up."

When they were finally alone, Calanthe looked around. "This used to be my old drawing room."

"I know. I mistakenly thought this was where you did arts and crafts," Dani admitted. "You know: Drawing. Room."

Calanthe tried to cover her mouth, but a gurgle of laughter still managed to escape. "Arts and crafts?"

Dani winced. "Yes."

"I'll have to remember that one." She gestured to the sofa Dani had vacated. "Can we sit?"

"Of course."

Nerves quivered in Dani's belly as she wondered what Calanthe wanted to talk to her about. Jameson had decided not to tell his mother about his newest deal with the queen because he didn't want her to worry, and he knew his mother would never have allowed him to enter into that agreement on her behalf. But maybe Calanthe had her suspicions. It would take something major for Jameson to willingly step back into the spotlight and Calanthe was aware of the terms the first time the queen had called on Jameson.

Is that why she was here? To grill Dani for answers?

Calanthe settled next to Dani. "Your friends are quite accomplished, although I shouldn't be surprised. Like attracts like."

"Thank you."

"The past few days can't have been pleasant, with the tabloids and the headlines. How are you holding up?"

Dani appreciated the woman's kindness. "I'm okay."

"We've all been through it, some to a harsher and more relentless degree than others. I wanted to let you know how grateful I am to you. You're subjecting yourself to this unfair scrutiny to save the monarchy's reputation when you didn't have to, simply because you love Jameson."

Dani ignored the twinges of guilt that riddled her with Calanthe's words. She did love Jameson, but it wasn't the only reason she was doing this.

Calanthe continued. "He never wanted to be a Counsellor of State, so I was worried, but I needn't have been. Since you've come into Jameson's life, I've never seen him happier."

"Really?"

"Yes. Watching the two of you interact while representing the queen and seeing you stay true to yourself, I couldn't have asked more for my son. You let him be himself while still encouraging him to occasionally step out of his comfort zone. And he does because he knows you'll be there with him. You're exactly what he needed." Calanthe covered Dani's hand with her own. "So . . . be careful. Now that the media has turned, the queen won't be pleased."

First Catherine. Now Calanthe. That's two people who felt the need to warn her. What in the hell was about to happen? Should she be worried about some *Get Out*–type shit?

They *did* drink a lot of tea over here . . .

Dani frowned. "She places so much stock in how the press sees the family."

Unexpectedly, she felt a moment of kinship with the queen. Apparently, in this new age they were in, even monarchs had to concern themselves with the external perception of their brand.

"That's your first mistake, dear," Calanthe said. "Thinking of us as a family. We're a business. That's why we call it the Company.

Don't misunderstand me, the Lloyds are capable of caring, familial relationships and no one could deny the love between her and Prince John. But her main duty, and the duty of everyone around her, is to ensure the survival of the monarchy . . . their monarchy. And if she has no problem exiling her own child for his poor decision-making, she won't allow you staying true to yourself to get in the way of what she needs to do."

Calanthe's words were still buzzing in Dani's head several hours later, as she and Yolanda sat in her private suite, wrapped in the pristine white terry cloth robes that bore the hotel spa's insignia.

"God, I needed this," Dani said, referring to more than just the treatments. She'd missed her girls. She needed to be with people who knew her and had her back.

"I could tell," Yolanda said, sliding her fingers through her russet-colored coils. "At one point when you were in the other room you moaned so loudly that if I hadn't known you were getting a massage, I'd have thought you were indulging in some self-love."

"I remember that part of the treatment," Dani said. "But I'm an excellent lover. Trust me, that moan would've been way more intense."

They both laughed.

Dani stretched on the chaise lounge, feeling the languid movement required too much energy. "I'm glad you're here. How have you been? I haven't seen you since the exhibition."

"I know, it's been a minute," Yolanda agreed from the chair next to her. "I gotta tell you, looking up at that box and seeing you . . . it was a moment."

"Awww . . ." Dani reached out and clasped Yolanda's hand.

"Oh. My. God," Nyla said, drifting into the room.

Dani smiled. "All done?"

"Hmmmm," Nyla responded, her arms stretched high overhead.

"I was just telling Dani how it felt to look up in the Royal Box and see her sitting there," Yolanda said.

"That reminds me, congratulations on Wimbledon." Nyla slid onto a neighboring settee as if her body contained no bones.

"Thanks." Yolanda laughed, flexing her bare feet on the chair's matching ottoman. "But I didn't win Wimbledon."

"You made it to the semifinals!" Dani said. "The way you felt seeing me in the box is the same way I, and millions of other girls who look like us, felt seeing you on Centre Court playing your ass off. And it was close. You'll get there. I have no doubt."

"I appreciate both of you."

"Same, sis," Nyla said, her eyes closed.

"Speaking of being up in the Royal Box during your exhibition," Dani began, sliding a look at Yolanda, "did you know Liam Cooper couldn't take his eyes off you once you stepped onto the court?"

Nyla's lashes flew up and she pointed her finger at Dani. "Spill it!"

"I know you don't consider yourself an expert but that's how watching tennis typically works," Yolanda said dryly.

"Ha. Ha." Dani rolled her eyes. "But seriously, he seemed very taken with you. He mentioned he'd played tennis when he was younger and said he was a fan."

"Interesting," Nyla said, drawing the word out in several syllables.

"That's one word for it," Dani said.

A blush tinted Yolanda's light-brown, freckled cheekbones. "He signed up for the celebrity doubles tennis tournament I'm participating in to benefit the Arthur Ashe foundation. We're supposed to be partners."

Nyla smirked. "Seems like 'interesting' might be the right word after all."

"I'm focused on my career. I don't have time for anything else right now."

Dani jerked her head back. "I know Liam's young, but how much stamina do you think he has? How long do you think it takes? I didn't say relationship. I said you need to get that puss patted."

"Ride the bologna pony," Nyla added.

"Get some sour cream on that taco!"

"Foxtrot, uniform, charlie, kilo!"

"You two are so fucking childish!" Yolanda laughed and threw a pillow at Nyla.

"Maybe," Dani said, sobering, "but I'm grown enough to know how lucky I am to count you both as my friends. You're giving up valuable vacation time to be here and Nyla is in the middle of shooting—"

"I'll have to fly back tomorrow afternoon and that jet lag will be a bitch. But you know I'd do anything for you."

"And that brawny D!" Yolanda crowed.

"That *will* make it easier to tolerate," Nyla conceded. "But I was truly worried about you. First, these tabloid headlines, then . . . did you tell Louisa you got into a fight with Jameson?"

Dani nodded. "We did."

"What about?" Yolanda asked.

"He's angry about the press coverage and the things they've been saying about me."

"That's understandable," Yolanda said. "I imagine he just wants to protect you."

Dani could feel herself becoming irritated. "But I don't need him to protect me. I've been taking care of myself since I was fourteen."

Maybe she needed to get some fucking shirts printed!

"Because you had to. Part of finding someone who loves you is allowing them to shoulder some of your burden." Nyla frowned. "But I don't understand how it turned into an argument."

"He's angry enough to leave and I . . . I don't think it's necessary."

"By 'leave' you mean—"

"Walk away from his official duties for the royal family."

"And you don't want that?" Yolanda asked.

"*He* wants it, and of course I support him, but . . . not yet."

"I know the coverage this week hasn't been ideal, but you could come back to L.A.," Nyla said, her tone making it clear she thought the solution was obvious. "Attend some charity galas, hit a few more premieres."

Dani recoiled. "Jay would hate that."

"Why? It's the same type of stuff you did here, and you'd be killing two birds with one stone. A few events in L.A. to shore up the whole positive branding angle and you're out of the U.K. and away from the media here. Seems like a win-win to me. Why would he object to that? It doesn't make sense. Unless you—" Nyla broke off, her expression contorting into disbelief.

Yolanda glanced between the two of them. "What?"

Nyla didn't take her gaze from Dani's. "You never told him, did you?"

"Let me expl—"

"Oh my God!" Nyla sputtered, rising. "I can't believe it! You never told him what happened during your meeting with Genesis and the compromise your team came up with? Are you crazy? Did you really think you could go through all of this without him ever knowing?"

Dani clenched her jaw and crossed her arms.

"And *that's* what the argument was about. He's seeing how you're being treated by the press and he's willing to leave but you'll put up with it because you need him to stay in a little while longer." Nyla shook her head. "What are you doing?"

"What I have to do to secure my deal. The state visit is next week."

Yolanda stood. "What's going on?"

"I'll fill you in on the details later," Nyla said. "Long story short, Dani is on the verge of screwing up something great."

"You don't understand! He hates this life so much. The only reason he's staying is because of his mother. His *mother,* Nyla. He's already said if it weren't for her, he'd walk away. I'm just some woman he's been dating for a few months."

"But he loves you. He disobeyed the queen and told the world what you meant to him. I'm sure if you asked—"

"And are we forgetting, I shouldn't need his involvement!" Dani unfolded from the chaise and jerkily got to her feet, the anger flaring inside making it impossible for her to remain still. "It's my company. The fact that I need him to do *anything* for this deal to go through is preposterous."

"You're right," Yolanda said. "It's bullshit. But you do. And based on what I'm hearing, I agree with Nyla. He needs to know about it."

"I'm sorry, but no. Mela-Skin begins and ends with me. It's my responsibility. I can't let its future, or my own, ride on the actions of anyone else."

Nyla rolled her lips inward until they practically disappeared. "I hope you know what you're doing. You're a fighter, Dani, but this time you're fighting the people who are already on your side. If you continue on like this, he'll leave. Not because he doesn't love you or want to be with you but because you're going to push him away."

Chapter Twenty-One

DUCHESS TO PRINCE JAMESON: "CASTLES FOR ALL OF MY FRIENDS, OR ELSE!"
The Sun

Jameson sat at the large oak desk in the drawing room of Hillsborough Castle, the royal family's official residence in Northern Ireland. He'd been unable to stop his conversation with Rhys from repeating in his mind. He resented his friend questioning Dani and her loyalty to him. But he couldn't deny he sometimes had a blind spot when it came to her.

Or a blind canyon, as Rhys would call it.

Still, he knew something was going on and he was disappointed that she wouldn't trust him to help her with it. Hadn't he proven he'd do whatever he could to protect her?

Breaking their agreement and assenting to the queen's request to take up official engagements for the Company had been a mistake. He'd known it would be, but Dani had been insistent they could handle it. Seeing where they were now, he should've stood firm. Throwing their nascent relationship into the spotlight had caused damage. There was a distance between them that hadn't been there since their early days of dating. They needed to put all this family business behind them and refocus on their relationship. He refused to let his family situation ruin the best thing to happen to him.

It had been only three days, but he missed her terribly. They hadn't had a chance to talk, outside of a few texts, since he'd left. Between stopping at centers, receiving visitors from various organizations, and attending several receptions, including one at the Belfast Empire Music Hall, he'd been quite busy.

He needed to see her, hear her voice.

"You are the best man I've ever known," Dani said when she accepted the call, her expression soft, brown eyes bright.

His pulse quickened. He couldn't stop himself from responding to her; it was instinctive. "So you liked your surprise?"

"I did."

"Good." Warmth unfurled in his chest at pleasing her. "Did you enjoy seeing your friends?"

"Yes! How did you know it would be just what I needed?"

"I took a chance. You mentioned them during our walk last week and I remember after Nyla's premiere you said the two of you missed spending time together. I figured you may not have gotten the chance before you left to come here."

She briefly averted her gaze, before inhaling and offering an overly bright smile. "That was so thoughtful, baby."

There it was. Something was going on. He might have thought he'd imagined it but now that he was looking for it, it was obvious. And he wouldn't let her convince him otherwise.

He narrowed his eyes. "And you're feeling better?"

"I am." Dani laughed. "Are you auditioning for a role on *Law & Order*?"

The TV series? Why was she ask—

She was trying to distract him, but it wouldn't work. "I want you to tell me what's wrong."

She sighed. "There's nothing wrong."

"You've been saying that to me for the better part of two weeks and I've let it slide. But no longer. Love, I'm worried about you."

"Jay—"

"No, Dani. I know something is wrong. Why won't you tell me what it is? Do you want me to beg?"

"God, no, baby. I—" She squeezed her eyes shut. "You win."

He nodded, gratified by his victory. "I'm leaving for a youth center visit shortly. We can talk this afternoon."

"It's not pressing. Let's wait until this is all over. We'll have held up our end of the bargain and you'll have a chance to figure out what you want to do next."

That timing was suspiciously vague. When would it be all over? After the invention of flying cars or when they'd returned from their six-month tour of the moon?

She must've sensed his impatience because she said, "I promise I'll tell you what you want to know but can you wait a little while longer? Please?"

He exhaled. "Okay. But this is the last time you'll put me off."

"I never put you off," she said, looking affronted.

"Hmmm . . . lucky me, then."

He wished she were here with him. He missed holding her. Among other things . . .

"I really want to kiss you."

Her gaze dropped to his mouth. "Same. When do you get home today?"

Home. He liked the sound of that. Unfortunately—

"It won't be today. They've added two more events to my schedule. I'll be back tomorrow before the state dinner."

"Oh. Are you coming to the apartment?"

"There won't be time. I'll fly into London and meet you at the palace."

"I'll see you then. I love you," she said, before ending their call.

At least he was finally going to get some answers. And as impatient as he was, Dani had been right. Waiting until all the family stuff was behind them meant they wouldn't have to worry about headlines or official royal events or anyone else's opinions or input other than their own.

◊ ◊ ◊

DANI LOOKED AROUND the room she'd been escorted to. It had been easy to be quippy when she'd been here with Jameson. His presence had lent a comfort she'd taken for granted. Now the grandeur of her surroundings was making her nervous and uneasy.

Because you know why you're here.

Without Jameson, who was in Northern Ireland drumming up the only positive press the palace had managed lately.

Column inches and camera lenses were shifting to the upcoming state visit and the banquet tomorrow evening with the prime minister of St. Lucia. Considering the current mood in light of the royal family's scandals, many were questioning the purpose of the visit and asking if St. Lucia was close to holding a public referendum on the issue of separating from the monarchy. An issue Dani would have followed with a curious but detached interest if not for her conversation with Andrea that morning.

"Parcellum was troubled by the sudden downturn in positive coverage, even though you're still trending on social media and receiving a lot of engagement online," her CEO said. "But then someone brought to their attention the news about the state banquet and the fact that you're expected to attend."

"Yeah, I've been reading up on it. It's a mess."

"Why do you say that?"

"Colonialism," she said, as if the one word summed up everything. Which, to her thinking, it kinda did. "The visit feels weighted, you know? There are many people from St. Lucia who take exception to the queen being their head of state and yet unwilling to acknowledge or apologize for the shit done in her name."

"It sounds heavy and not an issue that can be solved during a dinner or by a foreigner. So try not to start a revolution over the fish course," Andrea said, her tone laced with humor. "Parcellum was impressed by the access you've managed to gain. According to Greg Martin, unmarried partners of members of the royal family have never been legitimized by the Company. But with your appearance at this dinner, you have."

"Damn. Royal stalker, much?"

"He did seem rather giddy during our conversation. Long story short, this event is make or break. If you do well, and the coverage is positive, they're ready to sign the contract. But if there are any issues and the negative trend continues, they'll reject the compromise and figure out their next step."

No pressure.

It was unfair that despite everything she'd done the past three weeks—fuck, the past eight years!—it all came down to one dinner. Mela-Skin's growth and Dani's own financial future rested on whether she wore the right outfit, smiled brightly, and gave good small talk.

She didn't have a lot of time to reflect on it because she'd ended the call with Andrea only to be greeted by a text from Louisa:

"The queen requests your presence at Buckingham Palace at half past two this afternoon."

She should've been expecting it. The queen had to be displeased with the recent media coverage. From her outburst at the hospital to what happened at the regatta, Dani's missteps were playing out in the headlines, to the exclusion of anything else. Someone had leaked to the papers that Jameson had arranged for Nyla and Yolanda to visit and now the media was debating whether she should reimburse the Crown for the expense. It was overwhelming. And she was certain the queen had something to say about it all.

"Her Majesty the Queen," the footman announced as the door opened and the queen entered wearing a calf-length pale yellow dress dotted with pink tulips and a matching fuchsia cardigan.

Dani peeped around her, confirming she was the room's sole occupant save the servants. It was obvious Dani knew who she was here to see, and the queen knew who was waiting. Did they have to formally announce her each time she entered a room?

Marina stood in front of the blue chair she'd occupied the last time they'd met. Dani sank into a curtsy and waited for the queen to take her seat before she perched on the edge of the love seat.

For several long moments Marina didn't utter a word, and Dani realized it was an old-fashioned test of wills. She forced herself to remain still and return the older woman's gaze.

Don't you dare speak. No matter how long it takes or how uncomfortable it gets, you will not go first.

Yes, it was petty, but then Dani's application for membership in that club had already been vouched for, accepted, and approved. She wasn't coming to the palace in a position of power, but she had to win something, dammit!

Marina broke first. "These aren't the results I expected when I sat in this room three weeks ago and agreed to let Jameson step away from his official royal duties in exchange for your help with our image problem."

Other than an internal celebratory fist pump, Dani didn't respond. What could she say?

Me neither?

Marina pressed a button and a second later, a footman entered.

Dani almost groaned. Not another periodical-filled silver tray!

"We're on the front page of every newspaper and tabloid that matters, but the headlines are all negative," she spat. "We're in the same position you were supposed to help us out of. I hope this isn't an indication of how you run that business you're so fond of?"

Dani resented the slight but clenched her jaw to keep a harsh retort back and said, "I know and I'm sorry."

"Your apology is pointless. I want to know what happened."

Now the queen of England was to be added to the list of people she had to answer to?

She knew what she *wanted* to say, but it wouldn't do her any good to antagonize the queen before the state dinner. Afterward would be an entirely different story.

Dani swallowed. "With the event at the hospital, I was alerted at the last minute, and I didn't read the dossier. Totally my fault. At the regatta, all I did was enjoy some music. I still don't understand the problem there."

"None of you ever do." The queen pursed her lips. "What do you think happened to the other royal families? Why have we prospered while other great dynasties have fallen?"

Dani shrugged. In all her twenty-eight years, she'd never given any thought to royal dynasties until this moment.

"Humility." Marina answered her own query. "We are here by the grace of the people. They have told us what they want from us, and we must listen. The monarchy depends on the support, acceptance, and, ultimately, the love of the working class."

Again, Dani didn't know how to respond. She wasn't a royal and this didn't apply to her. Should she add it to her small talk arsenal?

"They don't want us to be like them. They want us to be idealized versions of them. Talking politics, losing our temper, expressing ourselves through our dress, boogeying with a band—those are things regular people can do that members of this family cannot."

"Why would anyone want to live that way?"

"That's why 'anyone' doesn't. This life requires duty and sacrifice, notions we instill into our children from birth. It's only the unmitigated gall of people like you and this Samantha Banks who think they have what it takes when they weren't born into it."

If Dani had wanted to spend the afternoon being insulted by someone British, she'd have turned on BBC One or gotten her own stack of newspapers.

"Was there anything else?" she asked, feigning nonchalance while inside she seethed..

Marina's nostrils flared but instead of the hostile response Dani expected, she sighed. "Your attendance won't be required at the state dinner tomorrow."

Dani froze, stunned by the queen's declaration. "What?"

"You're no longer of use to me."

No!

Panic tightened her chest and she struggled to draw in a breath. "Your Majesty, please, I'm happy to participate."

For the first time, the queen's haughty demeanor faltered. Divots appeared between her brows. "I don't understand. Jameson will be mollified. He never wanted you involved."

"This isn't about Jameson. It's about me, and what I need."

Interest sparked in her blue eyes. "And that is?"

Dani glanced around uneasily, reluctant to give this woman more ammunition against her. But what choice did she have? The state dinner wasn't like a gala or a museum opening, where she could persuade Jameson to take her as a guest. If the queen didn't want her to be there, she wouldn't be allowed to attend.

And her last chance to save the deal with Genesis would be gone.

"The state dinner. I need to attend and be a part of it or I'll lose a very important contract for my business."

"I see. It appears this dinner is important to both of us."

"It is," Dani responded with bated breath.

"And this contract . . . Did it play a role in your willingness to cooperate these past few weeks?" she asked, appearing almost fascinated.

"Yes."

"And I'll hazard a guess Jameson has no clue about your ulterior motives?"

Dani flinched at the bluntness of the statement, but no lies had been told. "He doesn't."

"And you feel conflicted," Marina presumed, nodding slowly. "Will you allow advice from someone who's been where you are now and had the privilege to go even further?"

Was the queen comparing herself to Dani? How could she refuse, considering the power this woman once again held over her future?

"Of course."

"In the beginning, it's a good idea to heed romantic ideals dictating complete and open honesty with the object of your affection. But the one thing I learned after all my years of marriage? It wasn't necessary for John to be aware of all my comings and goings, my thoughts and deeds. And the reverse held true. We acted under the guiding tenet that what we did was for the good of our partnership. I think it served us well."

It was similar to Dani's own thoughts on the matter. She hadn't kept her plans from him out of malice or spite but because she knew it was the only way they could both get what they wanted.

"Since it's important to you, I'll change my mind and let you attend. But I hope you understand your presence must benefit me, too."

Dani briefly closed her eyes and resisted crumpling in her seat. "Whatever you want."

"Good. Because it's clear that your approach has stopped working." Marina crossed her hands in her lap. "It's time to do things my way."

Will you walk into my parlor? said a spider to a fly. Dani could almost feel the durable, silken, gossamer strands wisp along her skin, wrapping all around her, ensnaring her in its trap.

Seemed she was well and truly fucked.

And she had no one to blame but herself.

"SO, YOU DIDN'T heed my advice?"

Dani started at the sound of Catherine's voice. She rose from the mahogany bench she'd snagged in an effort to get her bearings after the meeting with Marina. "Excuse me?"

"I've heard that Mummy has requested her favorite stylist be sent to Jameson's apartment."

Dani resumed her seat. "This place is too big for gossip to travel that fast."

Catherine settled across from her in a navy blouse and wide-legged, rust-colored slacks. “That you think that proves just how little you understand our world.”

“I appreciate the heads-up, I truly do. But at this point I have no other choice.”

“So says everyone who’s been in that very same position,” she said with a touch of condescension and a tiny smile.

Dani lifted her chin. “Are you happy?”

“What a silly, American question.”

“So that’s a no? I figured. I’ve never seen this amount of misery masked by this much blatant wealth. And that’s saying something. I’m a celebrity in America.”

“My personal happiness is irrelevant. My family is the steward of a dynasty that dates back more than a thousand years.”

“Whoop-de-doo. But what does that mean?”

Catherine tilted her head back. “The queen is a living symbol of our nation, our head of state.”

“A figurehead who gives people something to focus on when they’re unhappy about their own lives and the conditions that may have caused it.”

Dani was pretty familiar with that play because it wasn’t all that different in America. They sold people on the American dream. Had everyone believing they could achieve it. But no one ever questioned who that dream was for.

Catherine narrowed her eyes. “The monarchy provides stability and continuity.”

“Ahhh. Being raised to value the old ways means it’s difficult to accept change. You know that saying about old dogs and new tricks? Just because it’s what you’ve always done doesn’t mean it’s what you should always do!”

Spots of color dotted Catherine's cheeks. "Our entire existence is devoted to service."

"And you're the only ones? Is the good you do superior to what's done by other countries just because you have a monarchy? Couldn't your family set up a huge charitable trust and do the same things you do now? Except then people wouldn't bow and scrape to you, right? Is it about doing good for your fellow man or getting off on your own power?"

Catherine crossed her arms over her chest. "Does it make you feel better to denigrate an entire system of government because of poor choices you made?"

"I'm glad you brought up choice. For people here, there is none. They are ruled, led, whatever"—Dani waved her hand dismissively—"based on a genetic lottery. Instead of Queen Catherine, they'll get King Julian. And you can't tell me, with a straight face, *that's* in the best interests of the monarchy."

"You . . . you couldn't possibly understand," Catherine said, her jaw tight.

"Y'all can keep saying it, but it's not true. I comprehend your words; I just place a different value on them than you. Have you ever asked yourself why this shit has to be ingrained in you from birth? Could it be that otherwise, you'd all get how ridiculous this is in today's world?"

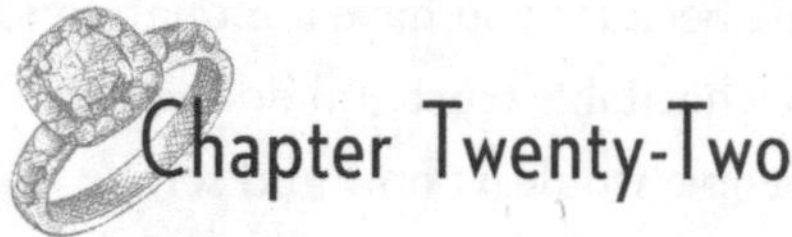

Chapter Twenty-Two

QUEEN MARINA WELCOMES SAINT LUCIAN PRIME MINISTER VERONICA AUGUSTE FOR CEREMONIAL VISIT

Leader Visits as Her Country Decides Its Future with the Commonwealth

The Telegraph

Dani knew she would never learn her way around the palace.

It was huge and disorienting. It reminded her of a game she used to play as a kid, where she and her friends would spin around until they got dizzy and then try to race each other. That's how she felt coming here. She'd been to several of these rooms multiple times and yet until she entered them, she had no clue where she was.

But she knew *this* room. It had been designated for the royal family to assemble in before state functions. But for Dani it was where she'd realized her relationship with Jameson had gone beyond a fling. That she was in much deeper than she'd ever imagined.

Interestingly enough, she felt similarly about her current situation. Giving in to nerves, she smoothed a hand over her hair—which had been parted in the middle and slicked back into a chignon at the base of her neck—then down the front of the sleeveless, mock neck, floor-length gown in pale blue, with a tulle cape overlay adorned with beaded embellishments. It was an exquisite gown, but one she'd never have chosen to wear. It wasn't her style.

But she didn't have a choice.

Her contract depended on being at this state dinner and if she didn't conform to the queen's vision, she wouldn't have been allowed.

Then get to it.

Dani nodded to the footman, who opened the door.

The room was small by palace standards, but lavishly furnished, with a magnificent fireplace, chairs covered in gold and crimson silk damask and circular antique tables on an oversized Aubusson carpet.

A small group was already there, but Dani didn't immediately join them. She needed a moment to compose herself. Part of her wished she could've talked to Jameson but it was probably best she hadn't. If he'd seen her, he would have wondered why she was going through all of this. Hopefully, it was the last thing she'd have to do. She just needed to hold off his questions a little while longer.

She spied a gold glass display case that housed ornamental trinkets and she smiled, drawn to it. Whether it was black angels and state souvenir plates or snuffboxes and fancy jeweled fans, old ladies loved their tchotchkes. The fact that she could find a measure of comfort in something that reminded her of Nana, in a place that couldn't be further from where Dani came from, actually grounded her and lightened some of the tension constricting her chest.

"I spy the work of Mummy's longtime dresser," Catherine said.

So they were on speaking terms after their conversation yesterday?

Dani reinforced her spine and turned to face the Princess Royal, who looked stunning in a frothy ivory tulle gown, a diamond and pearl tiara nestled in her strawberry blonde hair.

"I'd hardly call it work," she said, clasping her hands in front of her. "More like advice. I have my own people."

Catherine eyed her from head to toe. "Well, you look lovely."

"Because I don't look like me?" Dani arched a brow, not ready to let up.

"They're just clothes. You're still you. And don't look so surprised," Catherine said, her tone light. "Reasonable people can disagree. It doesn't mean we must be mortal enemies."

In the real world, Dani knew that to be true, but she'd learned the rules in *this* world didn't always make sense. Catherine would have to excuse her for not letting her guard down. Isn't that what they did, lured people into a false sense of security?

And then it was off with their head!

"Are you ready for today?"

Dani had read up on St. Lucia, its history with the Commonwealth and the queen's objective. Marina seemed intent on holding tight to a former colony, situated thousands of miles away, that sought to claim the right to rule themselves. The monarchy as a jealous psycho ex. That seemed about right. Dani disapproved of the strategy the queen had in mind but all that was required of her was to look "presentable," be knowledgeable, and converse with their guests. All things she could do.

Just keep your eyes on the prize.

"As ready as I'll ever be."

"Make sure that you are," Catherine said, adjusting the blue sash that draped over her shoulder and across her torso.

Dani's gaze skimmed over the people assembled. "Where's Julian?"

"You didn't think he'd actually be here, did you? It would defeat the purpose of what we've spent the past month attempting. He and

Fi have been shipped off to Scotland. I'm sure Fi would've preferred staying here but until the baby is born, they're a packaged pair."

Dani wrinkled her nose. "Cynical much?"

"Realistic," Catherine said, shrugging her shoulder.

Earlier, Dani had noticed Bettina kikiing with a blonde whose back was to her. Now the woman shifted . . . and Dani went still. "What is Lady Imogen Harrington doing here?"

Catherine glanced over and her expression tightened. "Mummy wanted a word before the banquet began."

Dani couldn't swallow past the boulder lodged in the back of her throat. Marina didn't do anything without a reason. Why bring Jameson's ex into this small gathering?

Once this is over the queen will have no further use for you.

Is that when Imogen's usefulness will begin?

Catherine brightened. "He's here! Thank God. If you'll excuse me . . ."

She started then reached out and squeezed Dani's hand. Dani met her gaze, shocked by the sympathetic gesture, and the Princess Royal nodded to her before leaving to approach the man Dani had been introduced to as Lord Stafford, Catherine's husband.

An aide approached with a short, dark-skinned woman wearing a beautiful gray and turquoise dress with a matching turquoise jacket. Her locs were gathered at the crown of her head and cascaded down her back, almost to her waist.

"Duchess, please meet Veronica Auguste, prime minister of St. Lucia."

"It's a pleasure to meet you," the prime minister said, her English accented with a touch of Creole patois.

"Likewise, Madam Prime Minister," Dani said, shaking the hand of a woman who would fit in at any of her family's gatherings.

"Your music is very popular with a lot of our younger generation, but I find I'm a fan of your skin-care line."

"Really?" Dani asked, surprised and elated. "You use Mela-Skin?"

"Yes, you have a great moisturizing sunblock that is easy on the face. Since St. Lucia has a tropical climate, I use it daily."

"That means a lot to me. Thank you. I'll make sure to send some to you."

Mrs. Auguste nodded. "I was really disturbed to learn of the bombing of the childcare center that mainly serviced immigrant families. I believe you visited with some of the victims?"

Dani was still tormented by the experience. By the fact that the bombing had occurred, by her behavior at the hospital, and by the Company's refusal to name it and shame it.

"Yes. Princess Catherine and I both did."

The prime minister's lip curled. "And is it true the bombing was underreported in the U.K.? And the authorities hesitated to identify it as a hate crime?"

"It's true. Unfortunately."

"But in America, they looked into it, yes? And now the authorities here have backtracked and labeled it properly? All because of the attention you brought to it with your visit?"

Heat burnished Dani's cheeks. "You make it sound like I'm some sort of social justice mastermind. Trust me, I'm not."

"You made wonderful use of the power of your position," she insisted, capturing Dani's gaze and refusing to let it go. "Thanks to you the matter will not be shoved under a rug. It can't be. The eyes of the world are watching. And judging."

Dani swallowed and her stomach churned. She had a feeling the queen would not approve of this conversation. But then, the queen wasn't here. And Dani found herself unable to go against her home training and shut down a woman who resembled her Aunt Gladys.

"How have you found it being here?" Mrs. Auguste asked, narrowing her brown eyes.

"It's been interesting. Different."

"Hmmm," she said. She moved closer and lowered her voice. "Have you noticed it?"

"Noticed what?"

"You, me, and my husband. We're the only brown-skinned people in the room. Did you notice that?"

"Not actively, no."

But Dani had been aware. How could she not be?

"I know why my husband and I are here. Do you know why you're here?"

Dani could feign confusion about what the prime minister was asking, but she wasn't keen to do either of them the disservice by pretending not to know the deal now.

"I have a pretty good idea."

"I will admit to being fascinated, like everyone else, by your relationship with Prince Jameson. Seeing his declaration of love after the tribute ball was very romantic. I'm sure he meant it, but you have to know that you're only being tolerated because the queen wants to use your image to show a more progressive Commonwealth. To make us relinquish our plans to leave."

Dani caught Bettina and Imogen watching them, their disdain evident. She thought back over her interactions with the queen. Finally, she peered down at what she was wearing.

"I know." She nodded, looking up, tears burning in their desire to run free. "You aren't the first to say so."

At least not in so many words. Hadn't every warning she received insinuated the same thing?

"You seem like a wonderful young lady, quite different from what I'd been expecting. I wish it didn't have to be said at all."

The door opened and the footman announced, "Her Majesty the Queen and His Royal Highness Prince Jameson."

JAMESON'S GAZE SEARCHED the people gathered until he spotted her. He exhaled and his heart walloped his rib cage. It had been four days, but seeing Dani reanimated his spirit. As if he could now view the world in color where before it had been sepia-toned.

Without a word, the queen took his arm and exerted the right amount of pressure to steer them to where Dani stood with the prime minister.

She needn't have bothered. He hadn't planned to go anywhere else.

"Your Majesty," Dani said, dipping into a curtsy.

"You look splendid, my dear," the queen said, approval—and a touch of triumph—in her voice. "Doesn't she, Jameson?"

He drank in the sight of her, appreciating the way the dress hugged her curves and the ice blue color gleamed against her skin. With her hair pulled back and more subdued makeup, of course she looked gorgeous, just not like herself.

He furrowed his brow. If anyone would've been able to withstand the pressures of his family, he'd thought it would be Dani.

He may have underestimated the exertion of their power.

"She does. But then, she always looks beautiful to me."

Dani dipped her chin and regarded him from beneath her lashes. His body responded to a look it knew intimately.

"Well, a little refinement never hurt anyone."

To everyone else there, Dani appeared to absorb the barb without any outward expression. Except he knew her, and he saw her offense in the tightening at the corner of her eyes.

"Madame Prime Minister—" the queen began.

"Ma'am?"

"Please allow me to introduce my grandson, His Royal Highness Prince Jameson."

Before the prime minister could dip into a curtsy, Jameson held out his hand to shake. She smiled. A genuine one that lit her eyes and curved her lips. "It's a pleasure to meet you, Your Royal Highness."

"Thank you, Madame Prime Minster. We're happy to receive you at Buckingham Palace."

Marina patted his arm. "You were unable to meet him earlier because he's been on a very important trip to Northern Ireland, acting on behalf of his sovereign. It's why we were late. I wanted to wait for him."

"Don't let it concern you a moment further. I've been having the most enlightening conversation with Duchess."

"Is that so?" the queen asked, studying Dani.

Who averted her gaze.

He wanted to comfort her, but this wasn't the place. Marina frowned on public displays of affection, especially at extremely formal events. And for this banquet he was serving as her escort, not Dani's.

"Yes. We discussed her company and—"

"We're very proud of Duchess and her company," Marina interrupted. "In fact, we're considering granting it a royal warrant."

They were?

A look passed between the prime minister and Dani.

"Which one of you uses it?" the prime minister challenged.

Jameson widened his eyes, intent on seeing how this would turn out.

"I have dry skin and I've found the custard to be a tremendous help," Marina said with a tilt of her chin.

Point goes to the queen.

"Mummy," Bettina said, strolling over to join their group. "I brought Imogen as you asked."

Imogen? Why did the queen want her here?

The queen's lips pressed into a thin line, but she nodded to Imogen, who curtsied in response.

"Your Majesty. Thank you for including me." Imogen fluttered her lashes in his direction. "Hello, Jameson."

"Imogen," he said, inclining his head. "Madame Prime Minister, please allow me to introduce Lady Imogen Harrington."

"A pleasure." Mrs. Auguste smiled.

"She's the patron of various charities and trusts," Bettina inserted. "She and Jameson were very close. At one point we all thought they would get married. Isn't that right, Mummy?"

Dani stiffened and Jameson clenched his teeth. What fucking game was his aunt playing at?

The queen must've wondered the same. Her tone was tight as she said, "If you will excuse us, I need to talk to my daughter and Lady Harrington."

"And that's my cue to check on my husband. Please excuse me," Mrs. Auguste said.

Finally! He and Dani were alone.

"What's going on?" he asked.

"Nothing. Everything is f—"

"If you say fine one more time, I'll—"

"Do nothing," she said, pressing a hand to the blue sash he wore beneath his tailcoat. "Your manners are too deeply ingrained."

"Not when it comes to you. Tell me what's going on. Why are you dressed like this?"

"Your grandmother pointed out that my way of doing things hadn't worked lately and she suggested an alternative."

"You don't have to change. You're perfect the way you are."

"As Catherine said, they're just clothes. I'm still me. I just toned things down."

Now she was quoting Catherine?

The queen had gone too far. She'd purposely waited until he was away to summon Dani to the palace. Alone and without his protection.

He took her hand. Her skin was cold and her fingers gripped his. Alarm stirred the hairs at the nape of his neck. This wasn't his imagination. Something was wrong.

"I appreciate you wanting to help me, but you don't have to do this."

She squeezed her eyes shut. "Yes I do."

"No. You don't. This is what she's good at. Manipulation. Making you believe that her way is the only way. But if she's requiring you to change who you are, it's not worth it."

Her lashes lifted. "It's not what you think—"

"I'm quite aware of how my grandmother operates, love. When you don't buy in initially, she finds another way to get what she wants." Ah. Of course. "What did she promise you?"

Dani shook her head slightly. "Here they come. Can we discuss this later, please?"

"They are a striking couple, don't you think?" Marina asked, as she, the prime minister, and Bettina, sans Imogen, rejoined them.

"Indeed," Mrs. Auguste said.

Marina smoothed a hand down her white gown. "Some would say they are the future of the monarchy."

Jameson inhaled sharply. *What?* "That might be overstating things a bit."

"That's outrageous." Bettina fumed, before a look from Marina had her clamping her mouth shut.

Mrs. Auguste smiled derisively. "I thought the Prince of Wales and his line were the future of the monarchy?"

Jameson winced, embarrassed by the illogical twists his grandmother was employing to minimize Julian's damage. He glanced at Dani but her expression remained blank.

"Oh, it is. But I was referring to the freshness they bring to the institution. The younger generation has really taken to Jameson and Duchess. You've expressed your concerns about the future of the Commonwealth and your country's place in it. I assure you things are changing, but you can only take advantage of it if you remain in and help us do the work."

The import of the queen's words, all of it, suddenly dawned on Jameson. The insistence on Dani's participation, this makeover . . . it had been about more than ensuring Dani fit in. His grandmother was the grandmaster of this chess match; she'd grown up playing it. And now, finally, he understood her end game.

And how he and Dani had played their parts.

Fury burned through him, torching any last vestiges of familial loyalty. It would always be something. Some reason why she'd need him. Why duty to the family would be more important than his personal happiness. But to bring Dani into it? To get her to change who she was; to use her and put her on display solely to serve her own agenda?

He was fucking done. He'd meet with Catherine to guarantee she'd do what she promised and protect his mother's position in this family and then the hell with them. As long as he had Dani, he could function anywhere. Get a position lecturing in the States, research and write a book. They could even take time off and travel. The only thing that mattered was that he and Dani get away from the queen and her influence over his life.

The prime minister shook her head. "I'm afraid it's too late. We've lingered out of a sense of familiarity, not devotion. You mention looking to the future, and we have. We don't want to be governed by your son. How can we expect him to treat us with care when he can't manage to put his own family above his baser instincts?"

The room fell into a shocked silence so quiet one could hear the centuries-old palace foundation settling. Had the prime minister called out the Prince of Wales? It was his grandmother's greatest fear come to life.

Maybe he'd been too quick to declare his grandmother the victor.

"I am also disappointed in my son, but I've always maintained no one person is bigger than this institution." Marina cleared her throat and forced a laugh. "And this is a bit premature. I plan to rule for many years to come."

"With all due respect, ma'am, we can't wait that long. We are not willing to accept the idea of Britain as a mother country when you have no significant cultural tie to us. The ongoing role of the monarchy in St. Lucia cuts into our dignity as citizens."

Jameson exchanged startled glances with Catherine and Bettina. He'd never heard anyone speak to the queen in that manner before.

Except Dani.

"It seems I've been tried, adjudicated, and executed before I even knew the charges," Marina said, lines bracketing her mouth.

"That wasn't my intention and certainly not in this forum. But recent developments supported our decision. The bombing of children of color is a significant event and this country's refusal to highlight it and call it what it is epitomizes why we're ready to hold a referendum to gauge the mood of removing you as our head of state. How can you reconcile your role as queen of the U.K. *and* of St. Lucia? In that contest, it's clear the side you chose." The prime minister issued Dani a visual apology. "And trotting out your progressive grandson and his charming Black girlfriend doesn't change that."

Audible gasps greeted this statement.

Had this been part of Dani's conversation with the prime minister? Had she known? If so, his grandmother would never forgive her. Jameson placed a hand on Dani's lower back, letting her know he was here and he would always be on her side.

The queen shook with barely restrained anger. "I see. I assume you'll keep these thoughts to yourself?"

"If you're asking if I plan to share our decision with the guests this evening, the answer is no. I have an ordinary speech prepared. But eventually we'll make an announcement."

"We'll deal with that when the time comes." Marina acknowledged the footman's signal. "Right now we're going to line up and process into this banquet that the Foreign and Commonwealth Office has spent a year planning."

Everyone in her orbit shuffled awkwardly about, as if throwing off the stasis of the previous ten minutes. The aides began arranging them in the correct order.

"Her Majesty and Madame Prime Minister first, followed by His Royal Highness, Prince Jameson, and Mr. Auguste . . ."

Public displays be damned. He took Dani's hand and cupped her cheek. "Are you okay?"

"Yes," she said, although her chin trembled. "Go."

He kissed her, their lips lingering before he took his place next to the prime minister's husband. But Jameson vowed that after the banquet was over, they were going to find someplace private and talk.

"And finally, Her Royal Highness, Princess Bettina, and Duchess."

"No."

His head whipped around. "Dani?"

She tilted her head, her brows gathered inward. "I'm so sorry, Jay. I know what this means to you and your mother, but I can't."

"You very well can," the queen declared, a crack in her vaunted composure. "I have no doubt this is partly your fault. You will help us fix it!"

"Dani isn't to blame for this," he said, not willing to stand by and watch her be attacked.

"Have you been listening? The prime minister is talking about centuries of slavery and colonization. I got here three months ago! This has nothing to do with me, but you were willing to use me to clean up your mess and I refuse to do it. Being a part of this," she said with a sneer, waving a hand to encompass . . . everything, "cuts into *my* dignity as a woman of color."

Rage mottled Marina's pale cheeks as she registered Dani's reference to what the prime minister had said. "If you walk out of here now, you'll lose that business contract."

Jameson frowned. *What business contract?*

"I'll take my chances," Dani said.

The queen set her jaw. "I will ruin you."

"Take a number. You've all tried your best. And yet, I'm still standing," Dani said.

She looked his way, mouthed *I'm sorry*, and made her escape through the hidden door concealed by an enormous mirror and stone inlaid ebony cabinet.

Chapter Twenty-Three

"Visits from our commonwealth countries always remind me of the relationship we share with them. Your coming here shows the importance both of us attach to that relationship. As we face the challenges of the twenty-first century, please be reminded that we are stronger together than we ever are separated. And as we look to the future, I'm confident our common goals and shared values will continue to unite us."

From Queen Marina's speech at the State Banquet of the State Visit of the Prime Minister of Saint Lucia.

Her Majesty is pictured alongside the Prime Minister, Prince Jameson, and Duchess in the White Drawing Room at Buckingham Palace.

@TheBritishRoyalFamily, Instagram

Holy shit.

Dani staggered over to a yellow silk-covered accent chair grouped with a sofa, chaise, and table next to the large white hand-carved marble fireplace. She braced a hip against its golden crest rail and inhaled deeply, pressing a hand to her pounding heart.

Had she actually done that? Essentially told the queen to fuck off?

It didn't take long for the adrenaline to desert her and send her mood crashing to the Earth's core. She'd done it and the queen was right. Not attending the banquet meant kissing that contract good-bye.

But it had been worth it. Dani hadn't acted impulsively. She wasn't hangry, although she hadn't eaten since breakfast. She'd made a choice. She refused to let the queen tokenize her just to cling to a nation of people who wanted to be free.

All for a contract.

That would've been when she'd officially sold out, not the hurt feeling bullshit Cash had been peddling.

"This is getting to be a habit," Jameson said.

Dani whirled around to find him standing there, gorgeous in white tie and his full royal regalia.

For someone who'd never been particularly interested in or excited about assuming his role as a royal, it fit him well. But then, from her perspective, everything did.

"You should go back. Your grandmother will be furious."

"I don't care. What was all of that about? And what did she mean by 'you'll lose that business contract'?"

She took a step back. She couldn't tell him. He'd be livid. He'd think she'd used him, just like others in his past. The way his family was now. She couldn't bear for him to view her with that same disillusionment.

"It doesn—"

"No."

Her head jerked at his abrupt denial. The professor was in the house and he wasn't going to let her get away with brushing him off. Not this time.

"Are you ready to tell me what's wrong?"

Her vision blurred with unshed tears. "Oh, Jay, I don't know if it matters now."

He frowned. "Why?"

"Because after that," she said, gesturing behind him, "I don't think we can be together."

His nostrils flared. "So that's it? Don't I have the right to know what happened to end the relationship that was so important to me, I was ready to risk everything for it?"

Every word pained her like a dagger to the heart, and instinctively she wanted to meet his anger with her own. But she didn't. She absorbed the blows. As she'd said, what would it matter now?

"Genesis wanted—"

"Ohhhhh," he said, nodding as he mentally put the pieces together. "You said you hadn't signed the contract and I assumed it was a mere formality. Since you never went into detail and because you're *you*, it never occurred to me you wouldn't get the deal."

It was inappropriate to take pleasure in his faith of her considering the circumstances, right?

"Apparently, I did my job too well when I was last here. A new company bought Genesis and they loved the idea of us. Of you. They wanted to add you to Mela-Skin's marketing campaign."

"That makes no sense," Jameson said, rubbing his forehead. "Your products are marketed primarily to women of color. What would I have to add?"

See, even he *gets it!*

Yeah, bitch, he *gets it.*

"That's the same point I made. But they were royalty struck."

"And what did you tell them?"

"I told them no! But Andrea pointed out there was a possibility they could keep Mela-Skin tied up in court if I walked away. We all thought a compromise would be in the best interest of all parties concerned."

"We." A muscle ticked in his jaw. "But it wasn't 'we,' was it? It was you."

"Me and my team."

He winced and she realized her words made it clear she didn't consider him a part of her crew.

His hands clenched into fists. "Why?"

"Because I needed to do it on my own."

And that had been the answer all along. The only person she could ever truly count on was herself. She should've realized it back on the plane. If she had, they wouldn't be here essentially dealing with the same issue, but deeper in love and with more people affected than if they'd just broken it off the last time.

"It's like a bloody mantra with you," he growled. "You make it true because you keep saying it! When I stood outside at that airport and declared to my family and the world how much I loved you, I never intended for you to ever do anything on your own again. I meant it, Dani. Why couldn't you believe me? What did I do to make you doubt my sincerity?"

His anguish was killing her and she wished she could take his pain away. But this wasn't happening because she didn't love him.

"It's not just you. It's everything. All of this. It asks too much of me. Your family, the Company—they want the benefit of my skin, but not the burden of my humanity."

He pursed his lips, rolled them inward. Then: "You said your team came up with a compromise when you turned down their condition of including me in the campaign. What was the compromise?"

What? She narrowed her eyes. She'd just explained the reason they couldn't be together, and he was asking her about her business?

"What was the compromise?" he repeated. His hands flexed at his sides, almost as if he were preparing himself for her response.

Her chest tightened and she exhaled audibly. "We realized they didn't really want *you*. They wanted your clout and prestige . . . to rub off on me."

He closed his eyes, a wry humorless smile curving his lips. "Of course."

Dani swallowed but continued. "In the end, we told them you didn't have to be in the campaign for me to benefit from your influence. I could access it just by being seen and photographed with you."

Nausea roiled in her stomach even saying the words, knowing how he would feel hearing them.

"Hence your willingness to do all the events. Fuck!" He threw his head back, shoving his hands through his hair. "Here I was trying to protect us from the very thing you needed for your company."

"But I wasn't thinking only of Mela-Skin. I was thinking about our future."

"Were you?" he asked, his eyes wide. "Because you just admitted you never trusted me!"

"That's not what I said."

"It's how you acted. We spent a month working at cross purposes because you didn't trust me enough to tell me the truth! Why didn't you ask if I'd be willing to participate or allow me to be a part of the process?"

"Because I knew how you felt! You hate the press. You resent their intrusion into your life and—"

"Bollocks," he said, cutting her off, though his voice never rose. "You're doing it again. Judging my feelings."

"No I'm not. I'm saying using them as an explanation for your current behavior is bullshit. After what we've been through, do you honestly believe I wouldn't move the heavens to satisfy you? That I'd let my disdain for the British tabloid media stop me from taking a few pictures if you needed it for your company?" He flicked his gaze away from her. "Try again."

She flinched and scrambled to come up with a reply. Because a part of her *had* been afraid that he would. And then what? A fight? Or a choice to make, being caught between love and a hard place?

Heat flushed through her and she strode over to him.

"But you shouldn't have to! It's *my* business!" She pounded her chest. "It shouldn't have anything to do with you!"

He gripped her shoulders. "I'm not your enemy, Dani."

"I know that."

"Do you? Because everything you're saying sounds like it's you against them, instead of us against them."

"Why can't you understand that my life was on the line? I did what I had to do."

He dropped his arms. "You sound just like her."

That humorless laugh again. She fucking hated it.

"Excuse me?"

"The queen. You both believe that you alone must solve everything. That you're the only ones who can right the world's wrongs."

"Not the world's," she said, tilting her chin. "Just our own."

And then she could've kicked herself because she didn't want to be allied with his grandmother.

"I suppose she already knows about this? Does that explain your transformation?"

"Yes. I didn't plan on telling her, but she'd disinvited me to the state banquet."

"When?"

"Yesterday."

"Another instance where you could've talked to me."

Dani knew how it looked. That she'd chosen to confide in the queen instead of him. That she'd picked the queen over him. It wasn't true, but it's what she'd done. How could they ever get past that?

"Did you know what she had planned?"

"Not initially, no."

"But you and the prime minister figured it out?"

"Yeah. And I couldn't do it. I couldn't let her use me to prop up her agenda. Especially because I don't support it. Despite what Parcellum thinks, that goes *against* my brand."

He nodded. "What will you do now?"

"I'll have to figure something out." She weakly threw up a hand. "More meetings where I'll probably have to explain why my attending the banquet would've been a disaster."

"I."

For fuck's sake! She jammed her hands on her hips. "What do you want from me?"

"Everything!" he shouted, his voice cracking with emotion.

Dani gasped and pressed her fingers to her lips.

"I want all of it. All of you. I want your heart, your smile, your laughter. Your kindness. Your sense of humor. Your intelligence. I want your body. I want your soul." He moved closer. Cupped her cheek. "I want your faith. And I need your trust."

Goddamn this man. It would be less painful if he'd punched a hole in her chest and ripped out her heart.

She covered his hand. "I can't change who I am, Jay. I've given you all that I can."

His lids fell and he retreated. "Then it's not enough."

She whimpered as hurt made it hard to breathe.

You're not enough.

"Fine," she said, dashing away her tears with the back of her hand.

"That's it? That's all you have to say?"

There were so many things she wanted to say.

I love you.

You're one of the finest men I've ever known.

I can't imagine a future without you.

Don't leave me.

She shook her head.

He sighed and his shoulders slumped forward. "I've thought a lot about this total control you want over your life. But that shouldn't be surprising because I think about you all the time. You factor into everything I do. Every action I take. Every decision I make. It's a wonder I have the brain space to devote to anything else."

Her heart squeezed at the stark vulnerability of his words.

"But that control, it's a fantasy."

"No—"

"None of us have it. My grandmother is the queen of England, and she has to answer to an entire nation. We're here, in part, because she's lived her life, privileged as it is, deathly afraid the British people were going to get rid of her."

She crossed her arms over her chest, her mouth suddenly dry. "It's different."

"It's not, love. And I can guarantee you, as long as you deal with other people, you'll never be truly autonomous. There will always be someone you have to answer to, someone's feelings that will have to be factored into your decisions. You're not a woman on an island all alone."

He'd never get how different it was for her.

"Then I guess we should end it now, before anyone else gets hurt.

We're too different. And thinking we could make this work was naive."

"Too late. Because if you leave, I won't be hurt, I'll be devastated."

She couldn't respond, needing everything she had to fortify herself against his words.

"Whatever this new company or the palace wants you to do or not do, isn't really the issue. Leave because you don't love me like I love you. Leave because you'd rather have your business and career without a relationship to distract you. Those are reasons that make sense. But don't leave for this made-up reason that you don't have control over your life."

Tears flowed freely down her cheeks now. "I don't see it that way."

"I know." He slid his hands into his pockets. "And until you do, we'll end up in this same situation. You'll continue to find excuses to run and I . . . it hurts too much to keep chasing after you."

This time he was the one who walked away.

Chapter Twenty-Four

EXCLUSIVE: WHERE ARE DUCHESS'S PARENTS? JAMESON'S GIRL AIMING TO SWING FROM BROKEN FAMILY BRANCH TO ROYAL FAMILY TREE

The Mail on Sunday

Hi, Reggie." Jameson smiled, if one could call it that, at the older man who opened the door. "I believe my mother is expecting me."

"She is, Your Royal Highness. Please come in."

Jameson stepped into the foyer of Calanthe's Kensington Palace apartment. A large marble table sat in the centre of the open space, holding a porcelain vase containing peonies, his mother's favorite flower. Across from him a doorway framed the curved staircase leading to the upper floors.

Jameson followed the butler into the drawing room, stopping short at the sight of a wooden tray atop a large, tufted ottoman that served as a coffee table, set with his mother's favorite tea service, the china emblazoned with the House of Lloyd family crest.

"Is she entertaining?" he asked.

Reggie picked up the tray. "No, sir. The Countess of Winchester, the Countess of Harwick, and the Marchioness of Ainsley just left. Her Royal Highness should be down shortly."

Instead of sitting, Jameson strode over to the far side of the drawing room and stood staring, but unseeing, out the floor-to-ceiling bay window. In the week since Dani's departure, he had indeed been devastated. He was confident he'd done the right thing, but he hadn't heard from her and he'd been reduced to stalking her Instagram account again.

"Jameson, darling," his mother said, sweeping into the room in dark slacks and a beige jumper. She kissed his cheek then held him by the shoulders and studied him. "You look dreadful."

"Thank you," he said.

"How are you doing?"

"I've been better."

Wasn't that the truth!

"I've kept my distance because I figured you had some issues to work through. But I've had enough of watching you mope over in your garden."

He hadn't been able to go back to Primrose Park. Dani had gone there after their argument. He knew from Margery that she'd left two days after the state banquet, but he'd been unable to bring himself to return. Her memory would haunt everything, making it worse if they couldn't get past this.

"Come and sit down," Calanthe said.

Jameson dropped onto the love seat and his mother grabbed a small ottoman and placed it in front of him. She sat on it and took his hands.

"How long is this going to last?" she asked.

"Do you think I want this? That I want to be away from her?" he asked, miserably.

"Of course not," his mother soothed.

"She says she loves me and wants to be with me, but she won't let me in."

"Does this have anything to do with Marina and your decision to take Julian's place the last few weeks?"

He nodded. His mother had inquired about his arrangement with the queen before, but he hadn't divulged the full details. He did so now and watched fury contort her features.

"That bitch!"

"Mother!" he said, shocked. In all his years, he'd never heard his mother refer to the queen in that manner.

"I can't believe she used me to gain your obedience." She turned her heated gaze on him. "And I'm furious you let her do it!"

He widened his eyes. "What was I supposed to do? Sit by and let her force you out of your home? Out of this family?"

"I think you forget which one of us is the parent in this relationship. I don't need your protection. I'm an adult woman."

"Have you and Dani been comparing notes?" he muttered.

"No, but we're both very smart women so maybe you should listen to us. By the way, I was sad I didn't get the chance to say good-bye, but she did text me the next day. Now tell me how Dani got entangled in this."

He did, briefly summarizing the situation. "We'd agreed to not get involved in each other's business, so when the queen asked and she changed her mind, I thought she was doing it for you. Instead, she had this whole issue with her business that she didn't tell me about. That's why she was eager to participate in all the royal events."

"I see," Calanthe said slowly. "What did you want her to do?"

"She should've come and told me!"

"The way you came to talk to me?"

He opened his mouth to respond. Then closed it.

Calanthe sighed. "I agree she should have told you, but that's not what's really tormenting you, is it? What is it? What has you so upset?"

He took a deep breath. "What if she *was* using me all along? How will I ever know if she wants me for me or for my family? I thought I knew, but I was wrong."

"Oh, Jameson. I know what I saw between the two of you and I have no doubt that her feelings are genuine. Yes, she should've been honest, but didn't you withhold something important from her after the tribute?"

"And she made me promise to never do it again. Then she turned around and did the same thing!"

"Because, my darling, both of you are suffering from the same ailment. You've been defined by the death of someone integral to you when you were children. You come from different backgrounds, which means your experiences and attitudes about that event may have differed, but you're both still reacting to it, making choices and decisions based on what happened to you."

His head jerked back. How had he been so blind?

His father's death and the circumstances surrounding it had played a major role in who he'd grown up to be. So many of the choices he'd made could be linked to the belief he'd formed after that seminal event. Needing to protect his mother. Wanting a life away from the royal spotlight. Keeping the woman he loved away from the Company. It's what his mother and grandfather had done for him.

And he'd tried to do that for Dani.

But she'd continued to fight him, probably because she was dealing with her own issues, and the emotional fallout from the death of her grandmother had affected her in ways he'd never imagined. He thought back over their conversations where she'd talked about her life.

"Have you ever had your utilities turned off? Or come home to find a 'pay or quit' notice on your door?"

"I've been taking care of myself since I was fourteen."

"—I told myself I'd never be in that position again."

Was it any wonder she craved a say in her own life and the means to make it happen?

"There you go. I can see you using that big brain of yours," his mother said, brushing a lock of hair off his forehead. "It's amazing what you can figure out when you're not instinctively reacting in hurt."

"I wouldn't know. I haven't been able to move past the hurt since she left."

"Now that you have a better understanding, maybe you can give her what you were asking for. Faith and a little trust."

He could do that. Happily. But—

"How does that solve anything? Even if I'd understood all this back then, Dani still would've walked away. I can't make her trust me. And I don't want a relationship without it. Like—"

He broke off before he could say it.

"The one I had with your father," Calanthe finished quietly.

Now it was his turn to offer consolation. "I'm sorry."

"It's quite all right."

He looked away from her, glancing out the window that faced her gardens. "Can I ask you a question?"

"Always."

"Why have you stayed?"

"Here?"

"Yes."

She lifted her brows. "I guess we're two peas in a pod. Because I've been staying to protect you."

"Me? I haven't been a part of this family for years."

"I thought my presence would mean Marina couldn't forget her promise to me and your grandfather to leave you out of the royal spotlight. And if she did, I'd be here to support you. Instead, she found a way around me by using my . . . complacency to get you to do her bidding."

He'd marvel at his grandmother's shrewdness if he wasn't disgusted.

"If you hadn't been worried about me, what would you have done?"

Calanthe smiled. "I have my eye on a little chateau in Provence."

"Really?" Warmth flooded his chest. "How long have you been considering it?"

"I was going to tell you about it after my last visit, but—"

"You heard about me being the face of the tribute and you came rushing home."

"Yes."

The relief he felt made him giddy. His mother could finally carry on with her life. She'd given more than enough to the Lloyds. It was time she claimed some happiness for herself.

"If that's what you want, then I'm thrilled for you."

"Thank you, my darling. Who knows," she said, a sudden twinkle in her eye, "I might start working on my memoir."

She'd finally rendered him speechless.

"What? I've let other people tell my story long enough." She laughed, then sobered. "And you're right, you shouldn't be with someone who doesn't truly love and trust you. Who isn't all in. But that's not Dani, and deep down, you know I'm right. Do you still love her?"

He nodded.

"And you want to be with her?"

"Yes."

"And if she was going through something and wanted to reach out to you, would you want her to?"

"Of course."

"Then you know what you have to do," Calanthe said. "But if what you want is a damsel in distress, someone you'll always need to coddle and protect, you should know that's never going to be Dani. She's too strong, been through too much."

Jameson shook his head. "Her strength is one of the traits I love about her. I don't want to change that. I want to be included. Considered. I need to know my opinion matters to her."

"I believe it does." Calanthe smiled softly. "You know, part of loving someone is knowing their flaws and figuring out if you can live with them. Life isn't magically perfect after you say I love you or even I do. After all, neither of you are perfect people. But if you're aware of all your issues and you're still willing to work on them together? That's love that will last."

They rose simultaneously and he kissed her cheek. "Thank you, Mother."

"Will you allow me one more piece of advice?"

"Of course."

"You're going to be tempted to act right away, but I want you to take some time. Think about how much you love Dani and how you felt this week without her. Consider her flaws and your own. When you're absolutely certain she's the one, reach out. And when you do, offer her something she's been searching for since her grandmother died." She patted his chest over his heart. "A place to belong."

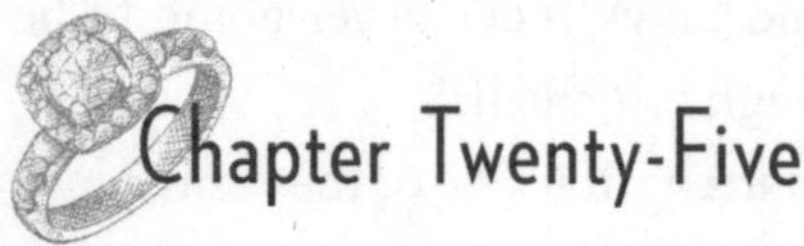

Chapter Twenty-Five

BOW DOWN? BOW OUT! PRINCE JAMESON TO THE YANKS: YOU CAN HAVE HER BACK!
Metro

Hampton, Virginia

You want me to come with you?" Antoine asked from the front seat of the midsized SUV.

"Nah, I'll be good. With this disguise and in these clothes, no one should recognize me." Dani opened the door and hopped out. "You don't have to wait here. I'll text you when I'm ready to leave."

If the press were looking for her—and she knew from the people who worked for her at her homes and business that they were—they might go to the house where she lived with Nana, but it would never occur to them to check out this park near her old middle school. She'd spent many an afternoon here after Nana's death, especially when she dreaded the place she was currently staying.

It wasn't the same as when she was little, thankfully. Growing up, it had been a poorer neighborhood, but like with a lot of areas, gentrification had come to Tidewater, and the neighborhood park was now a respectable recreational space with recycled rubber flooring and rainbow-colored structures that were a mix of ladders and bridges and tunnel slides.

Unlike the patchy grass, monkey bars, and metal slides that could burn your skin when it got too hot in the summer, that she remembered.

But she was happy to see the swings. They had always been her favorite. When she was swinging, she was in charge and she could soar and fly and pretend to escape to anywhere in the world. No one could ever get to her when she was up there.

She'd been right that no one was giving her a second glance, outside of the ones usually reserved for sullen teens by themselves. The swings were set off to the side, a long stretch that included bucket swings for babies, teeter-totter swings for a group, large full-support swings for people with disabilities, tire swings for the adventurous . . . and four solo swings. Dani approached the last swing of the last set, ensuring there was space between her and the kids still playing in the waning afternoon hours.

She dropped onto the plastic rectangle seat and used her feet to push herself backward. She didn't know how long it had been since she'd been on a swing, but her body recalled what to do. She let go and let her limbs take over.

And for the first time since she left London, she allowed herself to think about Jameson.

It had been a little over a week since she'd left and missing him was a physical ache, a pain unlike anything she'd ever felt before.

She loved Jameson and she knew he loved her. But it was the first time she understood the saying that love may not be enough.

Why couldn't he see that what she'd done hadn't been because she didn't care or love him, but because *she* needed to take care of it.

"Can I swing here?" a teen called, in a southern accent that felt more Richmond than Tidewater.

Dani tried hard not to roll her eyes. There were three other solo swings. Did the girl have to interrupt her ride and choose the one right next to her?

Sighing, she stopped pumping her legs, and as the swing slowly came to a stop, she looked up and—

"Nyla!" she shrieked.

"Shhh," Nyla said, motioning with her hands for Dani to calm down. "I thought we were being incognito."

Happiness bubbled in Dani's chest but she lowered her voice. "What are you doing here?"

Nyla winked and sat on the swing next to Dani. She was dressed similarly in sweatpants and a trucker hat pulled low, but glasses instead of shades.

"I heard my bestie was heartbroken."

"Who told you?"

"Tasha. You should give her a raise."

"At this point, Tasha probably makes more money than I do." Dani snorted, shifting in the swing and straddling the plastic seat so she could face Nyla. "You owe me several I told you so's."

"I know, but when you're looking this pitiful, it takes the fun out of being right."

Nyla copied how she sat in the swing and they both swung toward each other and away, just being silent. And Dani felt better because her friend was there.

"So why did you do it?" Nyla finally asked.

"Because I needed to—" Dani stopped and dropped her head. Even she was tired of repeating that same old refrain.

"I love you," Nyla said. "You're one of the fiercest women I know. And we've never blown smoke up each other's ass, have we?"

"No."

"So I'm going to tell you some truths whether you want to hear them or not." Nyla placed a hand over her heart. "But with love."

"Okay." Dani braced herself.

"Be real," Nyla began. "Do you think Jameson would've prevented you from doing what you needed to do to get the Genesis contract?"

Dani squinted her eyes. "He said he wouldn't."

"Did you believe him?"

Since there's nothing she'd ever asked for that he'd denied her . . . "Yes."

"Then why didn't you ask for his help?"

Dani's stomach churned, her mouth drier than her unmoisturized skin.

Which was hella dry.

"The truth?"

Nyla tilted her head, full of attitude. "I'm not asking these questions for my health!"

Fine! "I was afraid."

"Of what?"

"Of being wrong."

Nyla was relentless. "About what?"

"About him. And his feelings for me." Dani clenched her fingers around the swing's thick chain links. "I was afraid that I'd gotten it wrong. That I'd fallen hard for him and that if I asked him to do this for me he'd say no."

"And what if he did?"

"Then we'd argue and he'd leave. Or he'd try to make me choose and I'd leave. Either way, the relationship would end and I'd lose the man I'd come to love so much. I didn't want that to happen so . . ."

She shrugged and dug her toe into the recycled rubber.

"And nowhere in that mental consideration"—Nyla's tone was soft—"did it ever occur to you that he could say no but also help you come up with alternative ideas? That neither of you would have to leave?"

It took Dani several long seconds to respond. "No."

"Why do you think that is?"

Dani countered, "Why would he do that?"

"Because he loves you," Nyla said, as if it was obvious.

But what did that mean, really?

After Nana's funeral, family and friends had swarmed, full of hugs and kisses and food and promises. Emphatic in saying, "If there's anything we can do"; enthusiastic in their assurances that "of course we can take her in and provide for her."

The way her grandmother would've wanted.

But it wasn't long before time and reality changed their minds and it was "this is too much, we didn't sign up for this," and she was shipped off to the next person on the list who'd been emphatic and enthusiastic.

They'd professed to love her, too. Many had known her much longer than Jameson had. But they'd found it easy to leave. To turn her over to someone else.

And then there was Nana.

Dani hadn't been aware she'd said that aloud until Nyla asked, "You know Nana didn't leave you on purpose, right?"

What? "Yeah, of course."

Nyla grabbed Dani's chain, stopped them both from swinging. "Dani—"

"I know, Nyla!"

But her mother had.

Dani froze as understanding slammed into her.

Is that what this was about?

All these years later, she was still reeling from that original abandonment. Everything she'd wanted, strived for, and achieved had been to prove that she was worthy of love. That she wasn't someone to be left behind.

Was her need to be "in control of her life" really about her gaining the power to always be the one to decide who leaves?

Or who stays?

Dani was glad she was already sitting, the realization so overwhelming that her legs felt weak. She touched a shaky hand to the brim of her hat, thankful Nyla had remained silent and given her time to work her way through it.

Nyla squeezed Dani's hand. "You've been through a lot in your life. And instead of letting it break you, you used it to fuel you. That's great. But you've also allowed it to keep people at a distance."

"Not you."

"Not me. Or Yolanda. But have you noticed that other than us, and Jameson, the people you're closest to are people you pay?"

Well, damn. She hadn't.

Nyla pursed her lips. "I'll admit, I got it wrong."

"When?"

So far, she'd been right on the money.

"During the tribute ball. I told you not to take Jameson seriously or get involved with him. But that man is head over heels, crazy in love with you. And he wants to make you happy."

Dani knew that. She did. But as Nana used to say, there was a difference between knowing something and believing it.

"You have to let him in," Nyla continued. "That's the only way it's going to work. As a partnership where the decisions that affect you both you make together. And if you don't agree, talk it out and work through it. He's not going to leave."

"But he has to learn, too. He can be my partner, but I don't need a father. He can't keep things from me because he doesn't want to worry me."

"I think he learned his lesson about that the last time. But here's some more food for thought: Did you ever consider why you fell in love with a man who's clearly a protector? Maybe a part of you was seeking someone to take care of you. After years of having to do it all on your own."

"Wow." Dani tilted her head back and eyed Nyla down the length of her nose. "Have *you* been hiding things from me? Do you have a side hustle as a therapist?"

Nyla sucked her teeth. "Girl, no! I just got a new script. It's for the lead in a thriller. A psychiatrist. Even better, I don't have to audition. If I want the part, it's mine."

"Ma'am!" Dani said, snapping her fingers.

They laughed and hugged each other, and as they drew apart, Dani noticed they were attracting attention. Several people stared at them, then reached for their phones.

"That's our cue to audi this bitch," Nyla said, standing.

Dani glanced around and found what she'd been looking for. "See that walking path that borders the park? If you go left, it winds its way around a couple of apartment buildings and ends at a drugstore parking lot. We were never supposed to go that way because it's a little isolated, but you know kids."

"After you," Nyla said. Then she raised her voice. "Anyway, are you going to the homecoming dance? I don't know *what* I'm going to wear!"

"What is this, *Vampire Diaries* circa 2010?" Dani laughed and rolled her eyes.

"You'll thank me when we get out of this without ending up on TikTok," Nyla said, grabbing her arm and heading toward the path.

Once they were away from the playground—and it looked like no one had followed them—Dani sent a quick text to Antoine with instructions on where to meet. They hurried to the pickup spot while her head buzzed with all she'd uncovered.

The first thing she needed to do was figure out what she wanted. A bunch of answers flooded into her mind, and all would have to be identified and pondered, but there was one response that rang the clearest and loudest.

She wanted to be with Jameson.

So what did she need to do to make that happen?

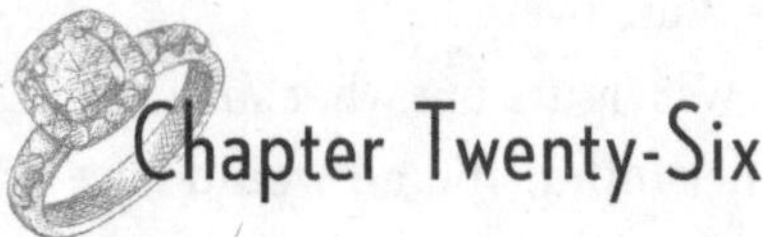

Chapter Twenty-Six

STOIC IN THE MIDST OF CHAOS!
ROYAL FAMILY CARRIES ON DESPITE
• Julian's Pregnant Mistress
• Growing Commonwealth Crisis
• People Asking, "Where's Jameson?"
The Sun

Thank you, Ellis," Jameson said, offering a weary smile to his butler.

Ellis nodded and closed the front door of Primrose Park behind him. "Sir?"

Surprised at this deviation from their routine, Jameson paused. After a long day of meetings with his private secretary, solicitors, and the heads of various charitable organizations, he craved the quiet stillness of his office. Whatever Ellis needed, it was delaying that indulgence.

"One of the housemaids reported an issue in a bathroom during her cleaning rounds. It's the one in the east wing near the Celestial Bedroom."

He wasn't a bloody plumber!

But he stiffened as Ellis's words penetrated.

East wing.

Celestial Bedroom.

Dread left a sour taste in his mouth. "Where's Margery?"

"Mrs. Shephard was already consulted, sir. She requested your assistance as soon as you returned home. She said it was rather urgent."

Are you going to avoid an entire wing of your house because the memories of Dani are too painful?

Of course not. With time—

It's been a month.

Thirty days of expecting her to walk through the door at any moment. Of knowing she got his gift and hoping she understood its message. Of fighting the instinct to fly to America to see for himself. Of rounding a corner and encountering a scent, a sight, or a sound that reminded him of her. Of being flooded with despair as each day ended like the one before.

Without Dani.

It was time to move on.

And the first healing step should involve returning to the scene of the crime, so to speak.

Taking a deep breath, he headed up the grand staircase and across the walkway that led to the east wing. The closer he got to the bathroom—her bathroom—the more his steps slowed. He paused just outside the door, leaning his forehead on the smooth panels and placing his hand on the knob.

Frothy lather sliding down one shapely raised leg—

"Did you just throw your sponge at me?"

"You needed to cool the fuck down."

"Can I taste you?"

Swallowing past the boulder lodged in his throat, he went in.

"Margery? Ellis said—"

Shock wrenched the breath from his body, and he blinked, unable to believe what he was seeing.

Dani sat on the blue tufted bench on the far side of the room.

The bench where they'd first made love.

Heat spread through him as his heart pounded, his blood roared, and everything within him jolted back to life.

"Hi."

"Hi," she said softly.

She wore a long, hooded dress in bright blue and her crossed legs afforded him a view of her white trainers. Her hair was a riot of dark brown and blond curls that tumbled over her shoulders.

She was a delectable visual treat.

But he didn't dare move. Not yet.

Not until he knew for certain.

"What are you doing here?" he asked, trying to force his burgeoning hope back in the box.

She uncrossed her legs and sat forward, her hands curling around the edge of the cushion. "I came to see you."

"Oh."

Because she regretted what happened as much as he did?

Or to finally put an end to everything?

Not knowing, but after a month of longing for this moment while simultaneously being aware this may be the last time he saw her, he went with the truth. "I've missed you, love."

"I've missed you, too. And I'm so sorry, baby."

She stood and rushed into his arms.

Thank God!

Shudders racked her body and he alternated between rubbing her back and readjusting his embrace, holding her tighter and tighter. He never thought he'd feel this—or her!—again, and he needed time to savor the experience. To imprint it on his heart and never take it for granted.

"Awww, Dani. Love. It's okay."

"No, it's not. You were right about a lot of what you said." Her words were muffled, spoken into his neck.

He shivered and pressed a kiss into her curls. "I should've been more understanding."

She pulled back to look at him and her beautiful brown eyes were luminous with unshed tears. Was it possible she was more beautiful than he remembered? "How about, in the future, you're more understanding and I won't run away?"

He exhaled, his chest finally releasing the tension it'd held in its grip all these weeks. So, there *would* be a future for them.

"Deal."

Her luminous smile began mending the cracks in his heart.

"Come, sit." She took his hand and led him over to the bench. "What happened after I left? Was the queen mad at you?"

"Yes," he said, pulling her down onto his lap and settling her ass over his growing erection, "but I didn't attend the banquet, so I wasn't privy to her wrath until later."

She wiggled her hips. "And was the state visit ultimately successful?"

"You didn't hear about it?"

"No. I couldn't. It was too hard."

"I understand," he said, sliding a hand to the nape of her neck and bringing her lips to his. Their kiss set his world to rights. "The prime minister kept her word, and the state visit went according to plan. Plenty of pictures, meetings, and the exchanging of gifts. She didn't utter one word on the topic of independence."

She frowned. "That's disappointing."

"As soon as she got back to St. Lucia, however, she issued a visit debrief statement where she mentioned it all, including the issue of the bombing of the childcare center and the palace's lackluster response. She declared St. Lucia's intention to call for a referendum and urged her fellow Commonwealth Nations to be proactive in determining the feelings of their own citizens."

Dani brought her closed fist to her mouth. "Damn."

Jameson nodded. "Just one of the words the queen was heard yelling."

"I'm sorry you had to go through that."

"It's fine," he said, marveling at his current largesse when actually dealing with the queen had been a nightmare. It proved his theory that having Dani in his arms meant he could deal with anything.

She gasped and shifted on his lap. "What about Calanthe? If the queen was that angry about the visit, did she take it out on your mother?"

"She tried to. But her threats were meaningless."

"Because Catherine was true to *her* word?"

"Because my mother is moving."

"What? Where? When?"

He filled her in on his mother's plans.

"A memoir?" Dani asked, tilting her head. "Well, go on, Mama Calanthe! Good for her."

"She's excited about the move and happier than I've seen her in a long time. For the most part."

"Oh?"

"Us. She thought I should've chased after you."

"That's why I love me some Calanthe." Dani snapped her fingers. "I hated leaving without saying good-bye."

"She was happy you reached out to her."

"Good. So, you're saying your mother thought I was right?"

He laughed. "That's not what I said."

"Hmmmm . . . that's what I *heard*." She sighed. "But back to the queen, what is she going to do?"

"Retreat. Reassess. For a while, the fallout from the state visit was the gift that kept on giving. After the prime minister's statement, our absence from the ceremony and any subsequent royal engagements has meant headlines here have been nonstop Sturm und Drang."

"They haven't been fun on my side of the pond, either," she muttered, dipping her chin to her chest.

He patted her thigh. "I imagine they'll fall back on the tried-and-true 'Nothing to see here, Keep Calm and Carry On' and try to weather this storm and figure out their next move. Whatever they decide, it's no longer my concern."

Dani covered his hand with hers, entwining their fingers. "Have they heard more from Samantha Banks?"

"Just her daily social media postings, I'm told." If he never heard that name again, he'd give daily thanks. "But enough about this dysfunctional wreckage. Don't keep me in suspense. What happened with Genesis and the new company? Did you sign the contract?"

Considering what they'd gone through because of it, he hoped for her sake she was able to come up with a solution that worked for all parties involved.

"No."

He was even more stunned than when he'd walked in here fifteen minutes ago!

"Did they back out because you didn't attend the state banquet?"

"*I*"—she pressed a hand to her chest—"actually told *them* I was no longer interested. I thought about what you said, and you had a point. There would always be something or someone to answer to and the more money they invested, the more they'd think their opinion mattered and the more entitled they would feel to my time."

"Weren't you worried about them suing you?"

"It could still happen. But we were never concerned about the merits, only whether it would affect other companies coming to the table. And we've decided that no longer matters because we're not taking on any new investors for the foreseeable future."

He didn't know how to respond. "That's quite a shift."

"I know, but not when you really think about it. Who knew the real key to negotiation is to be willing to walk away? And mean it! Parcellum immediately backtracked. According to Andrea, Genesis was furious that Parcellum cost them the deal, which would've been signed if they hadn't stepped in." Dani shrugged. "Everything happens for a reason and not having an investor is the right decision for me."

"Are you sure?"

"Absolutely. I've grown Mela-Skin into the success it is and there's no reason we won't keep growing. In fact, we're meeting with Oscar Michaels and Celebrity Gift Suites next month. You don't mind, do you?"

"Mind? I'm thrilled. Oscar is a good man. I think you'll work well together."

"Thanks, baby," she said, raising their clasped hands to her lips. "Would a nine-figure payout have been nice? Hell, yeah. But we'll get there. That doesn't mean I won't consider another investment somewhere down the line. If or when that happens, I'll be negotiating from a better position. And I may need to do one last world tour to line my pockets before I step back from music for good!"

Dani was a brilliant, marvelous woman and he was the luckiest bastard on Earth.

He hugged her around her waist, inhaling her sweet scent. "I can't believe you're here. This month has been torture without you."

"Then why didn't you listen to your mother and come after me?"

"After the initial hurt, I really considered it. Daily. But in the end, it was clear we both had problems that required sorting. I needed time to work on mine and I thought you needed the same. Me chasing after you and bending you to my will—"

"You wish!"

He grinned. "—wouldn't work. But you got my gift?"

"I did," she said, her expression softening. "Keys to Primrose Park and your apartment at Kensington Palace. That was sweet. And it gave me the courage to come to you. But you're right. I needed that time." She gazed directly into his eyes. "I started therapy."

He cupped her cheek. "I have, too."

Her expression brightened and his heart constricted in his chest at her telling relief. "I have some things to work through, but before, I thought I could live my life just fine without addressing them. But I want to be better for you and I want us to work. With our crazy, heightened lifestyles, it could all get messed up. I don't want that."

"I don't want that, either. We have to be honest with each other."

"You're right. And so . . . I don't want to be involved with your family. Not as a working royal. Any private family functions with your mom, obviously, or even Catherine, you know I'm all in. But I won't allow them to use me when it's clear they only see the color of my skin."

"Oh, love." He pressed his forehead to hers. "That's not an issue. At all. I never wanted you anywhere near them. I tried to protect you, but you don't need my protection, although that will always be my initial instinct. You just need my support. And you'll always have that."

"Thank you. I've learned, and am learning, that we are a team. That I—" She stopped and took a deep breath. "I trust you to love and want the best for me."

"I do. I'll never hold you back or dim your light. Your shine is a part of who you are. It's what drew me to you."

They kissed and he poured everything he was feeling into it. How much he loved her, missed her, was sorry for hurting her. Was overjoyed to have her back and how he'd never let her go again.

"Baby," she whispered when they'd parted.

She grasped him through the fabric of his jeans, the tip of her tongue peeking at him between her full lips as she reached inside and pulled him free. He closed his eyes and gripped the side of the bench to keep from coming in her palm like some inexperienced schoolboy.

"Oh God, love," he groaned, thrusting his cock into her hold. "I've missed this so much. My hand never felt as good."

"None of my toys helped."

Toys? He surged forward.

"Guess we have some sex to catch up on," he hissed.

She brandished a condom from her bra. "A girl was hoping."

"I love you," he said, overcome with happiness and desire as she covered him.

"Then don't make me wait." She tilted her hips and slid down his length.

Not even if Primrose Park fell to ruins around them.

"WHEN DO YOU think you could take some time off?" Dani asked, her head resting on his chest, his heart beating strong against her cheek.

She couldn't believe she was here, and they were together. She'd missed him, enduring a constant ache as a reminder of what she had lost. It might take a while before she'd forget the devastation of his absence in her life.

His fingers played in her curls. "What do you have in mind?"

"A trip. To Paris. More specifically, the northeast region of France."

Excitement bubbled in her as she scooted off the king-sized bed in the Celestial Bedroom and into the adjoining sitting room where she'd left her luggage. She grabbed what she'd been looking for out of her overnight bag and went back into the room, hiding the item behind her back. Jameson had pushed himself into a seated position, his back against the headboard. His chest and feet were bare, his pants unzipped, and his hair was tousled. He looked thoroughly fuckable, and she could feel herself grow damp between her legs.

Focus, Dani! You can get back to that *later.*

She had all the time in the world.

"The last time we were like this in this wing, I'd taken your grandfather's champagne. And even though we had some lovely moments as a result, I remember how upset you were."

Decades ago, Prince John had collaborated with a specific producer to create his own vintage champagne. When Jameson turned twenty-one, John had gifted him a crate of the rare bubbly with a promise that they'd enjoy a bottle each year on Jameson's birthday. The next year, John had died. Jameson had saved the last two bottles, wanting to hold on to them for as long as possible. Dani had helped herself to one. She hadn't known, but still . . .

"I've never gotten over that or how childishly I reacted. So, I tracked down the person your grandfather hired. Unfortunately, he passed away. But his son had taken over, and of course he knew Prince John. The producer said his father told everyone that making the special vintage for Prince John had been one of the highlights of his life. He'd kept all the notes. And the son has agreed to make another batch for you."

He stilled. "Dani, love—"

"It won't be the exact same because, well, grapes. But it'll be close."

He blinked rapidly and she hurried on, wanting to get it all out before the heightened emotions took over.

"And . . . since champagne is my jam, I thought you and I could also make our own brand. That we could drink every year on the anniversary of when we met to celebrate being in each other's lives."

She held out the bottle then, showing him the label and special logo, consisting of a scripted D and J surrounded by calligraphic flourishes, which she'd had created for their vintage.

His eyes widened. Then—

"Wait right here."

Dani was confused. "What?"

"I need to get something. Wait right here. Don't go anywhere."

He disappeared from the room. Dani shook her head. She hadn't been expecting *that* response.

She placed the bottle on the bed and headed over to partially open one of the French doors. It had been chilly, so she didn't step out onto the balcony that overlooked the back of the property. Instead, she stared out at the portion of the lawn she could see with help from the home's exterior lights. She exhaled as a peace settled over her. She hadn't known if she'd ever see this place again and it contained so many memories for her. She wondered how Jameson had been able to bear it.

After several minutes, Jameson's blurry image, as he reentered the room, was reflected in the door's pane.

"I remember standing here the first night I arrived. The view was gorgeous, but I was so angry at you, I couldn't appreciate it. Do you remember you told me I could call you 'Your Royal Highness'?" she scoffed.

His reflection moved but he didn't respond.

Frowning, she turned . . . and her gaze fell to where he'd dropped to one knee. Her heart began to race and particles of transcendent pleasure radiated out from her chest. Her hands flew up to cover her mouth.

"Oh my God! Baby . . ."

"In the moments when I felt the most hopeful, I practiced all sorts of proposals, trying to find the right words to express the effect you've had on my entire life. But nothing felt appropriate, and in the end, I decided simple would be best. So, Duchess, will you marry me?"

He flipped open the top of the box in his hand and she gasped. Nestled against the black velvet cushion sat an emerald-cut ruby, at least three carats, between two trapezoid diamonds of a carat each.

"It's spectacular," she breathed.

"They're flawless, hot, and passionate. Just like you."

That's what he'd told her the night of the tribute ball, when she'd told him rubies were her favorite gemstone.

He finally stood and took the ring out of its groove, sliding it on her finger. It fit perfectly.

"How did you know?"

"I asked Tasha, a while ago. I knew the night of the ball that I wanted to spend the rest of my life with you."

His words had the power to make her weak in the knees.

His head descended but Dani dodged his kiss, a thought occurring to her. She didn't want him to think her ungrateful, but—

"This isn't from the family vault, is it? I don't want to be wearing the Queen Mother's blood rubies or anything like that."

He laughed so hard it became soundless, his body quaking with amusement. He wasn't offended. He got exactly who she was. And he loved her.

"They're ethically sourced. And paid for from my own bank account."

"Then it's perfect," she concluded, accepting his kiss. "Oh, and Jay?"

"Hmmm?"

Dani bit her lip. "We're having a meeting next week. Bennie, Tasha, people from the music label, Andrea from Mela-Skin, everyone. And I'd like you to be there."

He smiled. The one that carved crinkles at the corners of his eyes and arrowed its way to her heart. And lower.

"Means a lot to me," he said, before nipping at her bottom lip.

Probably to remind her that was his job.

It would be. Always.

"I love you, Dani."

"I love you, Jay."

And they proceeded to show each other exactly how much.

Epilogue

Unidentified Male: Live from BBC Studios in London this is *This Morning in Britain* with Kelly Gibson and John Hayes.

Kelly Gibson, co-host: In a shocking move, Buckingham Palace has just announced that Prince Julian has chosen to surrender his and his children's positions in the line of succession. He will no longer be the Prince of Wales. Catherine, formerly the Princess Royal, has taken his place. Are you shocked?

John Hayes, co-host: I really am. It's unprecedented. There hasn't been a surrendering or abdication in the more than one thousand years of the monarchy.

Gibson: Could he do anything else? Once tests confirmed Samantha Banks was indeed pregnant and Prince Julian was the father, he couldn't be allowed to ascend to the throne.

Hayes: Not when, as king, he would be the titular head of the Church of England.

Gibson: Recent poll numbers have been very interesting. A majority of the people polled, fifty-nine percent, believe the prince has made the right decision, while a small amount, only twenty-two percent, thought he should stay. What's even more interesting are the numbers on the viability of the monarchy, which breaks down among age lines. Eighty-four percent of Britons aged sixty-five and older say Britain should continue to have a monarchy, while a whopping sixty-seven percent of people aged eighteen to twenty-four believe it's time for the institution to end.

Hayes: And it's clear who our new Princess of Wales may be listening to. In her statement she said she's honored to serve the Welsh people but hints that the monarchy of the past may not be required in the future.

Gibson: Our royal correspondent, Felicia Thorp, has more on the ever-dwindling royal family.

Felicia Thorp: Thanks, Kelly. It's been an interesting month for the royals, today's announcement coming on the heels of the engagement of Prince Jameson and American rapper Duchess, *and* their decision to step back from senior royal duties and live away from the royal spotlight. Prince Jameson also announced his decision to devote himself full-time to running his grandfather's charitable trust and administering the JFL Prize in his honor. Meanwhile Duchess will have her hands full. You may recall last week we reported the demand for Duchess's Bow Down World Tour broke the ticket sales company's website.

We asked Britons outside of Buckingham Palace to share their feelings about the engagement between Prince Jameson and Duchess.

Spectator 1: Ahh, I love them together. He's so fit and she's gorgeous and a lovely person.

Spectator 2 [face blurred]: In my day, she'd be his mistress, not his wife! [*laughs awkwardly*]

Spectator 3: Isn't there another one? Bettina? What does she do besides show her tits?

Spectator 4: I don't exactly know what the royals do, but I'm sure it'll be fine.

Spectator 5: Whether they're here or not, or step back from royal duties or not, Duchess will still be a princess, yeah?

Acknowledgments

Being back here again is a blessing and a curse. Most of the names remain the same and I'm gratified by that. It means I have a stable core of people in my life and, as a lot of these people can testify to, I'm someone who needs stability.

So I'm going to make this one short and sweet. Refer to novels 1–8 (helpfully listed in the front of this book) to read more about why these people are the bomb dot com. #ISaidWhatISaid.

Continued love and appreciation to:

My agent, Nalini Akolekar, and my editor, Tessa Woodward.

My writing besties and confidants, Mia Sosa and Alleyne Dickens.

My morning writing group, Adriana Herrera, Alexis Daria, and Zoraida Cordova.

The other authors who continually make being in Romancelandia enjoyable: Sarah MacLean, Nisha Sharma, Adriana Anders, Tif Marcelo, Nina Crespo, Priscilla Oliveras, Michele Arris, LaQuette, Andie Christopher, and Joanna Shupe.

Erick Davila for hitting it out of the park again with his amazing cover art.

Victoria Colotta, VMC Art & Design, for the badass graphics that make all my social media look good.

Kristin Dwyer and the ladies at LEO PR, who used their superpowers to help the world learn about *American Royalty* and *The Duchess Effect*.

A new one! The Bookstagrammers and BookTokkers who posted pictures and reviews of *American Royalty* and helped shout that book to the high heavens. Thank you so much! It means a lot!

The friends who dare to drag me out of Romancelandia when I need it: Tanya Smith-Evans, Dr. Imani Williams-Vaughn, Cassandra Williams, Alvenia Scarborough, Petra Spaulding, Sharon McGowan, Leigh Florio, and Ashley Motley.

And, as always, last in my Acks but first in my heart: my mother, Elsie; my three children, Trey, Grayson, and Will; and the absolute love of my life, James. (Any similarity between my husband's name and the hero's name is definitely on purpose.)

Until the next one,

TL

About the Author

A former criminal defense attorney, TRACEY LIVESAY finds crafting believable happily ever afters slightly more challenging than protecting our constitutional rights, but she's never regretted following her heart instead of her law degree. She has been featured in *Entertainment Weekly*, the *Washington Post*, and on *CBS This Morning*. Tracey lives in Virginia with her husband—who she met on the very first day of law school—and their three children.

READ MORE BY TRACEY LIVESAY

AMERICAN ROYALTY

LIKE LOVERS DO

SWEET TALKIN' LOVER

LOVE WILL ALWAYS REMEMBER

ALONG CAME LOVE

LOVE ON MY MIND